ABOUT THE AUTHOR

Jane Peart, award-winning novelist and short story writer, grew up in Asheville, North Carolina, and was educated in New England. Although she now lives in northern California, her heart has remained in her native South—its people, its history, and its traditions. With more than twenty-five novels and 250 short stories to her credit, Jane likes to emphasize in her writing the timeless and recurring themes of family, traditional values, and a sense of place.

Ten years in the writing, the *Brides of Montclair* series is a historical family saga of enduring beauty. In each new book, another generation comes into its own at the beautiful Montclair estate near Williamsburg, Virginia. These compelling, dramatic stories reaffirm the importance of committed love, loyalty, courage, strength of character, and abiding faith in times of triumph and tragedy, sorrow and joy.

THE BRIDES OF MONTCLAIR SERIES, VOL. IV

BY JANE PEART

FEATURING:
MIRROR BRIDE
AND
HERO'S BRIDE

ZONDERVAN PUBLISHING HOUSE
GRAND RAPIDS, MICHIGAN
A DIVISION OF HARPER COLLINS PUBLISHERS

Mirror Bride
Copyright © 1993 by Jane Peart

Requests for information should be addressed to:
Zondervan Publishing House
Grand Rapids, Michigan 49530
First Combined Hardcover Edition for Christian Herald Family Bookshelf: 1993
Library of Congress Cataloging-in-Publication Data

Peart, Jane.
    Mirror Bride / Jane Peart.
        p. cm. - (Brides of Montclair series : bk. 10)
    ISBN 0-310-67131-0
    I. Family—Virginia—Williamsburg Region—Fiction. I. Title.
II. Series: Peart, Jane. Brides of Montclair series ; bk. 10.
PS3566.E28M57   1993   93-22213
813'.54—dc20   CIP

Edited by Ann Severance
Interior design by Kim Koning
Cover Design by Art Jacobs
Cover illustration by Wes Lowe, Sal Baracc and Assoc., Inc.

Printed in the United States of America

Mirror Bride

Book Ten
The Brides of Montclair Series

JANE PEART

ZondervanPublishingHouse

Grand Rapids, Michigan

A Division of HarperCollins*Publishers*

Mirror Bride
Copyright © 1993 by Jane Peart

Requests for information should be addressed to:
Zondervan Publishing House
Grand Rapids, Michigan 49530

Library of Congress Cataloging-in-Publication Data

Peart, Jane.
    Mirror bride / Jane Peart.
        p. cm. – (Brides of Montclair series : bk. 10)
    ISBN 0-310-67131-0
    1. Family—Virginia—Williamsburg Region—Fiction. I. Title.
II. Series: Peart, Jane. Brides of Montclair series ; bk. 10.
PS3566.E28M57   1993
813'.54—dc20   93-22213
                                                                        CIP

Edited by Anne Severance
Interior design by Kim Koning
Cover design by Art Jacobs
Cover illustration by Wes Lowe, Sal Baracc and Assoc., Inc.

Printed in the United States of America

Prologue

Arbordale, Virginia
At Avalon, Jeff Montrose's Studio

"OH, JEFF, it's wonderful! Rod will be so pleased!"

Blythe Cameron glanced from the portrait of her ten-year-old twin daughters to her artist son. The painting was still on the easel, the smell of oil and turpentine pungent. "I really don't know how you managed to do it . . . I mean, capture the twins' individuality while showing how much alike they look!" She smiled fondly at the tall young man in the paint-smeared smock standing beside her. "You caught the mischief in Cara's eyes and the sweetness in Kitty's without losing the essence of their relationship."

"I hope Rod will share your opinion, Mother, but—"

"Oh, darling, you know your stepfather. He doesn't pretend to know or understand a thing about art, but I'm sure he'll recognize the skill it took to do this marvelous portrait of the girls."

"It wasn't easy," Jeff admitted ruefully. "Especially Cara! What a little scamp she is! I had to use all my creative imagination to keep her still. It's a good thing I know most of the stories of King Arthur by heart, but I must confess I made up a few along the way. I was *that* desperate at times!"

They laughed together. Cara's restless, madcap personality was a family joke.

5

"And Kitty, I suppose—"

"—was an absolute angel, of course," he finished.

Mother and son exchanged a meaningful look. It went without saying how different the twins were. Cara was high-spirited, stubborn and sassy, while Kitty, although vivacious and bright, was quieter and eager to please.

"Now, what about the framing?"

"I'll see to that, Mother. You don't want anything ornate. We need to retain the subtle delicacy of little girlhood—" Jeff paused as if unsure his mother was following him. "A heavy frame would overwhelm them."

"Of course." Blythe nodded in agreement. "I trust you, dear, to select something that will set the painting off to the best advantage. Just so it's ready by Christmas. I want it to be a surprise for Rod."

"I'll find just the right thing, Mother. Don't worry," Jeff assured her.

"Well, I must be off." Blythe gathered up her fur, picked up her handbag, and slipped on her kid gloves.

"I'll walk out with you." He opened the studio door.

As they stepped outside, the wind of the early winter afternoon felt damp and chilly. Blythe shivered and adjusted her mink stole. Walking down the path carpeted with sodden pine needles to the ferry dock, she put her hand on Jeff's arm.

"I do hope that you and Faith will be joining us for Christmas dinner."

Jeff shrugged. "You'll have to check with Faith. She makes all our social arrangements."

"But we're *family*, for pity's sake. Besides, you rarely ever socialize," Blythe chided gently. "You two live over here at Avalon like two hermits."

"Now, Mother, that's not entirely true. As a matter of fact, Faith is visiting Davida at Montclair this very afternoon."

Blythe's expression was thoughtful, considering the young woman who was now mistress of Montclair, the property adjoining their plantation. "Well, I must say I'm glad to hear that. Having someone as cheerful as Faith about will do Davida a world of good." Blythe sighed. "I should probably do more for her myself. I

6

have invited Davida several times to go riding with me, but she usually refuses. She doesn't like horses—" Blythe's voice trailed off as if wondering why anyone, given her choice of fine horses and beautiful countryside in which to ride them, wouldn't jump at the chance.

"I wouldn't worry about it, Mother. I'm sure Davida is happy enough. Faith says she absolutely dotes on her children."

"True. Almost *too* much, I'd say."

"And of course *you don't!*" he teased.

"Well—"

"In your defense," he put in gallantly, "I'd say all mothers are much the same, aren't they? At least that's what I've observed."

"But I don't think I hover over Scott and the twins as much as Davida does Meredith and Kip, do you?" Blythe asked in all seriousness. "Especially Kip."

"He's her only son," Jeff reminded her. "And I don't suppose *I* was spoiled at all, was I?"

"Oh, that was different. I was a single parent for much of your young life. After Malcolm died, you were my whole world." She gazed at him through misty eyes.

"Well, the Montrose children *have* a father. They have Jonathan."

"Jonathan!" Blythe made a gesture of dismissal. "Jonathan is much too passive where they're concerned. He doesn't assert himself at all."

Jeff shook his head. "Mother, you can't solve everyone's problems."

"That doesn't keep me from *trying!*" she retorted with a touch of girlish spunk.

Just then, Harry, the Montrose family groundskeeper, emerged from the little shed and approached them, tipping his cap and asking, "Ready to go across, Miz Cameron?"

"Yes, thank you, Harry." Then Blythe said to Jeff, "Good-bye, dear. Thank you again for a beautiful job. I *know* Rod will be pleased."

Jeff leaned down and kissed his mother's cheek, then helped her into the wooden boat. He untied the tow line and threw it to Harry in the prow, who shoved off from the dock.

7

As he stood watching the boat glide over the smooth surface of the water into the distance, Jeff unconsciously composed a painting. What a picture his mother made against the gray November sky, he thought—her auburn hair a flame under the brown velvet tricorne hat, the still-firm chin in profile, the slim lines of her body so gracefully erect.

Returning Jeff's farewell salute, Blythe sighed. He was probably right. Perhaps she *was* as much of a smothering mother as she considered Davida Montrose to be. But Jeff was so special. Born after the death of her first husband, Malcolm, Jeff had been brought up in England. Even though Blythe herself was now happily remarried to Rod Cameron, with whom she had three young children, her firstborn held a unique place in her heart.

She had wanted only the best for him always—happiness, love, success. Now he seemed to be achieving most of her dreams for him. His chosen career as an artist was progressing nicely. His paintings were more and more in demand. His wife adored him— his marriage ideally happy.

She remembered how she had had to reconcile herself to his elopement. Faith Devlin was the daughter of Garnet, whom Blythe had considered her rival because she had once been in love with Malcolm.

But that was a long time ago. *I will not dwell on the past,* Blythe told herself resolutely. Instead, she concentrated on how delighted Rod would be with the portrait of his two little girls! She recalled how thrilled he had been when their son Scott was born less than a year after their marriage. The birth of the twins had been an added blessing.

Unconsciously, Blythe shook her head, remembering the night they were born, a night marked by a wild storm that had lashed Mayfield County. So furious was the wind and driving rain that several of the towering elms surrounding their house had been badly damaged. Cara's birth had preceded Kitty's by fifteen minutes—slightly before midnight—so that their birthday was not shared, a fact that never diminished the enthusiasm with which they celebrated the two separate events. A year later, a daughter,

Meredith, had been born to Davida and Jonathan Montrose, and since babyhood, the three little girls had been staunch friends.

"Here we are, Miz Cameron," Harry called out. His voice brought Blythe back to the present as they came alongside the landing dock on the other side of the river. From here, it was only a short walk to the Arbordale livery stable where Blythe had left her smart little buggy and Deirdre, her mare.

Soon Blythe was heading back to Mayfield. She always looked forward to going home after an outing, back to Cameron Hall, to a glowing fire in the library, to her husband Rod, whom she would welcome at the end of a long day, to her children, with whom she would share those precious moments just before dinner and an early bedtime.

Part I
New Year's Day 1900
Cameron Hall
Mayfield, Virginia

chapter
1

THE DOOR TO Blythe's bedroom inched open and a child's face peeked around the edge. Taking a quick look inside, she turned to her companion and spoke in a conspiratorial whisper, "Come on, Kitty, coast's clear."

A minute later two little girls tiptoed into the room. They were about ten, dressed in matching blue striped pinafores.

"Oh, Cara, look what Mama's going to wear tonight!" exclaimed one softly as she went over to the canopied bed where an emerald green satin dress was spread. Kitty's small hand smoothed its lustrous surface, fingered the heavy black lace overlaid on the bodice.

But her sister was busy at the dressing table taking the stoppers out of the assortment of crystal perfume bottles, first passing them under her pert little nose, then running them along the inside of her wrist.

"Mmmm, smell this, Kitty!" Cara closed her eyes ecstatically.

Kitty joined her and sniffed appreciatively.

Just then they heard their names being called from down the hall, and they both looked up startled. Their images reflected in the large gilt-framed mirror were identical—red-gold curls; wide, dark eyes; small straight noses and rosy cheeks.

"Uh-oh! That's Lily." Kitty's mouth made a round O. "She's looking for us. If she finds us in here going through Mama's things . . ."

"Let's wait and see if she goes by—" was Cara's advice. "Maybe she'll think we went down to the kitchen."

Both held their breath as they heard footsteps outside their mother's door, then their nurse's voice talking to herself. "Now where did those two git to whilst I was laying out their party dresses?"

Cara clapped one chubby hand over her mouth stifling a giggle. But Kitty looked worried. "We better scoot, Cara."

Cara rolled her eyes and gave an elaborate shrug. "Oh, what can Lily do but fuss? She won't upset Mama by telling on us. Not tonight anyway with the party and guests coming." She started to lift the lid of the velvet jewel box when her twin grabbed her arm and jerked it away.

"No, Cara, don't! I don't want to get into trouble tonight with Meredith and Kip coming—"

"Oh, all right." Cara sighed. Impatient but persuaded, she reluctantly turned from her fascinating exploration to follow her twin. Kitty opened the door and cautiously peered into the hallway. Seeing that no one was about, she motioned with her hand to Cara and the two scampered back to their own bedroom.

A half hour later, Blythe, wrapped in a silk quilted robe, came from her bath in a mist of fragrant rose-scented talcum. She paused briefly outside the twins' door. From behind it she heard the sound of children's voices and laughter punctuated by another scolding adult one. Lily was in charge, she could tell. Blythe smiled and hurried down the hall toward her own bedroom.

She settled herself at the dressing table to do her hair. She liked doing it herself, knowing just how to twist its heavy length into a Roman knot, a trick her maid, Tisha, had never quite mastered. After slipping in the ornate amber shell comb at just the right angle, Blythe opened her jewel case and took from it the double strand pearl choker Rod had given her on their wedding day. Could it really be thirteen years ago this October? They had been the happiest and richest years of her life. Rod was still as devoted, as much in love with her as ever and the children, their son Scott and the twins—what angels they were and how blessed she was in her family.

She fastened in matching pearl drop earrings, then opened one of the dressing table drawers to replace the jewel box. There she saw another jewel case at the bottom. Involuntarily she shivered, feeling a sudden chill. It contained the Montrose bridal set, a ruby and diamond necklace and earrings. Of course, she had never worn them, had never wanted to. She rarely opened that box. Even looking at the jewels now brought back unhappy images of her ill-fated first marriage to Malcolm Montrose.

Seeing them brought to mind her recurrent conflict about the jewels. Since the 1700's Montrose men had gifted their brides with the magnificent set, with the understanding that it should be passed down from generation to generation.

A flood of memories swirled through her mind—the loss of Montclair, her first home in Virginia, to Randall Bondurant in payment of her first husband's gambling debts; Malcolm's subsequent death; her odyssey in England, where she had fled to escape that turbulent time; Jeff's birth there—

For a moment, Blythe thought again of Jonathan—Malcolm's other son by his first wife. Blythe herself had not met the young man until her marriage to Rod Cameron when she had come to live here at Cameron Hall, but now they were neighbors. Jonathan had inherited Montclair and now lived there with his wife, Davida Carpenter.

Just as she had attempted to forget her brief and tragic first marriage, so Blythe sometimes almost forgot about this intricate web of relationships woven by Malcolm's passion and pride. She knew that as a young man he had married Rose Meredith, a young New Englander he had brought as a bride to Virginia. But the Malcolm of her memory was a dark and brooding man. When she met him in California so many years ago, he was broken in spirit by his young wife's tragic death and the bitter years of war that he had endured.

Under unusual circumstances Blythe had married Malcolm Montrose. Eager for a life of her own, she had followed him gladly to his world—Virginia . . . and Montclair.

Hesitantly, almost with aversion, Blythe now pressed the little button that sprung the lock, opening the long velvet box in her hand. The Montrose rubies and diamonds lay against the satin lining, winking and gleaming as if to spite her. To whom did they rightfully belong? To the wife of Malcolm and Rose's son . . . or to her son's wife?

With a sigh, Blythe closed the jewel box and put it away. She would have to give the matter more consideration It wasn't something that she could decide now. But soon she really should.

At that moment, Blythe heard the sound of the children's voices coming down the hall from the nursery wing. Not that it was actually a nursery any longer. The children were growing up fast— *too fast*, she thought with regret. She had been overjoyed to have a second family with Rod—first, a son, Scott, to carry on the Cameron name and preserve the family dynasty; then two years later, the twins.

She could hear Cara's voice above the others, raised in a perennial argument of some kind. This child was always at the center of any storm, and Blythe wondered if having been born in the worst storm in the history of Mayfield County had anything to do with her temperament.

She rose and hurried to the bedroom door to see what her little daughter was making a fuss about now.

Opening the door to investigate the ruckus, Blythe saw the girls running down the carpeted hallway. They were already dressed in their new party dresses—royal blue velvet with wide bertha collars of Irish lace. Lily, hairbrush in hand, was following them as fast as her girth would allow. Cara's rosy face was screwed into a stubborn protest and she was shaking her head from side to side. Blythe could not tell whether Lily was trying to use the brush on the child's mass of russet curls, or to apply it to her derriere for chastening.

"Now, looka hyah, missy," Lily scolded. "You stand still and doan gib me no nonsense! Them Montrose chillen ain't come yet, and you doan hab to be out on de veranda waitin' for 'em, neither."

Catching sight of her mother standing at the bedroom door with a reproachful expression on her face brought Cara to a standstill.

"Well, all right, Lily!" she sighed dramatically. "Go ahead, but do hurry up. Kip will be here in a few minutes and—"

Kitty had also seen Blythe. "Oh, Mama!" she called out. "You look so pretty in that dress."

"Thank you, darling. I'm glad you think so." Pleased, Blythe leaned down and patted her little daughter's cheek, then turned to admonish Cara. "Don't make such a fuss, Carmella, and stop making Lily cross. You're getting to be a young lady and so you must start acting like one, not wiggling and squirming like that."

"But, Mama, Lily's already done my hair once, and Kip will be here and I—"

"Don't argue. Just do as you're told. Later on, you can all watch the dancing from the balcony . . . *that is*—" and Blythe's voice took on a severe tone, directing the rest of her remark to Cara—"if you're good and behave yourself."

With this warning, Blythe returned to her room to get her fan and gloves before going downstairs. She must consult with the serving staff, see that there were no last-minute emergencies, and check the refreshment tables to be sure that everything was in readiness for the many expected guests.

The twins stationed themselves on the steps, their faces pressed between the spindles of the stairway. From this vantage point they could see the front door, not only to watch for their friends, Meredith and Kendall Montrose, but also to observe the arrival of their parents' elegantly attired guests. Half the fun, they thought privately, was seeing which of the ladies was most done up and which of the gentlemen was most courtly and handsome.

Although an "outsider" from California, her mother had embraced all Virginia's holiday traditions enthusiastically and incorporated them in decorating Cameron Hall at Christmas. Not only did she observe all those passed down by Rod's mother, Kate, but had studied books describing the customs of the early Colonials and had applied them with precision.

Looking about her now, Kitty loved Christmas, especially the decorations that transformed their house into a wonderland. Greens native to the Virginia countryside—pine, waxy magnolia leaves, soft red cedar, rosemary, and laurel—decked the halls, while fragrant garlands of spruce were looped down the stairway banister. At the landing hung a plaque centered with pomegranates, grapes, Seckel pears, and Jerusalem cherries. Red candles scented with bayberry were everywhere—in the chandeliers, at each window, and on the tree, having been lit only once, on Christmas Eve. Every mirror and window frame was adorned with holly bright with crimson berries and a red satin bow tied with streamers at the top. On the double front door, twin arrangements of cloved lemons in evergreen wreaths, embellished with pine cones and cotton pods, welcomed all comers.

The centerpieces on the long refreshment tables were works of art, carefully crafted by Blythe herself—great pyramids of polished red apples encircled by shiny laurel leaves and flanked by bouquets of poinsettias and tall red tapers in gleaming silver candelabra.

The Christmas tree, a twelve-foot cedar standing in its usual place in the entryway between the drawing room and dining room, dazzled the eyes of the beholder. Each year the trimmings seemed more imaginative and spectacular than the last. This year, glittering with gilt beads, the tree was hung with gold balls and colorful exotic birds perched on its branches. Glass bells tinkled merrily each time the front door opened, admitting a breeze.

Music from the quartet playing in the small room adjoining the parlor accompanied the mingling of voices lifted in holiday greetings and the hum of conversation. Soon there would be dancing, and Kitty would be lost in dreams of the distant day when she, too, in a beautiful dress, would be waltzing on the polished floor in the arms of a Prince Charming who would assuredly come to whisk her away.

Satisfied that everything was under control, Blythe took her place beside Rod in the elegant foyer to receive the guests now streaming through the front door that never seemed to close before another group arrived.

They had been receiving for perhaps a half hour when Jeff and Faith appeared. *How stunning Faith looks,* Blythe thought with affectionate pride as her daughter-in-law swept into the front hall. Tall and willowy, she was wearing a peacock blue gown that set off to perfection the dark, wavy hair and English rose complexion. She wondered if Jeff had designed the gown, as he often did Faith's dresses. Certainly he must have chosen the color, his sure artist's eye selecting what would be most becoming to his wife. Perhaps Faith should have the Montrose bridal set. She could certainly display it to advantage.

As the couple came up to exchange New Year's greetings, Faith embraced Blythe. Then, clasping both of Blythe's hands in her own, Faith leaned forward and whispered, "Oh, Auntie Blythe, I have the most marvelous news. Jeff and I . . . we're to have a child, a baby this summer!"

"Oh, my dear, I am so happy . . . for both of you." Blythe smiled back into Faith's shining eyes. "I thought you had a special sparkle about you this evening!"

"It's still a secret. We haven't told anyone else yet. Not even Mama. I plan to write her just as soon as the holidays are over."

"She'll be on the next ship!" Blythe laughed, thinking of her old nemesis, who was living in England with her publisher husband, Jeremy Devlin. How thrilled she would be with this news of her first grandchild. Or would she? Garnet had always been vain and a bit shallow. Perhaps she would feel she was much too young for grandchildren!

Faith rolled her eyes. "Oh, no, I hope not!" She blushed at her own slip, then added, "You know I adore her, but she *does* have a tendency to take over. And Jeff is working on a very important painting, so I don't want anything to disturb his concentration until it's finished."

Jeff took Faith's arm, while giving his mother a slow wink. "Come, darling wife. You made me promise I'd dance tonight, so let's get it over."

"Get it over—the idea!" Faith pretended indignation, then linked her arm with his, and they strolled off together.

Blythe gazed after them. What a handsome couple they made and what a beautiful baby they were sure to have. Suddenly a startling realization dawned. *Fancy me about to become a grandmother when I still feel like a bride myself!* Glancing up at the tall, splendid-looking man beside her, an amusing afterthought followed. *Why, I'm in love with a grandfather!* Somehow, that notion struck her as even more preposterous, and she started to feel a giggle bubble up inside.

"Now what are you smiling about?" Rod asked, frowning. "You look like the cat that swallowed the canary."

"It's a secret."

"A secret? I thought we weren't ever going to have any more secrets from each other. Wasn't that part of our wedding vows?" he demanded with mock severity.

Blythe was saved from a reply by the next flood of arrivals, and there wasn't a chance to tell Rod about Jeff and Faith's news.

Several times during the evening, she watched the young couple circling the floor, admiring the grace of their movements, observing the way they gazed into each other's eyes. Blythe remembered the first time she had seen them waltzing together. How startled she had been at the time to see how perfect they looked together. And how strange and rather frightening that *her* son and *Garnet's* daughter might someday fall in love and marry—the children of the two women who had both been in love with the same man. Life is incomprehensible.

Perhaps she should give Faith the Montrose rubies, for Jeff was just as much a Montrose as Jonathan. When Jonathan's mother, Rose, had died, Blythe, as Malcolm's second wife, had been the logical one to have them. By the same token, Faith was eligible to receive them now.

Almost on the heels of Blythe's thoughts, Jonathan and Davida arrived. In contrast to Faith, Davida looked diminutive and fragile in a pearl-gray taffeta. Still, she was very attractive with her delicate features and wide eyes.

As Blythe went forward to greet her latest guests, she noticed that Davida was wearing the stunning diamond snowflake pendant that had belonged to Jonathan's mother, Rose. The sight of it eased her conscience a bit as to the possible disposition of the family heirlooms. Certainly the current mistress of Montclair did not lack for beautiful adornment and should have nothing to complain about.

On the contrary, however, the first words out of Davida's mouth were laments about the icy roads and the freezing weather, accompanied by her rueful glance at Jonathan as if he were somehow to blame. *Surely winters in Davida's native Massachusetts must be worse than Virginia winters*, Blythe could not help thinking.

She studied the couple. Was Davida unhappy? The next silent question followed the first. Was Jonathan? Blythe couldn't be sure. For all her good intentions, in the ten years since they had become neighbors, Blythe had never been able to get very close to either of them. Not that she had really tried, she thought with some guilt.

Perhaps it was her fault. Was there some inner resistance on her part? Jonathan resembled the young Malcolm to an uncanny degree. Was there, therefore, some hidden resentment in Blythe that prevented her getting to know and love Malcolm's other son?

Much, she knew, lay unspoken between them—most obviously, the fact that Jonathan was the son of Malcolm's first marriage, and Jeff was the son of Malcolm's second bride. Jeff had never known his father, and since coming to Virginia to make his home, the two young men had managed to gain a mutual respect for one another without ever really forging a strong fraternal bond. Perhaps too many barriers separated them, thought Blythe, not the least of which were the circumstances of their birth and having grown to manhood in different countries and developing different values, different goals.

Jonathan was now a gentleman farmer, overseeing Montclair after it had been deeded to him by his cousin, Drucilla Bondurant; and Jeff was pursuing his art at Avalon, the home where he had lived with Blythe until her marriage to Rod Cameron.

Almost as if thinking of Dru had precipitated her arrival, she appeared on the arm of her husband, the man who had won Montclair from Malcolm in a card game. Even now it was difficult for Blythe to be polite to Randall Bondurant, but her role as hostess demanded a charming and gracious welcome. Besides, she sincerely liked Dru.

While not beautiful, Dru had the proud carriage, the aristocratic features of the Montrose family. Since her marriage to a worldly, well-traveled man, she had also achieved a certain sophistication, a glamor and style, Blythe thought, admiring her ermine-banded velvet evening cape and the superbly beaded gown of ice-blue satin she was wearing.

The instant that Dru spotted Jonathan, she hurried toward him with a glad cry of greeting. The two, who had grown up together at Montclair during the War, had always been close. They hugged and then Dru embraced Davida, too, before coming to greet Blythe and Rod.

"It's so wonderful to be here and to see everyone!" she exclaimed.

"Where's Aunt Dove?" was Rod's first question, referring to Dru's mother, whom they had come from Charleston to visit for Christmas.

"Oh, Evalee had the sniffles, and Mama elected to stay home and keep her company. They were snuggled up reading *The Twelve Dancing Princesses* when we left. You know, Mama is the dotingest grandmother in the world!" Dru explained, laughing. "But Evalee was disappointed not to see the twins and Scott, of course."

"Yes, that is too bad," Blythe fibbed, knowing that her twins considered Evalee Bondurant a "spoiled brat" and would be mightily glad that she had not come.

Hearing this, the twins, who were sitting on the steps just beyond the curve of the stairway, exchanged exaggerated sighs of relief.

The two Montrose children had arrived with their parents and stood waiting beside them. To Blythe's eye, Kendall, nicknamed Kip, a handsome, rosy-cheeked lad of eleven, quite overshadowed his younger sister, Meredith, a plain-looking little girl with straight, light brown hair and wistful hazel eyes. She was quiet and shy, with none of her mother's prettiness nor her father's outgoing charm, and seemed destined to walk in her more outgoing brother's shadow.

Seeing their friends, the twins dashed down the steps to meet them, Cara tugging at Kip's sleeve and Kitty taking Meredith's hand.

"I've got a wonderful idea! Just wait 'til you hear!" Cara told Kip.

Kip eyed Cara warily. Cara was great fun, and he was usually willing to go along with any suggestion she made. But there were times he'd regretted it—like the time he'd broken his arm jumping from the shed roof—

"What kind of idea?" he asked.

"I'll tell you in a minute, but first you've got to promise to keep it a secret."

Kip glanced up and caught Scott Cameron at the top of the steps, leaning over the banister as the four other children approached.

At twelve, Scott felt much too old to join in games with his sisters and their friends, but tonight had the potential of being tediously boring since the younger generation would be confined to the upstairs for the most part. If nothing more interesting developed, he would retreat to his room to read one of the new books he had received for Christmas.

As much as Kip liked Cara, his masculinity was in the balance now that he had seen Scott. If there was an option tonight, he'd rather be with the older boy. So, until Scott indicated what he was going to do, Kip decided to reserve his decision.

"Wait 'til you see the dollhouse we got, Merry," Kitty was telling Meredith. "It looks just like our own real house outside, but it's got different kinds of rooms and furniture and a little family of dolls that goes inside."

Kip turned to Cara with a disgusted look. "Is *that* what you wanted to show me?"

"A silly old dollhouse? Of course not! Come on." And Cara proceeded to drag him down the hallway.

Overhearing this exchange, Scott raised his eyebrows, evidently coming to the conclusion that whatever the others were going to do didn't interest him. So, putting his hands in his jacket pockets, he sauntered nonchalantly in the other direction to his own room, leaving Kip to throw in his lot with Cara for the evening.

Kitty and Merry had disappeared into the nursery where the miniature three-story replica of Cameron Hall was set up, and the two little girls were immediately involved in the make-believe lives of the dollhouse family.

"Now what the's secret?" Kip demanded.

Cara put her finger to her lips. "We've got to be real careful. Follow me."

She tiptoed down to the end of the hall where her parents' suite was located, an area of the house usually off limits to the children, though they had violated that restriction more than once.

Easing open the door to Blythe's small sitting room adjoining the master bedroom, Cara beckoned Kip forward and asked in a stage whisper, "Cross your heart and hope to die?"

"Sure."

"'Member last Saturday at your house?"

He nodded vigorously, eyes alight in anticipation.

The week before, when looking for a place to hide while they were playing "Sardines" at Montclair, Cara and Kip had accidentally discovered a hidden panel in the now unused nursery. Inadvertently, Cara had leaned against the wall and sprung a concealed hinge that released the lock. To their astonished eyes, the panel had slid back, revealing a secret room. Creeping inside, they had found another door that led down some narrow steps to an underground passage. Swearing secrecy, they had emerged, covered in cobwebs and dust, determining that when the weather was better and the opportunity presented itself, they would follow it to see where it led. Both had felt the thrill of fear along with a heightened sense of adventure. Sharing such a momentous secret had strengthened their bond of friendship even more.

"Well, my idea is this—" Cara began. "Next time I'm over at Montclair, we'll find a way to go up to the nursery again, slide back the door, and . . . put a time capsule in there—"

"A time capsule?"

Yes, you know the kind people bury and don't dig up or open for years . . . sometimes even a *hundred* years—"

"A *hundred* years?"

"Well, it doesn't have to be that long. Maybe, twenty—"

"Twenty?"

Cara gave a sigh of disgust. "Kip, you're repeating everything I say! Anyway, we'll put all sorts of things in it. You know, tomorrow will be 1900, Kip! Can't you just imagine what it will be like twenty years from now when our time capsule is opened up?"

"What sorts of things would we put in it?" Kip asked cautiously, hoping it wouldn't mean giving up some of his new Christmas presents.

"They should be important things—secret things. Documents, sort of."

"Uh . . . what do you mean?"

"Documents like . . . ummm, maps, certificates—"

"Certificates?"

"Oh, Kip, use your imagination, can't you?" Exasperated, Cara put her hands on her hips.

"Sure, but I don't have any certificates."

Cara's eyes grew very big and she leaned closer. "Well, I *do!*" She waited for his reaction. "At least, I know where some are. And *that's* my secret. But you've got to promise you'll never tell anyone what I'm about to show you."

"I promise," he agreed solemnly, now thoroughly intrigued.

"Say it then. Repeat after me: I, Kip Montrose, choose to be hung by my thumbs from the tallest tree if I ever tell what I'm about to see."

Kip, excited now, rattled off the pledge.

"Now, I'll show you," Cara declared. "See that desk?" She pointed to the graceful fruitwood desk with inlaid marquetry. "It's my mother's now, but it used to belong to *your* great-grandmother, Sara Leighton. It has her initials carved underneath and 'Savannah, 1820'."

Kip looked impressed.

"My mother found it in an antique shop and bought it," Cara told him. "But that isn't the best part. It has a secret drawer. Here, I'll show you." She went over and ran her chubby hand along the underside, and a small drawer slid open. "And here is an important document—something we could put in our time capsule," she crowed triumphantly.

"But wouldn't your mother find out? I mean, wouldn't she miss it if she's hidden it?"

"She's probably even forgotten she has it. Besides, it should be preserved for history in our time capsule. Here, read it." Cara handed him a folded parchment, yellowed with age.

Kip's eyes raced along the faded print, the paper so old it crackled in his hands. "MARRIAGE CERTIFICATE. Lucas Valley, California," he read aloud, then looked at Cara. "California!"

"In 1870 too!" she said in a hushed voice.

"Malcolm Montrose and Blythe Dorman." Kip looked at Cara again. "*Your* mother."

"Yes! And *your* grandfather!"

"Yes, and there's more." Cara put her hand in the drawer and drew out a plain gold band and stretched out her palm to show Kip.

"Cara, I don't think we should take this," Kip said solemnly.

"It's history, Kip. It belongs in a time capsule. It's important to both families . . . even if Mama's married to Papa now."

Just then Kitty's voice called down the hall. "Cara! Kip! Where are you? Lily says we can go down to the kitchen for refreshments now. Come on, you two!"

"You better put this back, Cara." Kip thrust the certificate at her.

"What's the matter? Afraid?"

"No, I'm not afraid, but—"

"Don't you think a time capsule's a good idea?"

"Yes, but I think we should put our own stuff in it, not these old things that don't belong to us. We could get in plenty of trouble, Cara."

"Kip, Cara!" Kitty's voice came again, this time closer.

"Oh, all right—" Cara sounded disappointed, but she was beginning to agree with Kip. She put the ring and certificate back in the drawer and closed it. Then they slipped out of the room, pulling the door behind them.

In an alcove at the side of the dance floor, Jonathan brought two cups of eggnog over to where Dru was seated, handed her one, then sat down beside her. Glancing at the young man dancing with his mother, he sighed. "I do sometimes feel guilty about Jeff . . . I mean, about Montclair. He's a rightful heir, too. Shouldn't he have some part of it?"

Dru put a hand on his arm. "You shouldn't feel guilty, Jonathan. We didn't even know Jeff existed when Randall and I deeded the property to you. If anyone should feel guilty, it's Blythe. It's *her* fault. Disappearing for all those years after your father's death, never letting anyone know where she was nor that she had a child, Malcolm's son—" She paused, frowning. "Besides, you are the firstborn, and the law of primogeniture declares the oldest son inherits everything, doesn't it?"

Jonathan smiled ruefully. "In England, maybe. But, after all, didn't we break away from England during the Revolution? So I'm not sure that law holds in Virginia. Anyway, I'm more than willing to share with Jeff—"

"Why, Jonathan? Jeff is perfectly content with his life at Avalon, and Faith certainly seems radiantly happy," she remarked as Faith danced by with her father-in-law.

Just then the band stopped in the middle of a popular dance tune, and the leader held up his hand, his baton poised dramatically. The dancers stood still and everything grew very quiet. Very slowly the grandfather clock in the hall began striking the hour of midnight. At the last chime there was a burst of applause and loud cheering.

"Happy New Year!" people greeted one another as strains of "Auld Lang Syne" poured over the happy crowd.

Jonathan smiled at his cousin. "It's midnight! The start of a new century. I'll have to go find Davida, but first—" He leaned over and kissed Dru's cheek. "Happy 1900, Dru."

"Happy New Year, Jonathan," she replied and hoped with all her heart that *this* year would mark the beginning of a new happiness for him.

Sitting on the back stairway off the kitchen, Kip and Cara enjoyed an assortment of leftovers from the grown-ups' buffet.

"I still think a time capsule in the secret room is a great idea," Cara insisted as she spooned strawberry ice cream and lemon sponge cake into her mouth, "don't you?"

Kip found balancing his plate on his knees too much, put it down on the step, and moved to the one below before replying. "Sure," he agreed, taking a bite of the cake.

"We could use a shoebox and seal it and nobody but us would know about it."

Enthusiastically they began to plan what they would put in it.

"And we wouldn't open it for . . . how long? Ten years?"

27

"Longer than that—" mumbled Cara, her mouth stuffed full.
"But we want to be alive when it's time to open it, don't we?"
"Twenty or fifteen years, then."

"How about . . . twelve years . . . when we're both twenty-one?"
suggested Kip after a little mental calculation.

Cara's spoon halted halfway to her mouth. "Right. Twelve years
from now, on New Year's Eve at midnight, we'll open it." A dreamy
look crossed her face. "I wonder what the world will be like in
1912—"

Part II
New England

chapter
2

Cape Cod
Summer 1909

JUNE SUNSHINE sparkled on the water as the ferry from New Bedford eased to the landing dock at Oak Bluffs where Meredith Montrose was to meet them. The Cameron twins leaned against the deck rail, searching the crowd waiting for the passengers for their friend. They had been invited to spend the summer at Meredith's Grandfather's Cape Cod "cottage." Finally spotting her, Cara exclaimed, "There she is!" and pointed to a slender girl dressed in a light blue chambray dress just below them. Waving her hand wildly she called, "Yoo-hoo, Merry!"

Seeing them, Meredith took off her wide-brimmed sailor hat and waved it back at them. "Hello, twins!"

Within a few minutes they were running down the gangplank toward her with shrieks of greetings. This was the first time they had all seen each other since March, when Kitty and Cara were home on spring vacation.

"It's so good to see you!" Merry said, hugging first one, then the other.

"You look wonderful!" Kitty told her.

"You're already brown as the proverbial berry!" Cara regarded her admiringly. "I can't wait to get rid of *my* 'prison pallor'!"

"I didn't know you considered Fern Grove *prison*." Merry laughed, gaily referring to the women's college near Charlottesville where the twins had just completed their first year. "We've been here two weeks. Mama and I came up at the end of May to be with Grandfather. He was a speaker at the local Veterans Memorial Day ceremonies in Milford. Then we all three came here to open the beach house for the summer."

As they collected their baggage, Merry said, "Oh, I'm so glad you've come. We're going to have such fun; it's going to be a wonderful summer."

She hailed one of the dockside porters to help them load the twins' things into the "beach wagon" Merry had driven in to meet them. Then they all climbed into the "basket," as Merry called the small pony cart, and, chatting and constantly interrupting each other, they started off.

While they drove along the cobbled streets in the main part of town, Merry gave them a capsulized background of the island, since this was their first visit. Cape Cod, a crescent shaped slice of land lying just south of the coast of Massachusetts at its most southeastern point, had a long, fascinating history. The capture of the first whale in 1668 brought with it a burst of prosperity, until the whalers almost brought the whales to extinction.

But toward the end of the last century, it had become popular mostly as a summer resort for New Englanders, Merry told them. "It's also a favorite spot for summer 'revival' Camp Meetings." She gave them a mischievous glance. "That is *if* you're so inclined."

"Not *me!*" declared Cara. "I'm here to relax, enjoy myself, and have a good time."

Merry and Kitty smiled at her enthusiasm, feeling the welcome shade of the tall elm trees lining the board walkways, and noting a few old brick houses of Federal architecture set back from the streets in the residential areas a short distance from the downtown section.

At the edge of town, they turned onto an unpaved road, plodding along at the fat little pony's leisurely pace. Here they could see only the slanted roofs of buildings half-hidden by high dunes. Merry told them they would soon be meeting the people who lived here.

"I've known most of them all my life, since the same families come back year after year. There are lots of young people our age. I think you'll like them. People are so friendly on the Island. And Kip's friends from Harvard come in droves!" She laughed. "In other words, there's plenty of social life, but it's different from Mayfield . . . much more informal."

"Sounds like fun!"

"Oh, it is! Worlds of fun! Here we are now. Whoa, Peggotty!" Meredith called to her pony, who stopped, then had to be prodded with a long stick before being persuaded to turn into a narrow driveway marked with a wooden sign: "Fair Winds."

"Welcome," she announced, jumping down from the driver's seat.

Hopping down after her, Cara and Kitty drew in a deep appreciative breath. The air was clear, pungently salty with the smell of the ocean—a far cry from the humid Virginia summers. Then they exchanged a surprised glance. The beach "cottage" they had expected was, instead, a sea-weathered, gray-shingled Victorian house three stories high, built on a bluff overlooking the Atlantic.

"See up there!" Merry pointed to the railed cupola on the roof. "It's called a 'widow's walk.' There are a lot of them on Cape houses, built so the sea captain's wife could catch the first glimpse of her husband's ship returning. This house was originally owned by a family of sailing men, many lost at sea. Unfortunately, the name was true more often than not."

Just then Mrs. Montrose, looking healthier and more fit than they had ever seen her, came out to welcome them. She was followed by a distinguished-looking man with a shock of thick white hair and a mustache, whom she introduced as her father, Colonel Carpenter. He greeted them cordially and invited them to come inside.

He led the way onto a wide veranda that wrapped around the house and overlooked the beach and the blue-green ocean beyond.

"What a gorgeous view!" Kitty said.

"It's one of the things I enjoy most about Fair Winds," Colonel Carpenter commented, pleased with her praise.

"Sit down, girls," invited Mrs. Montrose, gesturing toward the rush-seated rocking chairs arranged in a conversational grouping along the porch. "Now, how about something cool to drink? You must be thirsty after your long trip."

As they sipped refreshing iced tea from tall glasses, the twins related their traveling experiences since they'd boarded the train in Richmond for Boston—an overnight journey and their first time in a sleeping car. Before long, Cara had them all in hysterics with her graphic account of taking a wrong turn on her way back from the Ladies' Room and frightening an old woman when she tried to climb into the woman's newly made bunk by mistake.

"We're so glad your parents allowed you to come this year," Davida said after the laughter had subsided. "I'm sure you'll come to love our Cape summers as much as we do."

"I'm sure we shall, Mrs. Montrose," Kitty said, looking at Cara.

"I told them *this* summer is going to be the best one ever, Mama, now that *they've* come!" Meredith beamed, looking happily from one twin to the other, hoping they'd noticed how much more relaxed and happy her mother was here than at Montclair. During the summers at Fair Winds, Davida underwent a noticeable change. It was one of the things Meredith loved most about these Cape Cod summers.

After they had visited a while, when Mrs. Montrose suggested that the girls might like to get settled in their room, Meredith took them inside. They went down a wide center hall that ran the length of the house, with doors on either side opening on the bedrooms occupied by Colonel Carpenter and her mother, then up the stairs.

At the landing Merry paused and pointed to a narrow stairway leading to the top floor. "We call it the loft," she explained. "It's for Kip's friends, who'll start coming soon. That's when the summer really gets into full swing!" She giggled. "Want to take a peek? After the boys come, that floor is off limits."

Setting down their assorted luggage, the three scrambled up the steps and inspected the men's dormitory, a long vaulted room with narrow cots lining both sides.

"They might even arrive this weekend," said Merry. "I believe Kip's already primed them for two of the prettiest Southern belles from Virginia! So be prepared."

"I can think of worse fates than too many fellows," quipped Cara.

As they went back down the steps, Merry added, "Kip was going to stop over in Milford for a few days to see our Meredith cousins and pick up some things Grandfather wanted from his house." Back on the second floor, she opened a door into a room with two white elaborately scrolled iron beds and two bureaus. "This will be yours."

"Oh, what a view!" cried Cara, running over and looking out one of the large windows at expanse of sky, sand, and sea. "I know I'm going to love being here!"

"I do hope so. I've wanted to show you my summer world for a long time." Merry smiled. "Now, the bathroom's just down the hall, and I'm right next door. If my cousin Emily Meredith comes down to spend a week or so, she'll room with me," she told them, then suggested, "Why don't you two put on something comfortable, and we'll go for a walk on the beach before supper?"

It did not take any more urging for Cara and Kitty to get out of their linen traveling suits and unpack cotton skirts and blouses. Taking out their hairpins, they braided each other's waist-length hair to swing over their shoulders.

Appetites were keen when the girls came in from their stroll and found a supper of breaded halibut, served with baked potatoes and summer vegetables, and for dessert, a berry cobbler. Afterward the three friends took another walk on the beach, chasing shore birds and picking up shells. By bedtime they were thoroughly relaxed and ready to turn in early, the end of a picture-perfect day.

At Fair Winds, the twins soon discovered, everything moved at a different pace, as if capturing the moments to be sifted slowly, one by one, like grains of sand through an hourglass.

A stout, cheerful Irish cook named Aggie came in every day to consult with Mrs. Montrose about menus and meals. Housekeeping seemed mainly a matter of sweeping the constant inroads of sand tracked in by bare feet from the beach. The furniture was spartan, mostly of wicker, with sofas and easy chairs covered in blue-and-white-striped cotton and brightened by piles of plump pillows of flowered cretonne. The walls were bare, the curtains of plain unbleached muslin. Life was as pared down as possible and wholly enjoyable.

Meals, too, were not elaborate but hearty, with lots of vegetables, fruit, and fish. At breakfast, a buffet was set up, where each helped himself to oatmeal still on the stove, cinnamon buns, and coffee in an urn on the golden oak hutch in the dining room.

It was clear that the only thing that took place on schedule was the daily raising and lowering of "Old Glory." There was a flagpole out front, and the ceremonial running up of the Stars and Stripes and taking down the flag each evening was conducted with military precision by the Colonel and attended by all.

By the end of the first week, Kitty and Cara felt as if they'd never known any other kind of life. Long, lazy days were spent beachcombing and swimming. They waded out into the tingling-cold surf, jumping and riding the breakers. Getting caught in the swirling waves, they rolled, laughing, onto the beach. They searched for shells, picked berries, spent hours walking the beach, built elaborate sandcastles, and talked endlessly.

In spite of Mrs. Montrose's suggestions about protecting their fair complexions from the sun, they largely ignored the warning and slowly acquired becoming tans.

On Friday, Kip arrived, and immediately everything at Fair Winds changed entirely. From the moment he stepped onto the porch and announced himself with a shout, the atmosphere was charged with a new intensity. Everyone reacted to his magnetic personality, from the Colonel to Aggie, whom Kip teased unmercifully, imitating her brogue and snitching her hot rolls before they were even out of the baking pan.

And Davida Montrose basked in her handsome son's attention, delighting in his flattery.

Mealtimes became unrehearsed comedic scenes with Kip at his playful best. As usual, he and Cara set each other off, sparring and baiting one another. Their verbal battles were so frequent and furious that it was hard to tell if they were serious or merely having fun. No matter what subject came under discussion, they took opposite sides of the argument, whether designed to needle each other or to provoke a lively exchange. Whenever the two of them were together, sparks flew.

Kip was hard to resist, and his goading was usually good-natured. It was only when Cara's response became a little too sharp, a little too critical, that Kip showed any irritation. It was at such times that he flung down his napkin and left the table in an apparent pique over one of her well-aimed barbs. But most of the time, their encounters ended in hilarity, and the two of them seemed continually stimulated by each other's company.

In fact, within days after Kip's arrival, Cara was spending more time with him than with the other two girls. He was teaching her to sail and, since there was only room for two in his catamaran, Kitty and Meredith were often left to their own devices.

The other two girls left to themselves grew even closer. Although Meredith loved both twins and considered them her best friends, she and Kitty actually had more in common. They both kept journals, sometimes sharing the thoughts and feelings they recorded in them. Cara, on the other hand, was too busy living her life to write about it.

One evening shortly after Kip burst on the scene, Davida and Colonel Carpenter were sitting on the veranda when Kip and Cara walked past on their way down to the beach.

"What a handsome couple those two young people make," her father observed, taking in Kip's tall, well-built frame and Cara's sun-lightened hair, her slender graceful walk. "That girl's definitely a beauty, no mistake."

"In the eye of the beholder, maybe—" Davida began.

"What do you mean, my dear?"

"Pretty is as pretty does." Davida sighed. "She's a difficult young lady, to put it mildly. Any young man who falls in love with her is taking a risk."

"She seems quite charming to me."

"You don't know her, Papa."

"Well then, she's innocent until proven guilty, isn't she?"

"Perhaps I shouldn't judge her," conceded Davida. "All I really know is what I've observed in Mayfield. She's had dozens of beaux, and that may not mean she's fickle, but it *may* mean she's careless with other people's feelings."

Her father did not disagree but added, "Sometimes those are the ones who are most irresistible."

Davida turned to give him a long, searching look. "Well . . . I only hope Kip doesn't get hurt."

"Little girl," said the Colonel gently, "you can't protect your son from that kind of hurt."

If Davida had not been so preoccupied with her concern over the flirtatious twin and Kip's infatuation, she might have noticed the faraway look that crept into Kendall Carpenter's eyes. He was remembering his own hopeless love for Rose Meredith. If she had, she might have recalled hearing once that the only love that lasts, unchanging, is unrequited love.

chapter
3

THE NEXT WEEK everything changed with the arrival of three of Kip's Harvard classmates, whose families came to the Cape every year. The same Friday, Scott and Vance Langley showed up. They were staying with some university friends who had rented a beach house for the summer. When the Montrose cousins, the Merediths from Milford, opened their summer cottage, their son and daughter, Emily and Norville, joined the group of young people that soon made Fair Winds their headquarters.

For all of them that summer, life was a party—an endless round of sailing excursions and lobster bakes, volleyball games on the beach, and songfests on the veranda.

A month of perfect days passed before Cara awakened out of a dream one morning with the tantalizing sensation that something wonderful was about to happen. Wide awake now, she lay quite still, savoring the pleasant tingle. Knowing it would be impossible to try to go back to sleep, she slipped out of bed and went to the open window.

The scene before her was so pure and lovely that her eyes misted with tears. The rising ball of sun slanted its rays off the deep blue water, and in the canopy of clear sky, white gulls dipped and dived for their breakfast, their hoarse cries announcing the success of the catch.

Cara found her clothes and dressed quietly so as not to awaken her sleeping sister, then tiptoed downstairs, carrying her shoes. She stopped only long enough to take one of Aggie's cinnamon rolls set out in a basket on the hutch, wrap it in a napkin, and tuck it into her cardigan pocket. Then she let herself out the door, breathing rapturously of the tangy salt air.

Being out so early with no one about appealed to her sense of adventure, and she felt the rush of exhilaration. She ran down the porch steps, over the dunes, and onto the beach, feeling the cool, damp sand between her toes. On and on she ran, feeling completely free and at one with the world around her.

The beach was deserted, the ocean, a smooth sheet of blue glass. After a while, she slowed to a walk and began wading along the ocean's edge, stopping every once in awhile to pick up a shell, hold it in her hand, and examine it briefly before tossing it into the water. She'd never had much use for collecting things. Life was too exciting to spend precious time hunting for objects. Not when the world was so full of fascinating *people*.

Cara had gone quite a distance down the beach when she saw a figure approaching from the opposite direction. He was tall and lean, and his head was hunched into his shoulders as if he were in deep thought. They passed each other with a nod and a mere glance, as if in recognition of a "kindred soul," assuming anyone walking the beach at daybreak must crave solitude.

She had gone only a little farther when she heard someone calling. Turning, she saw that it was the man who had passed her moments before. In his hand he was holding something bright and colorful, waving it high above his head.

She halted, frowning. Who was he and what did he want?

Then, as he drew nearer, she saw that he was holding out her scarf.

"I'm afraid it's soaked . . . the tide's coming in—" He panted, a little breathless from running.

"Oh, yes, thank you." She took the slip of sodden silk, shaking it out a little.

He smiled, and she noticed even white teeth against a golden tan.

"It's great out here this time of day, isn't it?" he asked. "I love it when there's no one around. I feel like I own it all—" He laughed, spreading his arms to encompass the scene.

"Yes—" She studied him more closely, thinking he must be a new visitor to the Island. "Are you on vacation?"

"Well, not exactly. I'm staying with some friends up the beach. But I'm also working part-time at the Dover Inn to earn money for next year's college expenses." He made no move to leave, then said, "I'm Owen Brandt." The way he offered his name almost required that she give hers.

Well, there was no reason not to, Cara told herself. Here at the Cape everything was informal with no need to stick to silly old rules of protocol. "Cara Cameron."

His eyes lighted up. "Cameron?" He paused. "Are you possibly any relation to Scott Cameron?"

Cara was flustered. "Why, yes! He's my brother."

"Small world. We're both staying at the Langleys."

"Of course!" Cara exclaimed. "Vance said some of his friends from the University of Virginia were coming this weekend, and Scott—"

As they stood there smiling at each other, suddenly Cara felt she could not draw a deep breath. At the same time, she was aware that Owen's eyes were the color of the ocean . . . just past where the swells end and before the waves begin to roll toward the shore.

"Cara—" He repeated her name, a pucker of a frown drawing his sun-bleached brows together over a strongly molded nose. "Cara . . . it's Italian, isn't it? I mean, from my meager knowledge of the language, it means 'heart' or something affectionate like 'beloved'—" He looked to her for confirmation.

"No." Cara hesitated. Her heart was beating unnaturally fast. She wondered vaguely what was happening to her. This kind of bantering usually slid so easily from her practiced tongue. Instead, she seemed temporarily spellbound by Owen's eyes, so full of intelligence and merriment and all sorts of interesting possibilities—

"Cara's my family's nickname for me. My real name is Carmella. It's Spanish. I was named for my grandmother." She tilted her head to one side and continued. "She was a gypsy from Seville—a dancer, I'm told. Not a very proper background, is it?"

"I don't know if it's *proper* or not," Owen replied slowly, "but the

41

name . . . whatever it means . . . suits you—" He paused again, then, "Maybe we'll be seeing each other again. Are you staying around here?" he asked hopefully.

"My sister and I are houseguests of Meredith Montrose."

"At Fair Winds?"

"Yes." She nodded. "It belongs to Colonel Kendall Carpenter, her grandfather."

"What a coincidence!" He grinned. "I was told we'd been invited to supper at the Carpenters' cottage tonight!"

They looked at each other wordlessly for a long moment. Finally Owen backed away a few steps. "Well, then, I'll see you later . . . this evening!"

"Yes," Cara replied mindlessly, unable to think of a single breezy remark. And after Owen turned around and walked down the beach, she stood watching him.

That evening, when Owen showed up at Fair Winds with Scott and some of the other students from the university, their eyes met across the room. When Scott introduced them offhandedly, saying to Owen, "And this is the other half of my little twin sister set," Owen simply smiled and acknowledged the introduction as if they had mutually agreed to keep their earlier meeting a secret.

Supper was set out in the dining room—a steaming tureen of thick, creamy clam chowder, buttery poppy-seed rolls, a brown pottery crock of baked beans, and a large vegetable salad. Everyone quickly gathered, ready to enjoy it.

Scott held up his hand dramatically and, in his best thespian voice, declared, "Prithee, good folk, shall we then eat unblessed food?" With that, he made a sweeping bow to Owen. "I suggest we let the chaplain of this motley crew pronounce grace."

All heads turned in Owen's direction, but he seemed not at all embarrassed and said good-naturedly, "Well, I think the Selkirk Grace, written by the renowned Scottish poet Robert Burns, would be appropriate." He paused, then bowing his head, recited,

> *"Some hae meat and canna eat,*
> *And some wad eat that want it,*

But we hae meat and we can eat
And sae the Lord be thankit. Amen."

At once they moved to fill their plates and, in groups of three or four, found places to eat and talk. Before Cara knew it, Owen was at her side. "Let's take ours out on the porch," he said as if their dining together had been prearranged.

Finding a spot in a corner of the veranda, Owen drew up a bench where they could eat, undisturbed.

"I didn't understand—" began Cara when their meal was underway. "Why did Scott ask *you* to say grace?"

Owen took a sip of coffee, regarding her over the rim of the mug before answering. "You didn't know? I'm a divinity student."

Cara felt a sharp sensation of disbelief, then of disappointment. A divinity student?! Suddenly all the silly fantasies she'd had about him all day came crashing down.

"You mean you're going to be a *minister?*" Her tone registered her chagrin, and he laughed. She put down her fork and stared at him.

"Well, it's not as if I'd just told you I'm Count Dracula!"

Cara laughed too, albeit somewhat uneasily. Then she recovered herself. "And what does a divinity student actually study?"

"Right now we're heavily into the Old Testament and, of course, Greek and Hebrew—"

"Oh, dear!" she said in open dismay.

"Don't look like that," he pleaded in mock horror.

"It's just that I realized—"

But whatever she realized was never voiced because just then Scott, accompanied by Vance Langley, joined them and the topic changed. Before Cara and Owen could resume their conversation, Davida came to the door and invited them in for dessert.

After that, it was dark, lamps were lighted, and someone suggested a game of Charades. Owen and Cara ended up on the same team. To Cara's delight, Owen was not only creative in selecting ideas that confounded their opposition but quick and intuitive in guessing the other side's subjects.

"It seems you know much more than the Old Testament and a

43

few dead languages," Cara confronted him when the game broke up and Meredith and Kitty had set out pitchers of lemonade and oatmeal cookies.

"I'm interested in a great many things," he countered, smiling.

"Well, I'm relieved to hear that. I confess I was a bit taken aback when I discovered I was dining with a prospective man of the cloth!"

Owen threw back his head and laughed heartily. When Cara joined in, Kip glanced over at them and glared. Kitty intercepted the frown and knew that Kip was feeling the pinch of jealousy. Added to Vance Langley's attentions to Cara, he now must deal with the newcomer on the scene—Owen Brandt.

Later that night, long after Kitty was sleeping soundly, Cara lay awake thinking about Owen. Her thoughts tumbled chaotically. She had never met anyone like him or felt so quickly drawn to anyone before. Certainly none of the young men who came over to Fern Grove on weekends from the nearby men's college and circled her like the proverbial moth around a flame.

Of course, she had enjoyed flirting. But there was always an emptiness inside, a kind of "Is this all there is?" feeling at the end of the evening when the band played "Good-night, Sweetheart." With Owen, on the other hand, Cara suspected there were layers and layers to uncover and each one would be fascinating. Even on the surface he seemed ideal—considerate, intelligent, reserved yet fun-loving. *He has a wonderful laugh,* she thought, *and a smile that simply lights up a room.* But there was something more—deep spiritual qualities that, ironically, made him even more attractive.

Cara had a moment of doubt. What did she, who had never had a serious thought in her life, have to offer a man like that?

Still, when Owen's visits to Fair Winds became more and more frequent, no one seemed to notice how often he and Cara paired off for games or wandered off together to talk for hours. That is, nobody but Kip.

chapter
4

ON A TRIP into the village to collect the mail for Fair Winds, Kitty stopped by the harbor. Settling down on a bench to read her letters, she looked out at the ocean serenely smooth in the morning haze.

Shifting her gaze to the tangle of boats and nets in the foreground, Kitty scanned the harbor for a glimpse of Merry, who had come here to buy fish for supper from the fishermen who sold their fresh catch right from their boats. But Kitty knew that wasn't Merry's sole reason for her daily trip to the harbor. She also hoped to steal a moment alone with Manuel Sousa, a handsome young Portuguese fisherman she had met.

Spotting his dark head bent over Merry's fair one, Kitty saw that they were engaged in an intense conversation, and sighed. It hadn't taken long after her arrival to learn that Merry was smitten with the young sailor. And, knowing Davida Montrose's opinion of "fraternizing with people beneath one's station," she and Cara had entered into a protective conspiracy of silence about their friend's romance.

No doubt Merry's mother would put her foot down at once on any but the most superficial relationship with such a person. The twins knew she would have, as Cara privately put it, "a conniption fit" if she had any idea that her only daughter was entertaining romantic notions regarding the swarthy young man. Most of the men who made their living by fishing off this coast claimed Portugal as their native country and its traditions as a way of life, traditions as different as night from day in heritage, language, and religions.

Still, the twins agreed, Manuel Sousa did look like a hero straight out of a romantic novel—flashing dark eyes, a captivating smile, short hair curling like a well-fitting cap about his head. While the other men shouted back and forth to each other from their boats, Manny spoke to Meredith with a softness that was almost a verbal caress.

At last, flushed and breathless, Merry joined Kitty and they walked back along the beach road to Fair Winds, where the crowd was sitting on the porch planning the day's activities.

Everyone was there—the Meredith cousins with their house-guests, the Virginia contingent—all except Owen—and the fellows from Harvard. Kip was lounging on the steps beside Cara, doing his best to get her attention away from Vance, with whom she was flirting shamelessly.

"Here's the mail, everybody!" announced Kitty, passing out envelopes and postcards. There was a letter from her mother, describing a birthday party for the Montroses' youngest child, Bryanne. "Just listen to this—" Kitty read from the letter. "The party's theme was something right out of the Middle Ages, with knights and ladies. The children dressed in those wonderful medieval costumes and danced a Maypole dance with ribbon streamers—" Kitty laughed gaily. "Doesn't that sound just like Faith?"

"Who is Faith?" asked Jenny Aldridge, Emily Meredith's roommate.

"Our cousin, Faith Devlin Montrose. She's married to an artist, Jeff Montrose—"

"Another cousin," Scott put in laconically.

"Cousin married to cousin?" Norville raised his eyebrows.

"No, not exactly—" Kitty looked to Cara for help. "It's all rather complicated—"

"Southern families are *always* complicated," Norville commented. Scott shook his head, grinning. "Positively labyrinthine."

"Well, anyhow, they live on the most marvelous island in a house that was brought over from England stone by stone and—"

"It's almost medieval-looking," piped up Cara, "with dark panels and murals that Jeff has painted everywhere."

"Murals?"

"Yes, you wouldn't believe how wonderful they are! They really should be on display in a castle or church or somewhere for everyone to enjoy."

"Are these *religious* murals, like Italian frescoes?"

"Well, not exactly religious, except maybe for his illustration of *The Canterbury Tales*—you know, Chaucer's work. Jeff has painted the Abbess and the Priest and some of the others on their pilgrimage—"

"Chaucer!" groaned Kip. "I remember trying to wade through all that old English muck!"

"Muck!" Kitty sounded indignant.

"You're displaying your ignorance, old boy," remarked Scott.

Kip made an elaborate bow. "I admit my woeful lack of appreciation for the classics."

"And well you should," Cara said severely, frowning at him. "But you have to admire Jeff's painting."

"Oh, yes, I'm a fan." Turning to Norville, he remarked, "Avalon *is* a most unusual house, I can vouch for that."

"The only way to get there is by ferry," Kitty continued. "Avalon was named for the mythical island where King Arthur was supposedly taken after he was wounded—"

"And from where—that is, if you believe all the other myths about him—he will be 'the once and future King of England'," Kip put in.

"Oh, Kip, you're so annoying!" Cara said crossly. "You always put down anything you don't understand."

"Who said I don't understand? I've read *The Idylls of the King,* for pete's sake! What I don't understand is why my uncle and his wife choose to isolate themselves the way Jeff and Faith do."

"Jeff's an artist, Kip. Artists are different from other people, which proves my point. You simply don't understand!" Cara tossed her head. "You have to be sensitive yourself to really understand a creative spirit like Jeff."

Undaunted, Kip persisted. "Come on, you'll have to agree they are rather strange, reclusive really. I know my father has invited them dozens of time to Montclair, and they always have some excuse not to come."

"Well, of course, Jeff's always working on some painting. Artists have to concentrate," Cara went on. "They can't be distracted. Besides, I don't think Faith cares much for social life."

"She's not at all like her mother, our Aunt Garnet," Kitty tried to explain. "But Faith does the most gorgeous tapestries—"

"And that's another thing—" Kip interrupted. "It's positively medieval the way Faith dresses in those costumes and lets her hair hang down . . . and all that sitting at a tapestry frame . . . like the Lady of Shalott—" He threw out his hands. "If that isn't living in some kind of archaic shadow box, I don't know what is!"

"If they're happy, why should you care?" demanded Cara. "And they *are* happy. I've never seen two happier people than Jeff and Faith."

Kip seemed momentarily subdued. He returned Cara's irritated glance with a long, steady gaze, as if for once, he was seriously considering what she was saying.

chapter
5

THE SUNNY DAYS of June passed in a flurry of activity among the young college crowd. And before anyone realized it, July was upon them with plans for a gala Fourth. Each year, there was a real "Yankee Doodle Dandy" celebration, including a parade, picnic, fireworks, and, to top off the evening—a dance at the town hall.

A few days before the occasion, the dance was the main topic under discussion on the porch of Fair Winds.

"Where's Meredith?" someone asked. "She's spent all her summers here for years. She'd know all about it."

Cara and Kitty exchanged a surreptitious glance. They knew where Merry was, but, sworn to secrecy, could not offer an explanation. So they simply shrugged evasively.

"What I mean is, do we pair off or do we all go together?" asked Anny Baldwin, one of Emily's friends just arrived from Boston for the holiday, used to the rigid proprieties of Back Bay society.

"I suppose we could do either one—" Kip eyed Cara hopefully.

"We should fix Owen up with Meredith," Scott suggested with a mischievous grin. "I think they'd make a capital pair. She'd be perfect for him. She could play the organ, lead the choir, teach Sunday school, and be President of the Ladies' Missionary Society—"

"Idiot!" snapped Cara. "Meredith may have her own plans."

Scott gave her a quizzical look, and Cara realized she had overreacted to his remark.

49

Kitty nudged Cara with her elbow, afraid her twin might slip and give away the purpose of Merry's daily visits to the harbor. They both felt sorry for Merry, who had tried desperately to forget about Manny Sousa. She had even confided that she knew all the reasons that such a dream was pointless. The wide chasm that existed between them of family background and a different faith made any hope of a serious romance with him out of the question. It would only lead to heartbreak. Still, the attraction was there, pulsing in every encounter, and, in spite of everything, Cara and Kitty knew that Merry was looking forward to the Fourth of July dance. There she and Manny could be together without speculation.

On the evening of the Fourth, the young people gathered at Fair Winds and walked into the village together. From what Merry had told them, this dance was more informal than the ones given in Mayfield, and the twins had anticipated the event with as much curiosity as excitement.

"Don't be put off if a perfect stranger comes up and asks you to dance," Merry warned them. "In summer on the Island, people don't stand on ceremony."

"What fun!" exclaimed Cara. "I've always thought dance cards and having to be properly introduced were boring anyway. You could miss a grand time with someone you haven't met just to avoid shocking a chaperone. Besides, I like meeting new people."

The big hall or pavilion, as it was called, was surrounded by an octagonal deck with the doors thrown open to admit the sea breeze. Inside, the lamps, mounted in brackets and attached to the walls between the windows, were already lighted. Underneath, a wooden bench circled the room to accommodate weary dancers who were looking for a place to sit out a dance. Corn meal had been sprinkled on the floor to make it stick for dancing.

A small band was setting up in one corner, one of the musicians strumming on his guitar, another blowing some tentative notes on his horn. Groups of women and girls clustered together, ostensibly engaged in conversation, while casting hopeful glances toward the men and boys who were hanging around the open doors, as if unsure whether or not to come in and take part in the evening's festivities.

On one side of the hall, sawhorses covered with wrapping paper held refreshments. An assortment of cakes, layer ones, marble, coconut, were set out in a tempting display. Deep pails of lemonade afloat with wedges of lemon and chunks of ice were ready to be ladeled out to dancers thirsty from the first set of dances.

Merry knew most of the women present, all friends from previous summers, and immediately introduced Cara and Kitty. There were compliments on dresses and hair-dos until the tuning of instruments gave way to a lilting melody, signaling that the dance was about to begin.

"All righty!" shouted the conductor. "Choose your partners and March and Circle."

The twins were chosen right away and led out onto the dance floor. Cara cast a look over her shoulder at Kitty, who winked and smiled back.

Both band and dancers seemed tireless. From quadrilles to country dancing and the Paul Jones, there was never a lull in the music. Nor was anyone allowed to be a wallflower for long, as every person present found a partner—from the oldest man to the children who had tagged along with their parents.

When the dance ended, Ned Collins brought Kitty back to her seat, thanked her, and went in search of his next partner.

It was very warm in the hall now, and Kitty was thirsty. But the refreshment table with lemonade and punch was at the opposite end of the room. She looked around for Cara or Merry. The last she had seen, Merry was dancing with Manny, but she hadn't been able to keep track of her twin. Seeing neither of them, Kitty decided to look for them out on the wide veranda where they might be cooling off after this last set.

Even though it was stifling inside, Kitty knew the breeze off the ocean would be cool. Walking to the cloakroom, she looked for her light shawl among the assorted capes, stoles, and sweaters hanging there. To her surprise, it was gone!

Puzzled, she spent a few minutes looking for it, then spotted the lacy knitted one that Cara had worn—a match to her own except for its deeper shade of blue. In a hurry as usual, Cara must have grabbed hers by mistake. Flinging it around her shoulders, Kitty went outside.

The moon, nearly full tonight, cast a silver sheen on the rippling waves. In the faint light, Kitty could see that the veranda seemed to be occupied solely by couples seemingly engaged in romantic conversations.

Feeling rather self-conscious to be alone Kitty moved down to the far end of the porch and leaned on the railing, gazing out at the moon-swept sea. The moonlit beauty of the night was an ache in her heart. It was a night to be shared—with someone you love. She sighed, giving her fantasies full rein. *Kip, if you only knew*—

Inside, she could hear the music starting up again. This time it was a popular waltz, and she hummed a little under her breath and closed her eyes. In her imagination, she was spinning, circling the room in Kip's arms.

It was then that she sensed, rather than actually heard, footsteps coming up behind her. There was time only to stiffen in anticipation before strong arms went around her shoulders, turned her about, and drew her into an embrace. Then she was being kissed. Kissed as never before. Kissed as only she had dreamed of being kissed. Kip!

Without hesitation, her arms went up and around his neck, clinging to him, returning his ardor. His arms tightened, and the kiss lengthened and deepened.

Then suddenly it was over. The hands holding her loosed their grip. Dazed, she drew back and looked up into Kip's face, illuminated by the moonlight. It took her just another minute to see his eyes widen slightly. Then he smiled and gave an embarrassed laugh.

"I must have been moonstruck. Sorry if I startled you—"

Still in Kip's arms, Kitty knew the terrible truth. It was an embrace he had never intended. Kip had thought *she* was *Cara!*

In this light, with her back turned and Cara's shawl over her shoulders . . . well, of course, it would have been hard to tell them apart.

An agonizing lump rose in her throat, and she felt almost sick with disappointment.

"Come on. Let's go inside," Kip was saying. "I want the next dance."

Ever gallant, the debonair Kip was passing this mistake off with the savoir faire for which he was known, Kitty thought miserably, and she would have to rise to the occasion as well. He took her by the arm and led her back toward the lighted entrance into the hall.

Cara might have the dramatic ability in the family, but this is my moment to play a role, Kitty thought desperately, *to act as if nothing is wrong, to smile as if it didn't matter, not let on that my heart is breaking—*

The next afternoon after the dance, the three friends were at the cove, the sun hot on their backs, toes dug deliciously into the warm sand. They'd brought a thermos of iced tea and a basket of green grapes and fig newtons for nibbling as they lounged on the shore. Merry was reading, Cara was writing postcards to her friends at home, and Kitty was flipping through the pages of a new *McLean's* magazine and staring out at the water.

Then, from under the brim of her large straw hat, Kitty saw Kip leave the house and head toward them over the dunes. At the sight of his tall, lean figure, she felt the familiar excitement stir through her again. The night of the dance, the dark porch, the kiss all came back to her in breathless detail.

He had said nothing especially significant since—not later that night when they had all gathered in the kitchen after the dance to make cocoa, nor when they had all assembled for church that morning. But it had happened—the kiss—and surely he hadn't forgotten! Her heart lurched dismally. Maybe Kip kissed any girl he found alone in the moonlight.

Kitty felt heartsore. She knew her dreams were absurd, the midnight kiss on which she had built them like a castle made of sand. The daylight truth was that Kip loved Cara, while *she* would never have more than his friendship.

chapter
6

THERE WAS NO question about it. Everyone agreed that the Cameron twins were strikingly different. Or so Scott and Meredith decided one day when they were sitting alone together on the veranda as Cara and Kitty walked along the water's edge, obviously in deep conversation.

"It must be fun to be twins," Meredith said wistfully, feeling the loneliness of growing up without a sister to confide in.

"I don't know, of course," Scott replied thoughtfully. "Guess you'd have to ask Cara and Kitty. Although they look almost identical, I've never known any two people who are more direct opposites in almost everything else—taste, temperament, personality—"

"But it must be wonderful to have someone you can share everything with—"

Scott shook his head. "I'm not so sure they do. Oh, they probably have their moments. But you know as well as I do that they don't always get along. I've heard them go round and round." He smiled.

"Who's this?" Kip asked as he came out of the house and sat down with them on the top step.

"We're discussing the twins," his sister told him.

"What about them?"

"We were just saying that it's funny how much alike—"

"Maybe in looks, but there's only one Cara," Kip interrupted.

"Let me finish—" Scott continued. "That's just what I was about to say. How much alike they look to be so utterly different in temperament."

Meredith frowned. "To tell you the truth, I think their personalities are interchangeable."

Scott was a little taken aback. "What do you mean?"

"Simply that. I'm not at all sure either one of them enjoys being a twin all the time. I think sometimes they each want to be the other one, or better still, not be a twin at all but just be known as an individual like the rest of us."

All three commenters would have been surprised if they could have heard what the two under discussion were talking about at that moment.

Kitty, who lately was feeling that she saw less and less of Cara, was troubled and wanted to get her feelings out in the open. Sometimes she awoke to find Cara's bed already empty. Or her twin would come rushing, breathless, into the midday meal, usually served al fresco on the screened-in porch. Then she would fall into conversation with someone else. Kitty felt they never had any time alone anymore. The evenings, of course, were always filled with activity and other people.

What hurt most, however, was that there seemed to be a growing coolness between them whenever they chanced to be together in their rooms, dressing for the beach or dinner. To be honest, she thought, maybe she felt a little resentment that Cara seemed to find others more enjoyable to be with than Kitty herself, and most especially the time she seemed to divide equally between Kip and Vance Langley. Kitty felt instinctively that Cara was playing the two young men against each other, dispensing her favors alternately. *It is Cara's way*, Kitty thought, *a game she plays well and one in which nobody else knows all the rules*. What was so distressing about it, though, was that it set the young men against each other, creating an undercurrent of competition within the group that until recently had known only the spirit of camaraderie.

It troubled Kitty because she knew Cara did not mean to be unkind. Her sister must simply be unaware of the subtle repercussions of her actions. So, telling her twin that she wanted to discuss something with her, she had persuaded her to go for a walk after lunch. However, the talk took a very different turn.

"Just what are you getting at?" Cara asked indignantly.

Kitty sighed. "Actually, I guess I'm just trying to understand why you seem to be avoiding me."

"Do I always have to explain myself?"

"No, of course not. It's just that you used to tell me everything . . . and I miss our old times."

"Maybe I've outgrown the need to do that." Cara shrugged, turning away. "Anyway, sometimes it's easier to confide in a perfect stranger, someone who's not going to judge you or criticize you, or jump right in with advice—"

Kitty bit her lip. "I didn't know I did that."

"Well, I'm sorry if that offends you, but don't *you* ever want some privacy? We've been living in each other's pockets for years, but we're grown up now. I think we both should . . . well, branch out more."

Kitty remained silent.

"Oh, for heaven's sake, Kitty!" Cara burst out. "Don't look like that! I didn't mean to hurt your feelings."

After the Fourth of July, a troupe of New York actors arrived on the Island, opening Summer Theater. The advance program of productions to be presented by the players was varied, alternating Shakespeare with some of the more modern playwrights.

Colonel Carpenter bought a bank of season tickets, so theater-going became the order of the evening after long days of sailing and swimming. And, for the young women, it was a chance to dress up for a change. Auditions were held for minor roles, and some local Islanders got walk-on parts and one-liners. Since Merry and Kip knew some of the young actors, they were frequently invited to cast parties after the play closed. Cara particularly enjoyed these, finding this backstage glimpse into the world of theater very exciting.

This exposure stimulated some post-performance discussions at Fair Winds, *A Doll's House* by Ibsen provoking some of the liveliest debate. Cara, of course, sided with Nora all the way.

Awaking one morning to pewter gray skies and a slate-colored ocean, Cara donned a mackintosh she found and ventured onto the beach. The wind had churned the water to a froth and was swirling angrily onto the sand. Ever adventurous, Cara found this new glimpse of the Cape wildly exciting.

By evening the wind was blowing in powerful gusts, driving a downpour of rain against the windows at Fair Winds, but the fire in the living room fireplace crackled cheerily, sending up darting shafts of light and shadow onto the walls and giving the group gathered around a sense of cozy refuge from the storm outside.

Out came card tables to be set up for jigsaw puzzles and marathon games of rummy and checkers. As the rain persisted over the next week, books taken from the bookshelves became topics of conversation around the dinner table, where everyone lingered, since the after-supper strolls on the beach were out of the question.

The young people discussed endlessly such classics as Dickens's *Tale of Two Cities,* debating Sidney Carton's self-sacrifice for love of Lucie Manett, and romances such as *The Man in the Iron Mask* and *The Lady of Shalott.*

At these literary round tables, they were often forced to defend their reading choices. Cara took some badgering for hers, a book of Charles and Mary Lamb's, *Tales of Shakespeare for Children.* However, she reacted by challenging the others, one at a time, to relate the plot of some of the most famous of the Bard's works. All proved woefully unable to do so, hence she won the day.

During this week of forced indoor activity, the recent play-going jaunts inspired some amateur theatrics. It began when Scott gave an impromptu oration of "The boy stood on the burning deck." Challenges to perform followed and some unexpected and amazing talent emerged. Owen did a stirring recitation of "Under the spreading chestnut tree, the village smithy stands," accompanied by elaborate gestures. And Vance's rendition of "Be it ever so humble, there's no place like home" was met with teasing jeers and boos that he accepted with scraping bows and good humor.

Eventually it was Cara's suggestion that they put on some plays of their own. Bored with the monotony of confinement, most of them agreed it was a good idea, and they divided up into groups and began to make their plans.

With no formal scripts, each actor made up his or her own lines from a basic knowledge of the plot after a few read-throughs. The results were often hilarious, but the uproarious productions, full of mistakes and mishaps, only made for more memorable evenings.

Cara was declared the undisputed star, taking on any role assigned her without inhibition or self-consciousness. She won enthusiastic applause for her role as Rochester's mad wife, scaring not only her audience with her crazed screams but also poor Meredith, who was playing the indomitable Jane Eyre.

Owen, however, was the surprise of their theatrical season, showing amazing presence and flair in the role of John Alden in Longfellow's *The Courtship of Miles Standish*.

After another week of gray days there finally came a morning when they awoke to find the sun shining brightly. The ocean was blue and calm, the beach swept clean, as if the world had just been newly created.

Knowing that it was Owen's day off from the Inn, Cara slipped down to the kitchen early to put together a picnic lunch. She was pouring some of the iced tea made the night before into a thermos when Scott entered the kitchen.

Startled, she looked up from the basket she was packing. "What are you doing up?"

"Going fishing . . . and in search of a cup of coffee," he retorted, eyeing her activity curiously. "And where, may I ask, are you off to so early?"

"Well, if it's any of your concern, which it *isn't*," Cara said defensively, "I'm going to meet Owen."

"With *this?*" Seeing a book on the table, he snatched it up and read the title. "Aha! *The Lady of Shalott!* Are you and Owen planning to read poetry together?"

"Give that to me!" Cara grabbed for it, but Scott held it out of her reach and flipped it open. " 'She has a lovely face'," he read aloud. " 'God, in His mercy, lend her grace'—"

"Here, give me the book, Scott. I *mean* it!" She circled her brother, but he kept the book high above her head. "We *need* it!"

"*Need* it?" he scoffed.

"We're going over our lines for tonight's performance," she told him huffily.

"Need some extra practice, eh?" He raised his eyebrows. Then he closed the thin volume and handed it to her, still holding onto it. "All right, all right, here. But just a word of caution, little sister. Owen's way out of your league. He's not one of your eager lads looking for a romantic fling, a summer romance, like some of these other poor fellows who think you hung the moon. I'd suggest you not try to make something more out of this than—"

"Oh, Scott, for pity's sake! Don't try to dictate whom I can or cannot have as a friend!"

"We're not talking friendship, Cara. I've seen you operate, and I know how you enjoy twisting some luckless fellow around your little finger . . . like an industrious spider weaving a web around him until he's utterly helpless!"

"Thanks a lot, Scott," she said scathingly. "I really appreciate being compared to an insect I loathe and despise."

Scott laughed a little sheepishly. "Well, as they say, if the shoe fits—" He paused. "But then, I give Owen credit for being intelligent enough to see through any ploy you can come up with. Maybe this time it will be *your* heart that gets broken."

"That sounds like a prophecy."

"Sometimes our chickens come home to roost, little sister."

Cara flounced away angrily. "Oh, you're certainly full of proverbs and pithy sayings today, aren't you, big brother! Well, don't worry about me . . . or Owen, either, for that matter. I'm perfectly capable of looking after myself, and so is he."

She got a skeptical smile in return. "I'm not so sure—"

But he made no further objection, and Cara gathered up her basket, grabbed the wide-brimmed Panama hat off the rack by the kitchen door, and went out, letting the screen bang shut behind her.

Still seething from her brother's criticism, Cara walked briskly down to the beach and started toward the stone jetty where she was to meet Owen.

Today there was only a light breeze, skimming the surface of the sea, and leaving behind only a whitecap here and there to mar its glassy stillness. Gulls called to each other in their raucous voices, promenaded at the water's edge, then suddenly, with a flap of wings, took flight, diving into the sea.

Cara had been so happy before her conversation with Scott, looking forward to this day alone with Owen, a day as cloudless as the sky above her. Why had he said all those things and spoiled the day for her?

Unconsciously, Cara tossed her head, as if shaking off all those troubling warnings. Then she saw Owen and her heart began its excited race. He was waving, and she waved back, then started running to meet him.

That night everyone gathered for the final production of the Fair Winds' players' production. Cara had rehearsed well for her role as Elaine, which she was playing to Owen's Lancelot in Tennyson's *Lady of Shalott*. With Meredith as narrator, the two alternated lines, bringing a depth of meaning that mere rehearsal alone could not have produced. When Cara as Elaine, feeling the frustration of being compelled to view life through the mirror above her loom, quoted: "I am half sick of shadows," there was not a dry eye in the house.

The play ended to riotous applause, and Cara and Owen were given the Best Player's Award of the summer by a unanimous consensus of their peers.

Two weeks before the Meredith family was to leave the Island to return to Milford, they hosted a crab bake and invited all the young people who had become such good friends over the summer.

The twins were initiated into what was a New England and particularly a Cape Cod tradition. The crab bake was a day-long procedure with much ceremony. The crabs in their shells were buried in hot coals in a pit on the beach. At exactly the proper time, potatoes, ears of corn, and onions were added to the still smoldering coals. In the meantime, tables covered with blue-checked cloths were set up and laden with other typically New England dishes.

When the crabs were deemed ready to eat, they were shoveled out of the coals and spilled, clattering, onto a huge platter, where guests were encouraged to help themselves. Thereafter, all previously accepted table manners were put aside. Pots of melted butter were provided for dipping the luscious white meat, pried out of the shell with small forks or fingers. Finally, napkins were tied around necks for easy access to buttery chins during the course of the meal.

Afterward, when not another bite could be eaten, everyone gathered around the fire, sitting in a circle, Kitty across from Cara. Vance Langley had brought his guitar, and soon their voices were blending, rising above the pounding of the surf.

Kitty led out with her sweet, clear soprano, along with Vance, who seemed to know the words to every ballad ever composed. Someone would suggest a song—a school fight song, a popular ballad, or one of the old-fashioned tunes everyone knew by heart. Then Vance would try to finger the melody on his guitar, after which the others joined in.

When the air off the ocean grew chilly, Kitty decided to run up to the house for extra sweaters and blankets. Bringing them back, she began to distribute them and noticed that Cara was missing. It took her only another minute or two to realize that Owen was gone, too.

Shivering, Kitty sat down next to Meredith, snuggling under the blanket. She wondered if anyone else was aware that Cara and Owen had left the circle. She started to ask Meredith, then put the thought aside and joined in the singing again. Remembering Cara's complaint about "privacy," Kitty decided that maybe they did live too much "in each other's pockets," as her twin had suggested.

Suddenly the wind came up, sending a whoosh of sparks and embers everywhere. There was a great shouting and scrambling as people struggled to their feet, brushing the flying sparks from their clothing. By the time someone had the fire under control and everyone settled down again, Kitty saw that Cara had returned and was sitting in her place on the other side of the circle. Quickly checking, she saw that Owen was back, too. Kitty felt a sharp twinge in her heart. Cara was keeping something from her, and it involved Owen Brandt.

chapter

7

WHILE CARA dreaded to see the summer come to an end, Kitty had mixed feelings about it. In a way, she would welcome not having to deal with her feelings about Kip, not being in his presence constantly. She couldn't seem to act naturally around him any-more—not since the night of the kiss that had not, after all, been intended for her. Maybe, once she was away from the Island and all reminders of him, back at Fern Grove College, she could get over him.

The reality that their summer idyll would soon be over hit them when Merry received a letter from Peabody College, giving the date of the orientation week that all new students were required to attend. As they read the brochure enclosed, Cara breathed a secret sigh of relief that she would not be among those enrolled.

Poring over the information, they read with interest the stated objective of the school, printed in the brochure and pronounced solemnly at the beginning of each school year by its president, Miss Adelia Smythe: "This institution was begun for the purpose of educating young women, with its chief end to graduate women whose minds have been enlightened and uplifted but also who have been taught the great Christian lesson that the true end of life is not simply to acquire knowledge but to give oneself fully and worthily for the good of others, recognizing as their guiding rule that the Bible is the only true textbook of morality. We hope that our graduates will go out into the world to elevate and purify wherever they are placed."

To elevate and purify—It was a high ideal, and one which fun-loving Cara knew she might never attain. Not only that, but the list of rules to be obeyed was endless and, to Cara, impossible. A picture of a dormitory room showed that it was sparsely furnished, almost monastic—a narrow iron cot, washstand, bureau, desk, a small bookcase, and two straight chairs.

Other requirements specified that parents were not to send jewelry, expensive gifts, clothes, or food, to their daughters in the interest of maintaining the communal status for everyone.

Besides these rules, the daily routine was equally disagreeable, thought Cara. The rising bell rang at 6:30 A.M., breakfast in the dining hall to be served at 7:00 A.M. Tardiness for meals or classes resulted in demerits, which were calculated at the end of each week. Weekend privileges, which included walks into town, were permitted or withheld, depending on one's debit or credit status.

There was compulsory daily chapel, a weekly prayer meeting and, of course, Sunday church services. No one could leave the campus without special permission, and only visitors named in letters from parents were permitted to visit on Sunday afternoons.

Both twins agreed privately that they were glad to be returning to the more relaxed regimen of Fern Grove in the fall. Still, Cara willed the summer days to last, fearing that the end of summer might mean the end of her relationship with Owen.

Why can't he say the words? she wondered. *Tell me what I see in his eyes, what I sense in his heart?* Did he feel for her all the strong emotion that rocked her each time she saw him?

For the first time in her life, Cara knew the bittersweet anguish of being in love with a man who wouldn't declare himself. A line from a poem came to her now: *There is nothing held so dear as love, if only it be hard to win*—

It was his vocation that troubled her most. She knew what everyone would say, what they would think . . . that she was too restless, too volatile, too impatient, too *worldly* for a minister. Maybe they would even try to talk him out of loving her, too. But what did *they* really know about her . . . about the real Cara, her thoughts and aspirations? How judgmental people could be, and how very wrong about her—

With only a few days remaining before the house would be closed for the season, Kitty, Cara, Kip, and Owen volunteered to do errands in the village. On the way, they saw a canvas banner strung across the main street from one lamppost to another. In large red letters it spelled out: REVIVAL TONIGHT, 7:00 AT THE OCEANSIDE CAMPGROUNDS. ALL WELCOME!

"Have you been 'saved,' Carmella Cameron?" Kip asked in his most theatrical voice.

Cara threw him a disparaging look.

"Want to go to the Revival?" he persisted, half-teasing, half-serious. "You could do with some soul-searching."

"In the words of the immortal Priscilla Mullens of Pilgrim fame, 'Why don't you speak for yourself, John?'" Cara retorted.

"Well, it probably wouldn't hurt any of us after all that's gone on this summer," put in Kitty. "Remember when we were performing the *Haunted Castle*, Mary Shelley's story of Frankenstein, and you played the wicked Dr. Salavori, Kip?"

"Oh, come on!" Kip rolled his eyes. "Maybe our Massachusetts Puritan ancestors frowned on the theater, but surely our forefathers didn't *really* believe that sin falls upon their descendants."

"As usual, you've got your metaphors mixed and your quotations all wrong," Cara pointed out to him with acid sweetness. "It's 'The sins of the fathers shall fall upon the third and fourth generations,' and it's from the *Bible!* And, from what I gather from your Uncle Norville, the Meredith clan goes back to the witch-hunting days in Salem, so you'd better think twice before shrugging off the idea of going to the Revival meeting!" she warned him laughingly.

Afterward, Cara was to recall that Owen hadn't taken part in any of their lighthearted jesting. The following evening he didn't appear at Fair Winds, nor for the next four nights. Everyone simply assumed he'd been called to work the dinner shift at Dover Inn, so no one asked, nor did Owen offer an explanation.

Only Cara wondered where he had been. But she was too proud to let him know how much she missed him. Later when Scott told them that Owen had been asked to speak at the community church the following Sunday, she had a strong premonition that she couldn't put into words.

On Sunday morning, Cara yawned prodigiously and turned over, saying that she did not think she would go to church.

Kitty looked shocked. "Cara, you've *got* to! Everyone's going! We're *all* expected to be there. Besides, Owen would be hurt if we didn't show up—" She paused significantly. "Owen likes you very much, Cara. Haven't you noticed?"

Cara stretched. "Oh, Kitty, don't be such a monitor. Don't we have enough of that at Fern Grove? I don't see why they asked Owen to preach anyway, or why he accepted. We were all going swimming at the Cove today and take a picnic. Now our plans are all spoiled!" she declared petulantly.

"No, they're not spoiled at all. It just means we'll start an hour or so later," Kitty said sensibly. "Come on now, what are you going to wear—your blue dotted Swiss, or the yellow?" She pulled both dresses from the armoire and held them up on their hangers for Cara to choose.

Still, Cara sat on the edge of the bed, her full red mouth in a pout. "I don't want to go at all. Don't want to hear Owen sermonize! But, oh, well—" she relinquished. "I guess the yellow."

"And your hat with the daisies—" Kitty brought it out from the closet shelf and handed it to her sister. "It's so becoming."

Cara grabbed it out of Kitty's hand and jammed it on her tousled head, making a silly face and sticking out her tongue. "Oh, all right! But, please, no more lectures!"

The church was almost full when they arrived, with some of the people they had met at the dance the night before now in their Sunday best, looking properly serious and reverent. Kip managed a slow wink as he stood at the end of the pew to allow the ladies to enter. Mrs. Montrose went first, then the Colonel, followed by Merry, Cara, and then Kitty.

Sliding into the place next to Kip, Kitty felt breathlessly conscious of his nearness. She slipped to her knees, closed her eyes in the outwardly penitent position of private prayer, before seating herself again and trying to control her uneven breathing.

Beside her twin, Cara felt alternately too warm, then chilled. She hugged herself a little as the ocean-scented breeze swept in through the open windows.

Reverend Miles entered, followed by Owen, looking handsome in a navy blue suit, his white shirt accentuating the deep bronze of his tan. His expression was serious but relaxed, and it came to Cara very suddenly that Owen was in his "rightful" place here where he wanted to be, where he had been called, and that all her indignant, rebellious opposition would not change that elemental truth. Owen was God's man, like David, "a man after God's own heart."

The opening hymn was played with vigor on the wheezy ancient organ, and the voices of the congregation rose in happy praise. When Owen took his place behind the lectern and announced the text from which he would draw his sermon, Cara felt so tense she could hardly look at him. His voice, with the resonance so notable in the theatrical productions at Fair Winds, filled the small church with its mellow ring.

"This morning let us 'enter into His gates with thanksgiving, and into His courts with praise,'" he quoted. "'Be thankful unto him, and bless his name, for the Lord is good; his mercy is everlasting; and his truth endureth to all generations.'"

Most of what Owen said passed over Cara's head, but it was the sound of his voice that touched her heart, bringing with it a sense of separation. While a part of her felt proud, another was devastated. Her throat ached, and she dug her fingernails into the soft palms of her hands to keep from crying. Hearing him today brought home the truth that, despite the good times they had had this summer, on all the really important matters they were really worlds apart.

The truth was crushing. This had been the happiest summer of her entire life—*her* summer and Owen's. For the first time, someone besides Kitty had cared enormously how she felt, what she thought. She knew that Owen didn't think of her as one of a pair but as a unique individual. And loving him had changed her, no matter what anyone else believed.

Thinking of the carefree days just past—the sun and sand, the tingling cold of the ocean, the laughter and kisses—Cara closed her eyes, experiencing again the feel of his firm mouth on her own—its sweetness, its tenderness, its promise. There was music in the roar of the surf, the pounding of her heart like the pounding of the waves against the rocks. As she remembered it now, all the loveliness of this special summer seemed to be slipping away from her. No more the glances across firelit beaches, or moonlight strolls along the ocean's edge, or harmony sung together in the soft summer nights on the porch. If she had not realized it before, she knew it now. It was over, gone.

Finally everyone was rising. Hymnbooks were being opened again as the organ pealed through the raftered church, and the closing hymn was begun.

Outside the church, Cara unpinned her hat and shook down her hair. "Whew! That's done," she remarked to no one in particular.

Kitty glanced warily behind her sister. In Kitty's direct line of vision was Owen, surrounded by members of the church and friends wishing to congratulate him.

She would have liked to join the others to offer Owen her own congratulations, but Cara had already started out of the churchyard.

"Come on, Kitty, let's go. I'm dying for a swim."

Back at Fair Winds, Sunday supper was a casual affair, with friends dropping in and helping themselves to a cold buffet set out on the sideboard. By twos and threes they drifted out onto the porch to eat and watch the ocean roll onto the beach in foamy scallops as the day faded in pink and mauve glory.

Nobody seemed surprised when Owen showed up. There was a second round of compliments for his part in the morning's service. Over the shoulders of the others his eyes searched out and found Cara, but she moved over to the porch railing and leaned against it, staring out at the sea.

Then he was beside her. "I need to talk to you, Cara. Let's take a walk on the beach."

Her heart gave a little leap, aching with gladness but knowing it was all so hopeless. Still, she couldn't refuse. Silently they went down the steps and onto the sand. Though they were only inches apart, he had never seemed so far away.

They walked slowly along the water's edge, stopping every once in a while to watch the surf rolling in its relentless invasion of the shore, taking an occasional backward step to avoid being soaked.

Then suddenly Cara cried out. "Wait!"

Sitting down on a drifted log and unlacing her shoes, she pulled off her stockings. She looked at Owen almost defiantly, then rose, and swung her shoes by their laces over her shoulder. Holding up her linen skirt with one hand, she walked on ahead, curling her bare toes into the scallops of foam.

"Let's go out to the jetty," Owen suggested quietly, coming up beside her. But Cara hesitated, remembering the picnic on the day they had first kissed. "Come on." He held out his hand.

She didn't take it but continued walking in that direction.

"Cara, we have to talk."

"What is there to talk about?"

"About this morning . . . about me. About *us*."

She shook her head, dislodging some of the hairpins and loosening her hair to tumble about her face. She pushed it back impatiently.

Suddenly she stopped, faced him, and looked full into his eyes. She felt again the sting of threatened tears and willed them back. "Kitty says you have a call of God on your life," she said shakily. "I guess I really don't understand what that means. . . ."

"I don't know if I can explain it . . . at least, the way it really is." He looked far out toward the ocean, then, as if choosing his words carefully, said, "I can only compare it to what some men feel is the call of the sea, or the call to explore, or to climb the Himalayas. It is something deep within . . . something irresistible, insistent that, in the end, must be answered. That's what seminaries are for, Cara. To give those few—those lucky few who feel called—a chance to test the call to see if they really have been chosen."

"But—" Cara felt the pain in her heart pressing against her chest.

"I can't make any plans, Cara. I have to simply wait on the Lord to make straight my path."

She realized he was quoting Scripture, and she felt abandoned again. She had lost the power she had once had over Owen. He belonged to Someone else now, though he may have loved her for a brief time. There was no promise for the future.

Her eyes moved over his face, the strong line of his jaw, those clear, truth-seeking eyes. "I love you, Owen," she heard herself say, then looked away from the expression that came over him at her words.

She had not meant to say that. She felt humiliated by the confession, for she would not demean herself to plead for his love. "I know this isn't the right time . . . I mean, I understand you have a commitment to finish your training and—" Her voice faltered. "I'm sorry. Maybe I was mistaken . . . maybe this whole thing was only a figment of my imagination—"

"No, Cara. Believe me, it was I who was wrong . . . to lead you on. I shouldn't have—" Owen halted awkwardly. "But it just wouldn't be fair for me to let you think—"

"Oh, please, Owen, don't say anything more. You're right. Neither of us can promise anything—" Yet in her heart, Cara knew she would promise Owen *anything!* If only he would ask, she would wait for him however long it took . . . forever!

"I'm leaving next week," he said, breaking into her thoughts. "So, let's go on just as before. Let's enjoy the time we have left, just the way it's been this summer."

"Of course," Cara replied, managing a bright smile, even though she knew they couldn't go back, that nothing could be the same.

Lying sleepless in her bed far into the night, Cara wrestled with her emotions. After knowing Owen, how could she possibly love anyone else? She would have to wait, hope . . . and yes, *pray* . . . and if her love was strong enough, strong enough for both of them, maybe someday there would be a place for her in his life.

chapter
8

CARA'S OBVIOUS reluctance to leave Fair Winds was contagious and at last spilled over onto Kitty. In a reflective mood one day, Kitty began to consider what the next weeks would bring—new experiences, new friends, a whole different life at college.

This had been such a special odyssey. For the span of a few weeks, she and Cara had been living in another world altogether, a world thirty miles out from the mainland, a world apart from their ordinary lives, as if nothing and no one else existed except these special few.

On one of the last nights together they all sat cross-legged on the floor, eating buttery popcorn out of a big bowl placed in the middle of the circle as they played Twenty Questions. Cara made a sarcastic remark when Kip failed to guess the subject, one that Kitty had felt was too obscure all along, even though the rest of the team had consented to use it.

Now Kip was angry, and anger always made him caustic. Though he tried to cover it with retaliatory teasing, it usually came out as vindictive and mean-spirited, with Cara as his target.

As Kitty observed their verbal duel, it was easy to see that Cara was baiting Kip. This had been happening increasingly over the last few weeks, she realized, mostly in a crowd when Owen wasn't present. But Cara was too clever an adversary for Kip, able to turn his jibes around so that he appeared foolish.

Kitty gave her twin a reproachful glance, but Cara pretended not to see it and went on openly criticizing Kip. It was only when Owen arrived later, after his evening shift at the Dover Inn, that Cara's attitude changed. Kip was aware of it, too, Kitty noticed, and grew more morose as the evening progressed.

After the others had scattered to the cottages where they were guests, Kip lingered. While she and Merry began cleaning up, collecting the empty glasses and bowls and carrying them out to the kitchen, Kitty saw him corner Cara, take her arm, and lead her firmly out onto the porch.

After they went upstairs to get ready for bed, Kitty and Merry heard voices—Kip's first, loud and angry, then Cara's heated rebuttal. The voices, if not the words, carried all the way up the stairs and into the bedroom. There was no mistaking the fact that Kip and Cara were quarreling bitterly, shouting insults at each other that were gaining in volume and intensity.

Merry made an agonized face. "How sad that this had to happen at the end of our summer."

Kitty nodded. "That storm's been brewing all week. I'm just surprised that it didn't break sooner."

"If it had, maybe it wouldn't be so awful. They'd have a chance to make up before you have to leave." Merry sounded mournful.

Kitty shrugged. "Oh, well, you know Kip and Cara. It's always high drama with them. Maybe by tomorrow, they'll have forgotten whatever it was they were fighting about."

"You mean, kissed and made up?"

Just as she said that, there was silence on the porch below. Looking at each other, they scrambled over to the window to squint into the darkness. But while they were still leaning out on the windowsill, they heard the screen door bang and saw Kip's tall figure striding down the path toward the beach, kicking up sand as he walked. Next came the sound of running footsteps. Then the bedroom door opened and Cara came in.

The next day, remembering the argument the night before, Kitty risked Cara's resentment and asked, "Why have you been so odious to Kip these last few weeks? It seems so unfair when he obviously adores you."

"You're wrong, Kitty. I *am* being fair. I don't want him to be in love with me!"

"But why not? You've grown up together . . . everyone expects it—"

Cara responded with that mysterious smile that had always infuriated Kitty when they were younger. "Because there's someone else . . . but I can't . . . I mean, I don't want to say who it is."

Stunned, Kitty could hardly believe her ears. But feeling toward Kip as she herself did, it seemed safer not to pursue the subject.

At last the signs of the summer's end could not be denied. One by one, all the other beach cottages emptied, though Davida Montrose delayed their departure as long as possible, leaving open cardboard boxes sitting around and the packing unfinished to wander down to the beach for just one more stroll.

Meredith herself hated to see the summer end. But at least she and Manny had arrived at a plan to keep in touch. Still, the idea of keeping a secret this big and this important frightened her. She had never done anything like this before in her life.

Finally, there was no avoiding the inevitable. The twins were packed and ready to be driven to the harbor where they would board the ferry for New Bedford, there to take the train to Richmond and back to Mayfield.

Cara glanced around, ostensibly to check for items they may have left behind, but more accurately checking the road back into the village for signs of Owen. He had kept his word, she thought sadly. He had not come to say good-bye. The timing wasn't right for them, he had told her, when what she wanted to hear was that he loved her. But love could wait, couldn't it? Love could endure. Owen, of all people, should know that.

Even *she* knew what the Scriptures said about love. It was somewhere in a book called Corinthians, she thought, trying to recall the passage: "Love suffereth long and is kind; love envieth not; love vaunteth not itself, is not puffed up . . . love thinketh no evil; rejoiceth not in iniquity but rejoiceth in the truth; beareth all things, believeth all things, hopeth all things, endureth all things. Love never faileth."

Why couldn't he have come to say good-bye?

Then it was time for their departure. As they bade a tearful farewell to Meredith, who saw them off with hugs all around, they reminded each other that it wouldn't be long until Christmas when they would all be in Mayfield for the holidays.

"And, of course, there's always next summer!"

Next summer, Cara thought sadly. What did next summer matter? Maybe she would never see Owen again. All she had to cling to was a small book of Robert Burns's poetry—the one Owen had marked for her, indicating his favorites:

> *Had we never loved sae kindly,*
> *Had we never loved sae blindly,*
> *Never met—never parted*
> *We'd had n'er been broken-hearted.*

As the ferry pulled out of the harbor, Cara wondered, hoped even, that his heart felt as broken as hers.

Part III

Christmas Holidays 1909 to January 1910

Mayfield, Virginia

chapter

9

THE LOCOMOTIVE rumbled over the bridge and rounded the bend through the last length of Mayfield's picturesque countryside, then finally pulled to a hissing stop. Kitty, who had been waiting impatiently for the arrival of the train from Washington, D.C., ran along the platform, looking at each car for a glimpse of her sister.

At last she spotted a face identical to her own, pressed against one of the windows. Waving, she received an answering wave from a gloved hand. Two minutes later, the conductor swung down out of the train and placed a yellow stool underneath the high steps for the disembarking passengers.

Kitty had asked to come alone to the station to meet Cara. As she waited, her feelings had been mixed. Without knowing why, she felt that this homecoming was significant. She hoped that being home for the holidays, back in the warm family circle at Christmas as it was always celebrated at Cameron Hall, Cara would regain some of her natural gaiety and zest.

All fall, Kitty had been concerned about her twin. Something had happened last summer at Cape Cod, something she had never confided to her. But she had not really been the same since. Oh, there had been moments when she seemed her old self, like the time she had had the starring role in Fern Grove's dramatic presentation of *She Stoops to Conquer,* or when Vance Langley invited her to VMI for a special weekend. At those times her sister had seemed happy and excited. But her euphoria was always short-lived, and Cara had sunk again into the depression that had marked most of the semester.

After Thanksgiving, Cara had caught a bad cold that hung on so long she was sent to the infirmary to recuperate, missing midterm examinations as a consequence. So Kitty had preceded her home for the holidays, while Cara remained at school a few days longer to make up the tests.

She looks fully recovered now, Kitty thought, seeing the slender, russet-haired girl in a sheared beaver jacket step off the train. In fact, Kitty noticed, her sister looked positively glowing.

"Oh, Cara, it's so good to see you!" Kitty called, running up and giving her a hug. "How are you and how were the exams?"

"I'm fine—" Cara began, then grimaced. "But *they* were dreadful! The professors probably thought you'd crib me, so they changed all the questions and made them harder." She tucked her arm through her sister's. "Where is everybody? I thought you might at least have a brass band out to meet me!"

Kitty laughed. "Well, you *would* take the midday train. Mama's at a meeting of the Ladies' Guild, planning for the Christmas bazaar and appointing committees to decorate the church, Daddy's training a new horse, and Scott's gone riding with Kip—"

Cara's expression altered slightly. "Oh, is Kip home? I thought maybe Mrs. Montrose might have persuaded Uncle Jonathan to spend Christmas in Massachusetts with her Yankee relatives." There was a touch of scorn in her tone.

Kitty shook her head. "No, not this year. But from what Merry told me, Colonel Carpenter may be coming down to Montclair for the holidays." Then, almost as an afterthought, "Kip just got home yesterday. He spent a few days in New York with some of his Harvard friends, then came down by way of Washington. If you'd come a day earlier, you two would have been on the same train."

By this time, they had reached the end of the platform where the Camerons' chauffeur waited by the elegant dark green carriage drawn up in front of the station house.

He tipped his hat and smiled. "Welcome home, Miss Cara. It shor' is nice to see ya."

"Thank you, Willis. It's good to be home and to see you, too."

Cara dug into her handbag and handed him her baggage tickets. "Will you please get my trunk and suitcase?"

While Willis hurried to get Cara's belongings from the luggage cart, the two sisters got into the carriage.

"Oh, Cara, it's wonderful to be together again, isn't it? Do you realize that this is the longest we've ever been apart in our whole lives?" Kitty squeezed her arm excitedly. "We've had scads of invitations, but I didn't know which ones to accept 'til you got home."

Cara tucked the lap robe over their knees. "Have you seen much of Merry and Kip so far?" she asked with elaborate casualness.

"Not really. Meredith just got home two days ago, and you know how possessive their mother is. She seems to be jealous of anything or anyone who takes them away from Montclair for more than a few hours. But Merry has asked us over for an afternoon soon. I'm anxious to hear about her first semester at Peabody, aren't you? I remember that the brochure she showed us at the Cape last summer sounded awfully grim."

Cara recalled having read the orientation booklet that Merry had received from the New England college. She had tossed it aside and rolled her eyes, grateful that she and Kitty were returning to Fern Grove. Of course, some people, Merry's mother Davida, for example, considered Fern Grove more of a fashionable finishing school than an institution of higher learning. *Poor Merry,* Cara thought with sympathy.

As they traveled down the familiar road from Mayfield to their country home, Kitty looked about her with delight. She loved coming home to Cameron Hall, not realizing how much she would miss it until she had spent time away in college. Sometimes she longed to be home and was sure that if it were not for Cara as her roommate at Fern Grove, she would have been downright home-sick.

As they turned into the gates, Kitty felt a pang of nostalgia, seeing, as with fresh eyes, the pastures stretching away on either side, the meadows and woodland beyond. Coming up the curved drive toward the imposing house, they passed the horses grazing behind the white board fences, looking exactly like a picture of this special part of Virginia—her home, her heart.

She glanced over at her twin to see if she shared some of her feelings. But Cara was not even looking out the carriage window. She seemed lost in her own thoughts. *What were they?* Kitty wondered. Suddenly she felt shut out as she had so often last summer. Perhaps it was overly optimistic for her to think they could somehow capture their old intimacy while they were home for the holidays.

"Here we are, home at last!" Kitty announced cheerfully as they pulled to a stop in front of the house. "And just think . . . we have three glorious weeks of vacation!"

At this, Cara seemed to perk up and stepped down from the carriage. Moving out in front of Kitty, she ran up the steps and into the house.

Inside, signs of the holiday were already in evidence. The ornaments for the tree—brought to the house from the shed—were in boxes stacked in the hallway. Red candles waited to be unwrapped and placed in brass holders and set in every window.

Catching the spirit of anticipation that permeated the house, Cara whirled about. "What's the weather forecast, Kitty? I hope it snows soon!"

"I hope so, too!" echoed Kitty, glad to see Cara's enthusiasm.

At that moment, Willis stepped inside, bringing Cara's luggage as well as several packages bearing the names of Richmond stores.

Kitty looked at them askance. "You must have done some Christmas shopping!"

Cara looked secretive. "Well, if you must know, I did stay over with with Susie Mills, and we did go shopping."

Susie, one of their Fern Grove classmates, was a flighty kind of girl whom Kitty didn't respect much. This news bothered her, and her voice betrayed her concern. "You mean . . . you weren't at school all this time?"

"Oh, Kitty, don't be such a nit-picker! I finished my exams and then went over to the Mills' house. Susie's asked me dozens of times. It only meant an extra day or so—"

"But Mama didn't know," Kitty said slowly. "She was feeling so sorry for you, being at Fern Grove all alone, taking tests—"

"Well, I *was* there most of the time. When would I have gotten my Christmas presents for the family if I hadn't spent some time in Richmond?" she asked in a tone that instantly made Kitty feel foolish. Turning to Willis, who had been waiting patiently during the twins' exchange, she said, "Please take all that stuff upstairs," then deftly changed the subject.

"Be a lamb, Kitty, and go out to the kitchen and bribe Florrie for some food, will you? I'm famished! I didn't have a chance to eat lunch. As it was, I had to *run* to catch the train!"

With a sigh of resignation, Kitty went to do her sister's bidding and Cara ran upstairs to their bedroom. By the time Kitty came up with the tray, her sister had already opened her suitcases and was unpacking, strewing her clothes over every available surface.

At the sight of the plate of sandwiches and molasses cookies, Cara stopped immediately. "Ummm! I knew Florrie wouldn't let me down!"

"Well, she wasn't too happy about fixing all this so close to dinner time. She grumbled and said for me to tell you—" Here Kitty lapsed into the voice of their family cook—"Doan make a pig of yoself so's you doan do justice to the nice supper I spent all day cookin'."

"She needn't worry. After what they call 'food' at school, I can't get enough when I'm home," Cara assured her as she settled down on the bed and, spreading a napkin on her lap, picked up one of the ham sandwiches.

Curious to find out more about the two days Cara had been officially still at Fern Grove, Kitty decided to find out. "What happened? You know, Mama expected you on an earlier train. In fact, she was a little puzzled when we got your telegram saying you wouldn't be in until the 2:20. And frankly, Cara, I couldn't understand it, either."

"Well, she won't mind when she sees the present I got her!" Cara neatly evaded the question. Then she gave Kitty a long, speculative look. "Promise not to faint, or tell me I shouldn't have?"

"Oh, Cara, come on!" Kitty shook her head, wondering what her twin was going to spring next.

"I told you I went Christmas shopping, didn't I?"

Kitty nodded. "Yes, what about it?"

"Well, I bought myself a present, too!" Cara's eyes sparkled with mischief, almost always a prelude to some outrageous admission.

Kitty groaned. "What now?"

Cara polished off the glass of milk, then put aside the tray, got off the bed and down on her knees, and slid a dress box out from under the bed.

"Just wait 'til you see!" Lifting the top off a box imprinted with the label of one of Richmond's most expensive shops, she drew out a dress—flame-colored chiffon, embroidered with glittering beads—and held it up to herself.

"Oh, dear!" Kitty gasped.

"Is *that* all you have to say?" Cara swirled around to let the accordion-pleated skirt fan out as she spun. "Well? What do you think?"

In spite of herself, Kitty knew Cara would look spectacular in the dress, the shade enhancing her vivid coloring, its style setting off her slender grace. "It's . . . beautiful . . . but I'm just wondering what Mama—" She lowered her voice. "How much did it cost?"

Cara rolled her eyes. "You *would* ask that! Isn't it grand . . . worth whatever I paid?"

Wanting to agree, but knowing their parents might object, and rightfully so, to its daring, its sophistication, Kitty hesitated.

Cara looked peeved as she folded the dress and returned it to the box. "I thought you'd love it, too. I'm disappointed you didn't . . . well . . . rave about it more."

"I *do* think the dress is wonderful, Cara, but I only wonder what Mama and especially Daddy—"

There was a mild explosion. "Well, I don't care! The minute I saw it I knew I had to have it . . . no matter what anyone else said. I have to be *me!* I can't always be concerned about what other people think of me . . . even *you,* Kitty!"

"Don't say that," protested Kitty. "It's not the money that bothers me, it's—"

Cara looked somewhat chastened. "If you must know, it cost me two months' allowance." She paused, then tossed her head defiantly. "But it's too late to worry about it now. I can't take it back. Besides, I bought satin slippers the same color and a beaded evening bag to go with it!"

Kitty swallowed back the question of how her sister was planning to manage school expenses for the next few weeks. Surely, with all these purchases, Cara had overdrawn the joint bank account their father had set up for them. There was only one answer. *She* would become Cara's banker until the impulsive shopping spree was paid for.

Of course, what made her twin so irresistible was that she could be so high-handed, so irritatingly selfish one minute and incredibly sweet and generous the next. Kitty could never stay upset with her for long, and so she forgave the extravagance.

"It *is* stunning, Cara. You'll be the belle of the ball!"

The following afternoon, the twins rode over to Montclair to visit Meredith, their first reunion since the summer. They were always struck by the contrast between Meredith and her brother. Meredith was plain and small as Kip was tall. Her gentle nature and genuine sweetness of character more than compensated for what she lacked in beauty.

What the twins could not know was that Meredith was deeply troubled by a situation she had never confided to either friend. She had confided to her diary moments before they arrived: "Though I love my friends and can't wait to see them again, I've envied them since I was a little girl . . . for one thing only—their home. There's a difference between Montclair and Cameron Hall, and I've never seen it so clearly as now, after being away for the first time. Montclair is so cold. There's no laughter, no warmth. Perhaps it is because, and I hate to admit it, there is no real heart here, no love—" Then, hearing the front door open, she had shoved her leather book under the cushions of the window seat and hurried downstairs to welcome her guests.

After hugs all around, greetings and excited questions, Meredith brought them upstairs.

"Oh, Merry, your room is so neat!" was Kitty's first remark as she looked around with obvious pleasure, thinking of the mess they had left of their own rooms at Cameron Hall.

Cara's clothes were usually deposited wherever they happened to land. The dressing table was cluttered with her combs, brushes, and cologne bottles, the mirror practically invisible behind invitations, old dance cards, Valentines.

When they were at home, the room was cleaned at least once a week by the maids, who grumbled about the untidiness, but the room they shared at Fern Grove was like a small shipwreck most of the time.

"It looks different somehow," commented Cara, noticing the new rose-flowered chintz curtains and matching slipcovers on the two wing chairs flanking the small fireplace where a cheerful fire glowed in the hearth.

"Mama had it redecorated for me while I was away at school," Meredith explained. "Let's sit down. I can't wait to hear *everything!*"

They flopped on her high, canopied bed and began chatting.

"Now tell us all about Peabody," urged Kitty. "We've been anxious to know all about it. Your letters didn't say much."

"That's because our letters are censored!"

"Not really!" the twins gasped in unison.

"Well, not exactly censored, but the Dean of Discipline has a list of approved correspondents, and all letters must first go to her office, so everyone's sure she reads them," Merry told them. "In fact, some of the girls I know have been called in and questioned about the addressees on some of their letters, since all incoming mail goes through her office, too."

"However have you and Manny managed to communicate?" asked Cara.

Meredith flushed to her hairline and put her finger to her lips. "If Mama should ever find out—"

Excited by the prospect of a romantic adventure involving someone as shy as Meredith, Cara leaned closer and whispered dramatically, "Your secret is safe with *us,* for pity's sake, Merry!"

All three huddled, heads close, as Meredith continued. "Well, one

Saturday while we were visiting a museum in Boston, I had a chance to slip out from the group—"

"Yes, yes, go on—" prodded Cara.

"Manny met me and we went to a little café—"

"What happened? What happened?"

"Nothing *happened,* but we did manage to arrange a way to write. I have a post office box in town, and one of the day students picks up his letters for me—"

"Oh, I can't stand it! It's so utterly *romantic!*" sighed Cara, grabbing one of the lacy pillows and hugging it to her.

"Hush, Cara." Kitty gave her twin a disapproving glance. "Aren't you afraid you'll get caught, Merry?"

"Not really," she replied, her big eyes unusually bright. "Of course, I don't know what would happen if Mama ever found out."

As if on cue, there was a light tap on the bedroom door. Then it opened and Mrs. Montrose peeked in, a slight frown on her pale face. "Oh, I didn't realize you had company, dear. Hello, twins. I wasn't aware you'd come home for the holidays."

She nodded to Kitty and Cara, who slipped off the bed at her entrance and stood while they answered her polite questions about school and family. This completed, Mrs. Montrose turned to leave.

Meredith, looking anxious, put her hand on her mother's arm. "Did you want something, Mama?"

"No, dear, I just wondered what all the noise was about. I was lying down and—" Her voice trailed off weakly.

"Oh, did we disturb you? I'm so sorry, Mama."

The twins exchanged a knowing glance.

"That's all right, dear. I've taken something for my headache. . . . If you will, though, could you lower your voices a little?"

"Of course, Mama."

The door closed, and for a moment all three were silent.

"Don't worry. She couldn't possibly have heard what we were saying," Cara reassured Meredith.

"Now, tell us about school," prompted Kitty.

As Merry began a detailed account of life at the Massachusetts women's college, Cara's mind drifted a little. Who would have thought that docile, compliant Meredith would have a secret rendezvous with her love and carry on a clandestine correspond-ence? It was daring, even reckless of her, risking not only her parents' disapproval, but probable expulsion from the strict institu-tion she attended. Remembering again the rigid rules, Cara viewed Meredith with new respect.

Following Meredith's recitation, Cara's reaction was immediate. "Whew!" Everything in her free spirit rebelled against such confinement. "From what you're telling us, it's easy to see that the powers-that-be don't give you much time for fun."

"Couldn't you persuade your parents to let you transfer to Fern Grove?" Kitty asked sympathetically.

"Well, naturally, that thought has crossed my mind a lot." Merry sighed. "But Mama seems to think . . . it's just her opinion, you know . . . that I'll get a better education at a northern college."

"And for what?" demanded Cara, suddenly disgusted. "I mean, what will any of us *do* with our educations?"

Merry looked startled and glanced at Kitty who attempted an answer. "Well, I guess we could always . . . teach?"

Cara jumped off the bed and moved restlessly around the room. "And who wants to teach?" She went to the window and looked out. "I know what I'd really like to do, what I'd really like to be studying—" But before she could finish, she broke off, leaned closer to the window, and announced, "Here comes Kip, and Scott's with him!" She turned, her mood instantly brighter. "Come on, let's go down and say hello!"

Cara was out of the room in a flash, the other two following more slowly. At the top of the stairs, Kitty hesitated, expecting to feel self-conscious about seeing Kip again for the first time since summer. Whether or not the incident meant anything to him, *she* had not been able to forget that magic moonlight kiss. It didn't matter that he had thought she was Cara; the thrill she had experienced had lingered because even before that moment, she had been in love with Kip.

From where she and Meredith stood, Kitty could see down into the front hall just as the door opened and the two young men burst into the house. She watched as Cara ran to meet Kip, saw him clasp both her hands and swing her about, their acrimonious parting of last summer apparently forgotten.

Then suddenly Kip looked up and, catching sight of her, waved. "Come on, Kitty," said Meredith, taking her hand and starting down the steps.

Kip was handsomer than ever, Kitty saw. Now standing over six feet, he had the lithe build of a natural athlete. But Kip had more than good looks. He had a kind of casual charm and easy good manners so that his Harvard classmates had jokingly dubbed him "our resident Southern gentleman." It was all true, Kitty thought rather wistfully. No wonder half the girls in Mayfield were mad about him.

Seeing Cara chatting animatedly with Kip, Kitty thought how "right" they looked together, then realized it was like looking at *herself* standing there with Kip!

As she and Meredith joined them, Scott smiled. "What have you three ladies been up to?"

Before either could answer, Cara said flippantly, "What do you *think* we were talking about? *Men*? How attractive and irresistible you are?"

"That's possible." Scott shrugged, still smiling.

"Well, you're wrong, big brother," she retorted. "We were talking about how unfair life is for women, with so few opportunities to explore our talents and abilities!" she retorted.

At that, Meredith looked startled. "That's not exactly true, Cara."

Cara brushed off the correction with a smile, then linked arms with Kip as they all moved into the drawing room. "So, Kip, have you made the Dean's list yet?"

"That'll be the day." He laughed. "Scott's the scholar—and Owen, of course."

"Speaking of Owen," Scott spoke up, "he's going to be in Arbordale next week to help out with the special Christmas services at Trinity Church."

Trying to keep her composure, Cara asked, "Will he be coming over here?"

"I doubt if the Rector will give him much time off," Scott continued. "I understand that the Reverend Cranston is somewhat of a benevolent tyrant, fussy as an old hen that everything be done according to law and liturgy. My guess is that he'll keep Owen hopping the whole time . . . at least, for Christmas week. But maybe we can entice him over here for our New Year's Eve party and open house."

"Is he staying at the rectory, then?" asked Cara with careful indifference.

"No, actually, he has an aunt and uncle who live in Arbordale. I think he'll be staying with them," Scott said offhandedly, then turned to Meredith. "So how do you like college life?"

For the next few minutes the conversation became an exchange of "tall tales," each trying to top the other. Then Kip suggested that Merry go out to the kitchen to see if she could rattle up some refreshments.

"I definitely smelled gingerbread when we walked into the house, didn't you, Scott?"

When Meredith disappeared, Scott and Kitty got into a discussion about the new hunter their father had recently purchased on his last trip to Ireland, from his friend Dan McShane's horse farm near Dublin.

Kip turned to Cara. "Want to go riding tomorrow?"

"We're going to look for greens and holly to decorate the house, but you can come along if you like. You always were good at climbing trees. We'll put you to work cutting mistletoe."

"With the appropriate reward if I do a good job, I trust."

"Come and find out!" she said as she sat down at the piano and strummed a few chords.

"That's an offer I can't refuse." Walking over behind her, Kip gave the piano stool a strong push, sending Cara spinning around.

She threw back her head, laughing. "Stop, stop! You're making me dizzy!"

"I always have that effect on young ladies."

"What conceit!" Cara jumped up, picked up a pillow, and began chasing Kip around the room, batting him with it as he ran. Kip slid a chair in front of her to block the way, then ducked behind the sofa to miss the pillow she flung at him.

"Hey, you two, stop clowning!" ordered Scott. "Want to get us all thrown out for disorderly conduct?"

Just then, Meredith came back into the room with a tray. She set it down on a table, and everyone gathered around to help themselves to mugs of fresh apple cider. After a last pantomimed attack and defense, Cara and Kip collapsed on the sofa, side by side, breathless and laughing.

"My goal for this holiday is to talk my father into buying an automobile," Kip announced, helping himself to a large, still-warm square of gingerbread.

"Don't mention them around *my* father," said Scott. "He thinks that motor cars are an abomination."

"Well, naturally, he would, being a horse breeder. But they're the coming thing, you can't deny that. I mean, some of them can travel as fast as twenty miles per hour—"

Even Scott seemed impressed.

"Really?" Cara sounded excited. "If you do convince your father, will you take me for a ride? In fact, I'd like to learn to drive one myself."

"Ha!" scoffed Scott. "You do enough damage to Mayfield roads on horseback. No telling what you'd do if you tried driving a high-powered gasoline engine vehicle."

Pointedly ignoring her brother's remark, Cara turned back to Kip. "Do they really go that fast?"

"You bet! I've driven one," Kip declared loftily. "I tried one out when I was visiting Jed Hastings at his home in New York. He got one for his birthday."

At that, there was a collective groan of disbelief that Kip countered with a superior smile. "Can I help it if my roommate is a millionaire's son?"

"Oh, those *Harvard* men!" teased Cara.

"What do you know about Harvard men?" demanded Kip belligerently.

"All I need to know or want to know, for that matter!" she retorted airily.

"You couldn't! You haven't met any . . . except me!" flung back Kip.

"That's enough for *me* if *you're* any example—full of themselves, incredibly arrogant, believe they're God's gift to women!"

"A lot *you* know about it. You wouldn't even come to the dances I invited you to," said Kip, beginning to sound sullen.

"Well, I was invited to VMI, where all *real* Virginians go . . . or to the University of William and Mary—not some stuck-up *Yankee* college!"

"You don't know what you're talking about!"

"I know a great deal more than you *think* I do!"

Scott held up both hands. "Peace, peace. 'Tis the season to be jolly, or at the very least, civil. Cut it out, twin," he said to Cara sharply.

"Don't call me *twin!* I have a name," she snapped.

Ever the peace lover, Kitty got to her feet. "Why don't we sing some carols to get us in the Christmas spirit? Come on, Merry, you play."

Going to the piano, Meredith struck the opening bars of "Hark, the Herald Angels Sing." Kitty and Scott followed, and Cara joined them. Kip, hands plunged into his jacket pocket, went to the window and stared out for a few minutes. Then, almost reluctantly, he moved into the curve of the piano directly opposite Cara and added his nice tenor to the other voices. Meredith moved easily from one familiar Christmas song to another, ending up in a rousing rendition of "Go, Tell It On the Mountain."

"Better light the lamp, Kip. I'm having a hard time reading the music," said Meredith at last, alerting them to the lateness of the hour and the quickly falling darkness of the winter afternoon.

"Guess we'd better be heading for home," Scott said.

Kip came up behind Cara as she wound her scarf around her neck and pulled on her gloves. She tipped her head toward him coquettishly. "Has music soothed the savage beast?"

"You can be the *most*—" Kip sputtered, as if trying to find the exact word to describe her.

"*Tantalizing?*" she supplied archly.

"*Annoying, irritating, infuriating* is more like it," he growled.

"Want to call off our date for tomorrow?" She batted her long lashes comically.

He groaned. "No-o-o."

"Come on, Cara, it'll be pitch black before we get home if we don't leave now," called Kitty from the front hallway.

"Well?" Cara asked Kip as she moved toward the doorway behind Kitty.

"Your wish is my command. Your humble servant, ma'am." Kip made a sweeping obeisance, then grinned. "I'll be over about ten."

chapter
10

THE NEXT MORNING at Cameron Hall, the twins appeared for breakfast in their riding clothes. Kitty wore a well-worn, soft tweed jacket and brown gabardine skirt, her hair brought back and clubbed at the neck with a black ribbon. Cara's outfit was royal blue, the fitted swallow-tailed jacket molding her slimly curved figure. Her hair hung in a loose braid that ended in a swirl down her back.

Blythe looked up from the pile of mail beside her plate as the girls came into the dining room. "Where are you two off to?"

"We're meeting Merry and Kip to gather greens for decorations."

"Wonderful. I need more, so could you get some extras? I promised Reverend Wilcox I'd bring some by for the church."

Silently amused, Blythe watched the mutual serving ritual the twins had practiced since childhood. At the mahogany sideboard, where a silver urn, chafing dish and bun warmer were set out, Kitty poured coffee for both of them while Cara put sticky pecan rolls on two plates and brought them to the table. Kitty followed, setting Cara's cup before her, then sat down at the table opposite her twin.

Returning to her mail, Blythe picked up another envelope, slit it open with a pearl-handled letter opener, withdrew the letter, and scanned it quickly. "Well, Dru and Randall and Evalee will be here during the holidays, it appears. They'll spend some time with Dru's mother in Richmond, then they'll be coming down to Mayfield."

Cara put down her coffee cup in dismay. "Not *here,* I hope."

"No, they'll be staying at Montclair. You know Dru is very close to Jonathan. They grew up together during the War and—" She paused and frowned at her daughter who was making exaggerated gestures of relief. "What in the world is that all about, Cara?" she asked in mild bewilderment.

"Nothing, Mama!" fibbed Cara, putting her napkin over her mouth to suppress her smile. Across the table, Kitty was having a similarly hard time suppressing her giggles.

Every time the name of Evalee Bondurant came up, the twins always exchanged a significant glance. Their glamorous cousin was often the subject of slightly malicious discussion between them. Dark-eyed and beautiful, Evalee, the daughter of Randall and Dru, was a popular belle of Charleston society but not the Cameron girls' favorite person.

They had met her first during the Jubilee summer they had all spent at Aunt Garnet Devlin's country estate, Birchfields, in England. Since then, their negative opinion of Evalee had not changed.

After breakfast they said good-bye to their mother and went outside. The day was sunny, the air crisp, with the feel of snow. On the porch they whistled for their dogs, two Irish setters, descendants of their father's champion bird dog and companion, King, and started walking toward the stables. Now that they were alone, the twins could discuss their cousin's coming openly.

"If Evalee's here for the holidays, she'll spoil everything!" Cara said frankly. "She's such a brat and always has been!"

"Maybe she can't help it," suggested Kitty mildly. "She's been coddled and pampered by her family all her life. She just doesn't know anything else."

"Oh, fiddle! She's impossible, and you know it, only you're too nice to say so." Cara scoffed impatiently. "If you're so determined to be charitable, why don't *you* see that she has a good time while she's here?"

Kitty did not reply, knowing that when the time came, they would share equally the hostess duties. Cara might fuss and complain, but Kitty could always count on her when it mattered.

At the stable they found their horses already saddled and, after a few words with the groom, mounted and walked them down the drive, still deep in conversation. They were just about to turn into the woods when they saw Kip Montrose on his black stallion thundering down the path from Montclair.

At his unexpected appearance, Kitty's heart turned over. To hide her sudden confusion and the warm color flooding her face, she leaned forward and patted her horse's neck.

As Kip reined alongside Cara, she asked him, "Where's Merry?"

"Oh, she'll be along in a little while. Mama had one of her headaches, and Meredith decided to stay with her and read to her until she fell asleep," he explained. Then grinned. "But here *I* am to brighten your day!"

"Puleeze!" groaned Cara, then tossed her head and, giving Pharaoh a little flick with her crop, she rode on ahead, calling over her shoulder, "Well, come on then. I'll put you to work. Mother wants lots of greenery to take to the church."

She gave her mount a little kick with her boot heels and started down the drive. Kip urged his horse to a canter and followed. Kitty lagged behind purposely. Despising the sensation of being a fifth wheel, she hoped that Meredith would come soon and decided to look for a grove of wild holly trees and wait until she showed up.

Never one to resist an opportunity to tease or challenge, Cara took the fence at the lower end of the pasture, then gave Pharaoh his head and began galloping into the woods. From the sound of hoofbeats, she knew that Kip was not far behind. When the path narrowed, she had to slow her horse. She pulled on her reins and turned from the path into a clearing. The next thing she knew, Kip was beside her.

Reaching over, he took hold of her hands on the reins. "That was quite a chase you gave me."

She dismounted and Kip did the same. Leading their horses, they walked a little farther into the woods and came at last on a thicket of wild holly trees.

"This looks like a good spot," Cara said. "Let's cut some of these."

"Did you bring something to put them in?"

"Yes, some burlap bags fastened to the back of my saddle."

Kip tethered the horses, then brought the gunny sacks. They

94

worked in silence for a few minutes, cutting the greens and filling the sacks. But it seemed to Cara that wherever she went, Kip was close beside her.

"Why don't you find your own trees?" she snapped when she had had her fill of Kip's persistent pursuit. "Why do you keep following me?"

"Don't you know the answer to that?" he asked and began to hum, then to sing a few lines of a song that had been popular the summer before, one they had danced to and sung in the fire circle on the beach at Fair Winds: "I'll follow you wherever the heart leads—"

Frowning at him, Cara deliberately moved a short distance away.

"Come on, Cara, don't go all coy on me!" Kip teased. "I'm not immune to suggestion, and yesterday I got the not-too-subtle impression you thought it might be fun to be alone for a change. Don't forget I've known you for years. I can read you like a book."

"What kind of book? The trouble with you, Kip, is that you read whatever you want into anything."

Kip only grinned.

"*Honestly!*" Cara said with elaborate derision, then threw him an annoyed look and flounced away. She kept a little ahead of him, moving from tree to tree, using her clippers with pretended concentration. After a while she heard the sound of horses' hooves and Merry calling to Kitty. Though she couldn't see them through the thick foliage, she could hear them talking to each other.

"Ah, just what I've been looking for . . . mistletoe!" Kip exclaimed in triumph.

Knowing that the plant was hard to find, Cara turned back to face him. "Where? I don't see any."

Instantly Kip was at her side, pulling a sprig out of his pocket and dangling it over her head. "Just in case, I always bring my own supply."

Before she could make a move, he had grabbed her around the waist and pulled her into his arms. Startled, she struggled, but it was no use. His mouth covered hers in a kiss that was neither tender nor sweet but passionately possessive. Slowly the kiss ended, but Kip still held her close.

95

Looking down into her eyes, he whispered, "Just think . . . it'll soon be time for us to open our time capsule, remember? We each put in our secret predictions about the future. You're going to be surprised at mine. Even at age ten, I knew what I wanted . . . and how to get it. I love you, Cara. I guess I always have. I've just begun to realize how much.

Cara stared back into his eyes. What she saw there was more than she wanted to see. The intensity of his voice, his determination, frightened her. Fiercely she struggled out of his embrace. As it loosened, she swung back her arm and brought it up in a stinging slap across his face.

Kip stepped back, dazed at first, then angry. Then, even while his cheek was reddening, he burst out laughing.

"How dare you?" she hissed and whirled about, then stalked over toward Pharaoh and prepared to mount him.

Kip's mocking voice followed her. "You're acting like the outraged heroine in one of the melodramas we put on last summer at Fair Winds!"

Cara's heart was pounding, and she felt suddenly uneasy. She halted momentarily as Kip's jibe hit home. *Last summer!* She knew that she had used Kip then, the teasing and flirting, to cover her own secret. And she knew that once she'd learned that Owen was going to be nearby in Arbordale, she had almost unconsciously decided to do it again.

But Kip was too intense, too serious. Maybe she'd set in motion something she might not be able to control. What did Scripture say about "sowing the wind and reaping the whirlwind?"

Unnerved, Cara swung up into her saddle and tugged on the reins. Then, without a backward glance at Kip, she turned her horse down the bridle path toward Cameron Hall. But for the benefit of Kitty and Meredith who might wonder at her sudden departure, Cara called back some excuse, gave Pharaoh a kick with her booted foot, and trotted off.

"Hey! Not fair!" she heard Kip yell.

Not waiting for him to mount his own horse and catch up with her, she leaned into her horse's neck and urged him to a gallop.

Hot and breathless, Cara left Pharaoh at the stables and hurried into the house. Without taking off her riding boots, one of Blythe's unwritten house rules, she clattered up the polished stairway to her bedroom.

She flung herself down on the window seat and tried to collect her thoughts. She felt confused and a little worried. Just now, out in the woods, she had seen something new in Kip's eyes. Last summer, she had *wanted* to see that look. But Kip was so maddeningly sure of himself, his appearance, his charm. That's why she'd set out to see if she could make him fall in love with her. But that was at the beginning of the summer . . . before she'd met Owen. After that, everything changed. Realizing that she wanted something more than a summer romance, she'd done something unforgivable. She'd used Kip for her own purposes.

With Owen coming to Arbordale . . . what should she do? The look in Kip's eyes, the kiss, had changed things again. Maybe, after all, she wanted nothing more than for things to remain as they had always been between the three of them—Kitty, Kip, and herself. Could they recapture the past, keep things the way they were? Was it possible?

But more than her manipulation of Kip's emotions weighed on Cara's conscience. The two unaccounted-for days in Richmond. The note she had sent to the Seminary. The reply she had received while she was visiting Susie Mills. All that must remain a secret . . . at least for a little longer. Sometimes the end justifies the means, doesn't it?

She was still pondering this question when Kitty returned.

"Why did you rush off like that?" her twin asked. "Kip invited us to Montclair for lunch."

"I got bored," Cara replied indifferently.

"Kip said he thinks you've grown too sophisticated for all our old games. Says you don't play by our rules anymore."

"That's idiotic!" said Cara crossly.

But she thought of what had happened out in the woods and was ashamed. Maybe Kip was right. Maybe she wasn't playing fair. Then she shrugged. What was one kiss? It couldn't matter that much. Not to someone like Kip!

chapter

11

Jonathan Montrose was in deep thought as he rode over to Arbordale early on a December afternoon. Even though his half-brother Jeff had been back in Virginia now for nearly ten years, they had not achieved the closeness Jonathan had hoped for and anticipated.

It was understandable, as Davida tried to point out frequently. "What on earth do you two have in common except that you were fathered by the same man . . . and *that* nearly ten years and an ocean apart?" she would say as if astonished by Jonathan's expectations. "Besides Jeff is an artist . . . and artists are notoriously different from *normal* people," she would say with elaborate patience.

Jonathan could accept that explanation, and given the fact that Jeff's career had soared and he had many commissions to fulfill, Jonathan was even more aware of the contrast in their lives. Still, he longed to get to know his younger brother and to share with him some of the Montrose heritage.

In Arbordale, reaching the dock where he would take the ferry across the river, Jonathan was again struck by the strange history of his brother's house. Avalon—named after the refuge of the mythical King Arthur after the battle for Camelot—had been brought over from England, stone by stone, timber by timber, and rebuilt on the wooded island on which Jeff and Faith Montrose lived. Blythe, his father's second wife, had moved there when Jeff was only a little boy. Later, Jeff had returned there with his bride. Everyone said that Avalon looked more like an English manor house than most of the country homes in this part of Virginia.

Jonathan's visit had been an impulse of the moment, so he had not sent word ahead. When the massive oak door was opened by an elderly servant, Jonathan made sure that he understood if he had called at an inconvenient time that he had no wish to disturb either his brother or his brother's wife.

He was shown into the drawing room and told that the mistress would be informed but the master was in his studio and the house held to the rule that he should not be disturbed until he came out himself.

Jonathan walked to the center, looking about the oak-paneled room, waiting until his eyes adjusted to the dark interior. Pale December sunshine filtered through narrow diamond-paned windows, and a fire glowed in the stone hearth, scenting the air with the spicy smell of apple wood. Gradually he was able to see the arrangements of exotic flowers in handsome vases set about the room on tables and in bookcases. The whole effect was warm and charming.

"Jonathan, how lovely of you to come!" a low, English-accented voice greeted him, and Jonathan turned around to see the daughter of his foster mother, Aunt Garnet Devlin, standing in the doorway.

For a moment he was bemused by her appearance, for she looked for all the world as if she might have stepped out of a medieval painting. Her dark hair was down and fell around her shoulders in cascading waves, and she was wearing a royal blue velvet gown with flowing sleeves banded in bright embroidery and glittering with beads.

Her full, musical laugh broke the momentary silence. "It's no wonder you look startled. No, I'm not the ghost of Hamlet's 'Ophelia.' I've been posing for Jeff and didn't take time to change. I hope you don't mind."

"Of course not. But I apologize, Faith. I told your man not to interrupt you . . . I should have sent a note, but the desire to come and call on my brother and his wife was a spur-of-the-moment decision, I'm afraid. I do hope I haven't disrupted a modeling session—"

"No, Jeff finished with me a half hour ago, but wanted to work on another part of the painting. I'm the one who should apologize. But you know, Jonathan, I believe the ladies of old had a point in their choice of clothing. I can't tell you how much more comfortable this is compared to today's fashions—no whalebone stays, no narrow skirt requiring mincing steps! I confess I sometimes rather enjoy stepping back into the Middle Ages." She laughed delightfully and, for a second, Jonathan was reminded of her mother's same mischievous gaiety, typical of Garnet at her best.

"You will stay and have tea with me, won't you, Jonathan?" she asked.

"If you're sure I won't be intruding—"

"Of course not. Or, as Cousin Evalee Bondurant would say, 'Au contraire.'" Again the naughty sparkle brightened Faith's eyes. "Otherwise, I'd have to take it alone. There's no routing Jeff out of the studio when he's immersed in a project. That's one thing I've learned in nearly twelve years of marriage to a dedicated artist."

She crossed the room, a willowy, graceful figure, and tugged the tapestried bellpull that hung from the wall. Two minutes later the door opened, and Faith asked the same dignified man who had ushered Jonathan into the house to bring tea.

"Please sit down." Faith gestured to one of the high-backed Jacobean chairs upholstered in needlepoint and placed on either side of the fireplace. "Now, tell me what's going on at Montclair? I suppose Kip and Meredith are home from college and the house is full of fun and festivity."

"Yes, they've just arrived."

"Auntie Blythe is in seventh heaven now that all *her* chicks are home to roost . . . at least for a while. She has all sorts of things planned and, of course, the annual Open House. You'll be coming, won't you, you and Davida?"

"I plan to, that is if Davida—" He paused. "Davida hasn't been very well. She's been worried about her father, Colonel Carpenter. He's getting on in years, you see, and she hates the idea of his being alone for the holidays. I urged her to invite him to spend Christmas here in Virginia with us, even offered to go to Massachusetts and travel down with him. But she says it's too much to ask him to make such a long trip at his age—" Jonathan's explanation revealed his frustration, the residue of many discussions he and Davida had had on the matter. He was grateful when the door opened and a tea trolley was wheeled into the room, bringing the subject to a close.

As Faith lifted the round teapot to pour, Jonathan noticed the unusual ring she was wearing—a large amethyst in a gold setting of two clasped hands beneath a crown. With a start of recognition, Jonathan identified it as the same ring painted on the third finger, left hand, in the portrait of Noramary Marsh, the first Bride of Montclair, hanging on the stair wall in the front hall. *How*, he wondered, *did Faith come to be wearing it*?

"See this?" Her voice interrupted his conjecture. He nodded, thinking she meant the ring, wondering if she had seen his glance, read his thoughts? But he soon realized that she was referring to the cup she was holding.

"Aren't these exquisite? Auntie Blythe painted them. She's quite an accomplished china artist. She did quite a lot of it when Jeff was a little boy, but she's given it up now. Says it used to fill the empty hours for her when he was away at school and she was alone. I guess now that she's so happily married, she never lacks for interesting diversions to fill her time." Faith smiled and handed Jonathan the fragile teacup delicately hand-painted with pansies. "But it's clear to see where Jeff gets his talent, isn't it?"

To cover his own mental wanderings, Jonathan asked, "What is Jeff working on at the moment?"

"Well, it's a secret." She looked apologetic. "Although I don't see why I shouldn't tell *you*. After all, you *are* Jeff's brother and are as interested as anyone could be in his success. But artists tend to be superstitious about their work, you know. And this is quite an enormous undertaking, a kind of inspired theme. Jeff hopes to place it in the Waverly Exhibit next spring if it's finished by then. The Waverly Galleries gave him his start, you may recall, and Jeff's loyalties are long and deep."

Jonathan held up his hand to stop her. "Don't tell me, Faith. I wouldn't have you betray his confidence."

She dimpled. "Or change his luck?" She sipped her tea, then put the cup down on the tray and offered him a plate of currant scones.

"However, I think Jeff's success has been more than luck. He is extremely gifted, wouldn't you agree? Of course, I may be prejudiced—" She lowered her voice. "But I really believe this is going to be his masterpiece." She laughed, her sudden seriousness past. "And of course, I'd think so because *I'm* in it! Talk about being self-serving!"

Jonathan joined heartily in her spontaneous laughter. Just about then they heard the sound of scuffling, of giggles and childish voices outside the door, and Faith gave Jonathan a conspiratorial wink. "Are you ready for the onslaught?"

The words were scarcely out of her mouth before the door burst open and three little bodies came hurtling into the room. They ran non-stop until they tumbled pell-mell into Faith's lap.

Jonathan watched, fascinated, as she took them one by one, kissing and hugging them, tickling and ruffling the assorted curly heads. What beautiful children they were! He had often seen them on Jeff's canvases depicting cherubs or elfin woodland creatures or little royals in his illustrative paintings of courts and castles, his favorite medieval themes. In the rosy flesh, they were even more appealing—luscious skin tones, lustrous hair, shining, dark-lashed eyes.

An hour later, riding back to Montclair, Jonathan felt a certain heaviness of spirit. He had not seen his brother, but he had seen and experienced the loving circle in which Jeff's art was created and flourished. And in that, Jonathan had realized in some subtle way the emptiness and grayness of his own life.

As he turned onto the road leading from Mayfield toward home, a girl on horseback sped by, rider's hair and horse's mane flying like flaming silken banners. As she went by, she raised her riding crop, but the greeting she called was lost in the wind.

He knew it was one of the Cameron twins, most likely Cara—the one his son was infatuated with, the one who most probably would become his daughter-in-law someday. But what was she doing so far from Mayfield on the road to Arbordale this late in the day?

The small, gray church came in sight and, bending her head against the sharp wind, Cara hurried forward. It seemed an appropriate place to meet, ironic even, she might say. But Cara's heart was beating wildly. If he hadn't wanted to come, why would he have agreed?

She felt a little guilty that she had told her mother she was going to help decorate the Mayfield church for the Christmas services, using it as the excuse to be away all afternoon. Her sense of guilt was heightened when her mother had been so pleased that she would volunteer for such a good cause. Then there had been that dreadful moment when Kitty had almost offered to come along until she remembered that she had promised Meredith to help with some last-minute shopping for Mrs. Montrose.

Cara hoped she wouldn't be caught in her fib, hoped no one in the Ladies Guild would run into her mother and mention that there had been no representative from Cameron Hall to help with the decorations. She hated having so easily deceived her mother and murmured a quick prayer of repentance, knowing it was not enough. *It is so easy to deceive someone who trusts you,* she thought.

Pushing through the heavy church door, she went inside the dimly lit interior. Instantly she felt its stillness and realized that it was empty. Where was he? Why hadn't he come? If she had to wait too long, there would be other explanations to make. The late December day was chilly and, inside the unheated church, Cara shivered. She rubbed her bare hands together and turned up the collar of her jacket. Had he forgotten? Or worse still, decided not to come?

Just when her hope and anxiety had almost peaked, she heard the leather-padded back door of the sanctuary open with a swooshing sound. She turned to see a tall figure striding down the center aisle toward her.

At Montclair, Kitty and Meredith, back after their afternoon of shopping, were busy admiring the other's selections before wrapping them. It was a cozy time together as they selected ribbons to complement bright paper, nibbled on Christmas cookies, and chatted.

Suddenly Kitty noticed that night was coming on. "I'd better start for home, Merry." She wound her scarf around her neck, buttoned her coat, and tucked her hair under her knitted cap.

"I'll come downstairs with you and tell Jeb to bring the phaeton around and drive you home. It's getting too dark for you to walk, Kitty."

They left the bedroom and stood at the top of the staircase while Kitty pulled on her gloves. "Then I'll see you tonight?" she asked.

Just then a voice spoke from behind them, and they turned to see Mrs. Montrose in a mauve velvet tea gown coming down the hall from her room.

"Oh, is there a party planned for this evening?" Davida asked, frowning slightly.

Kitty saw Meredith give her mother a quick, anxious glance. "We've all been invited over to the Langleys for supper and dancing," she began, then asked, "Aren't you feeling well, Mama?"

Davida smiled wanly and shook her head. "Just one of my headaches coming on, I fear. Nothing for you to bother about, darling." She passed a thin hand across her brow, then turned and gave Kitty a long appraising look. "I suppose your sister is out gallivanting all over the countryside. I never knew a girl with so much *energy*—" Her emphasis on the word made it sound like some kind of vice. "Jonathan said he saw her on the road as he came home from Mayfield earlier. I believe he said, 'She was riding hell-bent for leather'!" Mrs. Montrose's faint smile suggested that she did not consider it in the least humorous.

She let her implication linger as she moved slowly back toward her own room. "I suppose she'll be at tonight's party, keeping everyone dancing until the wee hours."

Kitty did not know whether to be indignant or to laugh.

But Meredith, of course, failed to see beneath her mother's words and, instead, took a few steps as if to follow her. "Mama, could I get something for your headache?"

"Sweet girl, it always helps when you stay with me, read to me. Seems to make my headache just fade away. But no, of course not, dear. Go on to the party with the others. I want you to enjoy yourself."

"But I wouldn't enjoy a minute knowing you were feeling ill—" Meredith's resolve was already wavering.

"I wouldn't dream of keeping you from your friends. Of course, you must go have fun . . . I won't hear of anything else."

But, Kitty thought, *that is exactly what you do want, Mrs. Montrose. You want Meredith to miss the party and stay home with you—*

chapter

12

IT WAS ALREADY dark by the time Cara returned to Cameron Hall. At the stable she left Pharaoh with a brisk order to the stableboy to rub him down well and give him plenty of water and oats. Then she went to the back of the house and let herself in the kitchen door. Running up the back stairs to her bedroom, she let the door slam behind her, shedding her jacket, hat, and scarf haphazardly. She hoped to pull herself together before having to face anyone.

She felt wretched, almost ill with disappointment. She had been so sure it would happen the way she wanted it to, the way she had hoped and dreamed—

But it wasn't the end of things, not by a long shot. Oh, he was stubborn, but so was she! She'd never yet lost something she really went after, whether it was a horse-show ribbon, a recitation prize at school, or an extra privilege from her indulgent parents. She'd think of a way to convince him—

Just then she heard Kitty's voice, then Scott's deeper one outside in the hall as they came upstairs. Quickly she grabbed her robe and went into the bathroom adjoining their bedroom and turned on the faucets hard, filling the tub.

She was lying, eyes closed, in a froth of scented bubbles when Kitty poked her head in the door. "You look relaxed and comfy."

"I'll be out in a few minutes, then you can have your turn," Cara replied lazily.

When her twin emerged, Kitty teased. "You look glowing.

Decorating a church must suit you." She laughed. "I heard all about your 'gallivanting' around the countryside when I was at Montclair today!"

Cara registered surprise. Was it her imagination, Kitty wondered, or did her sister suddenly turn pale?

Cara gave her head a little toss, flounced over to the dressing table, and started to take the pins out of her hair. "Oh, is Mrs. Montrose gossiping about me again?"

"Not really. You know how she is. But sadly enough, I think she heaped enough guilt on Merry that she'll not be going to the Langleys tonight."

"That woman!" Cara flung down her hairbrush onto the glass top of the dressing table so the perfume bottles rattled. "Why doesn't she let her children grow up? I declare, I believe Kip will always be tied to his Mama's apron strings!"

"Well, at least she won't keep Kip from coming tonight," Kitty said, then changed the subject. "What are you wearing . . . your glamorous new gown?"

"No, I'm saving it—"

"Saving it? For what?"

"A special evening."

"What could be more special than the first big party of the holidays?"

Cara's eyes narrowed and, as she looked up at Kitty's reflection in the mirror, she smiled a mysterious little smile. It was one Kitty recognized, and it meant that her twin was keeping something from her. Miffed, Kitty went to take her own bath.

Cara was still fussing with her hair when their mother tapped on the bedroom door to tell her that Kip was downstairs waiting for her.

"Oh, Kitty, be a lamb and go down and keep Kip happy," Cara begged. "I'll be just a few minutes more."

Kitty was torn. The last thing she wanted to do tonight was play second fiddle to Cara with Kip. On the other hand, she couldn't pass up the opportunity to be with him for a little bit, even to pretend it was *she* he'd come to take to the party.

So with a suppressed sigh, a quick glance in the mirror, and a pat to her hair, Kitty acquiesced. "Oh, all right, but don't be long. You know how he hates being kept waiting."

Cara laughed and said over her shoulder, "Oh, fudge! Keeping them waiting is the secret to my success with men!"

Kitty let the bedroom door slam shut behind her. *It's probably true,* she thought indignantly. *Cara never lets any young man know how she feels, while I'm so transparent they see right through me! I guess that's just another difference between us.*

Twenty minutes later, Cara was satisfied with her appearance and, gathering up her white rabbit-fur jacket and beaded evening bag, she glided out to the hall, practicing a few dance steps in her new French-heeled satin slippers.

Hearing voices in the hall below, she imagined it must be Tuck Henderson come to take Kitty to the Langleys' party. Curious to see him in his VMI dress uniform, Cara leaned over the balcony for a peek.

She saw more than she had bargained for. The tall blond cadet was carrying on an animated conversation with their mother, while Kip stood at the foot of the staircase, talking with Kitty. *How lovely she looks tonight,* thought Cara affectionately, noticing how her sister's head tilted as she gazed up into Kip's eyes. *Why, she looks absolutely enchanted.*

The truth dawned slowly. *Kitty is in love with Kip! Kitty . . . Kitty and Kip!* With the revelation, Cara felt as if the breath had been knocked from her body.

Now what was she to do? Kip had fit so neatly into her plans. It had all been so natural. They went back ro far, shared so much—their childhood, their sense of fun and adventure, many of the same traits. *They were almost more alike than she and Kitty*, Cara thought with some irony. The big secret they had kept all these years—the time capsule in the secret room at Montclair and the discovery of the staircase leading down and out through the garden to the river—

All at once something Meredith had said to her one day on the beach flashed to mind. "It's inevitable, you know. Kip is bound to fall in love with one of you."

If I hadn't deliberately used Kip for my own purposes, would he have fallen in love with Kitty? she wondered miserably and drew a long breath. Kip would eventually inherit Montclair and settle down to be the country gentleman he was born to be, once all the wildness— the wildness *she* loved in him—played itself out. *That's what his parents are counting on and, in the end, that's what will happen. And Kitty would be much better suited to that kind of life than I—*

As she was standing at the top of the steps, these thoughts crowding her brain, Kip looked up and saw her and frowned ferociously. "Well, there you are at last, slowpoke. Do you finally think you're beautiful enough to appear in public? Come on, you've kept us waiting long enough."

The Langleys' home was a holiday fairyland. Their drawing room and hallway had been converted into a long ballroom with swags of evergreens and holly decorating the windows and red candles in brass sconces burning brightly. A popular dance band was playing the current musical favorites while couples whirled on the polished floor, the men's black evening tails sailing, the young women's bright dresses spinning like colorful pinwheels.

In spite of her own full dance card, Kitty found her eyes unconsciously following Kip. Most of the time, he was either dancing with Cara or gazing at her. Kitty remembered how she had longed to be grown up, how when they were children, nothing was more fun than dressing up in their mother's clothes, pretending to be a ballerina or a bride. Now she desperately wished for those days again! How simple things were when she and Cara were best friends, when they could talk together about anything, no matter what.

How she longed to be able to talk with Cara now. But they had both changed. Circumstances had changed. And now there was this awful barrier between them: Kip Montrose.

In the midst of all the music and laughter and gaiety, Kitty felt her heart wrench, swept by inexplicable sadness. Finally it was the last dance before supper. Soon she could go home.

"I've invited Vance Langley to escort me to the Christmas dance at the Tollivers," Cara said lightly the next morning as they were getting dressed.

Wide-eyed, Kitty turned to regard her sister. "But I thought . . . I mean, what about Kip?"

"What about him?" Cara forced a carelessness in her tone.

"I'm almost sure he expected that you—"

"I don't care *what* he expected." Cara shrugged, bending to straighten her stockings so that Kitty could not see her face. "Did he say something to you about it?"

"Not in so many words, but I just think . . . I mean, it's obvious he cares about you . . . and I assumed—"

For a moment Cara could not speak, hoping that when she did, her voice would not betray her. "Well, he assumed wrong. Why don't *you* ask him?"

"But, Cara, it's *you* he wants to take," Kitty protested.

"If he does, that's not my fault. I never meant to give him that impression." Cara picked up the silver-handled brush from the dressing table and began brushing her hair vigorously, so hard, in fact, that her eyes stung and watered. But she kept her tone even as she said, "Oh, Kitty don't be such a shrinking violet. For heaven's sake, it's not as though we haven't all known each other forever. Ask him!"

With the discussion seemingly at an end, Kitty felt there was yet much left unsaid. But something had happened to that warm intimacy she and Cara had once shared. There was tension between them now. She didn't know what had caused it, nor did she know how to ease it.

Since coming home, Cara was different, argumentative and touchy. So all the things Kitty would have liked to say to her sister, especially about Kip Montrose, had to remain uncomfortably locked in her heart.

Later that morning Kitty and Cara were starting to trim the Christmas tree that had just been set up when Kip showed up unannounced.

"What brings you over here so early?" Cara asked him coolly, continuing to loop strings of cranberries through the boughs.

"Just wanted to start my day off right by getting one of your incomparable greetings. You always make a fellow feel so welcome!" Kip quipped back, then sent one of his heart-rocking smiles

Kitty's way. "Good morning, twin—the sweet-tempered one, that is."

He walked over to the ladder on which Cara was standing and gave it a little shake, causing it to wobble slightly. "As for *you*, I guess I could wait until you were in a better mood, but I just wanted to remind you that tomorrow night's the Tollivers' party and—"

"So?" came Cara's indifferent comment.

Kitty stiffened, realizing that she was going to deliver her blow and that Kip was not prepared for it.

"So—" he imitated her tone of voice—"I just wanted to know what time we should go. The invitation said seven."

"I don't know what time *you* should go, but Vance Langley's coming for *me* at quarter to seven."

"Vance Langley?" Kip repeated. "You're joking."

"No, I'm not. What makes you think I'm joking?"

Then, realizing she was serious, Kip spoke with steely precision. "I was under the impression you promised to go with *me*."

"Well, you were under a mistaken impression," Cara retorted. "You know, Kip, you take a lot for granted. But I wouldn't worry if I were you. I'm sure you'll have no trouble at all finding a date, what with every girl in Mayfield dying for the chance."

Kitty tensed, knowing instinctively that Cara had hit a nerve with the remark. She glanced at Kip, saw his face turn white, his expression stony.

"Fine, just dandy! *Now* you tell me." Kip was furious. "Well, thanks a lot, Cara!" he shot out, turning on his heel, his boots loud on the tile floor of the foyer. He marched across to the front door. Its resounding slam made Kitty wince.

She turned to see her twin's reaction and saw her give an involuntary shudder. Maybe even Cara realized she'd gone too far this time.

In spite of Cara's impatient insistence, Kitty could not bring herself to invite Kip to the dance—not after she had heard their argument and knew how hurt and angry he was. Instead, she pleaded a bad headache and did not go to the Tollivers' party at all. The lovely emerald-green velvet hung outside the armoire in their bedroom, a lonely reminder of all the fun she might have had. But it would have all been pretense, she sighed, stroking the soft nap. If she couldn't go with Kip, and know he *wanted* to be with her, it would have all been a waste anyhow.

The hours ticked by endlessly. She heard the grandfather clock downstairs strike midnight, then one. It was sometime after that she heard wheels on the icy crust of snow on the driveway, voices murmuring, the sound of the front door closing.

Kitty pretended to be asleep when the bedroom door opened with a soft squeak, and Cara slipped in. She could tell that her twin was moving about, undressing quietly. Under partially closed lids, she saw her shadow move across the room to the window, then stand there looking out. Cara parted the curtains so a narrow shaft of moonlight slanted in, outlining her figure.

Kitty could not hold still any longer so she shifted and said, "I'm awake, Cara. You needn't tiptoe. You can turn on the light if you like."

She saw Cara turn toward her, shake her head, but she drew the curtains back and let the moon shine into the room, making bold squares on the floor.

"How was the party?" Kitty ventured. "Fun?"

"Yes, I guess so. Well, you know, it was just a party . . . lots of dancing, music. You should have come." A pause, then, "Are you feeling better?"

"Headache's all gone."

Cara traced her finger down the length of the window pane, outlining something with her finger on the frosty glass. Then suddenly she spoke up. "Vance Langley asked me to wear his fraternity pin tonight. I thought you'd like to know."

Kitty could not speak for a moment. Her first thought was Kip . . . how had Kip taken this news? "That's sort of like being engaged, isn't it?"

"Yes, I suppose . . . but not for ages and ages . . . it's, well— engaged to be engaged."

"He's awfully nice, good-looking, too . . . and a splendid rider," Kitty said, trying to sound enthusiastic, while all she could think of was the hurt in Kip's eyes, the anger in his voice—

Cara, still standing at the window, did not respond. But before Kitty could think of anything more to say, she remarked indifferently, "It's freezing cold . . . The lake will be frozen hard tomorrow, I think."

"Oh, good. Maybe we can go skating."

Cara did not answer but walked over and got into her bed. There was a long silence, both of them remaining perfectly still.

In a few minutes, Kitty thought she heard the sound of stifled sobs from Cara's side of the room. She leaned up on her elbows and asked anxiously, "Cara . . . Are you crying?"

"No! Of course not! Why should I be crying?" There was another silence, and Kitty distinctly heard a sniffle, but for some reason, she could say nothing more. Unless Cara wanted to confide in her, or indicated that she needed comfort, Kitty felt that she was not free to offer any. The barricade that existed between them now was impenetrable.

"Cara—" she began hesitantly. "I hope . . . I hope you'll be very happy."

"Of course I will," Cara said sharply. "Why ever wouldn't I be?" Another pause, then, "Well, good-night, I'm exhausted."

Kitty lay awake long after Cara fell silent, not sure whether her twin was really asleep or not, her thoughts in turmoil. *What was really going on with Cara, Kip, and Vance Langley?*

Cara pretended to be asleep when Kitty got up the next morning, tiptoeing around so as not to disturb her twin, then went out and shut the door softly behind her. Cara lay there for a few minutes, plotting just how she would manage the day.

She did not know how she could avoid going skating today, but she knew she had to make another trip to Arbordale before the New Year's party. Still, it would have been such fun to be out on the frozen pond again. She loved the sensation of gliding on the ice. She was a good skater, and she knew it. Her skating outfit with its swirling, fur-trimmed skirt and the tight little jacket with Russian braid was sure to attract attention, for she had seen the admiring glances cast her way as she skimmed and weaved in and out. *It is like dancing*, she thought, *only better, with the fresh air and the cold wind in your face and the feeling of total freedom! But . . . first things first.*

Cara threw back the covers and got out of bed. Flinging on her quilted robe, she slid her feet into fuzzy slippers and brushed her hair back, securing it with the first thing she saw, which was the narrow sash of the dress she had worn the night before.

Taking a look in the mirror, she wondered if she looked pale enough to complain of a scratchy throat. If so, she could mention that she felt achy, not up to the long walk through the woods to the pond. Or would Mama get all solicitous and put her to bed with a mustard plaster and a hot brick at her feet, declaring she'd better stay in bed until all danger of the "flu" that was going around, was past?

She *had* to get to Arbordale today. Maybe if she just said she was tired . . . after all, it was long after midnight before she had come up to bed. Just maybe she could get away with it . . . if she was very, very clever.

Kitty wanted to be sympathetic when Cara told her she wouldn't be going skating. But down in the tiny self-centered spot she tried hard not to indulge, she was glad. If Kip realized that Cara was not in love with him—

And Cara had certainly given her the go-ahead in every way, hadn't she? If she really was engaged to be engaged to Vance, didn't that give Kitty clear sailing?

The morning was bitingly cold, and frost had traced an icy lace on the grass as Kitty and Meredith, skates slung over their shoulders, made their way to the pond. The path underneath their boots was hard with a slight overlay of frost and crunched with every step they took. The sun, pale at first, emerged gradually into mellow brightness, sharpening the winter landscape of brown fields and dark evergreens.

The boys had gone out earlier to test the ice and had declared it solid. There was a mood of anticipation in the air, and voices rang with good humor as they called back and forth from group to group along the trail, everyone eager to begin the first skating party of the year.

The sight that greeted them when they arrived was spectacular—the gleaming surface of the frozen pond, ringed with snow banks and stately pines, their branches heavy with snow. Then the skaters themselves, garbed in colorful mufflers and mittens—bright spots of warmth and life against the wintry backdrop.

Gaiety and good-humored greetings resounded as skates were put on and laced up tight and the first skaters glided out onto the ice.

To Kitty's dismay, Kip was all moody and miserable. Cara, of course, was the cause. Kitty could not deny the fact that his face had brightened at the sight of her. It was a common mistake, and not the first time he had mistaken Kitty for Cara.

She put on her skates and moved out onto the ice, telling herself that she must be sensible. How could she ever be sure of Kip's love when she and Cara looked so much alike? Even if he managed to get to know and love her for herself, would he always fantasize that she was her twin?

Suddenly Kitty heard the scratch of steel on ice behind her and executed a figure eight just as Kip skated alongside. A split second afterward, he held out his hand, inviting her to skate with him. Determined to seize the moment, Kitty thrust away all her disturbing thoughts and smilingly took his hand.

Kip made an amusing comment and she laughed in delight, feeling the wind on her face, the glow of happiness. For now . . . it was enough—

Wind-driven snow blew in chilling gusts around the corner of the building. Cara huddled against the stone wall in the arched passageway. In spite of her fur jacket, she felt cold. She clenched her teeth together to keep them from chattering and chafed her hands inside the fur-lined gloves.

From inside the church, through the cracks of the stained-glass windows under which she stood, she could hear the muted sound of the organ and voices lifted in some hymn or carol. The choir must be practicing. She dared not go in, afraid someone might ask why she was here.

Shivering, Cara found herself saying frantic prayers. The light was fading quickly. If he didn't come soon, she'd have to leave without seeing him, or she would be missed at home and there would be questions—

Then she heard booted footsteps along the stone walk, and turned. Her heart leaped with joy. He was here. He *had* come.

"I'm sorry I kept you waiting. You must be freezing."

She shook her head impatiently. "Well, can you come?"

"I can't. I can't leave now. There's a Vigil service, Watch Night—"

"But—" She wanted to plead with him but checked herself. "There's no way?"

"You knew it might turn out like this when I—"

"I know . . . I just thought—" Then, "Can we go somewhere for a little while?"

He hesitated.

"You're afraid someone might see us, aren't you?'"

"Well, I suppose—"

"Never mind." Her voice quavered.

His arms went around her, holding her. "You shouldn't be standing here in this wind," he said, his lips warm on her cold brow.

She shifted slightly and lifted her head, searching the clear eyes of the young man in whose embrace the world seemed to begin and end. Slowly, everything else—the shrill whistle of the wind, the voices of the choir inside raised in anthems—receded, as if coming from a long distance.

For a moment all Cara was aware of was the pounding of her heart before she felt the seeking sweetness of his kiss.

Too soon it ended, and she heard him say huskily, "I have to go. It's getting late. You'd better leave, too—"

"No," she protested, her voice muffled against his tweed jacket.

"Oh, Cara, sometimes I wonder if—"

"Don't say that! Don't even think that!"

"I don't like meeting this way. At least, shouldn't we tell Scott?"

"No!" She cut him off. "It would just cause . . . difficulties. Not yet—" She sighed. "You're sure about New Year's?"

"It's impossible." He kissed her again, a long, lingering, tender kiss. "I have to go now. You must, too. It will be dark soon—"

"I know—" Still she was reluctant to move out of the comforting circle of his arms.

He held her tight in one long hug, then released her. "You'll write?"

"Of course."

She watched his tall figure, head bent against the snowy wind, hurrying across the churchyard. She felt miserable and abandoned, her heart as cold and frozen as her fingers and toes.

chapter
13

ON THE LAST DAY of the year, Cameron Hall hummed with activity. Everything was in preparation for the smaller party to be held that night for family and close friends, with the Open House to follow on New Year's Day.

Cara had never felt less like celebrating. It all seemed so pointless when the one person in the world she wanted to be with was not here. The future was a blank. The new year promised nothing.

The game she was playing was utterly false, but she couldn't stop now. It would have been easier had she been able to keep up the charade. Everyone was used to their sparring, their teasing, but for Kitty's sake, she must once and for all end things with Kip.

To make that more evident, she had introduced a new player into the game—a "pawn," Vance Langley, who had been constantly dancing in attendance since the summer at Cape Cod. One unexpected complication, however, was that her family was delighted with her new beau. An excellent horseback rider and hunter with the manners of a born Virginia gentleman, Vance had won both Rod's and Blythe's approval.

Maybe she could have handled that for the few days left of Christmas vacation if Kip hadn't made such a nuisance of himself. He had taken her new preoccupation with Vance as a direct challenge not to miss a single party, and there he would sulk and stare, generally disrupting her plans.

Cara felt helpless, trapped, and resentful. And it showed. She was snappish with her family, picked petty quarrels with Kitty, and argued with her mother. Everyone was finding her behavior tedious and tiring.

To make matters even worse, sandpapering her nerves was the unexpected arrival of Evalee Bondurant. She had wheedled an invitation from Blythe to spend the New Year's weekend at Cameron Hall instead of Montclair, which Evalee found deadly dull.

"Aunt Davida's always sick, and my mother and Jonathan are always out somewhere together," she complained, so the twins found themselves unwilling hostesses to their cousin.

Although she had been given a guest room to herself, Evalee popped in and out of the twins' room without so much as an "if you please," imposing her company on them constantly. Evalee put on so many airs, going on endlessly about her sister, Lady Blanding, and her country estate, her London townhouse, and all the social events she attended while visiting there, that Cara was ready to scream.

"Lalage has *promised* that she'll arrange for me to be presented at Court!" Evalee told the twins, posing and practicing what she assumed to be proper court bows in front of the full-length mirror in their bedroom.

Kitty watched nervously as Cara's temper grew shorter and shorter. Besides Evalee's annoying presence, she knew that there was something else bothering her twin. As the tension tightened, Kitty began to dread the inevitable explosion.

Arriving home on New Year's Eve afternoon, Scott Cameron was in an unusually introspective mood, his thoughts full of possible plans for the future. He had had several long talks with his father during this vacation, and he knew that Rod expected him to join the family business when he graduated next year.

But there was one big problem. Scott had his heart set on a career in the practice of law. With a strong legal tradition in the Cameron family, he didn't know why his father wouldn't be pleased with his choice. Great-Uncle Logan had been very successful, had even gone to Bermuda and become a well-known solicitor there.

Still, Scott wasn't sure how to break the news to his father, who had already suffered the disappointment of one son's refusal to join him in the Cameron Hall Horse Farms. Scott's stepbrother Jeff had made another choice, too, one that had almost caused a permanent rift in the relationship between stepfather and son. History had a way of repeating itself. He didn't want to be the second to let his father down, but—

As he walked in the front door, he was annoyed to hear voices raised in argument. *That Cara's at it again,* he thought with some irritation. It was unmistakably her voice arguing with their mother. Why was it that his younger sister always managed to cause a minor hurricane whenever she was home from school?

"It's *not* too sophisticated!" he heard her protest. "After all, I'm twenty, almost twenty-one!"

Then there was Blythe's quiet, reasonable tone, though he couldn't quite hear what she was saying. He felt like giving his sister a piece of his mind, but, gathering their discussion had something to do with a dress, decided it was not his area of expertise. Instead, he strode through the hall and out to his father's office above the stables.

Maybe it wasn't the best time to approach Rod, to come to some decision about his future. Then, what better time than New Year's Eve?

Upstairs, when Blythe left the twins' bedroom after issuing her ultimatum that either Cara change her dress or wear the fringed Spanish shawl over her bare shoulders and daring décolletage, the discussion continued in lowered tones.

"It's so unfair!" Cara said furiously. "Mama didn't say a word about *Evalee's* dress! Black velvet and rhinestones is perfectly all right for *her* to wear, it seems, so why should she make such a fuss about *my* dress?"

"Why don't you just do what Mama says, Cara?" pleaded Kitty.

"Because I'm sick to death of people telling me how to *be,* how to *act,* how to *dress,* for pity's sake! Everyone . . . Mother, Father, Scott, and you . . . yes, *you,* Kitty!" Cara accused her, then pacing the room, she went on. "I know they all want me to be more like

120

you. Even our friends expect us to behave exactly the same. Well, I'm not *you!* I'm *me!* And if this family can't accept me the way I am, *who* I am . . . well, that's just too bad!"

Crushed by her twin's outburst, Kitty was silent. She knew from experience that there was no reasoning with Cara when she was like this. She glanced at the clock. It was getting late. Mama would be expecting them downstairs to help receive the guests, especially with so many of the younger crowd invited. So Kitty began to dress while Cara flung herself on the window seat, pouting.

At length, Cara got up, yanked down the dress that had caused all the controversy, and slipped the filmy chiffon over her head. Then she sat down at the dressing table.

Out of the corner of her eye, Kitty watched her lean toward the mirror and bite her lips to redden them. Sweeping her hair up off her neck, Cara twisted it into a coil, anchoring it with an ornate comb. Then she fastened glittering gold hoops into her ears.

Pushing back the dressing table bench, she stood, and stepped back to survey her appearance. Something in her sister's reflected expression sent an involuntary shiver through Kitty. She *knew* that look, and it always meant trouble!

Seeing Kitty's gaze upon her, Cara struck a dramatic pose and whirled around, flinging one bare arm over her head, the other fanning out the pleated skirt. "Ta-dum!" she exclaimed. "How's this?" Then she picked up the Spanish shawl and spun it around her shoulders. "See you downstairs."

When Cara left the room, Kitty ran after her, whether to halt her in her collision course or to warn her, she was never sure. But she was too late. As she reached the top of the steps, Cara was already running lightly downstairs, humming to herself.

When Kitty reached the ballroom, she found the party going splendidly. Throngs of people mingled, congenially flowing through the beautifully decorated rooms and enjoying the conversation and the bounteous buffet. Another annual Cameron Hall celebration to welcome in the new year was in full swing.

As the evening progressed, the guests broke into two groups— Blythe and Rod's friends congregating in the drawing room, the younger set gravitating to the second parlor that had been cleared for dancing. Here, the gramophone was on, spinning out all the most popular tunes, and soon couples were dancing.

Kitty could see that Vance Langley was trying to monopolize Cara but not succeeding very well. As usual, her twin was circulating, seeming more vivacious than ever. In fact, Cara was "showing off," as their nurse, Lily, used to say, and Kitty tried not to feel annoyed. A quick glance at the glowering Kip told her that he too was obviously incensed by Cara's ignoring him.

Kitty suspected that her sister's behavior was more than a mere reaction to the argument she had had earlier with their mother, or even her impatience with Evalee who was flirting openly with everyone. It was something more, something deeper. Whatever it was, she wished Cara would share it with her.

Suddenly Kitty's attention was diverted from Tuck Henderson's attempt at conversation. Whatever he had been trying to tell her was drowned out by the sound of vibrant music being played very loudly. It was a Spanish dance record, a favorite of Cara's, the ballad sung by a romantic Latin musical comedy star.

Even before she turned around, Kitty felt a tremor of apprehension. She could sense a murmur rippling through the crowd. Then she understood. A circle had formed, and everyone had stopped dancing—that is, everyone except Cara, who was in the center of the floor, dancing to the music, snapping her fingers like castanets, and swirling the Spanish shawl.

Kitty suppressed a horrified gasp. Her parents would be absolutely appalled! At least her mother would.

But Cara danced on, adding a staccato click of her heels to the music that intensified as it reached a crescendo. Kitty watched her, seemingly caught up in the pulsating rhythm. Did her impulsive action spring from some long-buried connection with that other Carmella, the dark-eyed Spanish ancestor with her exotic beauty and adventurous soul—their gypsy grandmother?

Cara's heart was pounding, every drop of Spanish blood in her throbbing. She was experiencing something beyond herself as she spun around and around on the polished floor. With a final flourish of the shawl and a rap of her high heels, Cara finished with an

"Olé!" to a burst of enthusiastic applause from the group of young people surrounding her.

It was only when the music stopped and the clapping had faded away, leaving an abrupt silence, that Cara snapped back to the present moment. Standing in the archway with shocked expressions on their faces were her parents. Cara flinched before her mother's wide-eyed gaze, her father's cold fury.

Cara's little moment of triumph fled. In its wake she felt only shame and regret. Suddenly everyone began to talk, chattering together, turning away from the embarrassing scene being enacted between parents and daughter before their eyes.

Then Rod and Blythe turned away, too, and returned to their friends in the drawing room, to attempt to smooth over the undercurrent of tension.

Impulsively, Kitty moved toward Cara, ready to lend sympathetic support, though Kip reached her side first. But Cara brushed him away, saying, "Let me alone!" and rushed blindly past Kitty.

Kitty hesitated, momentarily stunned motionless, watching her sister leave the room and run up the stairs. Ordinarily she might have followed, tried to help in any way she could. But this time something held Kitty back. She had seen something more than rebellion in Cara's eyes, much more than parental displeasure in their father's.

Instinctively, Kitty had the feeling that this night marked some kind of turning point for their family, and she felt chilled by the premonition.

Upstairs in her room, Cara breathed rapidly, feeling the rage slowly drain away, leaving frustration and despair. She had successfully wrecked the evening for everyone. But then nobody understood. Nobody cared. When finally she could draw a breath without experiencing a sharp pain in her breast, she covered her face with her hands and felt the tears slide through her fingers as they ran down her cheeks.

It was after midnight by the time all the guests had left. Cara, lying on her bed in the dark, heard the good-nights and New Year's greetings ringing out in the cold night air from below her bedroom window.

A few minutes later, the bedroom door opened and Kitty came in. Cara felt her sister approach the bed, stand there for a full minute before touching her shoulder gently.

"Cara, are you asleep? If you're not, do you want to talk?"

"No, I'm not asleep. How could I possibly sleep after that dreadful scene tonight?" Cara replied drearily. She reached out, pulled the cord on the bedside lamp, and the room sprang into light. Punching up her pillows behind her, she sat up and leaned back. "Well, I suppose you want to write me off, too."

Kitty shook her head sadly and sat down on the edge of the bed. "No, Cara. I just want to know . . . why?"

"Why what? Why I danced? Or why I yelled at Kip and defied Daddy?" She gave a helpless shrug. "How do I know? Maybe I just *felt* like it." She sighed, then asked with a wry smile, "It did shake everyone up a little, though, didn't it?"

"But you really hurt Daddy, Cara. And poor Kip . . . he looked so—so . . . crushed—"

"Oh, Kip. He'll get over it. Don't worry about him. He's pulled enough stunts of his own not to dare point a finger at anyone else." She tossed the covers back and got out of bed, then went over to the dressing table and picked up the nail buffer. "What about Vance?"

"He excused himself and left right after you did."

"I'm sure his mother will get an earful from all her friends who were here. They won't be able to wait to tell her what a disgrace I was! He'll probably ask for his fraternity pin back." She gave a short laugh.

There was a long silence, filled only with the sound of Cara filing her nails. She examined her fingertips and flung down the buffer. It clattered noisily onto the glass top of the dressing table. Then she stood and walked to the window, staring out into the darkness.

When she turned to face Kitty at last, her eyes were flashing. "I think maybe the reason everyone was so shocked is they don't really want to see me as I am. Maybe in this family it isn't all right to be *different*. And I *am* different, Kitty, whether anyone wants to admit it or not."

"I know, Cara, but . . . it just seems like tonight you set out deliberately to cause . . . trouble."

"Because I danced? That's crazy. I don't know why Mama should be all that upset. After all, her own mother, the one I'm named for, was a dancer." She sighed. "I guess dancing is just not considered a proper profession for all the blue-blooded Virginia Cameron clan! Or even to acknowledge that I have gypsy blood in my veins!"

"Oh, Cara, you're just being dramatic. I have the very same blood in my veins, and I don't feel the need to exploit it—" Kitty began but never got to finish.

"Even you don't understand, do you?" Cara looked almost sad, then shook her head.

"I do, I mean, I'm trying to. You're my twin sister. I *want* to understand!" Kitty cried.

"Yes, I know we're twins, but *who* am *I?*" demanded Cara hotly. "We're not paper dolls cut out of the same cardboard!"

"I suppose Daddy is furious with me, isn't he?" asked Cara tentatively as the twins got dressed the next morning.

Kitty tried to soothe her. "It's just that he loves us so much, wants to protect us—"

"Protect us? From what? From life? From anything outside this small world of Mayfield and raising horses and hunting foxes? There's a whole other world out there, Kitty, and if he thinks I'd be content to stay in this provincial little town while I'm young and talented—" She broke off, pacing a little. "No, Kitty, you're wrong, and so is Daddy. Protect us? You mean *trap* us, keep us penned up here at Cameron Hall, keep us his little girls forever. What does he expect us to do . . . settle down in Virginia for the rest of our lives, content to ride horses and serve tea to company?"

Since that was exactly what Kitty wanted to do with the rest of *her* life, she remained silent. Personally she could think of nothing more fulfilling than marrying someone like Kip Montrose, living at Montclair, and having his children. But knowing Kip was in love with her twin, she didn't dare say anything for fear she might set Cara off more.

Cara twisted her hair up in a knot and adjusted the bow of her blouse. "Well, I guess I might as well beard the lion in his den or the autocrat at the breakfast table, whatever the case may be," she said with a shaky smile. "At least I got an A in English Lit." She laughed, then looked mournful. "I suppose Daddy expects me to apologize—"

"Well, it isn't just Daddy. Scott was upset, too."

"Oh, Scott. Well, I don't care if he *is* angry! He doesn't think anything I do is worthwhile."

"Oh, Cara—," Kitty began. But her words of caution died on her lips as Cara started out the bedroom door. She had a dreadful feeling that to assert her independence, her twin would alienate everyone.

Almost in fulfillment of Kitty's unspoken prediction, Scott came down the hall as Cara left her bedroom on her way downstairs.

Pausing on the stairs, Scott turned to glare at her. "Why is it you can't let us have a peaceful holiday without throwing one of your public tantrums? What are you really trying to prove, Cara?"

Cara felt a choking fury. "Maybe I'm not trying to prove anything. Maybe I'm just being myself, hoping this family will see me as I really am for a change," she flung back.

"Oh, we've seen you all right. We see a selfish little brat who doesn't care if she spoils an entire evening for everyone!"

With that, he preceded her down the steps, leaving her trembling with rage but unable to think of anything to say in her own defense.

Only Blythe was at the table when Cara finally worked up enough courage to enter the dining room. Scott had evidently had his coffee and left. Her mother raised her eyebrows but said nothing.

"Is Daddy . . . at the stables . . . or has he gone riding?" Cara asked warily.

"He went out early, but he should be back shortly," Blythe replied evenly. "He wants to talk with you."

Impulsively, Cara went over to her mother. "Oh, Mama, I'm sorry if I did anything . . . well, if I embarrassed you last night. But *you*, of all people, should understand my loving to dance and—"

"That's not the point, Cara." Blythe rose, pushing back her chair. "But I agreed not to discuss this with you until your father has had a chance to see you." With that, she left the dining room.

For a minute, Cara closed her eyes wearily. With only two days remaining of the Christmas vacation, she had managed to make a mess of things. Somehow she'd counted on her mother's usual support. She dreaded facing her father. And all because—

She gulped down two cups of coffee, but still her father did not appear. Maybe she could put this off a while. She'd go riding, she decided. A good canter always cleared her head, made her feel refreshed and invigorated.

Passing Kitty on the stairs, she told her what she was planning to do, and hurried by. In her room, Cara dragged on her boots, pulled on her heavy sweater and tweed jacket, and rummaged in the bottom of the closet to find her twill riding skirt.

She was nearly ready when the knock came on the bedroom door. She stiffened and waited a full second before calling out, "Come in."

Another short pause, and the doorknob twisted and Rod entered.

One look at his expression, and all Cara's intentions to be calm and accept her father's rebuke with proper respect left her. All the emotion that had built up in anticipation of this confrontation, hardened into a long self-justification. What had she done, after all, that was so wrong?

Straightening her shoulders, Cara did not wait for him to speak first but lashed out recklessly. "I suppose you expect me to apologize. But what am I supposed to apologize for? For being myself? For using a talent I happen to have? Some people would even call it a 'gift.'" She gave a nervous laugh. "Aren't 'all good and perfect gifts' from above? What if my talent for dancing is a God-given gift, like Meredith's music, or Kitty's singing?"

"You may apologize or not, as you wish," Rod said in a low voice. "That's up to you. I have to deal with my own feelings. So what I came to say to you this morning is this, Cara. I can forgive you for making a spectacle of yourself, but I find it hard to extend forgiveness for embarrassing your mother and me and for your rudeness to our guests."

He halted, his expression softening as he looked at his daughter, but he continued in the same even tone. "I realize that it may have been the impulse of the moment—we all make mistakes of judgment one time or another—and so I'm willing to forgive you."

Cara willed herself not to betray her pain at her father's words. Furthermore, she had always prided herself on not crying if she could possibly help it. Even as a child, when Kitty would burst into tears at the slightest reprimand from Rod or a gentler reproach from their mother, Cara would stubbornly resist the urge. She was determined not to give way now.

"I don't *want* your forgiveness. I've done nothing to be forgiven for."

Rod regarded her steadily. Whatever emotion he was feeling when he spoke, his voice revealed nothing. "All of us need forgiveness sometime in our lives, Cara—either to extend it or to receive it. I hope you learn that before it's too late."

chapter
14

IN SPITE OF everyone's best efforts, the rest of the holiday at Cameron Hall was strained. Everyone went through the motions like actors who had rehearsed their lines well and now performed them woodenly. But there was no spontaneity, no joy, for the embers of the hot flames of emotions still smoldered.

Although Cara had made an abject apology to Blythe and been forgiven, her father remained aloof. There seemed nothing Cara could do to bring back their old affectionate relationship.

The usual flow of visits between the families at Montclair and Cameron Hall ceased abruptly after New Year's Day. No one said so, but Cara felt certain that she was the cause. Even Kip stayed away. Although Vance continued to court her, seemingly unaffected by the New Year's party scene, gossip soon reached Blythe that his mother, Cornelia Langley, had been deeply shocked by Cara's "performance" at the party.

No one questioned Cara's decision not to accompany the rest of the family to Williamsburg to visit relatives the following Sunday. In fact, there seemed to be a corporate sigh of relief when she mentioned going to the late morning service at the Mayfield church. This, she knew, would satisfy her mother, who had been upset when Cara had spent Christmas Eve with the Langleys instead of attending the midnight candlelight service with them.

This church dated back to Colonial days, and the Montrose and Cameron families had worshiped there ever since. But the service itself, although individualized somewhat by the various pastors who had graced its pulpit, retained many of the same traditions observed by the older Virginia congregation.

There was a garden that in spring was abloom with lovely old lilacs and other perennial flowering plants set out in a rectangular form enclosed with a scrolled iron fence. Behind the church on a sloping knoll was the church cemetery, where many of the familiar names of the county were engraved on the headstones and crosses.

While the Cameron name appeared again and again on the markers, the name Montrose was absent, for the Montrose family had their own graveyard on a hill above Montclair. *How appropriate,* Cara could not help thinking. *The Montroses have always kept themselves a little apart.* There was an element of pride that held them aloof, made them sometimes maddeningly arrogant. Kip certainly manifested that trait, and Cara knew with some guilt that she had used his weakness for her own advantage.

As she knelt, she was feeling a rare mixture of emotions. She had been humbled by what had happened during the past few days, the havoc she had wrought. Even though she knew that it was her own secret unhappiness that had fueled her behavior, it was wrong. It was nobody else's fault that she was so frustrated, so depressed.

The one little glimmer of hope she had was that Owen had agreed to meet her here. Here they could be alone, no watchful eyes observing. She intended to say what was in her heart to say, ask him to tell her what was in his.

She couldn't give up. Not now, not when she believed as she did, loved as she did. Nothing made sense if Owen wouldn't admit what she felt in her soul was true. *Please, God, let him see me as I really am.*

Kitty, who had been rather dreading going back to college after the long holiday, now found herself looking forward to it. Since the disastrous party on New Year's night, an event she now privately referred to as the "fiasco," life at Cameron Hall had not been comfortable. An uneasy truce between Cara and the rest of the family prevailed, but it was certainly not the old easy camaraderie they had always enjoyed.

Today both the Montrose and Cameron families were at the

Mayfield train station to see their young people off to their respective colleges. The atmosphere, however, was much changed from what it had been only a few weeks before.

After the first exchange of greetings, the two groups kept to themselves, engaging in the inconsequential conversation indulged by people waiting for trains, making trivial kinds of last-minute remarks.

Davida Montrose, dressed with her usual understated elegance in a pale mushroom-beige coat, a stone-marten fur thrown around her shoulders, clung to Kip's arm as if loath to let him go. *Why is there always that air of melancholy about Davida?* Kitty wondered, observing the mother and son.

Kip was concentrating on whatever his mother was saying, stoically avoiding making eye contact with Cara, who stood a little apart on the other side of the platform.

She, on the other hand, stared down the railroad track, willing the train to be on time or even early, although she hated the thought of going back to the monotonous routine of college so ill-suited to her nature and personality. Had it only been three weeks since her arrival here, a homecoming filled with anticipation?

As time passed, the small talk gradually drifted off and an awkward silence grew as they all stood stiffly, straining for the sound of the train's approach. Rod moved from one foot to the other restlessly. Blythe's hands clenched nervously inside her mink muff, her mind oppressed by the unhappiness that surrounded her. The mood of gloom was so pervasive that even those not directly involved in the individual quarrels could not fail to be affected.

Gamely, Meredith and Kitty struggled to keep up a light patter of conversation, hoping to bridge the noticeable gap between the two families. But as valiantly as they tried, they could not seem to lift the heavy pall enveloping the little group, nor recapture the gaiety and happiness of their recent reunion.

The train for Richmond, the one that would carry the twins back to Fern Grove, arrived first, its whistle shrill in the cold, crisp air, its plume of steam white against the dark gray winter sky. In rapid order, carts piled high with luggage were wheeled onto the tracks to be loaded, the final warning whistle blew, and the conductor shouted, "All aboard."

Meredith rushed over to say good-bye, hugging Kitty hard and whispering, "There's still this summer. Everything will be all right when we're all back at Fair Winds!"

When Cara and Kitty were settled in their compartment, the train began to chug slowly forward, moving away from the station. Kitty looked out the window for a final glimpse of the little group waving on the platform. As they grew smaller and smaller, she wished again that things could have been different and wondered what she might have done to make it so.

Next summer, she thought, trying to cheer herself. *Like Merry said, there's always next summer*.

But there was to be no "next summer" at Fair Winds, because in late spring, Colonel Carpenter died suddenly of a stroke.

As a result, Fair Winds remained boarded up through another lovely Cape Cod summer. No young people sang or laughed or played music on the wide veranda overlooking the sandy beach. Only the great gray house kept its vigil by the sea.

Part IV
Spring 1912

chapter
15

FROM THE *Arbordale Advocate*:

Internationally known local artist Geoffrey Montrose will be leaving for England to attend the opening of his one-man show at Waverly Studios, the prestigious London gallery where his recent painting *Mary of Bethany at the Feet of the Master* will be featured this spring.

Mr. Montrose will be accompanied by his wife, who was the model for this principal figure. Art critics who have seen the painting at a private viewing in New York have acclaimed it as a modern masterpiece. Jesus is never shown. The luminosity of Mary's upturned face gives the viewer the illusion of reflected light emanating from Christ's presence.

Although Mr. Montrose will return to accept an award from the American Artist Guild, Mrs. Montrose will remain in England for a visit with her parents, the Jeremy Devlins, at their country home, Birchfields. Mrs. Devlin is the former Garnet Cameron of Mayfield, Virginia.

*   *   *

Birchfields,
The Devlins' English Country Estate

As usual, everything was perfection. Garnet had carried through the "Bon Voyage" theme without overdoing it. That was always the greatest challenge in giving a party, not to wreck it by being too obvious. But, of course, this was a very special occasion—a once-in-a-lifetime event. Davida and Faith going on the maiden voyage of

Britain's great new ocean liner. For a moment, Garnet felt a flicker of envy. She wished that *she* were going. And she could have been. Jeremy had tickets for both of them, purchased by his publishing firm, but he had gallantly surrendered them to his daughter and Jonathan's wife.

Ah, well, there would be another time, Garnet comforted herself. Jeremy had practically promised her that on her next trip to Virginia he would book passage for her on this luxurious new passenger ship.

She moved around the long table, surveying it with satisfaction— the Battenburg-lace tablecloth, the centerpiece of spring flowers, delicate golden daffodils and blue delphinium arranged in a Waterford glass bowl. She circled again, checking the place cards, the napkins folded into fans at each place, the beribboned gifts awaiting Davida and Faith.

It had been gratifying to see Davida so much better, apparently recovering from the depression into which she had fallen after her father's death. This European trip, at Jonathan's insistence, with a stay at one of the famous Austrian spas, had done her a world of good. It was also marvelous to see that they had seemed to recapture some of the affectionate companionship missing in their relationship the last time Garnet had seen them together.

At the sound of a child's laughter Garnet glanced out the window and saw Faith in the garden with chubby little Bryanne, her four-year-old. Holding the child by her hands, she was swinging her around and laughing with delight. Unconsciously, Garnet moved a silver setting more precisely, wishing she could have had more time with her daughter during her stay in England. But, of course, Faith had spent most of her time with Jeff in London. For a grown man, he seemed totally lost without his wife by his side. She was so competent in dealing with art dealers, collectors, and gallery people. *Jeff would probably give his paintings away if it weren't for Faith*, Garnet thought with some irritation.

One compensation was that Garnet would get to keep Bryanne for a few weeks longer after Faith and Jeff left. Lalage Bondurant, now Lady Blanding, would be taking her along when she and her own children sailed to America later in the month to visit her parents, Druscilla and Randall.

Hearing the sound of voices, Garnet realized that Jeremy had returned from the village train station with the rest of her guests. With a final look at the festive table, she went out in the hall to greet them.

*   *   *

April 15, 1912

EXTRA! EXTRA!

DISASTER AT SEA

R.M.S. *TITANIC,*

WHITE STAR LINE'S "UNSINKABLE" OCEAN VESSEL,

SINKS AFTER COLLIDING WITH ICEBERG.

HUNDREDS PERISH!

Only four days after being launched on its maiden voyage and fewer than twenty-four hours before the luxury liner was expected to arrive in New York, the unexpected tragedy occurred.

A release of the list of passengers and crew members who have lost their lives in this historic maritime accident will be withheld pending notification of next of kin.

chapter

16

Cameron Hall

May 1912

IT WAS ALMOST time to leave for the memorial service for Faith and Davida at the church in Mayfield. Blythe, still in a kind of apathetic inertia, sat in front of her dressing table, unable to move, barely able to think. Her mind seemed numbed by the double tragedy that had struck the two families in the span of a single afternoon. How strange that Fate should bind the Montroses and the Camerons so closely in both happy and sorrowful circumstances.

She looked pale. Black was not becoming to her, and Rod had never liked to see her wearing it. But a funeral, after all, demanded it. Propriety also dictated that only certain jewelry other than one's wedding ring be worn on such occasions.

With a deep sigh, Blythe opened one of the drawers to take out the mourning jewelry where she had put it away once the requisite year's mourning for her beloved mother-in-law, Katherine Maitland Cameron, was over. She had hoped never to wear it again. Certainly not for someone as young as Faith or Davida.

As she drew out the black moiré silk jewelry box containing the set of onyx earrings and brooch, she spotted another box at the bottom of the drawer—the blue velvet jewel box. Remembering what was in it, her hands shook, suddenly clammy. It was the Montrose bridal set.

Stricken with guilt, she dropped the box. She had almost forgotten about it . . . again! Undecided as to who should wear the jewels—Jonathan's wife or Jeff's—she had procrastinated . . . and now it was too late for either of them!

The other ring, the betrothal ring—an amethyst in the heavy gold setting of clasped hands and crown—Blythe had not had the slightest hesitation in giving that to Faith, because Davida was wearing Jonathan's mother's engagement ring.

Heartsick, Blythe realized that the ring would never be worn by another Montrose bride. It was probably at the bottom of the sea. From the accounts of the frantic rush to the too few lifeboats on the *Titanic,* panic had prevailed. Passengers, wearing only their night-clothes, were routed from their cabins and instructed to don life jackets. There had been no time to collect possessions. Surely Faith, in her haste, would not have grabbed her jewel box when her very life was in danger!

But she had lost her life anyhow, and now a decision about jewelry seemed so trivial in the light of everything that had happened—

Blythe had been in shock for weeks after learning of the disaster, while they waited for details of how Faith and Davida had lost their lives. In fact, she had been so emotionally paralyzed by the enormity of her loss and how it would affect all of them that she had not yet been able to cry.

Now she felt herself begin to shudder, and racking sobs welled up from deep within, begging release. She got up and stumbled over to her bed, throwing herself on her knees as paroxysms of grief trembled in waves through her body. Burying her head in her hands, she allowed the tears to flow, unchecked.

All the useless regrets, the self-recriminations common to the bereaved beset her now. How she could have been a better mother-in-law to Faith, a better friend to Davida. All the hopelessness of being too late, ungenerous, insensitive, of having left unsaid so much that could have brought healing or encouragement—

Then Blythe heard Rod's voice in the hall below, speaking to one of the servants. She knew that he was probably asking about her, if she was ready to leave for the drive in to Mayfield. Soon he would come up to check for himself.

Wiping her eyes, she started to drag herself up from her knees when she saw her Bible lying open on the table beside her bed. Earlier, she had tried to find some word of comfort, something from which to gain strength for all the day held. She had turned the pages distractedly but now couldn't quite remember what she had read.

She drew the Bible to her now and read the passage marked at Proverbs 8:11: "For wisdom is better than *rubies*; and all the things that may be desired are not to be compared to it." How ironic. When had she marked that passage? Yet it was true. What good had been all her worry and concern as to which daughter-in-law should wear the ruby jewelry? What possible difference did any of it make now?

At the memorial service in the small church where the Montrose and Cameron families had worshiped for generations, Kitty and Cara, seated in the third pew back, saw Jonathan enter with Meredith and Kip beside him. Across the aisle was Jeff, face set like flint. Only his little son Gareth accompanied him. Lynette had been considered too young, and little Bryanne was still in England with her grandmother, Garnet. The plan that she would travel home by ship with Lalage, now Lady Blanding, and her children was now postponed indefinitely.

To the right of the altar and directly in front of the pew where Jeff was sitting was the baptismal font, where the children had all been baptized. Behind that stood the triptych he had painted—the figures of John the Baptist baptizing Jesus in the Jordan River, surrounded by clouds of cherubs whose faces were those of Gareth, Lynette, and Bryanne!

Meredith, beside Jonathan, reached for his hand and pressed it gently. She knew her father was struggling with the poignant memories of times they had attended services here as a family, sitting in this very pew. If she closed her eyes, she could almost sense her mother's presence—the way she inclined her head, her delicate, graceful movements, the exquisite yet subtle scent that always enveloped her.

Meredith was also remembering other things about her mother and hoped, with all the faith she could muster, that Davida had found the happiness, the peace and joy that had eluded her here in Virginia.

Reverend Ludlow, his feathery white hair like a halo about his head, entered from the sacristy to the center of the altar, signaled the beginning of the service, and the congregation stood.

He looked at them, his benevolent face composed, yet sympathetic. "Today we gather to offer a memorial to the two young women, Davida Carpenter Montrose and Faith Devlin Montrose, beloved members of these families who have come to pay their last tribute of devotion. Let us pray.

"Most merciful Father, Who has been pleased to take unto Thyself the souls of these Your children, grant unto us who are still in our pilgrimage and who walk as yet by faith, that having served Thee with constancy on earth, we may be joined hereafter with Thy blessed saints in glory everlasting, through Jesus Christ our Lord. Amen."

Lifting his head, he looked into the faces of the sorrowing family. "Because we believe, in our finite minds, that these two were taken at the peak of their womanhood and, as far as we know, without the comfort of a minister, I have chosen the following blessing for those who die at sea as appropriate for this commemorative service.

Unto Almighty God, we commend the souls of our sisters departed and we commit their bodies to the deep, in sure and certain hope of the resurrection unto eternal life, through our Lord Jesus Christ; at whose coming in glorious majesty to judge the world, the sea shall give up her dead; and the corruptible bodies of those who sleep in Him shall be changed and made like unto His glorious body, according to the mighty working whereby He is able to subdue all things to Himself.

The organ began a slow roll as if from a mighty tide. In Meredith's imagination, she could see her mother standing on the shore watching the waves, as she had so often at Fair Winds, her face revealing a rare contentment. Meredith felt a peace steal over her, an assurance that at last her mother was happy. It was almost as if she saw her mother turn to her, smiling, and say, "Don't grieve, love. It is all so beautiful, so splendid—"

Then she heard the minister announce the hymn, and she leafed through the hymnal she held and read the words, even before finding her voice to join in the singing:

> *Eternal Father! strong to save,*
> *Whose arm hath bound the restless wave,*
> *Who bidd'st the mighty ocean deep*
> *Its own appointed limits keep:*
> *O hear us when we cry to Thee*
> *For those in peril on the sea.*
>
> *O Christ! whose voice the waters heard*
> *And hushed their raging at Thy word,*
> *Who walkedst on the foaming deep,*
> *And calm amidst its rage didst sleep;*
> *O hear us when we cry to Thee*
> *For those in peril on the sea.*
>
> *Most Holy Spirit! who didst brood*
> *Upon the chaos dark and rude,*
> *And bid its angry tumult cease*
> *And give for wild confusion, peace;*
> *O hear us when we cry to Thee*
> *For those in peril on the sea.*
>
> *O Trinity of love and power!*
> *Our brethren shield in danger's hour;*
> *From rock and tempest, fire and foe,*
> *Protect them wheresoe'er they go;*
> *Thus evermore shall rise to Thee*
> *Glad hymns of praise from land and sea.*

Meredith's voice grew stronger with each succeeding verse, and although Jonathan's seemed to falter now and then, at the end his rich tenor rang out with conviction.

She was sure they felt that Davida was now with her beloved father and with the mother who had died when she was a very little girl, safe and happy, free from all the trials and burdens she had carried in life.

Meredith was grateful for this assurance as she glanced first at her brother, who was shouldering his sorrow manfully but with a stoicism that rejected any offer of compassion or sympathy, then over at Jeff, with his haunted eyes, his irreconcilable grief.

Her tender heart ached for both of them, and she whispered a prayer that someday, somewhere, they would be comforted.

Birchfields, England
1912

BIRCHFIELDS that summer was particularly lovely, the lilacs' pale lavender and purple clustered plumes scenting the air with their marvelous fragrance.

Garnet, still dressed in mourning, looked out through the French doors that opened onto the terrace facing the garden, and saw Bryanne running across the velvety green lawn, her young Irish nursemaid in pursuit. The little girl's red-gold curls glistened in the sunshine, and the sound of her merriment as she evaded her would-be captor made her grandmother smile. Just then the little girl turned to glance over her shoulder at her pursuer and she stumbled and fell, her plump, white-stockinged legs kicking wildly, displaying ruffled, upturned petticoats. Nanny snatched her up, then whirled her around, their mutual laughter filling the morning air.

Garnet watched as the two, hand in hand, made their way back across the lawn in the direction of the gazebo. There they turned down the path leading to the lake at the bottom of the estate, probably to feed the swans, Garnet surmised and then moved over to her desk where her correspondence waited.

She didn't begin the task of answering her mail right away. The sight of her granddaughter had brought with it all the memories that the little girl evoked, and she must take time to sort them out. Was it possible that six months had elapsed since the tragedy? The awful disaster that had left the child motherless and Garnet mourning both husband and daughter?

It had been a day much like this one, Garnet recalled, when she had received the news of the sinking of the great *Titanic.* Only days before, she had accompanied Davida and Faith to Southampton from where they would board the new, "unsinkable" luxury liner, headed for New York on its maiden voyage.

She thought of the gala luncheon she had given for the departing travelers here before they left. How excited and elated they had all been as they crowded into the luxurious cabin for a farewell party before the women set sail. It had been such a happy occasion, no long separation was anticipated. Jeremy and Jonathan were booked on a smaller ship to follow and would meet them in New York, where Davida and Faith planned to do some shopping and theater-going before returning to Virginia. Jeremy was leaving to be gone only a few weeks on a business trip.

They were all so happy that day. Davida had seemed particularly well and animated, and Jonathan was relieved that she seemed to be coming out of the long depression. Garnet had not seen them so openly devoted in a long time. Again she sighed deeply.

Jonathan was so dear to her, almost like her own son, their deep bonding the result of her care of him immediately after the death of his mother, Rose, who had died when he was only three. Garnet had wanted so much for his troubled marriage to be restored, and she had felt she was beginning to see the answer to her prayers. Then . . . this. Jonathan had still not fully recovered from the loss of his wife among the countless drowned when her overloaded lifeboat capsized.

Most of all, Garnet grieved for her own daughter. Faith had survived the dreadful ordeal of the sinking ship, had drifted in a crowded lifeboat for hours in freezing weather, dressed only in a thin nightdress and silk robe. Then, after a miraculous rescue at sea, she had been taken aboard the *Carpathia,* the ship that had steamed to the aid of the stricken *Titanic.* Weakened by exposure and shock, she had later died of pneumonia.

Garnet had always prided herself on her strength, having lost so many dear to her during the War but still was not spared another cruel blow. Only a few days after the disaster, Jeremy had had a fatal heart attack. In one short week, both husband and daughter were taken from her.

Garnet put her head in both hands, suppressing an involuntary shudder. She had once been the envy of many, a woman whose whole life seemed charmed, a brilliant triumph. But overnight everything that meant most to her had been taken away. Her child, her beautiful bright Faith . . . and Jeremy—

At first, she had not thought she could bear it, that she would surely go mad with grief. For more than half her life, Jeremy had been everything to her—husband, lover, companion, protector. The one person in the world who knew her best, and loved her most, in spite of her flaws and failings. How, she asked herself, could she go on without him?

A few weeks after her double tragedy, a package was delivered to her at Birchfields—a small box of Faith's belongings that had finally been released by the hospital where she had been taken after her rescue and later died. It was sent to Garnet, since that was the address registered on her reservations aboard ship.

When Garnet could bring herself to open it, she found inside something both familiar and unexpected—the amethyst betrothal ring. She had never expected to see it again!

Now the sight brought fresh tears and, as she put it away, she decided she would soon pack it among her other things and send it to Jonathan for safekeeping.

The tragedy had shattered each family in a different way, Garnet mused. Jonathan had been stunned, but with a crush of business affairs to settle, he had taken little time for his own grieving at first. Since Jeremy's fatal collapse had occurred in New York, Jonathan had managed all the details, cabled Garnet, arranged for Jeremy's body to be returned to England for burial. All this, in addition to his own sad tasks—the arrangements for a memorial service for Davida, whose body was never recovered, the comforting of his own two children—

Garnet thought then of Kip and Meredith. Kip had gone off with a college friend to a ranch in Montana to spend the summer as a cowboy, and to the surprise of some, mild little Meredith had married the Portuguese fisherman she had known since her childhood at Nantucket and had gone to stay with him there. This left Jonathan alone at Montclair. She wasn't sure what he was going to do.

Somehow Garnet had gone on. She had had no choice really, for there was Bryanne to think about now that her beautiful young mother was dead. Jeff had completely collapsed. Later, he had left with their young son, Gareth, and gone to live with a friend in New Mexico, leaving Lynette, their nine-year-old daughter, with her other grandmother, Blythe Cameron.

Strange, wasn't it? Garnet reflected, that once again her life and Blythe's should be inexorably bound, each caring for a grandchild. The two women who had loved the same man, Malcolm Montrose, whose lives had crisscrossed dramatically for years, who became sisters-in-law when Blythe married Rod, and then even more closely tied when Blythe's son by Malcolm and Garnet's daughter Faith, fell in love and married. Now they shared grandchildren.

Life was filled with irony.

Six months ago life had seemed impossibly bleak, empty, sad, without meaning for Garnet. Now Bryanne had become the focus of her life. Plans for her future were the most important yet troubling aspect of Garnet's day-to-day existence.

Nothing had been settled about Bryanne, and Garnet knew that she could not put it off indefinitely. No word had come from Jeff in months, not since his few cryptic notes from New Mexico, with little in them to give a clue as to his plans for the future of his lost little family.

It seemed it was up to Garnet to make some decisions . . . about Bryanne, at least. There was no alternative but to go to Virginia and discuss their mutual concerns with Rod and Blythe. Yes, something must be settled—and soon.

Part V

Mayfield, Virginia
Fall 1912

chapter

18

Cameron Hall

IN THE MIDDLE of September, a cable from Garnet was delivered to Cameron Hall, saying that she would be arriving in Mayfield the first week in October. She would be traveling alone.

"She says nothing about Bryanne," Blythe said, puzzled.

Rod shrugged. "Maybe she didn't think it was necessary."

"Perhaps—" Blythe's voice trailed off uncertainly. A tiny shred of suspicion that she could not quite name stirred in her heart.

Three weeks later Garnet was on the afternoon train pulling into Mayfield. From her compartment window she saw the small yellow-frame station as the train pulled to a stop. *How little it had changed in all these years!* In all the decades of comings and goings, arrivals and departures . . . young men had been seen off to war, veterans returning met. How many hopeful youths had set out to seek their fortunes, how many come back wiser, richer, poorer, humbled, sometimes broken. She herself had come and gone countless times. But this was perhaps the saddest time for her.

Kitty had been delegated to go to the station. There was no mistaking her aunt as she alighted gracefully from the train. Dressed in a pale gray suit trimmed with a ruff and cuffs of silvered blue fox fur, wearing a velvet toque adorned with blue and gray feathers, Garnet was elegant as usual. As she started down the platform, in her wake was a porter wheeling a cart loaded with monogrammed luggage.

"Aunt Garnet!" Kitty waved.

At first Garnet wasn't sure which twin it was. Both were stunning young women, so alike it was hard to tell them apart. Unless they dressed differently, uniquely reflecting their opposite tastes and personalities, it was a wonder that anyone could tell them apart!

Suspecting her aunt's uncertainty, Kitty came forward. "It's Kitty. Could I carry something for you?"

On the ride from the station out to Cameron Hall, they were silent. Kitty knew that her aunt was lost in nostalgic memories as they drove over the familiar road. After all, even though she had lived abroad for years, Garnet had spent her childhood, girlhood, and young womanhood in the magnificent house they were approaching. She had first left it to become the bride of Bryce Montrose, returning five years later as a widow. Then she had left again, as the wife of Jeremy Devlin, to live in England, visiting many times over the thirty-two years of that marriage. Now she was returning, a widow once more.

Blythe was in the front hall when they entered the door and came at once to greet Garnet, hands extended. Whatever negative emotions her mother might be experiencing, Kitty saw that they were masked perfectly behind her gracious welcome.

It was the first time the two women had seen each other since their mutual tragedy. As their eyes met in a long look, the souls of both were exposed in their mute agony of loss, the clasp of hands acknowledging the sorrow they shared and receiving the mutual sympathy offered.

"Garnet, my dear, it is so good to see you. You're looking well . . . splendid, as usual. But you've had an exhausting trip. Come in. We'll go into the library. There's a nice fire going, and we'll have tea."

Kitty excused herself, knowing her mother and aunt had much to discuss in private.

Entering the library, Garnet took one of the wing chairs by the fireplace and glanced around appreciatively. Nothing much had been changed in here. It was very much the same as it had been when she was a child. Her gaze halted on the family portrait still hanging over the mantel, the one commissioned by her father and painted when she was five years old and her twin brothers, Rod and Stewart, were eight. How young and handsome her parents were then . . . goodness, could it really have been so long ago? Garnet gave an unconscious little shudder, reminded that she had passed her sixtieth birthday.

Blythe busied herself pouring tea from the silver service. She was sure that Garnet recognized it from the Cameron crest engraved on the rounded surface. Perhaps all the family silver should have gone to her as the only daughter. Blythe wondered if she should mention it. She had always felt a little unsure about such things, having come into the family late and as an outsider, at that. Well, but this was surely no time to bring it up.

"Lemon? Cream? Sugar?" she asked, then handed Garnet her teacup and offered the plate of cheese biscuits and rolled ham sandwiches. But underneath the polite exchange, Blythe felt the discomfort of past intimidation.

She had always been a little in awe of the older woman's confidence, her instinctive air of belonging, while Blythe herself suffered the sensations of inadequacy and insecurity. And when she had learned that Garnet had once hoped to marry Malcolm, Blythe had felt even more ill at ease around her.

The passing years had put them on a more equal footing, however. Blythe had acquired a new poise in her many life experiences of travel and cultural exposure. She now gave every evidence of being a well-loved woman, wealthy in her own right, and held an unassailable position in Mayfield society.

The two spoke of trivial matters while each continued her private assessment of the other. Although many things connected them— they were, after all, sisters-in-law twice over—it was the marriage of Blythe's son Jeff to Garnet's daughter, Faith, now deceased, that had been the strangest twist of fate.

And therein lay the challenge. What had brought them closest might yet be the thing that divided them most, for all their new civility. Uppermost now in both women's minds must be the future

153

of their two motherless granddaughters, Lynnette and Bryanne Montrose.

As she sipped her tea, feeling its energizing warmth, Garnet could not help comparing the composed, fashionably dressed woman sitting opposite her now with the coltish young girl in the outlandish outfit she had first seen in the pantry of Montclair—the bride that Malcolm had brought home from California.

Today in a lavender dress, softened by the lace collar fastened by an amethyst pin at the neckline, her auburn hair against the emerald green velvet chair on which she was seated, Garnet had to admit she made a stunning appearance. The unlined creamy smoothness of her skin reminded Garnet sharply that Blythe was some ten years younger than she.

The first exchange of pleasantries past, the room was suddenly quiet. Only the sounds of the log crackling in the hearth and of a clock striking the quarter hour somewhere deep in the house disturbed the silence.

Well, thought Garnet, *there is no use delaying what I've come to say.* But something stopped her, something in Blythe's posture, her demeanor. Looking over at her sister-in-law, Garnet was struck with the expression in her wide, dark brown eyes—a kind of innocence much like she had seen on that long-ago day when Malcolm had introduced her for the first time.

As Garnet hesitated, there came the bang of the front door, the sound of a child's voice, then laughter.

The two women looked at each other, and Garnet read in Blythe's face a pleading, a questioning that disturbed her. She spoke only a single word. "Lynette?"

Blythe nodded. "Yes," she said in a whispery voice.

"I'm anxious to see my other granddaughter." Garnet made a move as if to rise from her chair, but Blythe stood first.

"I'll call her in," and Blythe went to the library door. She opened it. "Darling, come in. There's someone here you'll want to see."

Garnet felt her throat tighten and instinctively put up a hand as if to ease the tightness. When the little girl entered the room, Garnet drew in her breath.

How like Faith at that age she was!—dark hair, heart-shaped

face. But she had the Montrose eyes—those extraordinary, intensely blue eyes, passed on from Sara Leighton Montrose to her sons, her grandson. The child held herself very erect. *A small, slender, dignified little creature,* Garnet thought, *but with a look of vulnerability that is very appealing.*

She was wearing a red coat with a little cape. Blythe helped her out of it, revealing a plaid dress with lace collar, bowed at the neck.

"We've a nice surprise for you, darling," Blythe said. "Your grandmother Devlin has come all the way from England to see you."

Lynette glanced at Garnet a little shyly and slipped her hand into Blythe's as they crossed the room toward her.

"Precious child, come here! Let me look at you! Give Grandmother a hug." Garnet held out her arms. She felt a twinge of annoyance as Lynette hesitated, looking up at Blythe as if asking permission.

When the child was standing in front of her, Garnet cupped her face in her hands, then kissed both rosy cheeks. "Well, my darling, it's been such a long time since I've seen you and you've grown into such a pretty, big girl. I wouldn't have recognized you!" Garnet's voice wavered at the thought of Faith, and a renewed sense of her loss threatened to overtake her.

The last thing she wanted was to upset the little girl, so she quickly controlled her emotions and tried to smile brightly. "I'm so happy to see you."

"I'm glad to see *you,* Grandmother," Lynette said shyly, one hand stroking Garnet's velvet sleeve.

"Now, tell me, where have you been this afternoon?"

"To my dancing class."

"The Mayfield Junior Cotillion. You remember, Garnet. They've reactivated it. It's a very nice way to get the children together early enough so they'll find it easy and natural to move into social situations when it's suitable," Blythe explained.

"Ah, yes." Garnet recalled her own cotillion days.

"She loves going," Blythe continued. "She has so many friends—"

155

"I'm sure she does," Garnet said quickly. "But I find children make friends easily *wherever* they are."

Suddenly Lynette twisted free of Garnet's hold and directed her attention to Blythe. "Nana, Dabney Carrington is having a birthday party. May I go?"

"Well, I certainly don't see why not. When is it?"

"He said they would be sending invitations."

"Well, then we shall see."

"I'll need a new dress, don't you think?" Lynette's voice was tentative.

"And you shall have one!" Garnet said, turning the child toward her again. "Just wait 'til you see what I've brought you in my trunk!"

"A dress?" Lynette sounded excited.

"Yes, darling, a dress, and many other things besides! And a special present from your little sister Bryanne!"

There was a moment's pause, and Lynette put one chubby hand up to her mouth, rounded into an O.

"What is it? What's the matter?" Garnet was concerned.

Lynette's expression was suddenly solemn. "I . . . well, sometimes I almost forget I *have* a little sister."

Over the child's head, the two women's eyes met, and the look they exchanged was inscrutable.

Garnet recovered first. "Well, of course, you haven't seen her in so long . . . but she knows all about *you* and she wanted to come with me to see you. But you'll never guess what happened! She came down with the miserable old measles and is in quarantine, so I couldn't bring her. Still, she picked out your present herself and was sure you'd like it."

"Can we go open your trunk and see it now?"

"But, Lynette, your grandmother hasn't finished her tea—" began Blythe.

"Nonsense," Garnet dismissed her concern with an airy wave of her hand, and got out of her chair. "I've had it, and it was lovely, but now the important thing is that Lynette have her gift from her sister. Shall we go now, darling?"

Taking the child by the hand, they started toward the door, then stopped and turned. "I don't know where you've put me, Blythe," Garnet said apologetically.

"Your own room, of course, Garnet, your old one," Blythe said quickly and moved with them out into the hall.

At the bottom of the winding staircase, Garnet paused again. "No need for you to show me, Blythe. I certainly know the way."

Although Garnet's remark was spoken lightly, Blythe felt rebuffed. She realized that her sister-in-law still had the power to make her feel unneeded, unimportant. Watching the two start up the steps together, chatting animatedly, she suddenly felt left out. She stood there until the figures of the woman and little girl rounded the bend in the stairway and disappeared down the corridor.

Blythe returned to the library. Despite the fire still burning brightly in the fireplace, she could not get warm. Sitting down, she rubbed her hands together.

Why did she feel so tense, so apprehensive? She knew there was more, much more for the two of them to discuss, and she dreaded it. Blythe closed her eyes for a moment. At least, Garnet had not brought up the subject of Jeff, though Blythe had steeled herself for a tirade. No doubt that Garnet would mention his irresponsibility, his neglect of his duty as a father, running off to New Mexico the way he had, and taking only Gareth with him. Jeff had been away almost a year now, and there was still no word, not an inkling of when he planned to return, to reunite his family—

But did Garnet, or even Rod for that matter, realize how devastated Jeff had been after the tragedy? Without Faith . . . literally, *without faith*, Blythe thought sadly . . . she had feared not only for his sanity but for his very life. His wife had meant everything to Jeff.

It was the prize-winning painting he'd done of her as Mary of Bethany at the feet of Jesus that had won him new acclaim. Perhaps he had never forgiven himself for returning to America before her to present the painting at the gallery in New York for a month's exhibit, leaving her to follow him on the *Titanic* a month later—

Wearily, Blythe got to her feet and rang the tapestried bellpull by the fireplace to call Fanny to come for the tea tray.

She and Garnet would have another chance to talk about the grandchildren. Blythe hoped that Rod would agree to sit in on any discussions they had. She needed his level head, his firm support, though she knew his views—that the sisters should not be separated any longer, that the cruel blow dealt the family should be healed by bringing up the two little girls together. Of course, they wanted to bring Bryanne here to Cameron Hall to grow up with Lynette, while Garnet . . . well, it was obvious how *she* felt—

Blythe also knew how her husband felt about Jeff's single-minded "selfishness," as Rod expressed it. In his own grief, Jeff had left his little daughters to others to comfort and nurture. Still, Rod and Jeff had never been close, perhaps never would be. Rod had never understood his stepson's sensitive, artistic soul. Not that she could defend what her son had done after he lost Faith, but in some ways, she could sympathize with it. Hadn't she, too, run away . . . after Malcolm's death?

But that was different. Yes, she knew that, and although she was not going to defend Jeff's action, neither was she going to blame or condemn him. After all, he had not left his daughters alone or with strangers. He had left them with grandparents, knowing that they'd be lovingly cared for.

Blythe put her fingertips to her temples to still the drumming that had begun. She mustn't start thinking of all this now. It would have to wait. Surely she and Garnet would have the opportunity to discuss all this rationally, intelligently. There would be time later. Now, there were other pressing problems to solve.

chapter
19

GARNET HAD learned through bitter experience that loss must be faced, pain walked through. If nothing else, the War years had taught her that, so she knew that a visit to Avalon was inevitable, not only to pick up some of Bryanne's things but to confront the fact that Faith would never be coming back.

The day that Rod drove her to Arbordale was the first time during the week she had spent at Cameron Hall that brother and sister had been alone. On the way, they spoke little. Garnet's heart was too full, her thoughts preoccupied with how quickly the years had passed since Faith had left her home in England, eloped with Jeff, and come here to Virginia to live.

Leaving the road, they boarded the old ferry to the island, then drove up the narrow trail guarded by sweeping pines and bordered with lush ferns. Seeing the house at last, she was struck again by how very English it looked with its buff-colored stucco and dark oak timbers, the low, slanting roof and diamond-paned windows.

Rod unlocked the heavily carved front door, stepping back so that Garnet could precede him across the threshold.

Though Jeff had arranged for the butler and housekeeper to remain on the place as caretakers, there was an empty feeling as they walked inside, their footsteps echoing hollowly on the slate floor of the foyer.

Garnet's first impression was of the pervading gloom. Then, remembering how happy Faith had been here, how fulfilled and

159

joyous in her role as Jeff's wife and mother to their three children, she realized that even the tragedy that had come to it could not completely diminish those memories. Everywhere she looked were reminders of the golden hours her daughter had lived here.

In the front hall were Jeff's Renaissance murals depicting legendary heroes, costumed ladies, angelic children at play. Silently they walked through the oak-paneled rooms hung with more of Jeff's paintings. Upstairs, they toured the children's wing, its walls aglow with fairy-tale stories Jeff had painted, some of the characters's faces bearing a strong resemblance to the children themselves! How this must have amused Faith, pleased and delighted the three little ones.

Garnet struggled with the increasing urge to weep for all the loveliness, the joy, the affectionate gaiety this home had held that now was forever lost. What was to become of these children, with their mother dead and their father who knew where? How could he have forsaken his two motherless girls? And what kind of life would poor little Gareth have with a depressed and unstable father?

Suddenly, overcome with outrage at the emotional wreckage that Jeff had left behind, Garnet whirled around to face her brother. Hands clenched at her side, eyes flashing, she burst out, "I never wanted Faith to marry him in the first place! He's always been irresponsible, self-centered. It was what *Jeff* wanted, what was best for *Jeff*—that's all that has ever been important to him, no matter what havoc he causes in other people's lives! Blythe has always coddled him, excused him for his weaknesses, and Faith, my poor darling, continued the pattern—"

She paused only to draw a deep ragged breath. "I pity his children, Gareth, especially. Why he took his son with him, I'll never understand. What kind of example has he set for the boy? That when life deals you a blow, you run away?"

Rod did not attempt to answer, allowing his sister to vent her grief, her anger. "Well, if I have anything to do with it, Bryanne will have a different kind of upbringing. She will be taught that life isn't always fair, and doesn't grant special treatment for wealth or talent. *Nothing* gives you the right to abandon your duty and responsibility to others—"

She broke off once more. Then, as if determined to bring her anger under control, she spoke with icy calm. "I have tried to understand the shock Jeff has endured, but I cannot condone his dramatizing himself, wallowing in his own grief while the rest of us get on the best we can with our lives—" She paused, then regarding her brother with a steady gaze, said, "I've come to a decision, Rod. I'm not going to bring Bryanne back here. She will remain with me at Birchfields until Jeff comes out of whatever he's in. When he does . . . or maybe I should say, *if* he does, and wants his daughter . . . he can jolly well come to England and get her!"

Once Garnet had made up her mind, there was no dissuading her. She packed, made her reservations, and prepared to return to England. When Blythe finally realized that Garnet did not plan to reunite the two little girls, she was deeply shaken.

In the privacy of their bedroom, she confronted her husband. Looking at him incredulously, she said, "I can't believe that you agreed with what Garnet plans to do!"

Rod shrugged, spreading his hands. "What could I do or say to stop her? You know Garnet."

"I thought you believed, as I do, that it is wrong for these little sisters to be separated, to be reared in different environments half a world apart!"

"It wasn't *our* doing, Blythe," Rod replied, his meaning implicit.

"You blame Jeff, don't you?"

"And who else is to blame? Should I blame God, the iceberg that crashed into the *Titanic* . . . whom? . . . what?"

Blythe gave a moan and buried her face in her hands. At the sight of his wife's distress, Rod was at her side in an instant, kneeling to take her in his arms. "Darling, darling, listen to me," he murmured. "Just remember *we* have each other—our daughters, our son, and now our granddaughter. But Garnet has lost everything. All she has now is Bryanne. How long she will have her, God only knows. And whether it is the wisest thing or the right thing, how are we really to know? Jeff *has,* at least for the time being, relinquished his responsibility, and we must do the best we can."

161

"For Lynette's sake, we shall try to make Christmas as happy as possible," Blythe announced bravely at breakfast the morning after Garnet's departure. "I don't want to spoil anything for her, so let's just be as cheerful as possible—"

Knowing her mother's heavy heart, Kitty promised to help make it so. This would be the first season since the double tragedy that they would be hosting their New Year's Day open house, and Kitty knew at what cost Blythe had made that decision.

A week later, when they received word that Cara would be home for Christmas, Kitty made plans to meet her at the train station. On the way, she thought of the different directions their lives had taken in the past year.

While Kitty had finished college and stayed home to help with the added responsibility of caring for Lynette, Cara, at the end of her sophomore year at Fern Grove, had convinced her parents that it would be "a waste of time and money" for her to return to college the following fall. Then she had laid out a well-rehearsed plan to stay with the family of her friend Susan Mills, in Richmond, where both would help out in a fashionable boutique owned by Susie's aunt. With Washington, D.C. nearby, there would be many opportunities to attend concerts, lectures, visit the great art galleries, and generally avail themselves of the cultural advantages of the capital city. All in all, she argued, these experiences would be much more educational than the curriculum offered at Fern Grove.

Blythe and Rod, still recovering from the shock of the two deaths as well as their care of Lynette, had neither the will nor the strength to resist Cara's persuasive arguments and finally consented.

What they did not know was that Cara's plan had been greatly influenced by Richmond's proximity to the Theological Seminary where Owen was enrolled. Nor would they have guessed that she was using her small salary to take singing and dancing lessons as well.

Waiting on the station platform, Kitty struggled with feelings of elation and apprehension at her sister's coming. Ever since that disastrous Christmas holiday years ago, the relationship between Cara and their father had been, at best, an uneven one. But all that had happened in the meantime—the tragedy, the changes, the fact

162

that so much time had passed—gave Kitty renewed hope. As she saw the engine round the last bend and head into the curved tracks in front of the station house, she prayed that Cara's strained relationship with their parents would be reconciled.

Kitty watched Cara swing gracefully down the trains steps and speak to the conductor who had assisted her. In the moments before she turned to look for her, Kitty had time to study her twin.

She was fashionably dressed in a cinnamon brown suit of nubby wool, trimmed with darker brown velvet and a matching tam, a tangerine silk scarf tied at her throat. But there was no time to study her face, to read the message there, for at that moment, Cara saw her and started toward her, smiling.

Kitty hoped that in spite of her new sophistication, Cara was really no different on the inside, and maybe they could be close again. But as her sister came nearer, a kind of cold sensation chilled her. Behind the smile, something was altered. Though her lovely face did not betray it, in those luminous eyes lurked some secret.

An inner knowing stirred in Kitty that it was not, after all, an "old wives' tale." Even separated twins *do* have a special empathy; they can sense if the other is happy or sad or in danger. Kitty was convinced that Cara's coming was like a pebble spun out into a pond, causing ripple upon ripple, spreading wider and wider, changing the smooth surface just as Cara's presence *always* changed things.

chapter

20

As Blythe had hoped, Christmas at Cameron Hall took place with all the trappings of their traditional way of celebrating the holiday. The tree was glorious to behold, hung with glittering new ornaments, some especially lovely hand-painted ones sent by Garnet from Germany. The house shone with candles and was fragrant with the pungent scent of masses of evergreens brought in from the surrounding woods. Stacked beneath the tree, to Lynette's delight, were piles of beautifully wrapped presents.

Rod had selected and bought a pony for the child and gave her her first riding lesson that very afternoon. Scott arrived, laden with gifts and games, then romped and played with Lynette in a noble attempt to replace the missing father. Kitty had spent weeks painting and refurbishing an old dollhouse for her, and from the boutique, Cara had brought her a white rabbit-fur hat and muff to wear to church on Christmas Day.

In spite of the sincere efforts of all, the day was difficult for the adults. There were too many memories, too many "ghosts of Christmas Past," with no new joys to take their place or to part the clouds of sorrow that still hung over them.

The weather had not helped. There was no snow. Instead, rain fell intermittently from leaden skies, making the atmosphere damp and gloomy. Most depressing for Kitty was the fact that, although she and Cara again shared their old bedroom, the old intimacy she had hoped to regain was lacking. Although Cara was consistently cheerful and entered into all the activities with determined good grace and a willingness to participate, some spontaneity was gone.

Kitty noticed Cara's strange reaction to learning that Montclair had been shut up for the last few months. Meredith had decided to spend the holidays with her Massachusetts relatives. Jonathan, unable to bear facing the season alone, had gone to Bermuda. And, as far as the Camerons knew, Kip was still in Montana.

"Maybe it's all for the best," Cara had remarked when she was told.

Cara pushed the heavy church door open and went inside.

The pale December sun filtering into the church from the arched stained-glass windows brought little illumination to banish the shadows lurking within its raftered ceiling and stone pillars. Inhaling deeply, she breathed the spicy fragrance of pine, spruce, and cedar from the Christmas decorations still in place.

The stillness was palpable and, although the church was empty, she felt at once the awareness of an unseen Presence.

The last hectic hours had been filled with anxious preparation for Christmas. *The remembrance of Christ's birth shouldn't be like that*, Cara thought. Then suddenly, the dodging and avoidance, the circling around the truth, the tension of deception in which she was engaged, smote Cara like a blow. With a groan of conviction, she slipped to her knees in one of the last pews, rested her forehead on clasped hands, and almost unconsciously began to pray—

Kitty was sure that every detail of that winter afternoon would remain clear in her memory as long as she lived. The instant that she entered the bedroom late on Christmas afternoon, she felt a curious chill. Later she wondered if it had been a premonition. She went over to the window to see if it had been left open by mistake. There she paused to look out and saw windblown flurries of snow falling in the darkness.

Unconsciously she shivered, drew the curtains against the coming night, then lighted the lamps. It was then she saw the envelope propped up against the mirror on the double dressing table. In Cara's bold backhand was written "For Kitty."

Holding her breath, she drew out the folded letter inside. "Dearest Twin," she read. Even that struck Kitty as strange. Cara hated the term when applied to herself. She read on: "I don't like keeping secrets and especially not from you. But there was no other way.

"Scott says I always stir up a storm in the family. Well, I guess this will be another one, but I thought it would be better this way. After all that's happened—Aunt Garnet's coming, the fuss over Lynette, the death of Faith and Mrs. Montrose—I wanted to make it easy on Mama and Daddy.

"Ever since we met that summer at Fair Winds, Owen Brandt and I have been in love. He fought it at first . . . well, it doesn't matter now. I managed to convince him that as long as we feel the way we do about each other, everything else can be worked out. So, since I've been living in Richmond, we've been meeting as often as possible.

"Kitty, the main reason I didn't tell you before now, knowing as I do what everyone will say, is that I didn't want to put you in the position of having to lie or cover for me. I realize that most people will think that Owen deserves someone sweet and docile, someone like Merry, maybe. I *know* they think I'm too reckless, too impatient, too *worldly* to be a minister's wife and, though I know it, too, I love him so much I'm willing to risk it. He is, too.

"Before I came home for the holidays, we met, talked it all out, and decided. Since the seminary allows students to be married, and since this is Owen's last year, we've decided not to wait any longer!

"Owen got the license and we're going away. I wish it could have been different, but I didn't want everyone trying to talk us out of it.

"Oh, Kitty, do be happy for us. I love you, and I hope . . . yes, I *pray* that someday you'll be as happy as I am now. Cara."

Kitty's hands, holding the hastily written note, began to shake, then her legs. She had to sit down quickly on the stool in front of the dressing table. She saw her face staring back at her in the mirror . . . Cara's face. She looked pale, her eyes dark and frightened. *Oh, Cara, how could you do this to all of us who love you?*

Kitty knew that her mother would be heartbroken. And her

father? She closed her eyes. What would he say? And Kip would be devastated.

Kitty turned off the lamps and went to sit in the window seat. Outside, the wind whistled eerily around the eaves, and icy pellets of sleet fingered the glass panes with small, tapping sounds. Were they out in this storm? She closed her eyes, felt the slow trickle of hot tears escape from under her eyelids and roll down her cheeks.

She never knew how long she sat there in the darkened room, lost in her own thoughts, mourning her runaway twin. Then she heard an unusual amount of activity downstairs, voices raised in surprise, exclamations. What was going on? Unexpected guests?

Kitty remained seated for another minute or two, straining to listen, trying to make sense of the flurry below. Then one voice, clear and distinct, drifted up from the hallway. Cara! At the sound of running feet on the stairs, Kitty started up from her seat. But before she could reach the bedroom door, it burst open and Cara was there.

After the first excited hugs, they sat down together on the bed, arms around each other, just like in the old days when they had shared everything.

"Oh, Kitty," Cara began, "I never imagined such happiness! We planned to elope, at least *I* did. I wanted to avoid all the fuss. But after Owen thought about it, he wouldn't hear of it. He said we owed it to my parents and that we simply couldn't start our life together without their blessing. Kitty, he's so wonderful, so good and pure! I don't know how I'll ever live up to him." Her eyes were moist, soft and shining. "All I know is . . . I'd follow him to the ends of the earth—"

Stunned by all that Cara was telling her, Kitty waited. Then she had to know. "But . . . what about Kip? All along I thought it was you and Kip. I know you tried to make us believe you were interested in Vance, but I never did. In spite of everything, I thought it would eventually be you and . . . Kip."

Cara looked pensive for a moment, then shook her head vigorously. "Kip and I are too much alike . . . you know, temperamental, independent, wanting our own way and trying to get it. We'd make each other miserable. I'm sure in time he would have realized that on his own . . . or talked me into marrying him and destroying us both!"

Then her frown melted into a radiant smile. "Oh, Kitty, don't look so sad. Be happy for me . . . please?"

"I *am*, really I am, Cara. It's just that I remember what we talked about one day that summer at Fair Winds—the summer you met Owen. Of course, I didn't know you'd fallen in love with him—" Here she gave her twin a reproachful look. "I was chiding you about the way you were treating Kip, and you told me there was someone else, only you wouldn't say who. But I remember something else you said, and that's why I'm reminding you of it now—"

Amused at Kitty's serious manner, Cara's mouth twitched. "What in the world did I way that was so profound?"

"You said, 'Being first in someone's life, being the most important person . . . *that's* love.' Don't you realize, Cara, that you can never come first with Owen? You can't be the most important person to him, because he's made a commitment to Someone else. . . . *God* will always come first with him."

"I know that, Kitty." Cara lifted her shoulders in a shrug and gave her a sidelong look. Then her smile came back. "But I guess I'm willing. Somehow I think it will be enough."

The two looked deeply into each other's eyes for a long moment. Then Cara's eyes twinkled with mischief. "Since you have such a phenomenal memory, do you remember when we did all those dramatic performances at Fair Winds? Remember the night we acted out Tennyson's *Maud*? Well, let me quote you a quote, and this should satisfy you about my decision to marry Owen: 'I embrace the purpose of God and the doom assigned.' Only, Kitty, it's not going to be 'doom,' it's going to be *heaven!*"

For a moment Cara closed her eyes as though in rapture, but Kitty saw with surprise that she was praying. "Dear God, thank You, thank You for Owen! I know I don't deserve him, but I'm so grateful, and I'll try, I'll really try to make you both glad he married me!" She clutched Kitty's arm. "Come on now, Kitty, come downstairs with me. We have so much to talk about, so much to plan." She got up and pirouetted across the room, pausing at the door. "Owen and Daddy are having one of those man-to-man talks, and I don't want to leave them alone together too long!" She laughed gaily. "Daddy might tell him all my faults and talk Owen out of marrying me." She held out her hand to her sister. "Come on, Kitty, I need you to back me up with Mama, too. As you might guess, she's all in a dither about getting a wedding together in such a short time, so I need your support to convince her it will really be very simple—"

Kitty had to smile. To Cara, of course, who floated above the earth most of the time, everything seemed simple. She would continue to occupy her particular cloud while everyone else scurried about, doing what needed to be done. Kitty took her twin's hand gladly, feeling the mix of joy at her happiness, and sadness at the knowledge that soon they would really be living in different worlds.

In the drawing room they found Owen, his expression rather dazed but his manner composed and confident. The three—Rod, Blythe, and Owen—were already deep in conversation when the twins arrived. At the sight of Cara, Owen's face lighted up. All during the subsequent discussion, his eyes never left Cara, and again Kitty felt the bizarre sensation of pleasure and pain. She was truly happy for her sister, yet grieved over the prospect of parting with the one person with whom she had been most closely bonded since before birth. What her life would be like without her literal "other half," she couldn't imagine.

"It will simply be impossible to have any kind of real wedding on such short notice—" Blythe was saying, looking distracted yet smiling at the shining faces of the two sitting opposite her together on the love seat. "We'll just have to do without some of the traditional things one always has—invitations, a reception—"

"Oh, Mama, you know I've never been one for tradition," protested Cara. "Owen and I will just start some new traditions of our own."

"But what about friends . . . especially the Montroses—" Blythe's voice faltered.

"Please, we just want everything kept very simple . . . *truly*. Just the family, Mama."

"But couldn't you at least wait until spring, until after Owen graduates from seminary and is ordained?" Blythe pleaded.

"No, Mama, we've waited so long already." She cast an appealing look at Owen for support.

At the same moment, Blythe's eyes met Rod's penetrating gaze, and in that glance was communicated all the agony they themselves had endured in their long separation before they could be married. They would not wish that pain on their daughter.

"No, we can't wait," Cara was saying as Blythe redirected her attention to the young couple. "That is, Owen has to be back the day after New Year's to apply for a married students' apartment for us, and right after graduation, he's due to report to the little church in Ohio where he's been accepted as pastor—"

"*Ohio!*" the three Camerons echoed in unison.

"Yes, Owen went for an interview and helped at the services during Easter week and . . . they want him, need him as soon as possible really, since their former pastor is retiring."

"But Ohio . . . is so far." Blythe's voice sounded weak.

"Not so far, Mama."

Kitty saw her mother's eyes brighten with unshed tears which she managed to control before changing the subject to more immediate practicalities. "But what will you wear? There's no time to have something made—"

"I can wear the dress we had made for our coming-out party . . . it's never been worn, remember?" Cara reminded her that the twins' debut ball, planned for the summer of 1912, had been canceled after the sinking of the *Titanic*.

"Oh, yes, of course. What a good idea," Blythe conceded and rose. "Well, come along, both of you. We'll have to get the dresses out of the storage room. You, too, Kitty. You'll be your sister's bridesmaid—"

In the next twenty-four hours, Cameron Hall was the scene of frenzied activity. Cara insisted that no one outside the family be informed of the four o'clock ceremony scheduled at the small Mayfield church. On a weekday afternoon and with holiday services over for the season, it would be unlikely to attract any special notice. At least, she was hoping.

As the twins dressed that gray winter afternoon, Cara was uncharacteristically quiet, although quivering with excitement.

Kitty thought that her sister had never looked more beautiful—paler than usual but with her dark eyes sparkling with deep confidence and joy.

The debut gowns had been made by the same well-known Williamsburg seamstress, yet designed to suit their different personalities. *Today,* Kitty thought, as they put them on for Cara's wedding, *they might have been fashioned for this very occasion.* Kitty's dress was an Alice-blue silk, with fluted chiffon panels floating from the shoulders, while Cara's was of shimmering gold satin with an overskirt of beige net sprinkled with amber beads.

Cara was just putting up her hair when Blythe came in, carrying something wrapped in tissue paper. "Look what I've found among my treasures!" she said happily, then proceeded to unwrap an exquisite piece of ecru lace, intricately embroidered with gold threads. "It's a mantilla I bought in Spain years ago. I'd forgotten all about it actually. But won't it be perfect for you to wear on your very special day?" she said triumphantly, holding it out for Cara to admire.

"Oh, Mama, it's—it's . . . beautiful," Cara said in a hushed voice.

"Here, let me drape it just so—" Blythe placed it carefully on the twist of shiny hair.

As Cara had insisted, the wedding was private. Just Owen's elderly aunt and uncle, his only relatives since his parents had passed away several years before, and the Camerons were present. The Reverend Canby, feeble now at seventy-five, his voice a little quavery, conducted the ancient ceremony.

The church, still decorated with evergreen boughs, bright poinsettias, and holly wreaths, held the scent of spruce and pine, mingled with beeswax candles.

Kitty, standing beside her twin and hearing her speak the eternal promises of love, faithfulness, and devotion, fought back tears, but it was the final benediction that caused them to fall upon the small bouquet of white hothouse roses she held.

"My blessing for this young couple as they start out life's road together is taken from Colossians 1:9–11," intoned the Reverend Canby. "We ask that Carmella and Owen may be 'filled with the

171

knowledge of His will in all wisdom and spiritual understanding; that they might walk worthy of the Lord unto all pleasing, being fruitful in every good work, and increasing in the knowledge of God; strengthened with all might, according to His glorious power, unto all patience and longsuffering with joyfulness.'"

After the ceremony, back in their bedroom at Cameron Hall, Cara flew about, flinging things haphazardly as she packed. Just as typically, Kitty picked them up, refolded them, and placed them neatly in the suitcase open on her bed.

At last, Cara looked around. "Well, I guess that's everything." Then she turned to her twin. "Oh, Kitty, thank you!" she said, hugging her hard. "I'll write and you must, too, and maybe you can get up to Washington for a weekend." Even as her eyes misted, they danced with mischief. "And maybe we can even find you a suitable seminarian to escort you to the theater ... Oops! I suppose I should say *lecture!* I'm not quite used to my role as a parson's wife!"

To hide her own rising emotion, Kitty busied herself detaching the nosegay of violets from the circle of roses in Cara's bouquet, taking a full minute to pin it on her sister's muff. "There!" she said finally. "You're all set."

"Aren't you coming down to see us off?"

Struggling with the threat of tears, Kitty shook her head. "You know how I hate good-byes."

Cara looked at her steadily for a moment, her own eyes glistening. "Promise you'll come to see us once we're settled?"

Unable to answer, Kitty nodded, then Cara gave her another hug. "Good-bye, darling twin," she said, then twirled across the room. At the door, she blew Kitty a kiss and disappeared from sight.

Standing alone in the middle of the room, Kitty pressed her hands tightly together. She could hear Cara's voice singing out, "I'm coming, Owen!" and heard the tap of her sister's high-heeled fur-trimmed boots as she ran downstairs to her new husband.

Kitty moved over to the bedroom door, leaning against the frame, listening to the farewells in the downstairs hall.

"You *will* be back before you leave for Ohio?" Blythe's voice caught, betraying her emotion as she and Rod walked with the couple to the door.

"Of course, Mama. Won't we, Owen?"

"Until June then, Mrs. Montrose, sir." Owen kissed Blythe lightly on the cheek, turned to shake hands with Rod.

"It was a lovely wedding, exactly what I dreamed it would be. Thank you, Mama, Daddy—"

"There's Willis. He's brought the carriage around." That was Rod's voice, a little husky now.

"We'll have to go, or we'll miss the train," came Owen's gentle reminder.

"Yes, darling, I know. Well then, good-bye, Mama, Daddy . . . Thank you so much for everything!"

"Good-bye, dear. Good-bye Owen." By now Blythe's voice was faltering.

Kitty ran to the window, knelt on the cushioned seat, and looked out. There were Owen and Cara running, hand in hand, down the terrace steps. The snow was swirling around them. Willis stood to assist them into the closed carriage, then mounted the driver's seat, and with a flick of the whip, the carriage moved down the winding drive. Kitty saw Cara's face pressed to the icy glass pane until it disappeared around the bend.

Cara was gone, really gone . . . and Kitty felt as if a part of herself was missing, too.

She turned away from the window, back to the room still full of visible as well as subtle traces of her departed twin. Discarded articles of clothing—silk stockings, Cara's quilted robe, her maribou-trimmed slippers, a scarf, a pair of gloves, the golden wedding dress tossed on the bed.

Even the gossamer lace mantilla lying abandoned in a glittering heap on the dressing table—left behind, like a symbol of her transition from maidenhood to wife. Kitty went over and picked it up, letting the fragile fabric slip through her fingers. She held it for a moment. Then gazing into the mirror, she lifted it and placed it on her own head, letting it fall over her hair, the light from pink-shaded dressing table lamps catching the red-gold glints under the gold-threaded lace.

Kitty did not know how long she had stood there, regarding herself, fantasizing herself as a bride, when she became aware of a slight movement behind her. Still looking in the mirror, she saw the reflection of her father standing at the open bedroom door.

Before she could turn around or speak, he left, his expression saying all there was to say.

After the impromptu wedding, the household returned to normal much too soon, Kitty thought in alarm. It was almost as if they were denying that Cara's sparkling presence had left a void, one that Kitty felt could never be filled by anyone else.

Of course, Rod had his horses, a business that never ceased to be demanding, and Blythe was totally occupied with Lynette.

Kitty was the only one who seemed to be at loose ends. Without Cara, she was only half alive. She couldn't even begin to get her back by trying to imagine what Cara's new life was like. She knew that her sister had found work in a small dress shop while Owen continued his studies at the seminary, but it was beyond her to think that now Cara belonged more to her husband than she did to her twin.

Several weeks after the wedding, she got a note from Kip, who had finally returned to Virginia. He wrote that after working on the ranch in Montana, he had traveled even farther west, roaming aimlessly in other states. She knew he had lost his bearings after his mother's death, and now there was Cara's unexpected marriage to contend with.

Reading his note, Kitty sensed the pain in the scrawled words, asking her to meet him. Even the suggested meeting place was significant. It was the clearing in the woods halfway between Montclair and Cameron Hall, where they had met to play as children. Here was the snug little house called Eden Cottage, now abandoned and boarded up, where the Brides of Montclair traditionally spent their honeymoon year.

Kitty hesitated. Was it really wise to go, feeling the way she did about Kip? His need overcame her own self-protective reluctance. Finally she put on her warm coat, grabbed a scarf and mittens. She would go to meet him, but first, she needed guidance. All the way there, she prayed earnestly to know what to say, what to do, how to comfort.

"I've lost her," Kip moaned when he saw her.

Instinctively, Kitty leaned toward him, feeling his grief, wanting to console him. "Oh, Kip, I'm sorry, so sorry."

"I know."

But he *didn't* know, he *couldn't* know that she was sorry, not only for his pain, but for her own, sorry that he couldn't have loved *her,* who loved him so much.

Oh, Kip, she thought, *I want to give you so much more*. But, of course, she couldn't say that. All she could do was look at him, eyes moist with love and pity. She couldn't even offer him the solace that in time he'd get over losing Cara. For she was afraid that Kip, like her, loved this passionately only once and then for a lifetime.

After a moment, Kip gave a harsh little laugh. "And we didn't even get to open our time capsule."

"Time capsule? What do you mean?"

Kip shook his head. "Nothing. Never mind. Just one of Cara's and my silly secrets."

But from the tone of his voice, Kitty knew that he didn't consider it silly. None of the things he had shared over the years with Cara would be anything but precious to Kip. She also knew that there would always be those "secrets" that bound them together, separating Kip from her even more.

Then, suddenly, he reached out for her, pulled her against him and held her close for a long time. "You're so sweet, Kitty. I appreciate your understanding," he said huskily.

She lifted her head. "Kip, I just wish I could—" She started to say "help you," but unexpectedly Kip kissed her, and there was sweetness and tenderness in the kiss. But as he drew away, holding her at arm's length, Kitty knew it wasn't enough. It wasn't the kiss Kitty longed for, the one that was *really* for *her*.

It wasn't enough to *look* like Cara. For that kind of kiss she had to *be* Cara. Kitty knew that she loved Kip, would go on loving him for the rest of her life. She couldn't help it.

175

Part VI
Birchfields, England
Spring, 1914

chapter
21

GARNET'S FIRST pleasure in receiving a letter from Jonathan soon faded. It was clear by its tone that he was seriously depressed.

"This house is like a mausoleum, Aunt 'Net," he had written. "I wander around like some kind of ghost myself, going from room to room, trying to remember what it was like when there was life here . . . like it used to be. I find myself wishing back the very things that used to bother Davida—the noise of children and dogs. I think sometimes I'm losing my mind— No, don't worry, it's not that bad. It's just that I think about the old days too much.

Suddenly that summer—remember the summer of '97 when we all came over to England to celebrate the Jubilee?—seems to have been the happiest time of my life. I know I shouldn't live in the past, but I can't believe that part of my life is over, that Kendall and Meredith are grown and gone, and that I'm sliding into middle age . . . alone."

Garnet's immediate reaction was to write him at once, insisting that he come to Birchfields on the next available ship and spend some time with her. Then, perhaps, she could persuade him to go up to Scotland for a vacation, a little hiking and fishing. She recalled how that sort of thing had always refreshed and renewed Jeremy.

To her relief, Jonathan responded by return mail, agreeing to come for a visit. But when he arrived at Birchfields, Garnet was gravely concerned, not only for his state of mind, but his appearance. He had lost a great deal of weight, looked tired, and his eyes had a haunted expression.

It was his emotional condition, however, that concerned her most. Jonathan had always had a buoyant spirit, an ability to weather the many storms life had dealt him from the start—losing his mother at an early age, not ever getting to know his father, being transplanted to an alien part of the country, where he grew up with his northern cousins. Throughout it all, Jonathan had maintained an optimistic outlook. If he had not been happy, at least he had remained cheerful and never burdened anyone else with his problems.

Now that positive view seemed sadly missing, and it frightened Garnet. She had to use all her persuasive powers to get him to follow her suggestion about the trip to Scotland. Although finally he agreed to go, even his apathy while complying disturbed her, for it was so unlike the Jonathan she had known and loved all these years.

From London, Jonathan was to take the overnight train to Edinburgh. As he left his hack and entered the station, a stop at an information booth warned him that the "Highlander" was already being boarded. Juggling his suitcases as well as a "tea basket" that Garnet's cook had prepared for him for the journey, Jonathan hurried through the doors out into the departure area.

A porter approached him right away, tipping his hat, and shouting above the din, "Your baggage, sir?" At Jonathan's nod, he made a grab for the two valises Jonathan was carrying. Then with a look around, he frowned. "No fishing gear or golf clubs?"

"None," Jonathan replied as he surrendered the leather cases.

"None?" echoed the porter in disbelief, as if going to Scotland without at least one was a kind of sacrilege.

Jonathan shook his head, knowing from the look on the fellow's face that no explanation would satisfy.

"First Class, sir?" was the next question. To this, Jonathan gave an affirmative nod.

Leading the way down the platform, the porter hurried to one of the few compartments whose door remained open even as the guard was moving quickly down the length of the train, slamming and securing the doors to the other compartments in the carriage.

The porter shoved the two suitcases onto the floor of the compartment, then turned. "There you are, sir, and 'ave a pleasant journey." To Jonathan's amusement, there was a note of doubt in his voice as to whether a trip to Scotland that did not include fishing or playing golf could be either enjoyable or worthwhile.

The train started up, gathering speed as it moved out from under the gloom of the station, while Jonathan settled himself comfortably. He was the only occupant, for which he was grateful. He would not be under any obligation to engage in conversation with some traveler craving companionship. It was not his nature to shun company. but over the past year and a half, he had been a stranger, even to himself.

It was probably a good thing that Aunt 'Net had persuaded him to take this trip to Scotland, the land of his Montrose ancestors. Perhaps he could do a little exploring, some sightseeing, maybe even take a ferry over to the Island of Skye. Yes, he'd have to do that. He was already beginning to feel a stirring of interest, a small sense of adventure at taking off on this serendipitous journey.

He had bought a guidebook, *Historic Scotland, The Land and Its People,* and planned to base his tour on the various suggestions to travelers. Mainly he intended to visit points of historic importance. He would arrive in Edinburgh the next morning and from there would map out the rest of his trip.

He recalled having debated the wisdom of accepting Aunt Garnet's invitation to Birchfields, precisely because it still held memories of his last visit there with Davida. That had been a bittersweet time when happiness, which had seemed to elude them for so long, again seemed a possibility. But his aunt had insisted, and finally Jonathan, unable to bear another spring at Montclair, had on impulse cabled her that he was coming. Before he changed his mind, he had gone to Richmond, then to New York, and booked passage on the first boat leaving for England.

His good sense told him that for the rest of his life everything would remind him in some ways of the past. He should try to apply all the good advice he had received since Davida's tragic death and build a new life for himself. It was easy to make the resolution, harder to put it into practice, he had discovered, but he was determined to try. This journey would be a good test of his resolve.

In Edinburgh, he boarded another train for Glasgow, and as the train left the city behind and rumbled out into the countryside, Jonathan got his first real glimpse of Scotland, the land of myth and legend.

The train rattled on its way, and Jonathan leaned forward, eagerly taking in the scenery. They passed through green stretches of land flanked by lavender hills, pulled to a screeching stop in picturesque towns full of whitewashed houses, window boxes trailing pink and purple petunias, then clattered into a valley cut deep into a pine-clustered hillside.

Jonathan thought it might be interesting to look up the places from which his Scottish ancestors had come. So, very soon after he had found lodging, he studied the map and, noticing a small town called Arbroath on the east coast, with the name *Montrose* appearing some six miles north, he decided to go there first.

He spent a pleasant day, rambling among the ruins. In the old church that was still standing, Jonathan learned that at ten each evening, the huge bell of St. Peter, cast in Rotterdam in 1676, was still rung to signal curfew. The castle, dating back to the tenth century, was the residence of King Edward I in 1296, though one year later it was razed to the ground by Scottish nationalists under William Wallace.

Amused, Jonathan scribbled on a postcard to Garnet: "Everything here is so very old that it makes America, even our historic Virginia, seem quite young by comparison!"

His interest in Scottish history taking its impetus from this first foray, Jonathan became quite excited at what he was learning. He began to love the countryside in which he was traveling. These stony cliffs, bulwarks against invading hordes, had given Scotland the independence born of solitude, while golden broom kindled a fiery glow on the hillsides under gray, cloud-laden skies.

He roamed the hills, the rough fern called bracken rustling in a chill breeze, the rising mist dampening his hair and cheeks. The peaty soil was soft under his boots, and he walked for a while under the tarnished sky, deep in thought.

He visited Glencoe, the site of the Massacre of February 13, 1692, remembered in infamy by most Scotsmen. The slaughter of the Clan Macdonald by the Clan Campbell, after they had been guests, was a horrifying betrayal of traditional Scottish hospitality. The ostensible reason for the attack was that old MacIan, Chief of the Clencoe Clan Macdonald, had not signed the oath of allegiance to William of Orange, the Dutch King of England. Jonathan was reminded of his grandfather Montrose, who had also refused to sign a loyalty oath after the War Between the States.

What a confirmation that human history repeats itself century after century, Jonathan could not help thinking, *probably because human nature, if unchanged by God, continues in its violence, its savagery, its bloodletting.* This haunted glen was a stark reminder of man's inhumanity to man.

Next, Jonathan visited Culloden, the ancient moorland on which the legendary Bonnie Prince Charlie fought for independence from the English. They stood no chance against a stronger foe, although the battle would go down in history as the gallant attempt of brave men to maintain their freedom.

Only a stone cairn stood as a modest memorial to their valor, if not the wisdom of their command. Mounds still marked the graves, the Highlanders lying with their clansmen in death, the English in a field nearby.

As Jonathan was contemplating this disaster, not unlike some of the Confederate battles fought in a hopeless cause, he saw the slim figure of a girl on a bicycle coming down the hill on the opposite side, watched her bend quickly over a grave, then remount her vehicle and pedal away.

Curious, he walked over to the headstone and saw a single golden daffodil, placed carefully on the rough marker over the name, Clan Stewart McPherson. *McPherson.* He repeated the name to himself, and the image of the pert young woman who had been employed as nanny to the children that enchanted summer at Birchfields, came briefly to mind. Phoebe McPherson. Wasn't that her name?

With some daylight left, he consulted his brochure once more, deciding to follow the road to Argyll into the land of Badenoch, and after several stops, found himself in Kingaren. It was a pleasant little town, hardly more than a village, with a cluster of houses built of gray stone and sturdy slate, hills all around and a river mumbling along nearby.

Lodgings, he was informed, were to be found at the local inn, where Jonathan found the most pleasant surprise of his trip.

Entering the large lounge, comfortably furnished with big easy chairs arranged around the stone fireplace where a splendid fire was burning, Jonathan saw that it was nearly empty, with only one or two people dozing or reading.

A tall man behind the registration desk looked up as Jonathan approached. He looked to be a typical Highlander, Jonathan mused, with his craggy features and ruddy complexion, and when he greeted Jonathan, his burr was pronounced. He introduced himself as Gordon McPherson, innkeeper, adding proudly that "Badenoch is McPherson country."

Jonathan's ears pricked up. Recently he had begun to think of Miss McPherson again, the young governess he had met that long-ago summer of the family reunion. Perhaps being in her native country had brought her to mind. To find that he had landed in the middle of her clan's territory seemed a strange coincidence.

"I have rooms, to be sure," said the innkeeper, rolling his r's delightfully. "But I'm very much afraid (sounding, to Jonathan's ear, like *verra mooch afred*) that ye've arrived past the dinner hour. Still—" he went on with a sly twinkle in intensely blue eyes, "no Highlander would iver send a guest to his bed hungry!"

Shown to a low-ceilinged room, its shiny brass bed piled high with pillows and quilts, Jonathan stowed his suitcases and washed up. Then he descended the staircase and returned to the now empty dining room, where a supper of poached salmon, potatoes, and hot tea awaited him as promised, served by the innkeeper himself.

Mr. McPherson then proceeded to keep Jonathan company while he ate his delicious meal. After learning that he was an American and that his ancestors were Highlanders, his host became loquacious and proved to be a great raconteur.

Pointing to an oil portrait hanging over the massive sideboard, he declared, "That's one of me illustrious ancestresses," he said and launched into a recital of her story. The Lady Jean was a supporter of Prince Charles and the Stuart cause. Her husband, a regular army officer who was expected to serve the king, whoever he might be, was on the other side.

As he listened to the tale of a family split over an issue that divided their country, Jonathan was sharply reminded of his own mother, Rose Meredith, and his father, Malcolm Montrose, who were bitterly estranged over the issue of slavery in the final years of their marriage before her premature death in a fire at Montclair.

Mr. McPherson spoke on about his little country's stormy history, with deep wounds not yet healed. Relics of their indomitable spirit filled the room—the shattered fiddle of one Jamie McPherson who was hanged for cattle theft, yet broke his instrument over his knee before he swung, saying, "No ither shall play my fiddle"; the McPhersons' green war banner, draped over the chimney place; and the set of bagpipes said to have survived the clan battles of the fourteenth century.

The more Gordon told him of the glorious and tragic history of his people, the more fascinated Jonathan became.

"'Tis too bad, though, that Christianity, comin' to us from Scotia," said Gordon, "has not done much to lift our spirits, lad. I fear 'tis the pride in us that makes it hard to bend to God or man!"

There was a companionable silence as Jonathan sipped the last of his tea and Gordon took a long draw on his pipe before continuing. "And we've lost some of our young to ither countries. Some of our brightest and best are searchin' for a better life elsewhere . . . in America, Australia. Even some of me own folk have left Scotland. One can't blame them, I guess." He shook his head sadly. "Well here now, lad, I've rambled on and kept ye up long after ye should hae been abed, gettin' a good night's sleep."

"Not at all, Mr. McPherson. I've enjoyed it immensely," Jonathan assured him. "You remind me in some ways of my Virginia relatives who are knowledgeable about their history. I appreciate hearing all this . . . makes me feel a part of my kin here."

"Well, then, maybe I should hae been tellin' ye the best places to fish—" Gordon chuckled.

"No, not really. You see, I'm not here to fish."

"Not here to fish?" Gordon seemed astounded. "Ye should at least drop a line while ye're here. The stream yon is alive with salmon." He walked with Jonathan to the foot of the staircase leading to the second floor. "I won't be here tomorrow. 'Tis my weekend off. My niece will be takin' over for me at the desk the next two days," he explained, then asked, "Would you want me to leave ye an extra rod and a creel, if ye've a mind to give it a go?"

Jonathan hadn't the heart to refuse. Mr. McPherson was so obviously proud of the abundance in the stream so near his inn. So, before bidding his host good night, Jonathan agreed to "give it a go" sometime over the weekend.

chapter
22

MUCH TO HIS surprise, Jonathan slept soundly and long. When he awakened and consulted his watch, he was amazed to see the time. Dressing quickly in the tweeds he had purchased in Edinburgh before setting out on his trip to the Highlands, he went downstairs, wondering if he had missed breakfast.

The wide hall was empty and so was the lounge when Jonathan looked in. Probably all the guests had already set off on their day's hike or a fishing expedition. Standing in the middle of the hallway, Jonathan heard the low murmur of voices coming from the dining room area, along with the click of china, the tinkle of glassware. The staff was probably setting up for the midday meal. Perhaps he should just venture out into the village and look for a small café—

While he hesitated uncertainly, he heard a door open behind him, and turning, he saw a young woman at the reception desk, her back turned to him, her head bent over a ledger. There was something vaguely familiar about the slim, graceful figure in a crisp shirtwaist and plaid skirt cinched with a wide leather belt. Then, as he stood making his assessment, she turned around.

"Miss McPherson!" he exclaimed in amazement.

She looked up, startled. Her face mirrored surprise, then gradual recognition as Jonathan approached her desk. "Miss McPherson! How extraordinary! I can hardly believe it!" He extended his hand. "Jonathan Montrose, here—Mrs. Devlin's nephew. We met the summer of the Queen's Jubilee . . . at Birchfields. You were governess to the Cameron children—"

He watched as two changes took place in the attractive face. The wide, dark-lashed eyes he now remembered so well widened, and a rosy color flooded her face.

Smiling, Jonathan persisted. "Do you remember me now?"

"Yes, of course—" she said, stumbling a little over the words. "Of course, Mr. Montrose. How nice to see you. How do you happen to be in Kilgaren?"

He explained quickly, then asked, "And *you,* Miss McPherson. I never expected to find you here . . . or even see you again. I thought you had planned to go to America or Australia."

"I was in America for a short while, did some traveling. But then my father became ill, and I came home to see him through a long, lingering illness. Both my brothers had emigrated, so there was no one else—" She paused, then continued. "After his death . . . well, there was a great deal to see to, and I stayed on. I've been helping my uncle here at the hotel—"

"Your uncle is Gordon McPherson? Of course! I've met him. A capital fellow!" Jonathan said heartily, adding with a chuckle, "He's been giving me a crash course in Scottish history."

Phoebe laughed and, hearing it, Jonathan recalled how delighted he had been when he had heard it for the first time.

"Oh, Uncle Gordie is a great storyteller. He'll keep you up half the night with his tales."

Jonathan agreed laughingly. "That's exactly what he did do! And I've slept most the morning away as a result."

Phoebe looked shocked. "Then you've had no breakfast, have you? Well, come along, and we'll see what we can do about that."

"I don't want to put you to any trouble. Perhaps I can just go down the street—"

"Nothing of the kind, Mr. Montrose. Uncle would have a fit if he thought any guest of his did without a proper Scottish breakfast."

She led the way through the dining room where rosy-cheeked maids in starched ruffled caps and aprons were putting fresh cloths on the tables.

Phoebe ushered him into an alcove and gestured to a small table set in the bow window, then disappeared through a door Jonathan assumed was the kitchen. Within minutes, a waitress appeared, bearing a pot of coffee. She poured him a steaming cup and almost immediately Phoebe herself came with a tray of oatmeal, a jar of heather honey, and a basket of currant scones, wrapped in a linen cloth to keep them warm.

"It's a little too late for a real Highlander breakfast, but perhaps this will do till lunch."

"Oh, this is more than enough, thank you, Phoebe," Jonathan said spontaneously. Then, realizing that he had called her by her first name, started to correct his gaffe by saying, "Miss McPherson," when it occurred to him she might no longer be *Miss!* Quickly, and as discreetly as possible, he checked her hand, now occupied with refilling his cup, and was relieved to see that her fingers were ringless.

"Well, I'll leave you to enjoy your breakfast."

She was about to leave when he halted her. "Will I see you later?"

"Yes, I'm on duty here until after tea in the afternoon."

"Perhaps then, we could . . . well, talk? I could catch you up on your former charges—the Cameron twins and even naughty Evalee Bondurant," he laughed half-apologetically, knowing full well that this was only an excuse to spend some time with her, and wondering if Phoebe guessed it, too.

"That would be very nice," she replied almost primly before she turned and went back to the lobby and her post behind the desk.

As Jonathan watched her walk away, he felt a happy anticipation at the thought of being with her again. Then he realized with a start of guilt that she must not know about Faith nor about Davida . . . and that he was now a widower.

Back behind the desk, Phoebe found it unusually hard to concentrate on the requests for reservations that she must reply to and have ready for the postman when he arrived with the day's mail. She felt flustered and yet excited at the unexpected encounter with Jonathan Montrose. She had certainly never expected to see him again. In fact, she had deliberately put him out of her mind after that idyllic English summer when they had met.

She recalled, with a helpless sense of impropriety, having been drawn to him from the first, drawn by his gentleness and good manners. As she had come to know him, she had also recognized the integrity, the depth of character, and later learned that his puzzling air of sadness was in part caused by a difficult wife.

The attraction she had felt for him, especially after the day they took the children to the village fair, was wrong, she had told herself. After all, he was a married man, and she had no business entertaining any thoughts about him at all. Phoebe had been brought up on Scripture and had learned it well. Whenever a thought of Jonathan Montrose had crept, unbidden, into her mind, she quickly whispered the admonition to herself: "Casting down imaginations, . . . and bringing into captivity every thought to the obedience of Christ."

It had been a difficult thing to do, but she had done it, and it had been years since the thought of Jonathan Montrose had bothered her. Now here he was . . . right at her doorstep, so to speak. And alone again. Where was his wife and the children he had spoken of so lovingly and longingly that summer at Birchfields?

"Miss McPherson" came the voice of one of the staff intruding into her reminiscence, and she immediately turned her attention to the task at hand.

So busy was she, in fact, that she had no time to ponder the strange circumstance of Jonathan Montrose's presence in Kilgaren until he returned at four o'clock, cheeks ruddied from his walk in the crisp air. Then there was only time for a brisk nod of acknowledgment.

Scotland had become a popular resort since Queen Victoria's vacationing here had made it fashionable. The inn was full. At half past four, a group of English ladies, here on holiday with their fisherman husbands, were scheduled for a "high tea" in the smaller dining room, so Phoebe had her hands full.

It wasn't until she was putting on her warm cape and hat to walk the few steps to the family home where she now lived alone that Jonathan presented himself as someone to be dealt with, for he was standing at the door as she was about to leave.

"Will I see you again?"

"Oh, yes, I'll be on duty tomorrow. I come in after church. Sunday dinner here is a regular event for some of the townspeople, and we're generally quite busy."

"Church?" he questioned. "Where do you attend?"

"It's the wee gray kirk on the other side of the bridge," she replied, unconsciously lapsing into the Scottish colloquialism he found enchanting.

"Perhaps I'll go myself," said Jonathan, realizing with some guilt how long it had been since he had attended a Sunday service anywhere.

Phoebe's cheeks became very pink again, and she occupied herself pulling on her gloves. "You'd be welcome, I'm sure."

Opening the door for her, Jonathan asked almost shyly, "Do you live far? I mean, may I walk you home?"

"It's only just down the street," she said tentatively.

"Then, if it's all right, I'll accompany you. I'm finding that a brisk walk does wonders for the constitution."

As they walked down the cobbled street, Phoebe questioned him about the Montrose relatives she had met at Birchfields.

"Well, the Cameron twins are all grown up, of course. Cara is married to a minister and—"

"You don't mean it!" Phoebe gasped. "Cara, the little mischievous one . . . a parson's bride?"

Jonathan chuckled. "Your reaction is typical. I'm afraid no one could quite believe it. But it's true."

"And is the other twin married as well?"

"No, and neither is Scott, their brother. He's in law school, with a legal career in mind."

"He was always quite bright and rather serious, as I recall. And then you mentioned Evalee, the *enfant terrible!*" Phoebe laughed merrily.

"Evalee has become a stunning young woman, quite the socialite. You may remember her sister, Lalage—"

"Of course. The Jubilee bride!"

"Yes, well, *she* married a member of the peerage, as you may remember, and that's just the sort of life Evalee revels in. It's known that American girls, especially American girls who are also heiresses,

191

are an attractive commodity in certain British circles. So Evalee is in her element, much to her mother, my Cousin Dru's, dismay."

They had almost reached the end of the street when Phoebe asked, "And your children, Mr. Montrose? I believe you have two, a boy and a girl about the twins' age, you said—"

"Yes, Meredith and Kendall. We call him Kip—" Jonathan paused and drew a long breath. "They, too, are in their early twenties now. My daughter is married to a fine young man, a fisherman from Cape Cod, where they are now living. And my son . . . well, Kip is going through a difficult time right now. You see, he lost his mother to whom he was very devoted . . . my wife, Davida, and Mrs. Devlin's daughter were both on the *Titanic*—"

Jonathan felt Phoebe's hand touch his arm gently. "Oh, I'm sorry! I didn't know—"

"Of course you didn't—"

They walked on in silence, then Phoebe spoke. "Well, here we are."

They were standing in front of a neat greystone with no unnecessary ornamentation, a solid no-nonsense kind of house, Jonathan thought.

At the doorstep, Phoebe put out her hand. "Well, good night, and thank you, Mr. Montrose."

"*Jonathan,* please. I mean, if you would—"

She seemed to hesitate, as if giving his suggestion consideration, then she smiled. "Well, then, of course," but she did not repeat his name.

Jonathan walked back to the inn in a strangely restless mood. Over and over he thought of the unique coincidence that had brought him to Kilgaren and Phoebe McPherson after all these years. How many? *Nearly seventeen,* he thought, quickly calculating the number. She must be thirty-five, possibly thirty-six by now. And he . . . why he was nearly fifty-five! Nearly twenty years difference in their ages. Now, what had made him think of *that*?

chapter

23

STARTING AWAKE as the first light of morning silvered the sky, Jonathan grabbed his watch from the bedside table, fearful that he might have overslept and missed the morning service.

Leaping out of bed, he shaved and dressed, then hurried downstairs through the quiet lobby and out into the misty morning.

The service had just begun, the first hymn being sung in thin, rather quavery voices by the sparse congregation scattered throughout the small church. But as Jonathan slipped into one of the back pews, he spotted Phoebe, recognizing the sweep of brown hair beneath the brown hat with its peacock-blue feathers.

The minister's burr was so thick that quite frankly Jonathan missed a good deal of the sermon. But somehow he felt a strong sense of reverence and combined strength in the bond of fellowship among the few worshipers. Curiously enough, as the service drew to a close, he was aware of a gradual peace enveloping him.

He remained where he was after the Doxology, waiting for Phoebe to pass down the aisle, hoping he might accompany her back to the inn.

On the way out, she spoke to a few people, and then suddenly seeing him, her eyes lighted up and she seemed to draw in a hurried breath. A slight smile touched her generous mouth as she approached, and Jonathan was encouraged to speak and walk out with her.

"Today there will be quite a bustle," she told him as they crossed the little arched bridge leading back to the inn. "As I mentioned, it's quite a popular gathering place for Sunday dinner. I'm afraid I won't have much time to visit until after tea—"

"Then I look forward to that," Jonathan said. "And maybe this afternoon I'll take your uncle up on his offer to lend me some fishing equipment and try my luck."

"Yes, why don't you?" She brightened. "You may find you enjoy it and become as serious a fisherman as most of our guests."

Phoebe found the rod and reel and creel her uncle had left out for him. With her good wishes ringing in his ears, Jonathan started off with not too much expectation on his part. For an hour or two, he worked a dark, promising pool in the stream to which she had directed him, but without result.

After a while the wind came up and Jonathan, in spite of his heavy sweater and tweed jacket, began to feel chilled. Admitting defeat, he packed up his gear and walked down to the harbor where he stood for a few minutes watching the sea gulls, who were apparently having much better success than he. Reading the names on a number of double-ended purse seiners that were moored there—*Fair Jane, New Dawn, Star of Hope*—he realized a stirring of hope in his own heart as he turned to walk back to the inn.

The hotel was still quite busy and so was Phoebe, so Jonathan went upstairs to his room, feeling both physically tired yet elated. He stretched out on the bed, thinking he'd rest until after the crowd left, then go down and find Phoebe. He'd ask to walk her home, and maybe this time she'd ask him in for some tea and conversation. He wanted urgently to be with her, talk to her—

To his chagrin, Jonathan fell asleep and, when he awakened, the room was dark. After a quick investigative trip out into the hall and a look over the banister down into the lobby, he realized that everyone was gone. Only one dim light was burning at the reception desk, where the night clerk was reading the Sunday paper.

Wide awake now, Jonathan returned to his room. He went to the window and pushed it open, breathing deeply of the salty air, the smell of fog and the sea, and leaned out on the sill.

One by one, thoughts of his life came to him, and he examined each with a courage and resolution he had not possessed before. He thought of Davida and their love—"that first fine careless rapture," of which the poets wrote—the gradual drifting apart, the sadness he had felt at the loss of that intimacy. Then, just as they seemed about to recapture what they had both thought lost, the tragedy had occurred.

It all came back, but by some mercy of Providence, this time without pain. For the first time since the horrible shock, Jonathan could think about Davida without the agony of regret, self-recrimination, guilt.

He felt warmth, a release as he remembered the sweetness they had once known together and, little by little, he let the dark years go. It was as if at long last, he was being healed, the keen edge of sorrow was mercifully softened, the suffering put aside. *Perhaps,* he thought, *when a sorrow is healed, the bitterness is gone, too, and only the best memories remain.*

Slowly, as all this came together for Jonathan, he realized that something else was happening. That numbness of emotions was disappearing, and he felt the tears come. But these were not tears of reproach but tears that somehow cleared his eyes so he could see the possibility of joy beckoning him, a hope that something wonderful lay ahead, and he was at last free to welcome it into his life.

Phoebe was not at the desk the next morning when Jonathan came downstairs. Instead, he found Gordon, ruddier and heartier than ever, ready to regale any audience he could find with stories of his wildly successful fishing weekend.

Jonathan was reluctant to ask about Phoebe, so, after a breakfast that introduced him to "bannocks," griddle-baked oat cakes served hot with "crowdie," a thick cream-cheese and marmalade, he went for a walk, hoping to encounter her somewhere in the village. He was, however, disappointed. There was not a sign of Phoebe anywhere in all Kilgaren. Although he strolled by her house several times, she was not in evidence there either, and Jonathan did not have the courage to go and ring her doorbell.

He had not planned to say in Kilgaren this long, but somehow he could not convince himself to leave. Aunt Garnet was not expecting him back until the following week. Even though he had not yet seen the famous castle or cathedral in Edinburgh, he knew that he could not go until he had spent more time with Phoebe, until . . . well, until he could explore what, if anything, might develop between them.

The weather turned cold and cloudy. The day seemed long to him after he had casually asked when Miss McPherson would be on duty and heard she was not expected until evening. He flipped mindlessly through all the magazines and periodicals available in the lounge, most of which were either on fishing or fashion, the latter for the patient wives who accompanied their husbands to this remote "paradise." At length, Jonathan grew bored and decided to walk down to the harbor again. No boats had risked setting out in the stormy weather, and only the sea gulls, screeching and soaring, gave him company. Impatient to see Phoebe, he returned to the inn.

On the way, an image of her rose in his mind—not the picture of the youthful Phoebe who had come and gone whenever he'd thought of that summer at Birchfields but the woman she had *become*. She still had the same clear-eyed serenity, but there was something wistful in their depths now, some shadow. Her girlish features had a new maturity, a new beauty. How was it she had never married? With such warmth, such wit and intelligence, he was surprised that she had not found love long ago.

That evening Jonathan was in plenty of time for dinner and sat in the lounge in front of the stone fireplace, waiting for the gong to signal the first seating.

Waiting for Phoebe, Jonathan fell into conversation with one of the other guests and learned, to his dismay, that on Monday nights a musicale was presented by local musicians in one of the inn's larger gathering rooms. Any idea he had entertained of having Phoebe to himself was banished.

Finally he saw her hurrying in the front door out of the wind, her face aglow, her eyes sparkling as she began to unfasten the braided clasp of her tartan cape. Wisps of brown hair had escaped from the tam she was wearing and blew in fetching curls over her forehead and around her ears.

At her entrance, Jonathan rose. She saw him and waved. Her smile of greeting was warm, sympathetic, understanding, and he felt something lift inside him, the feeling of possible happiness renewed, hope rekindled.

Although Gordon McPherson was back, Phoebe assumed the role of hostess not only to the hotel guests but also to townspeople who gathered for this weekly entertainment.

When he got her alone for a moment, she explained. "In the olden days, long before it was ever written down, the Highland Gaels made music with spoken words. They were great storytellers and even the lilt and cadence of their tales had a stirring effect on the listeners. Thankfully," she went on, "our old ways and old language are coming alive again." And before she glided off again to welcome some arriving guests, Phoebe whispered, "Save me a seat, and I'll join you for the concert."

Because he did not have a finely tuned musical ear, Jonathan had not anticipated enjoying the evening as much as he did. All the songs—"Annie Laurie," "Loch Lomond," "Flow Gently, Sweet Afton"—were familiar melodies, but it was as if he were hearing them for the first time. It did not occur to Jonathan that his appreciation of the music might be due to the awareness of Phoebe's nearness or the sweet scent she wore that reminded him of newly clovered meadows.

Afterward, she told him she would be going home in the company of friends. His disappointment was somewhat assuaged by the plans for the next day.

"If the weather's fair, I'll pack a picnic, if you like," she promised as he helped her on with her cape and went with her to the door.

"Oh, I would like that very much," he assured her and, after saying good night, Jonathan went whistling up to his room.

When he awoke the next morning, he lay on his bed for a few minutes, trying to recall something . . . a dream? Something hovered on the periphery of his mind . . . and then it came to him . . . a fragment of Scripture: "Forgetting those things which are behind, and reaching forth unto those things which are before—"

He lay there a minute longer, savoring the significance of those words, then bounded out of bed. There was something he must do without delay.

At the little post office that also served as the local telegraph office, Jonathan quickly wrote out a message to send to his Aunt Garnet. In it, he told her he would be staying in Scotland another week. He felt a little conscience-stricken that it would cut short his time with her at Birchfields. But he couldn't leave . . . not yet—

After sending off the telegram, Jonathan went back to the hotel, partook of a hearty Scottish breakfast of sausage, bacon, mushrooms, and tomatoes, then went over to Phoebe's house.

Jonathan had no idea whatsoever of what the day would hold for him as he and Phoebe started out. It was a rare Scottish morning with the sun slowly unveiling itself. Occasionally they stopped to watch lambs cavorting over the tawny hillsides, purple with heather and dotted with dark green pines and paler green larches.

They walked on, heedless of time's passing, telling each other bits and pieces of the years apart, sharing the events, the people, the incidents that had influenced and shaped their lives. When they stopped for lunch, they were barely conscious of what they were eating from the contents of the wicker hamper, they were so engrossed in conversation. Nor did they notice that the afternoon was far gone until they halted on the crest of a little bridge and saw that the river had turned amber with the soft light of approaching evening.

They had talked for hours, yet had not seemed to run out of things to say to each other. They had explored many topics—agreed on many, lightly debated others. Yet Jonathan was now suddenly struck with the panic of time's swift passage, of opportunity slipping out of his grasp.

Phoebe leaned on the ledge of the stone bridge, looking down at the water. Her profile looked so endearing that Jonathan could barely resist running his finger along the slightly upturned nose, or cupping the delicate chin in his hand to turn her face toward his. He thought Phoebe even lovelier than she had been as the vivacious lass, blooming with health and vitality, he had met when she was nineteen. There was character in that face now—the little laugh-lines around the eyes, the sweet, generous mouth. He longed to kiss that mouth . . . but he dared not.

Suddenly he felt the urgency of breaking through to her, of reaching some hidden part of her that he innately felt might respond to his honesty. He began to confide how meaningless his life had seemed in the past few years. Now with Kip out West and Meredith married and living so far away, how lonely he had been.

"Life *can* be very lonely," Phoebe agreed.

"Yes, that's true," he replied, then asked quietly, "Has it been lonely for you?"

She hesitated. "I suppose you might say I've been lonely all my life. As the only girl growing up on a farm with brothers, then living in other people's houses, taking care of other people's children. And, yes, you might say I've been lonely for Scotland, too, and that's why I came back—" She paused, then added thoughtfully, "But there's another kind of loneliness . . . a heart loneliness . . . a kind of searching for something—"

"Or some *one?*" Jonathan took Phoebe's hand and lifted it to his lips. "Phoebe, do you think it at all strange that I came to Scotland and, by some . . . happenstance . . . to Kilgaren and that we met again after all this time?"

Phoebe looked startled, thinking that he must have read her mind. Ever since Jonathan had appeared in the lobby that morning, the thought of Divine Providence, the belief that God arranges time and circumstances to fulfill His purposes in our lives, had thrust itself into her mind. Now, his question brought roses blooming to her cheeks.

"Yes, I suppose I do . . . I have," she murmured.

He put out his hand and turned her head so he could gaze into her eyes. "Phoebe," he said very softly, "would you . . . could you consider marrying me?"

To Jonathan, it seemed an eternity before she responded. Had she not heard him, or failed to understand what he was asking her?

He had to bend very near to hear her soft, "Aye."

"What did you say, Phoebe?"

She laughed, her soft mirth all the more heart-lifting in the gathering gloom and mist. "I said yes, Jonathan, I'd be most pleased to accept," she said in that musical lilting accent he had come to love.

There was no longer any reason to resist the temptation of those sweetly curved rosy lips so near . . . and as he kissed her, they both knew it was the end of loneliness for them both.

They were married at the "wee kirk," with all Phoebe's Kilgaren friends and many of the McPherson clan in attendance. Gordon, in full Highland dress, kilt and all, looking as proud as any clan chieftain, brought his niece down the aisle. She wore a heather-blue suit of softest wool, a hat trimmed with ribbons in the McPherson tartan, and carried a small bouquet of field flowers, centered with a sprig of white heather, the talisman of a long and happy wedded life for a Scottish bride. Yes, the time for loneliness was over. Only rejoicing lay ahead.

Since neither Kip nor Meredith were in Virginia to welcome their father and his bride, Blythe went to meet Jonathan and Phoebe at the station. Kip, restless and unhappy, was off on one of the several spur-of-the-moment trips he had taken since his mother's death. Meredith, living in Massachusetts now, was expecting her first baby and could not travel.

Blythe's own family was scattered, too. Cara, of course, was in Ohio with Owen in his first pastorate, Scott in law school at the university. Kitty had taken Lynette to England to visit her other grandmother in the hope of persuading Garnet to let her bring Bryanne back to Virginia. Jeff, still inconsolable, was in Taos, New Mexico, his little son Gareth with him. Blythe sighed. Would that little family, so broken by the terrible tragedy that had befallen them, ever be put back together?

Being at the station reminded Blythe of the day Jonathan came home after Davida's death. They had all gone down to meet him, hoping to be there, his family and close friends, to lend some comfort to this saddest of all homecomings. Ironically, in contrast to the grief they were all experiencing, the day had been one of the loveliest of the spring—the sky cloudlessly blue, the flowers in bright colored profusion all about the yellow station house. The sad part had been that even if Davida had come home with Jonathan, would she have seen its beauty?

Davida had not loved the peaceful Virginia countryside as Jonathan did, as did all the Montroses and Camerons. Her heart had remained in Massachusetts, and she had never consciously accepted her husband's home as her own.

Blythe recalled that in the months after the tragedy, everyone had wondered what Jonathan would do. He was still young, handsome, virile. Would he marry again, bring another bride home to Montclair? Someone who would share his affection and pride in the splendid house and plantation? Enjoy the tranquillity of the Virginia countryside?

Suddenly Blythe was brought back to the present by the sound of the engine rounding the bend, and the train was chugging into the station and pulled to a stop. In a few minutes the passengers began to emerge. Blythe searched the emerging passengers for a glimpse of Jonathan and his bride.

When she saw him, she was amazed at the change in him. He looked at least ten years younger! Turning, he held out his hand to help Phoebe down from the train. She was dressed in a navy-blue suit with a ruffled white organza collar and a wide-brimmed straw hat. Unaware that anyone was observing them, they exchanged a happy smile, and Blythe saw that what Garnet had written was true. This was truly a "marriage made in heaven!"

chapter
24
June 1914

"MAYFIELD! Mayfield! Next stop!"

At the conductor's sing-song call, Kitty Cameron began to gather up their belongings. "We're almost home, Lynette," she said to the small dark-haired girl whose tiny nose was pressed against the train window. "Please help me get your things together."

"Will Grandmother meet us?"

"I suppose so. Or somebody will, anyway. Here, put your book into this tote bag, and your crayons, too."

"Everything looks different."

"What do you mean?"

"I mean, it doesn't look like England."

"Well, of course it doesn't. We're in *Virginia* now. Back home."

"I wish Brynnie was with us. Why couldn't she come?"

"Your Grandmother Garnet will bring her later. 'In the fall,' she said."

"Really and truly?" The little girl's voice was plaintive.

"That's what she said," Kitty replied with more conviction than she felt. Her aunt had been less than specific in the message she had given Kitty to relay to the Camerons. Kitty knew that this latest change in plans would upset her mother. But there had been nothing she could do about it.

The quick trip to England had been a strange one, Kitty feeling some sort of subtle undercurrent when she had arrived at

Birchfields. Aunt Garnet had seemed aloof, remote, and Kitty had not been able to get through the wall she had erected. Perhaps she was still grieving. No wonder, Kitty thought with a rush of sympathy. The poor woman had lost more than any of them—her daughter to the *Titanic,* followed by her husband's passing only a short time later. The fact that Faith had left three children half-orphans was another kind of tragedy.

Garnet *had* mentioned Jonathan's visit with pleasure, but since he was in Scotland when Kitty arrived, she had not seen him until the newlyweds came through on their way home to America and Montclair. *What an affirmation of God's grace*, she thought. Jonathan deserved the happiness that was written all over his face when she had seen him for the first time with his bride, Phoebe McPherson, Kitty's former nanny from that unforgettable Jubilee summer!

Quickly her mind had turned to the other family that had suffered such pain with the passing of Davida Montrose. Kitty wondered how Kip was doing now. He had been so devoted to his mother, and the blow of her death had been cruelly severe. On top of that, his heart had been broken by Cara's marriage to Owen Brandt—

The grinding of the train braking to a jolting stop brought Kitty's thoughts back to the present. "Come on, Lynette, let's go."

"I don't see anyone waiting," said the little girl with a last look out the window.

"Oh, there's sure to be *somebody*," Kitty assured her, taking her hand.

Kip saw Kitty before *she* saw *him*. Slim and graceful, smartly dressed in a lime pongee traveling suit and wearing a perky braided straw hat, his old friend swung lightly down out of the train. Then she turned back, holding out her hand to help Lynette step onto the yellow stool and down to the platform. He saw her bend to straighten the little girl's wide-brimmed straw sailor hat and tie the ribbons under her chin.

"Kitty! Over here!" Kip called, striding toward her.

At his words, she raised her head. She looked startled, then happily surprised. "Kip! I didn't expect . . . how are you?"

As he came up to her, Kip had the strangest sensation that he was

203

seeing Kitty for the first time. For a moment he was speechless and simply stared.

"It's wonderful to see you, Kip." Kitty smiled. "I didn't know . . . When did you get back?"

"Just last week. You're looking splendid, Kitty. And, by golly, Lynette, *you've* grown two inches since I last saw you! Here, let me take your things." He reached for her hatbox and valise.

Kitty handed them to him, knowing that she was blushing, and why. "How did you happen to come for us?" she asked as the three of them walked down the platform.

"Your mother called when she got your telegram. Said she had some kind of meeting at the church this afternoon. Seems she's the chairwoman of a committee and couldn't get out of going. And your father's out of town at a horse show in Kentucky. Actually, she asked my dad if he would meet you, but I volunteered to do the honors."

Kip led the way over to a shiny jade green automobile. Kitty stopped short. "Is that *yours?*" she gasped.

"You bet!" Kip grinned proudly. "Isn't she a beauty? A birthday present from my father. You two will be my first passengers. Come on, hop aboard." He put their bags in the back, strapping them on behind.

Lynette's eyes sparkled as she climbed into the back seat. Then Kip made a ceremonial bow and opened the door on the passenger side for Kitty. The interior was upholstered in smooth russet leather, the dashboard panel made of gleaming polished wood.

Closing the door, Kip rounded the front of the vehicle and slipped behind the wheel. "All set? Hold onto your hats, ladies. Here we go!"

He shifted into reverse gear and backed the car out of the graveled space where horses with buggies were still hitched, and turned down Main Street. Kitty caught curious glances from pedestrians as they roared past. At the crossroads, they swerved, turning into a narrow lane, and within minutes, they were traveling at a high rate of speed along the familiar tree-lined country road.

"This unpaved road's hard on my tires!" Kip shouted above the roar of the engine. "But you should see how she rides on the paved streets! Just hear that sweet engine purr!" He smiled, tapping his hand on the leather-covered steering wheel as if keeping time to music.

"You sound like my father, bragging about a new hunter!" Kitty laughed. Leaning her head back, she felt the wind cool on her face and sighed happily. "It's so good to be home! I always feel like a part of me is missing when I'm away from here."

Kip glanced over at her. He'd forgotten how pretty she was. And there was something different about her, too. A kind of gloss, a self-confidence, a new poise.

"I guess, in a way, I do, too." He shrugged. "Everybody talks so much about California—the sun, the palm trees, the desert—and New Mexico, too. But I didn't think it was all that great."

"You were in New Mexico? You saw Jeff?"

Kip nodded.

"How is he?"

"Surviving . . . just. He's painting again. I guess that's a good sign."

"And Gareth?"

At the mention of her brother's name, Lynette leaned over the front seat. "Are they coming home soon?"

The two adults exchanged glances before Kip answered her. "Well, Gareth will, anyway. Your mother, I mean your Grandmother Blythe wants him to come back to Virginia. She wants to enroll him at Brookside Prep."

"Oh, goody!" Lynette gave an excited little bounce. "Will he live with us then?"

"You'll have to ask your grandmother about that."

"I hope so. I miss him. And Daddy, too, of course." She paused, then added solemnly, "I'm afraid Brynnie is going to forget us."

Kitty turned around quickly, patted the little hand. "Oh, no, she won't, honey. Remember, Aunt Garnet is bringing her to Virginia this fall."

Just then Kip turned into the long, winding drive leading up to Cameron Hall. Almost before he brought the car to a full stop, Lynette was scrambling to get out.

"Can I go down to the barn and see if Princess is all right?" she begged.

"Go ahead, honey. Mama's probably not home from her meeting yet anyway. But don't stay too long."

Lynette was already out of the car and running in the direction of the stables.

Kitty turned to Kip. "Well, thanks for the ride. I think your new car is the 'berries,' as they say," she teased. "So when are you going to let me drive it?"

"Just say when."

"You mean you'd actually trust a woman at the wheel of this—this chariot?"

Placing his hand over his heart, Kip intoned dramatically, "I'd trust *you* with anything, Kitty."

The words were barely out of his mouth when Kip suddenly knew he meant what he had just said. Looking at Kitty, he felt a melting warmth. In those dark brown eyes he saw something . . . the end of all the aching loneliness, the loss and emptiness of the last months. Was it possible that he had missed something before? Was it Kitty, after all, who could fill his life with hope and happiness?

His throat felt tight, constricted, but somehow he managed to ask, "When can I see you again?"

"Oh, Kip, any time. I've come home now."

In a funny sort of way, Kip felt that he had come home, too.

Cast of Characters in *Mirror Bride*

Mayfield, Virginia

At Montclair

Jonathan and Davida Montrose
their son, Kendall (called "Kip")
and their daughter, Meredith

At Avalon

Faith and Jeff Montrose

At Cameron Hall

Blythe and Rod Cameron
their son, Scott
and twin daughters, Kitty and Cara

Hero's Bride

Book Eleven
The Brides of Montclair Series

JANE PEART

ZondervanPublishingHouse
Grand Rapids, Michigan

A Division of HarperCollinsPublishers

Hero's Bride
Copyright © 1993 by Jane Peart

Requests for information should be addressed to:
Zondervan Publishing House
Grand Rapids, Michigan 49530

Library of Congress Cataloging-in-Publication Data

Peart, Jane.
    Hero's bride / Jane Peart.
      p. cm. — (The Brides of Montclair series : bk. 11)
    ISBN 0-310-67141-8 (paper)
    1. Family—Virginia—Williamsburg Region—Fiction. 2. Williams-
burg Region (Va.)—Fiction. I. Title. II. Series: Peart, Jane. Brides of
Montclair series : bk. 11.
  PS3566.E238H4   1993
  813'.54—dc20   93-19162
                                                                  CIP

Edited by Anne Severance
Interior design by Kim Koning
Cover design by Art Jacobs
Cover illustration by Wes Lowe, Sal Baracc and Assoc., Inc.

Printed in the United States of America

This book is gratefully dedicated to
Bob Hudson,
senior editor at Zondervan,
in appreciation for his supportive encouragement,
his enthusiasm and help

Hero's Bride

Prologue

August 1914

From: Katherine M. Cameron
      Cameron Hall
      Mayfield, Virginia

To: Mrs. Owen Brandt
      Good Shepherd Parsonage
      Harristown, Ohio

Dearest Twin,

The events of this past month are unreal, aren't they? Just a few weeks ago, Lynette and I were at Birchfields visiting Aunt Garnet in the peaceful English countryside, and now England is at war with Germany.

Mama is terribly upset. You know she lived in England for nearly ten years before coming back to Virginia and marrying Daddy, and still has lots of friends there. She has also traveled in Germany and remembers it as such a beautiful place, famous for its music and culture.

But she is mostly concerned because of Bryanne. She keeps saying that she wishes I'd brought her back with us when Lynette and I returned in June. But you know Aunt Garnet, Cara. She wouldn't hear of it. She said that one child was enough of a responsibility for me on a long ocean voyage and that she would bring Brynnie over herself later. Of course, that's out of the question now. With the Germans prowling the high seas, Aunt Garnet says it's much too dangerous to think of crossing the Atlantic.

As if that weren't all Mama had to worry about, Jeff still refuses to come back from New Mexico. Mama thinks Gareth should be in a more normal home situation, not living with a widowed father in an art colony. She thinks it's very bad for these three motherless children to be growing up in separate homes, under entirely different circumstances. How can they ever feel like a family again?

She's probably right. Brynnie has already acquired an English accent. Can you believe *that*?

It's hard to understand why these things happen, isn't it? How everyone could be so happy one minute, and the next, ripped apart by a tragic accident like the sinking of the *Titanic*. Remember how we used to think that Jeff and Faith and their children lived a kind of fairy-tale existence at Avalon? It was almost Camelot come to life.

How does Owen explain such things? As a minister, he ought to have more insight into the problem of pain in innocent lives than we do.

I still find it hard to think of you as a minister's wife, Cara. I just never imagined you teaching Sunday school and chairing the Ladies' Guild. I guess nobody else did, either. But when you said you'd follow Owen to the ends of the earth, I guess you meant it. Still, it's a good thing it was just to a little rural town in Ohio in a small country parish, not Africa, isn't it?

What did you think of the news that Jonathan and Phoebe Montrose have a baby boy? Kip seemed stunned that his father is starting another family. The christening was last Sunday—a lovely party at Montclair—and the baby is darling. They've named him Fraser, after Phoebe's oldest brother. Of course, she is disappointed that they had to call off their trip to Scotland because of the war. Also, she's worried about her nephews, all at an age for military service.

Things are as usual here. We miss you always. I don't think I'll ever get used to the idea of not having you near to talk things over with, or to wake up in the mornings and not see you in the next bed.

But I do know how happy you are, so that makes me happy, too.

Love, Kitty

Part I
Blue Skies

Mayfield, Virginia
Autumn 1914

Blue skies, smilin' at me,
Nothin' but blue skies do I see . . .
—a popular song

chapter

1

SUMMER FLOWED gently into fall, after lingering longer than usual in the Virginia countryside. The days were brilliant still, but darkness came more quickly now.

This autumn the colors were dazzling, the elms that lined the driveway up to Cameron Hall were golden against the dark green pines of the surrounding woods, the dogwoods were ruby-red and the maples on the lawn were butter-bright tinged with crimson. The gardens too were ablaze—saffron-yellow, russet, and amber chrysanthemums glistened like jewels in the September sunshine.

This was her favorite time of year, Kitty Cameron decided as she bent over her plants in one of the flower beds. Out in the crisp fall air, the combination of scents—ripening fruit in the orchards, distant wood smoke, the rich smell of earth—was exhilarating. Even the mundane chore of digging up tulip and gladiola bulbs for winter storage gave her enormous pleasure.

Rod Cameron, coming out onto the columned porch of the stately Georgian house that had been his family's home for generations, caught sight of his daughter. He stood at the edge of the steps and watched her work, her expression one of total concentration.

15

After a moment he strolled over, pausing beside her. "Must be in the genes."

Kitty smiled up at him. "Well, I *was* named for Grandmother, wasn't I?"

It was a family joke that Kitty's love of gardening must have been inherited from Katherine Cameron, who, in spite of having at least four gardeners at Cameron Hall during its "glory days," had insisted on doing much of her own work.

Looking into his daughter's upturned face, Rod was startled by a fresh recognition of how pretty she was. The sun, glinting on her auburn hair, enriched its vibrancy. One strand fell forward, and she brushed it back with an impatient gesture that left a smudge of dirt on her cheek. Her long-lashed eyes were softly brown, like his adored wife's. But where Blythe's face revealed the deep contentment of a long and happy marriage, there was something vulnerable about Kitty's that tugged at her father's heart.

He had tried to give his daughters everything possible to assure their well-being, but the one thing he had never been able to give them was happiness, so often found in unexpected places. Cara, Kitty's twin, was a prime example. She'd found hers in marriage to a penniless preacher! Unconsciously, Rod sighed. Impetuous and independent as she was, he missed Cara.

Turning his attention to Kitty again, he remarked, "I suppose you're right. As they say, 'blood will tell.'" Then with a wave he walked away, striding down the gravel drive toward the stables.

Kitty's glance followed his tall figure. Except for the slight limp, a token reminder of the wound he'd acquired during the War Between the States, her father appeared much younger than his sixty-odd years. He was still handsome with strong, aristocratic features, thick gray hair, an erect bearing.

16

Recalling her father's teasing, Kitty cast a brief look at the metal marker verdigrised with age, placed among the rosebushes years before by her grandmother and read the quotation: "The kiss of the sun for pardon,/the song of the birds for mirth,/You are nearer God's heart in a garden/Than anywhere else on earth." It spoke of her serene spirit, and Kitty was glad once again to be considered very like the other Katherine.

She returned to her digging, working steadily until she heard the sound of a motorcar roaring up the drive. *Kip,* she guessed, even before she saw the shiny green roadster round the bend of the driveway and pull up in front of the house, scattering gravel stones as he braked.

Kitty sat back on her heels and waved to him. "Good morning!"

Kip Montrose gave her an answering wave, then vaulted over the door of his open runabout and started over to join her.

At his approach, Kitty's heart flip-flopped foolishly. It happened every time, no matter how hard she tried to control herself. Everything about Kip—his saunter, the roguish smile, his tousled dark hair, the mischievous twinkle in his eyes—caused this ridiculous reaction.

Kitty felt her face grow warm. She ducked her head, pulled up a bulb, and pretended to focus on shaking the dirt from its root. "What are you doing up and about this early?" she asked with studied casualness.

"I'm about to let you in on a secret," he teased, grinning down at her.

Kitty looked skeptical. "What kind of secret?"

"What do you mean *what kind*? A secret's just that, a secret," he retorted. "Come on, 'Mary, Mary,' don't be contrary. Let your garden grow on its own for a while. I want to take you someplace."

"Oh, Kip, I can't," she protested. "I'm right in the middle of all this."

"Let it go," Kip demanded impatiently. "Come on, Kitty. Making mud pies can wait. This is important."

"And what I'm doing *isn't?*"

"Not as important as what I'm about to show you."

"Why are you being so mysterious? Why don't you just tell me? Let me decide—"

"Trust me, Kitty. Come on."

Slowly she dragged off her gardening gloves and brushed her skirt. Thrilled as she was that Kip wanted to whisk her away with him, she didn't want to appear too eager, ready to drop everything at his spur-of-the-moment invitation.

Feigning reluctance, she said, "Well . . . I'll have to change—"

"For Pete's sake, Kitty, you don't have to change!" Kip sounded exasperated. He grabbed her hand and pulled her to her feet. "You look fine. Just dandy."

Puzzled at his insistence, Kitty hung back. "Wait, Kip. I *do* have to tell Mother I'm leaving."

"All right. But hurry! We don't have all day!"

Kitty threw Kip a reproving look as she hurried past him, up the terrace steps and into the house. Kip was used to having his own way. She really shouldn't accommodate him so easily, she reminded herself. But, as usual, she didn't have the will to resist.

Inside, Kitty went to find her mother. Blythe was in her sitting room at her desk when Kitty stuck her head in the door and told her she was going for a drive with Kip.

Unbuttoning the brown canvas gardening smock, Kitty flung it on a chair and grabbed a cardigan sweater from the coat tree in the hall. With one hasty peek in the mirror, she gave an ineffectual pat to her hair, then ran out the front door and down the steps.

Kip was already behind the driver's seat, looking as if he were about to hit the horn. Seeing her, he reached over and opened the door on the passenger side.

"Where are we going?" she asked as they started off.

"You'll see."

At the end of the driveway, Kip shifted down and made a sharp turn onto the country road. They were soon bumping over the ruts at some speed. Hunched over the wheel, Kip was curiously intent on his driving, with none of his usual irritated comments about the road conditions or "Why didn't the county fund paving now with so many motor vehicles about!" Instead, he seemed wound up as if with suppressed excitement.

Suddenly, he jammed on the brakes and spun the wheel to the left, sending the vehicle bouncing down a lane that seemed hardly more than a cow path.

"Slow down, Kip, for goodness sake!" Kitty pleaded. "My teeth are being shaken out of my head!"

"Sorry, Kit! It's only a bit farther now."

"But where? This looks like a dead end to me."

Just ahead was a cattle gate. Kip slammed the brake pedal, then jerked the hand brake. Jumping out of the car, he walked over to open the gate and swing it wide. In a flash he was sliding under the wheel again, and they proceeded into an open field.

"Kip! We can't drive through here!"

"Don't worry, Kitty. It's all right."

She gripped the armrest as they plowed ahead over the uneven ground. Then straight in front of them she saw a large cleared space in the middle of the meadow. A few makeshift, weather-beaten sheds and a large barn-like structure stood at the end.

Kip brought the car to an abrupt stop and announced triumphantly, "Here we are!"

"Here we are . . . *where?*"

"Bell Park Flying Field."

"*Flying* field?" she echoed. "I don't understand."

"You will." Kip got out of the car. "Come see."

Kitty remained where she was, bewildered as to why he had brought her to this deserted place. While she was still wondering, the barn door slid back and a lanky man in coveralls emerged, wiping his hands on an oily rag as he walked out into the sunshine.

Kip waved and shouted to him. "Hiyah, Beau!"

"How's yourself, Kip?"

The two greeted each other like old friends. Kitty was puzzled as she observed them. She thought she knew most of Kip's friends, but this man was a stranger to her. Finally, as if remembering her, Kip jerked his head in her direction, and together they strolled back to the car.

Offhandedly, Kip introduced them. "Beau Chartyrs. Kitty Cameron."

At closer range, Kitty could see that the other man, in spite of his grease-smudged face, was quite good-looking. He grinned.

"Nice to meet you. Kip said he was going to bring you out soon."

The idea that Kip had discussed her with this stranger puzzled Kitty even more. Who was this fellow? And what was going on here?

"So, how's it going?" Kip asked Beau.

"She's a sweet little bird." Beau smiled. "I took her up this morning, and the engine's purring like a kitten." He paused, then asked, "I gather you want to take 'er up yourself, right?"

Kitty turned a startled gaze on Kip. He met it, his own eyes shining.

"You—you're going to *fly*?" Kitty was incredulous.

"Sure thing. I've been taking flying lessons for six weeks or more. In fact, I'm almost ready to take my test for a certificate to become a licensed pilot."

"Does your father know?"

"Not yet. Anyway, you're the only one I've told. So now you're in on the secret and can't say a word until I give you the green light." He fixed her with a fierce glare.

"Kip, that's not fair."

"Now, Kitty, don't turn all righteous on me. Besides, I wanted *you* to be the first to know, to see for yourself." He turned to Beau. "All set? Then let's go. Now, Kitty, this is a two-seater. Beau's an experienced pilot and he's going along . . . just in case—"

"Just in case of *what?*" she gasped.

"Don't worry, Miss Cameron. Kip's a natural," Beau reassured her. "He'll be fine."

Speechless, Kitty watched as the two men pushed the airplane out from the barn with the help of an even grubbier fellow in grease-spotted coveralls whom Kip called Mike. Then Kip shrugged into a leather jacket, donned a helmet-like cap, and after giving her a broad wink, pulled goggles down over his eyes and climbed into the front cockpit of the flimsy-looking little plane.

Beau clambered into the rear seat and signaled to Mike, who ran around in front and started spinning the propeller. It made such a roar that Kitty had to cover her ears.

She stood rigidly as the winged vehicle wobbled over the uneven grass down to the end of the field and made an uncertain turn. Then, before her eyes and with the engines making a huge racket, it began to race down the cleared path, faster and faster, until it lifted from the ground into the air.

"Oh, dear Lord!" she prayed aloud, clasping her hands tightly together in a heartfelt prayer.

Running out behind them, she followed the ascent of the plane as it climbed higher and higher into the blue September sky. Even as she tracked its progress, the plane seemed to be swallowed up in the clouds and finally disappeared from sight.

It all seemed like some kind of dream. When the two young men returned from their flight, Beau congratulating Kip on achieving a perfect landing, Kitty was still trying to take it all in. On the way back to Cameron Hall, she rode in shocked silence.

With the sinking of the *Lusitania* by a German submarine, in May 1915, all the tragedy and horror the two families had suffered in the *Titanic* disaster was brought vividly to mind.

The incident also served to point up the Germans' willful disregard of the basic rules of civilized warfare, the wanton pursuit of their power goals despite loss of innocent lives. Their determination to conduct unrestricted and intensified submarine warfare, regardless of neutral rights, persisted. The fact that 127 Americans had perished brought the United States closer to entering the European war on the side of the Allies. President Wilson, however, still refused to commit.

Kip was incensed. At the little café at the airfield, he and Beau discussed world affairs endlessly. "It makes me ashamed to be an American!"

Kitty was shocked. "Oh, Kip, you don't mean that!"

"Well, I *do!* Look, we owe France. *They* came in, sent men, money, volunteers to help us in our War of Independence, didn't they? It might even have been the turning point. The

22

British could have won! We might still be a British colony today if it hadn't been for France!" Kip banged his fist on the rickety table, causing their mugs to dance.

Beau, of course, agreed with Kip. But Kitty did not feel she knew enough about the situation to venture an opinion. She didn't want to take the opposite viewpoint from Kip on an issue that was so important to him. On the other hand, she had heard her father speak out strongly against America's intervention in a foreign war.

"It would be reckless and irresponsible for us to go in. President Wilson is right," Rod had said firmly. "Nothing is worth risking the lives of thousands of young men. Why can't people remember our own terrible war, the deep scars that have still not been erased? Any man who survived that bitter experience should applaud the President's decision." Rod added proudly—"You *know* he's a *Virginian!*"

Kitty knew, too, that there had also been opposing opinions about the war her father had served in. That war had pitted brother against brother, husband against wife. Whole families had been torn asunder over it. Kip's own grandfather and grandmother, Malcom Montrose and his wife, Rose, had been sadly estranged over the right and wrong of that war. She wasn't about to jeopardize her tenuous relationship with Kip by debating the issue!

So Kitty remained silent. War was a man's business. Men made war, fought wars. That's the way it had always been.

chapter
2

July 2, 1915

Dearest Twin,

Just a short note to tell you I'm taking Lynette to Cape Cod to visit Meredith. She's written so many times begging me to come for a visit, but there always seemed something to prevent my going. Last year, of course, I took Lynette to England to see her little sister at Aunt Garnet's. Now, with the war going into its second year, there's no telling when those two children will get to see each other again.

Mama has been real concerned about Lynette. She does seem sad sometimes, even though we all do everything we know to keep her happy and content. Father has been wonderful, has taken a real interest in teaching her to ride, and Lynette is doing quite well. She will soon be graduating from her beloved pony to a horse he has hand-picked for her.

Anyway, when Merry's last invitation came, it was decided that it would be good for Lynette to have a change of scene and that the sea air would do her a world of good. Summer is the best time for Merry to have us come, since Manuel is out on his fishing boat two and three days at a time, and she writes that she "longs for company." She is thrilled to have Lynette come, too, and says there are lots of children nearby to keep her company.

Remember our summer at Fair Winds? Well, of course you do! That's the summer you met Owen. I'll write from there, but I don't expect to hear from you. I know you're busy with Vacation Bible School. Good luck!

Love always, Kitty

When Kitty told Kip about her plans, he seemed not only surprised but angry.

"For the whole summer?"

"Not quite. A month or six weeks, actually."

"That's crazy! What in the world do you want to do that for!" he demanded.

"Kip! I don't understand why you're so upset. Merry's your own sister and my very best friend!"

"Well, but . . . why do you have to be gone so long?"

"For one thing, I haven't seen Merry in months, and we'll have a wonderful time together."

"Doing what?"

"What we always do at the Cape—swim, walk on the beach, *talk!* We have lots to catch up on."

Kip plunged his hands into his jacket pocket, pouting like a small boy. "Talk? For six weeks? That's ridiculous!"

"You don't understand. Men just don't." Kitty smiled and shrugged.

They were standing below the steps of Cameron Hall. Kip had just driven Kitty home from the airfield where they had spent most of the afternoon. Kip had been practicing landings and Kitty had sat in the little café, drinking coffee and holding her breath as she watched him.

"So, when are you leaving?" Kip asked.

"Next week."

"So soon?" Again he seemed offended. "Why didn't you tell me?"

"Kip, I'm sure I must have mentioned it. You just weren't listening."

He frowned, then said doubtfully, "I don't think so, or I'd have remembered—"

Kitty had to laugh. "Oh, Kip, your head is in the clouds so much of the time, you don't hear half of what's said to you!"

He gave her a doleful glance. "I'm going to miss you."

She shook her head. "No, you won't. You'll be too busy flying, taking engines apart with Beau."

"You're wrong, Kitty. I'm used to having you with me, riding out to the field with me, being there when I land and climb out of the cockpit. It means a lot to me that you understand, that you don't fuss or nag about it being dangerous or silly . . . which, of course, it isn't—" He paused, put both hands on her shoulders and stared down into her eyes. "Kitty, don't you know how special you are to me?"

With all her heart, Kitty wished Kip meant what he was saying. But deep down, she didn't believe he cared for her in the same way she cared for him. Not yet. Maybe he never would. She shouldn't put too much meaning into his words.

Sure, she was "special" to him. She was the one who had given him the proverbial shoulder to cry on when Cara left him for Owen, the one who sympathized, listened, bolstered his self-esteem, and encouraged him. She had comforted him when his mother had died so tragically on the *Titanic,* and tried to support him when he groped for new meaning in his life. She had been his friend. And she was wise enough to realize that "friend" might be all she would ever be to Kip.

Afraid she might betray her deeper feelings, Kitty leaned up and gave him a light kiss.

"And *you* are very special to me, Kip."

Then, with a casual wave, she turned and ran up the steps and into the house.

27

Besides, it might do Kip good to *really* miss her while she was gone. That is, if that old adage, "absence makes the heart grow fonder," is true!

chapter
3

Nantucket Island, Mass.
Summer 1915

THE CAPE SEEMED another world away, unchanged despite the seven years that had passed since Kitty and Cara had spent that last enchanted summer here. It even smelled the same—the salty tang of the sea air, the sharp aroma of geraniums spilling out of window boxes along the main street of town, the clean, wind-swept breeze.

Fair weather held long after Kitty's arrival with Lynette in tow, and they quickly settled into the leisurely pace of life in the Sousa house—a quaint sea-silvered "salt-box," as neat and orderly as Merry herself. Beyond a piled-rock fence, they could see the dunes, the dark blue ocean breaking in frothy foam onto the beach.

Occasionally Kitty felt a sad little twinge, aware that she had not yet found what both Cara and her friend had found—love given and returned in full measure. For Merry was lyrical about her darkly handsome Portuguese husband, Manuel, and the dimpled baby boy who filled her life.

A professional fisherman, Manny was usually up by dawn

and out on his father's fishing boat before the household stirred. And since his work sometimes took him away for two or three days at a time, Meredith and Kitty had plenty of time alone together.

Their days took on a pleasant pattern. Before noon, they took the baby in his carriage, a beach umbrella, blankets, and a picnic basket down to the beach. There was no lack of playmates for Lynette, for here other families from the cottages fronting the ocean gathered to while away the summer hours.

While the baby napped and Lynette joined her new friends to build sandcastles, search for shells, or wade near the shore, Meredith and Kitty had a chance to catch up on all the years since that enchanted summer.

Their long friendship dated back to childhood, and there had been few secrets between them. Meredith had sensed Kitty's love for Kip before Kitty was even willing to admit it to herself. Now they spoke freely about the things closest to their hearts.

"If Kip doesn't wake up and realize it soon, someone else will, Kitty!" Meredith declared. "You're much too special for someone not to fall madly in love with you and carry you off soon. *Then* my brother will be sorry!"

"You can't *make* someone love you, Merry. Kip thinks of me as a friend, someone he enjoys being with, someone he can trust. He doesn't think of me romantically at all—" She paused, then said haltingly, "I'm not sure he's ever gotten over losing Cara. Maybe he never will—"

Meredith shook her head. "That would never have worked, even if Cara had wanted it to. They were too much alike. Mama always said they were like flint and stone. Whenever they were together, sparks flew. Imagine what kind of a marriage that would have been!"

Kitty smiled pensively. Distracted for the moment by the shouts and shrieks of laughter on the shore where the children were splashing and rolling in the shallow waves, she did not reply to Merry's comment.

After nearly a month of sunshine came two days of overcast skies, rain, and high winds. The beaches were deserted, the ocean turbulent.

On one such afternoon, Lynette was invited over to play with some little friends at another cottage. While Merry was rocking Jonny to sleep, Kitty found herself alone in the small sitting room. Browsing through the bookcase for something to read, she came upon a photograph album. Reading its label, SUMMER 1908, she felt a clutching sensation in her heart. That was the summer they had all been together at Fair Winds, the rambling Victorian beach house that belonged to Meredith's grandfather, Colonel Kendall Carpenter. That summer held all sorts of memories for Kitty.

Curious, Kitty sat down on the floor, drew it from the shelf, and onto her lap. Almost reluctantly, she opened it. In Meredith's methodical manner, each snapshot was fastened in place by tiny black corners. Underneath, neatly printed in white ink, was the name, identifying the person in the picture and the date it was taken.

One of the first pictures Kitty came across was of herself and her twin, wearing identical middy blouses, sailor collars and ties, and pleated skirts, their hair whipped by the breeze off the ocean behind them. Looking at those laughing faces brought a lump into Kitty's throat. That had been the time when she and Cara had begun to tread their own paths, to find their separate selves. It was the summer of Cara's secret romance with Owen Brandt. Kitty could still feel the sting of that first separation, the first time her twin had ever shut her out of an important event. She was surprised to find that it still hurt.

There was a group picture of all the young people who had vacationed at the Cape that summer, several of them in makeshift costumes donned for one of the amateur theatricals they'd put on. As she studied that one, Kitty saw something she had failed to see at the time. Everyone was facing straight ahead, looking at the camera, except Owen and Cara. They were gazing at each other with such rapt expressions on their faces that a person would have had to be blind not to see that they were in love! But of course Kitty *had* been blinded by her own infatuation with Kip, so she was as surprised as anyone else when the truth came out.

Turning the page, she came upon a snapshot that made her heart stand still. Someone had snapped a picture of Kip in the sailboat. He was wearing a cable-knit sweater, his dark hair wind-tossed, his eyes squinted into the sun. There was that grin she loved so much—the white teeth, the tanned face. As she gazed at it hungrily, she saw another print of the same picture among several loose snapshots not yet pasted onto the page.

After a split-second's hesitation, Kitty picked it up and slipped it into her skirt pocket, telling herself that surely no one would miss it.

The first of August, Kitty left for New York City to be a bridesmaid in the wedding of a college chum, Babs Wescott, and her fiancé, Phil Bennett. Lynette was to stay with Meredith while Kitty spent a week on Long Island for the pre-nuptial parties and other festivities. After that, she would return to the Cape and she and Lynette would take the train back to Virginia in time for the beginning of school.

Lynette was delighted to extend her vacation, and Kitty

went off to meet another member of the wedding party in Boston. When she returned for Lynette, they knew at last that summer was over.

"I'm going to miss you both so much!" Meredith told them. "And I don't know what Jonny will do without his nanny." She took Lynette's face in both her hands and kissed the child's cheeks affectionately.

"Maybe we can come again next summer!" the little girl said hopefully.

"Yes! Please do!" Meredith looked at Kitty over the child's head.

Kitty hugged her friend. "Thanks for everything."

"I wish you'd let me give that brother of mine some sisterly advice," Meredith whispered.

"Don't, please. It's no good unless it's *his* idea."

"Can I help it if I want you for my *real* sister?"

Kitty sighed. "If it's to be, it will be," she replied. "I don't want it any other way."

Kitty got off the train at the Mayfield station a few days later and found Kip pacing the platform impatiently. When he saw her, he was beside her in an instant.

Before she had a chance to say "Hello," he was demanding, "Why did you stay so long? I mean, the wedding was two weeks ago, wasn't it? What were you doing so long in New York?"

Kitty's heart swelled with happiness. Then he *had* missed her! She had not dared think he would, busy as he was every day with his flying, tinkering with his obsession, the little plane he had dubbed "Bonnie Doon."

"I was doing some shopping . . . see?" She twirled about to show off the smart linen suit, touching the narrow brim of her braided silk hat.

33

"You look mighty fashionable, I admit. But you couldn't have spent all your time in stores. They do *close* at night, don't they?"

"Well, we went to some shows, too. Thax had tickets to the new Marilyn Miller revue—"

"Thax?" He scowled darkly.

"Thaxton Collinwood. You know him. A friend of Scott's and Phil's. He was one of the groomsmen in the wedding," Kitty explained. "He and Phil were roommates . . ."

"Oh, yes, I remember," he conceded, not too graciously. "He's a cousin of the Langleys, right?"

Could Kip possibly be jealous?

"Then we went to a *thé dansant*—that's an afternoon dance party to us provincials." Kitty laughed teasingly. "Babs's aunt gave one for the members of the wedding party at the posh Pierre Hotel. They're all the rage in New York now, and—"

Kip held up a restraining hand. "All right, enough! I don't need an itemized list of your social activities. I'm just glad you're back and we can get on with our life."

Our life? Kitty wondered just what Kip meant by that.

"Where's Lynette?" he asked, looking around as if he had just remembered the little girl.

"Mama met us in Richmond. She's taken Lynette to buy school clothes. Wait till you see her. She's grown a foot and is as brown as a berry."

"Well, then, I guess we're all set. I told your father I'd meet you and drive you home."

They were walking down the platform when Kip suddenly halted. "I've missed you like blazes, Kitty."

She bit her lower lip to control the surge of pleasure at his words. "Thanks, Kip. It's nice to know that one is missed."

When they reached the end of the platform, Kitty saw the

little green car parked at the curb. Kip opened the door on the passenger side and stood there absentmindedly.

"Kip, my bags—" she reminded him gently.

"Sorry, I forgot. Had something else on my mind. Wait here. I'll be right back."

Kitty laughed. "Of course, I'll wait! Where would I go?"

Kip was back within minutes, tossed her suitcase and hatbox into the back with abandon, and slid behind the wheel.

"Kitty, we've got to talk," Kip said firmly, shoving the car into gear and backing out of the parking space.

She felt her heart give another leap but spoke as casually as she could manage, "Oh, yes, how's the flying?"

"This is not about flying. It's about us."

"*Us?*" she croaked.

"Yes. You and me, Kitty."

She tried to look surprised, puzzled, but did not succeed. She could feel her lips part in a hopeful smile. "What about us?" she asked in a tremulous voice.

She looked over at Kip, saw the dear, familiar profile, the one she knew by heart. They were past Main Street now, turning onto the county road that led out to their neighboring plantations. Kip made the turn, pressed the accelerator, and they sped along until he made a sudden swerve off into a lane half-concealed by shaggy rhododendron bushes. Pulling on the brake, he stopped the car.

He turned toward her, one arm slid across the back of the leather seat. "You know I love you, Kitty." His eyes searched for some response. "You *do* know that, don't you?"

Kitty nodded slowly, not trusting herself to speak.

He rushed on. "I didn't realize how much until this summer. But it was this past month that I *really* knew. I don't want to be without you again. I don't want to lose you . . .

35

not to Thaxton Collinwood . . . not to *anyone*. Marry me, Kitty."

She started to speak but found she couldn't.

Kip reached for her hand. "What do you say?"

If she were smart, she'd hesitate, keep him waiting. But Kitty was much too honest. Besides, her ears ringing with what he had just asked, she felt a surge of joy that could not be denied.

"Kitty?"

Silly tears rushed into her eyes, but she could only nod. Then he took her in his arms and kissed her the way Kitty had long dreamed of being kissed, and she was lost in the ecstasy of the moment.

"Yes, oh yes," she murmured before his mouth covered hers again. She had waited so long for this. "Darling Kip, I love you so."

chapter
4
Winter 1915

Let me call you sweetheart, I'm in love with you,
Let me hear you whisper that you love me, too. . . .

And when I told them, they didn't believe me,
That from this great, big world you've chosen me.
      —from two popular songs

ON ONE OF THOSE brilliant mornings that come to Virginia in
early fall, each turning leaf—bronze, gold, and russet—
etched sharply against a vivid blue sky, Kip arrived at
Cameron Hall to take Kitty to Bell Park Field.

She had tried desperately to understand Kip's passion for
flying. She knew that he had always been restless, easily
bored, always looking for new challenges. Flying was the new
frontier for the bold, the adventurous, the young explorers. It
suited him, she had to admit. So she had gamely agreed to
accompany him twice a week to the airfield for his flying
lesson.

Today, however, she had other plans for them.

37

"Let's take a walk first. I have something to show you," Kitty said mysteriously when he appeared on the doorstep.

Uncharacteristically, Kip fell in with the plan, cocking an eyebrow inquisitively but obeying.

She whistled for Shamus, her Irish setter, and they set out down the drive. At the path leading into the woods, the dog took off like a red streak through the brush, then wheeled and bounded back to them before taking off again.

"Can't you tell me where we're going?" Kip asked.

"You'll see."

"I think you're trying to take your revenge," Kip teased.

Kitty did not reply but glanced up at him, eyes twinkling. They walked on quite a distance into the woods before she stopped.

"Close your eyes now. I'll lead you the rest of the way."

"Ah, Kitty, aren't we a little old for 'Blind Man's Bluff'?"

"Just be patient. It's only a little farther now." She took his hand and tugged gently.

They moved forward more slowly now with Kitty in the lead. The deeper they went into the woods, the more peaceful it seemed. Only the rustle of birds in the trees, the faraway sound of the creek rushing to the river, disturbed the deep silence.

When they came to a clearing, Kitty pulled on Kip's hand, drawing him alongside her. "You can open your eyes now."

A small house of white clapboard and mellow brick, the miniature of Montclair, stood before them, enveloped in sunlight. Dark blue shutters framed the eight-paned windows on either side of the fan-lighted door. A flagstone walk, bordered with late-blooming marigolds and purple asters, led up to the pocket-sized porch, and russet-red Virginia creeper climbed up the chimney.

"So this is your little secret?"

"Well, maybe not a secret . . . but almost forgotten."

"Eden Cottage."

"Yes." Kitty let out the breath she had been holding as she waited for Kip's reaction. "The traditional honeymoon house for Montrose brides—" She paused. "Kip, I want to live here. I mean, I want *us* to live here."

Kip stepped forward to look around. "Kitty, the place has been closed up for years. It's probably musty, full of mildew and mice."

She suppressed a little shudder. "But surely it can be cleaned up, painted, restored—"

Kip walked up on the porch, gripped one of the posts, peeled off a strip of paint, and shook his head, frowning.

"Oh, look, Kip!" Kitty pointed to the latticed arbor at the side of the house. Two built-in benches inside were shadowed by tangled vines, the leaves shimmering in jewel-like colors in the autumn sunshine. *What a perfect place for lovers to sit, sharing an intimate moment,* she thought.

But Kip had disappeared around the back of the house.

"The roof's been ravaged by squirrels, and the eaves over the windows look like they've nested generations of birds—" he called back.

"But it all *can* be fixed, can't it, Kip?" She caught up with him at the back door.

He gave her a long, reflective look. "You *really* want to live here?"

"Oh, yes, Kip, I really do!"

He brushed off the dust he'd accumulated and gave her a wide grin. "Well, then, consider it done. I'll talk to Pa and see about getting a consultation with a builder. We'll put a crew to work just as soon as possible."

"Oh, Kip, I love you so!" Kitty said, throwing her arms around his neck.

In retrospect, the only thing to mar her perfect happiness was Kip's seeming lack of enthusiasm. She wished he'd been the one to discover the little house and proclaim it the ideal place to start their life together. Wished he'd thought of carrying on the family tradition of spending the honeymoon year here. But what did it matter? At least, he had agreed to her plan. And they *were* going to be married and live happily ever after at Eden Cottage!

A few weeks later, Kip and Kitty were sitting in the small parlor at Cameron Hall. A fire blazed in the hearth, casting a warm glow over the room.

"Here, milady—the keys to the kingdom." Kip reached into the pocket of his tweed jacket and brought out a key ring from which dangled three old-fashioned brass keys. He took Kitty's hand, turned it over, and placed the keys in her palm. "Eden Cottage—all yours to do whatever your heart desires."

From his vest, he withdrew a legal-looking document. "It's all here in black and white, giving you the authority to contract for roofing, painting, whatever needs to be done. The deed to the house and the three surrounding acres are all in your name."

"But it should be in *both* our names, shouldn't it?"

He shrugged. "This just makes it easier when you're overseeing the repairs and restoration. You'll be on the scene, ordering paint, selecting the colors . . . all that sort of thing." He made a sweeping gesture. "We can change it after we're married."

Kitty's fingers closed around the keys. "Talk about dreams coming true." She sighed happily. "Ever since I was a little girl, I've always thought of Eden Cottage as some enchanted place, a fairy-tale house nestled deep in the woods, like the dwarfs' house in *Snow White*."

Kip looked puzzled.

"Didn't you read fairy tales when you were a child?" Kitty gasped.

"Guess not. Did I miss something?"

Kitty laughed. "Oh, Kip, darling! Never mind. We'll make up for it . . . we'll make up for everything . . . after we're married!"

"Well, just remember, I'm six-two, hardly a dwarf," he teased. "Just in case you're thinking of making any major changes in the ceiling height, that is."

Getting the house ready by June presented more of a challenge than Kitty had anticipated. In the first place, Montrose had stood empty for years, abandoned since Avril Montrose was married for the second time to Logan Cameron, and moved to Bermuda. Besides that, the structural restoration that had to be done took longer than anyone had foreseen.

In addition, since Avril had taken most of the furnishings with her, the house had to be completely refurnished. Kitty spent hours researching eighteenth-century materials to be used for curtains, haunting antique stores, and attending auctions. She wanted everything to be authentic, for the interior of the cottage to be as much like it might have been when it was built.

When she tried to interest Kip in helping her choose from swatches of fabric or pore over books of historical furniture, he proved irritatingly indifferent. "I haven't a clue about this sort of thing, Kitty." He threw out his hands helplessly.

"But you're going to live there, too. It's going to be *our* house, Kip, not just *mine*."

"Whatever you decide will be fine with me," he said firmly and that was the end of it.

The restoration of the little cottage became Kitty's project.

Much as she might have wished it were different, Kip rarely came over to inspect the progress of the work. Instead, he continued his daily trips to the flying field. She tried not to be jealous of Kip's preoccupation with flying, of the time spent away from her that they could have spent together, but it was hard when she wanted to be with him every minute.

Kitty comforted herself with the memory of a past experience, one that had made a deep impression on her. As girls, she and Merry Montrose had enjoyed wandering around the old tombstones in the cemetery behind the Mayfield church, reading the quaint epitaphs from long ago. One had stayed with her through the years: "What I gave, I have; what I spent, I saved; what I kept, I lost."

At the time, Kitty had not quite understood its meaning. But now, applying that bit of philosophy to her present situation with Kip, it made good sense. If she objected to his flying, made it into some kind of contest, made him choose, she would lose him. Just as Merry had confided to her how *she* felt about Manny's going out no matter what the weather, how afraid she was that there would be some kind of accident, that he would never come back.

"Finally, I knew I had to get rid of the fear. It was crippling me, crippling our marriage. For generations, the men in Manny's family have been professional fishermen. I knew that when I married him. I can't let my feelings spoil all the rest of our life together."

Wise words from her friend, Kitty thought. She'd have to learn to accept Kip's flying, too.

chapter
5

"WHEN DO YOU WANT to announce your engagement?" Blythe asked her daughter one morning at breakfast.

"Oh, I don't know, Mama. What do you think?"

"We could make the announcement at our annual New Year's Eve party. Or would you prefer a separate affair?"

"I think Kip's giving me my ring at Christmas—"

"Well then—" At Kitty's hesitation, Blythe took matters into her own hands—"since we'll need several weeks to make arrangements, maybe Valentine's Day would be nice. Such a romantic time to have an engagement party, don't you think?"

"I'll talk it over with Kip, then let you know." Kitty got up from the table, came around and kissed her mother on the cheek. "Thanks, Mama, for wanting to do so much for us."

"I just want you to be happy, darling."

"Yes, I know. And I will be ... I am—"

Blythe smiled. "Where are you off to?"

"Eden Cottage. The painters are coming today."

"Then have fun, dear."

From her place at the dining room table, Blythe had a clear view through the window. As she watched her daughter's slender figure walking down the driveway to take the woodland path, she thought of the little house in the woods.

43

Eden Cottage! What memories of her own that name evoked. It was there, during her disastrously unhappy marriage to Malcolm Montrose, that she and Rod had first recognized their feelings for each other. Although that love remained unspoken for many years, the cottage remained a special place.

The week before Christmas, Kip, at a loss to know what kind of present to give his stepmother, Phoebe Montrose, begged Kitty for help in selecting a gift. She was secretly pleased but teased him unmercifully, boasting that she'd had her presents bought and wrapped weeks ago.

He grinned sheepishly but had a ready excuse. "I hadn't the slightest notion what to get for her. Besides, you'd know how to please her better than I."

"Actually, Kip, I don't know her that well myself," Kitty replied doubtfully.

Of course, she remembered when the young Scotswoman had served as nanny the summer she and Cara spent in England as children. But Kitty had been away at college when Kip's widowed father had encountered Phoebe McPherson again in Scotland, had fallen in love with her and brought her home as a bride to Montclair. At first, the Montroses traveled a great deal. But now Phoebe was the mother of a toddler, living a very different life from Kitty's.

Kip suggested the city would have a bigger, better selection to offer than the Mayfield stores, so they left early one overcast morning to drive up to Richmond.

Leaving Kip's car in the parking garage of the fashionable hotel where they planned to have lunch later, they set out to shop. It was quite cold, and the wind blew in gusts, sending flurries of snow in a swirling dance about their feet as they

44

walked down the streets, gazing into the brightly decorated shop windows.

There was a bewildering variety from which to choose. By the time they had explored the third department store, Kip was ready to call it quits.

"We've been looking for hours," he complained. "Besides, I'm hungry. Let's go have lunch."

"But, Kip. We've barely started. Don't you have any ideas at all? Linens, china, crystal?" Kitty's voice trailed away. Montclair was already beautifully decorated, with many heirlooms passed down from previous generations of Montrose matrons. "What about something personal then . . . a silk scarf, a beaded bag—" Again she hesitated.

Kip's eyes brightened. "How about a piece of jewelry?" Once again in control, he took Kitty by the arm and propelled her down the street toward Simmons & Sons, a store on the next corner whose sign discreetly offered "Fine Gems, Estate Jewelry, Antique Reproductions."

Inside, the decor was understated elegance. Thick carpeting silenced their booted steps, and subtle lighting gave the place an atmosphere of hushed grandeur. The glass showcases were lined with mauve velvet with only a few selected pieces tastefully displayed.

A balding gentleman, splendid in a frock coat and striped trousers, a pair of pince-nez glasses perched on the end of a high-bridged nose, approached them.

"Good afternoon, may I be of assistance?" he asked in such a funereal tone that Kitty dared not glance at Kip for fear of giggling.

But Kip seemed equal to the occasion. To Kitty's surprise, especially in light of his initial uncertainty about Phoebe's gift, he responded confidently. "Yes, indeed. We'd like to see some of the estate jewelry, or perhaps some of your antique reproductions."

Kitty quickly stifled her urge to laugh, intrigued by the beautiful pieces they were shown. The salesman knew his jewelry and proceeded to tell them the history of each piece he showed them. One, in particular, caught Kitty's attention—a spectacular, deep blue sapphire ring surrounded by tiny diamonds in a gold setting.

Seeing the spark of interest in her expression, the jeweler spoke in reverent tones. "This is copied from a museum original. It is a reproduction of the engagement ring given by our Confederate President, Jefferson Davis, to his second wife, Varina."

"Oh, it's exquisite. Truly the loveliest ring I've ever seen." Kitty spoke in a near whisper. As a lover of history, especially the War Between the States, in which Virginia had played a part, she was fascinated by the story behind the ring.

Kip, however, seemed preoccupied. He was looking at a case displaying some necklaces and had missed the jeweler's discussion of the beautiful ring and its historical significance.

"What do you think, Kitty? Pearls?" he asked, spotting a nice strand in the case.

Kitty shook her head regretfully. "Sorry, Kip. I know Phoebe has pearls. She was wearing a double strand at baby Fraser's christening."

Kip looked discouraged. "Well, come on, then. I know she loves to read. Let's go to a bookstore. Maybe I can find her a book about Scotland."

Just then the jeweler cleared his throat and said diffidently, "Pardon me, but may I make a suggestion? Is this person of Scottish heritage, perchance?"

"Why, yes—"

"Then perhaps this—" He brought out a finely crafted

silver pin on which was sculptured a thistle set with a clear, lavender amethyst stone.

"Oh, Kip, look," Kitty breathed. "This would be the perfect gift for her. It's the symbol of Scotland, and I'm sure Phoebe would love it."

Kip was instantly agreeable. He asked the salesman to wrap the pin as a Christmas gift, and they were on their way.

In the hotel dining room, they dined on chicken *à la king*, rolls, and chocolate cream pie. Afterward, strolling through the hotel's arcade of fine specialty shops, Kip completed his shopping with a handsome leather writing case for his father and a cuddly Teddy bear for his little half-brother.

Kip was elated. "Now I have everything on my list. See how easy shopping can be! No problem to wait 'til the last minute!"

Kitty sent him a withering look. "You're hopeless!"

"Ah, Kitty, don't think I'm ungrateful. I'd never have been able to do this without you. Now let's go home."

"Don't forget. We have to go back to the jeweler's and pick up Phoebe's pin," Kitty reminded him.

"I'll tell you what. Since that's several blocks from here, we'll drive there. Then you can stay warm while I run in and get it."

Driving home, Kitty patted Kip's arm. "Well, that wasn't so bad, was it? Isn't it a satisfying feeling to find gifts that will please the people you love?"

"I hope so," he replied noncommittally.

In Mayfield, as they drove by the small Colonial church in the center of town, Kitty suddenly remembered her promise to deliver greens for the holiday decorations. Blythe had overseen the packing of the boxes, and Kip had placed them in the trunk of the car before they left for Richmond. But Kitty had almost forgotten they were there.

Kip followed her into the church, carrying the boxes of fragrant spruce boughs and holly, bright with red berries.

The ladies of the Auxiliary were still hard at work but greeted Kitty happily, exclaiming that they could always use more greenery. The choir was in the stalls, practicing Christmas carols, and the raftered sanctuary resounded with their joyous music.

Kitty and Kip emerged a short time later into a lovely purple dusk. A light powdery snow had fallen during the day and, driving through Mayfield, Kitty enjoyed seeing the houses adorned for Christmas with wreaths on the doors and glimpses of newly trimmed trees, their lights twinkling through the windows.

"Mayfield looks just like a Christmas card, doesn't it?" Kitty sighed happily. "I do love this time of year!"

It was already dark when they pulled up in front of Cameron Hall. Lights shone out onto the snow in welcome. When Kitty started to get out, Kip caught her arm and held her back.

"Aren't you coming in?" she asked. "I'm sure Mama's expecting you for supper."

"Yes, of course. But first, I have something for you."

"A Christmas present? But, Kip, it's too early. We always wait at least until Christmas Eve to open our presents."

"This is different. Besides, I picked it up today and, frankly, I can't wait till Christmas Eve to give it to you! I want to see if you like it."

"Of course I'll like it, Kip. I'd like *anything* you picked out for me."

"Yes, but this is special." She watched as he drew a small package out of his overcoat pocket. "I didn't want to give it to you in front of the others."

She took the small gilt-wrapped box, suspecting from its size what it contained, almost afraid to open it.

"Go ahead," Kip urged softly. "Open it."

With hands that shook a little, she undid the bow and carefully removed the wrapping. Inside was a gray velvet case bearing the name of Simmons & Son, Jewelers.

"Oh, Kip!" she gasped, looking at him.

"Go on, Kitty."

She pressed the spring that flipped up the top and saw within, glittering from its white satin nest, a sparkling sapphire surrounded by tiny diamonds.

"Oh, no, Kip, you didn't! It's Varina's ring!"

He was smiling broadly, obviously proud of himself.

Tenderness for him rose up within her. "How did you know? I didn't think you were paying any attention when I admired it."

"Nobody could have missed seeing your eyes light up, Kitty. I wanted you to have it."

"But you didn't say a word—"

"I only decided when we were there. But I wanted it to be a surprise. When I went back to pick up Phoebe's gift, I had the jeweler wrap it up for you. You *do* like it, don't you? I hope it's all right—"

His handsome face mirrored his sudden uncertainty. At the moment he looked so vulnerable, so like a little boy eager to please that Kitty hugged him impulsively. "Oh, Kip, it couldn't be *more* right! Here, put it on my finger."

"If it doesn't fit, the jeweler said we can have it adjusted."

She held out her left hand, and he slipped it on her third finger. It went on easily.

"Well, now, I guess it's official," Kip said. "We're engaged."

"Thank you, darling Kip. I can't begin to tell you how much this means to me."

"I'm glad, Kitty. You deserve the best."

She leaned across the seat, felt his cold cheek against her own, turned her face up for his kiss. His lips were warm, smooth on hers, and Kitty felt her heart soar. The kiss ended abruptly.

"Here, you're shivering. It's freezing out here. We'd better go inside."

Kitty hadn't noticed. She could have remained in his arms forever, but Kip had already hopped out and was running around to open the door for her. With his arm around her shoulders, they ran up the steps and into the house.

Kitty did indeed love her ring, but more important was what the ring symbolized. Kip must love her very much to have taken such pains to please her. He cared about her interests, what she liked, more than she'd realized. Though it *was* silly, she longed to *hear* Kip *say* more often that he loved her, but she decided that, with the ring, he had certainly *shown* her.

chapter
6

ON THE MORNING of the engagement party, the sky was heavy with clouds. The wind blew fiercely, and by afternoon a cold rain was coming down. Kitty peered anxiously out her bedroom window. If the temperature dropped and the rain turned to sleet, the roads leading to Cameron Hall would ice over, perhaps hindering the arrival of guests traveling from any distance.

At five, Kitty took her bath and, when she emerged into her bedroom, she saw that a fire had been lighted in her fireplace and a tray of tea and little sandwiches brought up for her. But she was much too nervous to eat.

Huddling in front of the crackling fire, she sipped her tea and tried to warm herself. But the chill seemed to penetrate bone-deep, perhaps more from anticipation than from the cold. Still, it seemed impossible that tonight her parents would be formally announcing her engagement . . . to Kip Montrose, the man of all her girlhood dreams!

Kitty gazed at her ring for long moments, turning it this way and that, the stones catching the fire's glow and refracting its light, winking and gleaming. As she had written in a letter to Merry: "I never quite believed that prayers like mine would be answered. It had always seemed too selfish, somehow too much to ask God to let Kip love me. And yet, wonder of wonders, it is true, and we are to be married in June!"

For a fleeting moment, Kitty wished Cara were here to share this evening. Then, quick to follow was a small, nagging admission that somehow her twin's presence might steal some of the shine from the occasion. This was *her* night, her moment. Immediately, she rebuked the unworthy thought. Still, she couldn't help recalling that once, not too long ago, Kip had thought himself in love with Cara.

At seven, Kitty took her dress out of its protective muslin cover. The rosy-gold satin shimmered in the firelight, igniting the tiny beads and crystals sprinkled over its tulle overskirt. It was the most beautiful gown Kitty had ever owned, even more stunning than she remembered it at her last fitting.

She was putting the tortoise shell combs in her upswept hair when a light tap came at the door, followed by her mother's voice. "Ready, dear?"

"Yes, come in, Mama." Kitty turned from the mirror as Blythe entered the room.

"How lovely you look! Kip will be dazzled."

As mother and daughter went down the stairs together, Kitty caught a glimpse of the transformation Blythe had created. Cameron Hall was a living Valentine! Bouquets of red and white roses in crystal vases had been placed under the mirrors on the marble-top tables in both parlors. The fireplace mantels and windows were festooned with red and white satin ribbons and bows, centered with lace-trimmed hearts and small gilt cupids. In the dining room, where later in the evening a buffet supper would be served, crystal candelabra held tall, twisted candles, and an elaborate floral arrangement graced the long table.

On the sideboard stood a three-tiered cake, decorated lavishly with swirls and pastry flowers on which Kip and

Kitty's names and the date, Valentine's Day, 1916, had been scrolled in sugared letters. At either end stood silver ice buckets cooling vintage champagne, awaiting the moment when the no-longer-secret announcement would be made.

Kip was standing at the foot of the stairs, talking with her father. His back was to her, and it was only when Rod's face lighted up at the sight of his daughter, that Kip turned.

He didn't speak but held out his hands, the gesture and the expression on his face speaking volumes. They had only a moment to smile at each other before Kip's father and Phoebe arrived.

"May I give my future daughter-in-law a kiss and welcome her into the Montrose family?" Jonathan asked as he and Phoebe greeted the honorees.

"Certainly." Kitty couldn't help thinking that in thirty years or so, Kip might look much like his handsome father, dark hair silvering at the temples, laugh wrinkles around his eyes.

Phoebe looked charming in an iridescent gray taffeta gown, and Kitty noticed that she was wearing the silver thistle pin on her shoulder.

"I love it," Phoebe confided as she greeted Kitty, then leaning forward, she whispered, "I'm sure you had a hand in selecting it, so thank you. It prompted Jonathan to give me these." She touched the delicate amethyst pendants swinging from her ears. "My Valentine gift from him."

"They're lovely!" Kitty was sincere in her admiration but felt a twinge of regret that Kip had not given her anything to mark the day.

Her momentary disappointment was fleeting because a moment later, Kip held out his hand to her. "Care to dance?" And he led her into the drawing room where the floor had been waxed for dancing.

The small band had been given all Kitty's favorite songs to

53

play. As Kip held her in his arms, they began playing "They Wouldn't Believe Me." She had always loved the lyrics to that song and, as they moved together to the music, Kitty could not help humming along with the melody. In a way, being here with Kip for the announcement of their engagement had the quality of make-believe. Some of the unsettling nervousness she had experienced earlier seemed to drift away with the music, and she knew that nothing mattered but being with him.

"Oh, Kip, I'm so terribly happy."

He smiled down at her. "I'm glad. You're absolutely shining tonight."

"Where do you think we should go for our honeymoon?"

He seemed puzzled. "Go?"

"Yes, after the wedding. Have you thought where we should make reservations? We really ought to do it since so many places book ahead."

Kip frowned. "I thought that's what all the renovating of Eden Cottage was about . . . for our honeymoon."

"*That's* where we're going to *live,* Kip. It will be our *home*. A honeymoon is different. That's when a couple gets away together, just the two of them, to get acquainted—"

"Acquainted?" Kip looked astonished. "Good grief, Kitty! We've known each other all our lives!"

Kitty laughed. "I know that. But we have to learn to know each other . . . as husband and wife—"

Kip shrugged. "Well, sure, but I don't see exactly why we have to go off somewhere. Everything and everyone we know and enjoy are right here."

Kitty looked startled for minute. "Maybe I'm being selfish, but I just thought we'd go somewhere without a flying field nearby!"

Kip threw back his head and laughed. "Ouch! I guess I deserved that. But I had no idea you were so devious."

"That's it exactly! There's a lot we don't know about each other. That's what a honeymoon is for . . . to get to know *everything* about each other."

"Oh, all right, I get it. So where would you like to go? The mountains or the seashore?"

Kitty was on the verge of answering when Rod tapped Kip on the shoulder. "May I dance with my beautiful daughter?"

Kip handed Kitty to her father, and for the remainder of the evening, the subject did not come up again.

The week after the engagement party, Kip suggested that the two of them go out for a quiet dinner. With several parties having already been hosted for the newly engaged couple, the two had been surrounded by people ever since the announcement of their forthcoming marriage, and Kitty welcomed the chance to spend some time alone with him.

He had chosen a new restaurant with a provocatively intimate atmosphere. Alcoved banquets upholstered in smooth, supple leather circled the room. Small peach-colored lamps shaded the tables, and in the corner a trio was playing soft music, creating exactly the right mood for a romantic evening. Kitty looked at Kip and smiled. How clever of him to choose this place.

When they were seated, Kitty studied the menu, glancing up occasionally to steal a surreptitious look at Kip's handsome face. She had never been so happy.

Kip ordered for them—an extravagant meal, explaining to the waiter, "It's a special occasion." And Kitty could not help thinking, *It's always a special occasion when I'm with Kip*.

They watched the waiter collect the menus with a flourish.

Then, with a stiff little bow, he left them to their conversation.

Kip leaned his arms on the table and cocked his head, giving Kitty a slow smile. "I have something to tell you . . . but I didn't want to spoil our evening."

"How could you possibly spoil it?" Caught up in the euphoria of the moment, Kitty was oblivious to any hint of trouble in Kip's words.

"I mean . . . we're supposed to be celebrating—" He seemed tentative, then added in a rush—"but you know how I feel about flying. You're the *only* one who does understand what flying means to me."

Kitty felt a small stab of disappointment. She hoped they were not going to talk about flying. Not tonight.

But he couldn't read her thoughts, and she was careful not to reveal her discomfort, so he went on. "Have you ever heard of the Lafayette Flying Corps?" The excitement in his voice was unmistakable.

She searched her memory. "Ye–es. I think I've read something about it in the newspapers."

"Well, then, you know that it's a single squadron composed of fifteen men. The Corps that was built up from this unit is a larger organization. A hundred or more Americans enlisted in the Foreign Legion for the duration of the war, then transferred to the French Flying Corps and are serving as part of the French army at the front."

"What has all this to do with you?" she asked, her heart already beginning to flutter with apprehension.

"Well, it's a fairly simple matter to join. Especially for someone who's already certified . . . I mean, someone who's been flying as much as I have."

Afterward Kitty told herself that she knew it was coming, knew what Kip was going to say even before he told her. She should have been prepared, but as she was to learn later, one is never prepared for some of the most important events in life.

Watching her closely, Kip took advantage of the pause. "Well . . . I've signed up with the Lafayette Escadrille—the outfit of American volunteers who'll be flying reconnaissance for the French Army."

Kitty's hand froze, holding her water glass halfway to her mouth, the ice tinkling against the crystal. She tried to respond but found her tongue frozen, too.

When she could speak, she asked the inevitable question, "When?"

"No more than three weeks at the most," Kip said, apparently relieved to have the news out at last. "All you need is a passport, which, of course, I have. Then fill out an application . . . Well, it's really quite simple, I'm told. While all the paperwork is being approved, you get your doctor to declare you fit . . . and that's all there is to it. Next thing you know, you're in France!"

"France?" Her stomach lurched, all desire for food vanishing.

"Yes, just imagine, Kitty! I won't be here champing at the bit on the sidelines of what's going on in the world. I'll be *part* of it. There aren't that many experienced aviators, so I've learned. I mean, the French are way ahead of us, and unfortunately, so are the Germans. But we'll soon catch up, give them a run for their money." His words were spilling out fast as his enthusiasm mounted. "It's a dream of an opportunity. How many people on this earth ever get to realize their dreams?"

Not I, Kitty thought dismally. Nor did it seem likely that her dreams would be realized any time soon. And what about the dreams they shared—marriage, home, family? Had he already forgotten?

Then, as if suddenly aware of what this decision would mean to her, to *them*, Kip looked anxious. "You see why I *must* go, don't you, Kitty?"

A hundred reasons why he shouldn't raced through her mind while Kip searched her eyes, begging her to reassure him, to let him go freely. But everything within her resisted. Now, when the happiness she longed for was just within her grasp, it was being snatched from her. Then a sobering thought broke on her consciousness. What if she did not give Kip her blessing? Wouldn't he go anyway? Either way, he would be lost to her.

"You do understand, don't you, Kitty?"

No! She didn't understand! She couldn't! *What about us, our wedding, Eden Cottage, all our plans?* She bit back all the arguments on the tip of her tongue.

Instead, she batted her eyelashes, mimicking one of those cupie-doll moving picture starlets. "I suppose you'll wear a blue uniform with a red-lined cape and visored hat, and look positively dashing."

Kip laughed. "You *are* marvelous, Kitty! I knew I could count on you." He reached across the table and took both her hands in his. "Of course, this means we'll have to postpone the wedding. But I don't think it will be long. This war can't last forever."

The night before Kip was to leave, Kitty found it impossible to sleep. Twice she turned on the light to check the clock on her bedside table. Finally, she gave up, pulled on her robe, and slipped quietly downstairs and out to the kitchen to warm some milk, hoping that would help her feel drowsy.

Still, she was almost afraid to go to sleep, fearful of the

recurring nightmare—one from which she always awoke, shaking and perspiring. She could never remember the details, except that at the point when she was jolted awake, she had seen a plunging rocket of fire.

Even after she went back upstairs to bed, she tossed and turned, awaking at dawn, exhausted.

Kip had arranged to say his good-byes to his father and Phoebe at Montclair, then would come by Cameron Hall, where he would collect Kitty and have her drive him to the station. He would be leaving his runabout with her in his absence.

Beneath the surface seriousness of his demeanor, Kitty sensed an underlying excitement. Here, at last, was the moment. Kip was on the brink of the highest adventure he could have imagined.

Kitty had already decided she would not spoil his image of her nor dampen his own high spirits by betraying the pain of this parting for her.

When they reached the Mayfield station, the train for Richmond and Washington, D.C., was already on the track. After parking the car, they walked onto the platform, then stood awkwardly, knowing they had only minutes to say all they had to say.

Kip put his hand under her chin and lifted her face so he could look into her eyes. "Well, this is it, darling. Now, I don't want you to worry."

She forced a bright smile. "Of course not!"

The conductor's call rang out, "All aboard!"

Kitty felt the edge of panic. She reached up and touched Kip's cheek. Her voice trembled as she pleaded softly, "Say it, please, Kip. Say you love me."

"Of course I love you, Kitty. I always have. I always will."

He kissed her. She closed her eyes, brimming with tears,

and clung to him, wondering how long it would be before she felt those strong arms around her again. Then she felt him pull back gently.

"Good-bye, Kitty. I'll write."

"Yes, I will, too."

The train whistle blew, and Kip looked over his shoulder. Kitty could tell that he was already thinking of the adventure ahead of him. "Gotta go."

He backed away a few steps, then turned and hurried toward his coach. The conductor had picked up the small yellow mounting stool and was preparing to board. Seeing Kip, he motioned him on. Kip broke into a loping run and swung up into the train. Leaning out, a wide grin on his face, he waved at her.

Kitty stood watching the train chug down the track, gradually gaining speed until it disappeared around the bend. The tears she had so valiantly checked, now spilled down her cheeks.

Overnight, it seemed, she had discovered what it really means to love someone. *Love means being willing to sacrifice one's own desires and goals for the beloved,* she thought, *even one's own needs.* She had let Kip go when everything in her cried out to hold him close. She had freed him to leave her and chase his dream. Even though she had always loved Kip, she had not realized before today how much love could hurt.

She walked back to the car in a daze, the echo of the train whistle as it crossed Mayfield bridge sounding hauntingly in her ears. Now she could release the tension of "keeping her chin up," of not giving in to her last-minute impulse to beg Kip not to go. He'd have hated it if she'd made a scene, but it had taken all her will not to.

Kitty got into the shiny green runabout, gripping the steering wheel, and leaned her forehead against it for a long moment. The rest of the day, the next week, month or who knew how long, stretched ahead of her in infinite emptiness. How could she bear it? What if the war lasted longer than anyone expected? And what if Kip didn't come back?

Finally she lifted her head, fumbled in her handbag for the car keys. She drew them out and held them, looking down at them in her open palm. The keys to Eden Cottage were attached to the same ring. Kitty felt her throat tighten. The keys to all her dreams, all she had hoped for, all she had wanted in life now seemed to exist in a dim and distant future.

What could she do? Wasn't there some way she could spend this waiting time usefully? Do something that would make Kip proud of her, something in the same cause he believed in so fervently? Something for poor Belgium, for France? Something that might even in a small way help bring the war to an end sooner?

But how? What? She must think, find a way. Kitty turned the key in the ignition, and the car pulsed to life. Suddenly, even as worn out as she was from tension and lack of sleep, Kitty's mind seemed clear. What was she good at? What came almost naturally to her? With remarkable clarity, Kitty began to remember her childhood—the parade of pets, the cats, the puppies, the birds that had fallen out of nests. All of these she had tenderly cared for and nursed to health—

In a war there was always a need for nurses. There were always the wounded, the injured and sick to care for. Kitty had read about Florence Nightingale, the valiant English woman called "the angel" of the Crimean War, who revolutionized the profession of nursing.

The more she thought about it, the more excited she became. Of course, she would have to take training. But what better way to use her time while Kip was away? And maybe

61

. . . just maybe, it would be possible to go to France. Surely, they would welcome American aid.

As she started down the road back to Cameron Hall, she could foresee only one obstacle—her parents. Would they object, try to stop her? Knowing her father's politics, how he deplored the idea of the States becoming embroiled in European battles, she felt a first wave of doubt.

He had certainly been outspoken enough, voicing his opinion of Kip's decision to fight for the French. "It's none of our business!" Rod had said. "It's not our war. The Germans and French have hated each other and fought among themselves for years. Let them settle their own affairs!" He was adamant. There had been no use arguing, no trying to convince him that for humanitarian reasons and in the name of Christian charity, America had an obligation to help.

Well, I'll cross that bridge when I come to it, Kitty told herself. First, there were other things to do, such as write for information about nurses' training.

Part II
Till We Meet Again

1916

Smile awhile, I'll bid you sad adieu.
When the clouds roll by, I'll come to you.
Until then, I'll pray each night for you . . .
Till we meet again—
        —from a popular song

chapter
7

On board the French steamer *Bonhomme*

Well, Kit, I'm really on my way. I could hardly believe it when I stood at the rail and saw the New York skyline drop away and knew I was actually en route to Bordeaux, from there on to Paris, and then to the secret air field "somewhere in France," where we'll be training.

I've met a great chap on board who, incidentally, is from California and on his way to join up with the Escadrille, too! What a bit of luck, right? His name is Vaughn Holmes, and he's about my age, although from an entirely different background. He's a real "cowboy." His family owns a ranch in the Central Valley, and he's practically grown up on a horse. At least, we have that in common, and, of course, our interest in flying. He's done a lot more reading and studying than I have about airplanes and the kind of equipment the French and Germans are using. I've already learned a great deal from him, although he's not yet actually flown. He'll get all his basic stuff from our French instructors, so I feel I have a leg up in this regard.

Vaughn also told me that the French airmen have been flying the Spad, a powerful one-seater that is the equivalent of the plane I checked out on in the States.

There are some French citizens on this ship, and at first they appeared to be somewhat aloof, even hostile, to the few of us

Americans traveling with them as fellow passengers. However, as soon as it was circulated via the ship's grapevine that Vaughn and I were on our way over to join up with the Flying Corps, their attitude changed dramatically. We are now looked upon as something of heroes! Sentiment seems to run high that it would be in America's best interest to come in and help defeat the Germans—

*   *   *

Paris, France

Dear Kit,

Know you would probably like more details about this place, the current fashions, art exhibits, etcetera, but I'm trying to concentrate on getting started with my training now that we're at last on French soil. Vaughn's father, I learned, has some friends in the diplomatic service here, and they took us out to see the sights. It was raining most of the time, and my sense of Paris at night is like a French Impressionist painting—vague and indistinct. They also invited us to dinner, and the French cuisine is everything it's cracked up to be! We're now waiting to get instructions on when, where to report—

*   *   *

Ecole Militaire D'Aviation, near Bourges

Well, Kitty, I'm here at last! And plenty ready to start flying. Even though I have my American certificate, I still have to go through the training steps here to qualify for a commission. I will be flying the neat little Blériot that I've had practice on in the States. It's a one-seater, so the pilot's in full control—start to finish—with no instructor with dual controls to take over. They feel that better pilots are produced with this machine.

Don't worry if you don't hear from me regularly from now on. Our daily routine is really full—every minute spent either studying or flying. My French is improving, but there is a whole new jargon emerging with the aviators.

We live in barracks—three big rooms, a hall dividing, shower at far end. There is a canteen on the field, a gathering place for the pilots, food strange but passable. I was relieved to find some very experienced men here, have been in the war since 1914, some Spaniards and Englishmen along with French. I'll be picking up a lot of tips from them. The conversation is an odd mix of languages, but all on the same subject—flying. We're all obsessed with it. But believe it or not, I'm doing a lot of listening!

Vaughn, it seems, is a born pilot. After only a few lessons, he's already got the hang of it. I think we'll move on to the next step together. It's a fine experience to be surrounded with men who have the same goal as I, to whom flying is more than some kind of hobby, as it is considered by most of the people we know, Kitty. Here it is serious business, and everyone is convinced it's the wave of the future and that, after the war, it will change the way the world thinks about transportation. Give my best to all your family.

As hungry as Kitty was for news from Kip, these were not the letters she had longed to receive from him. Even though she was interested in the new life he was living, Kitty yearned for one word of love, some hint that he missed her, regretted even a little bit postponing the life they had planned together.

To be fair, she realized that Kip was completely absorbed in the adventure, the thrill of it all. He wrote of the daily schedule, the camaraderie with the other men, the hours of study, the constant flying. She believed him when he said he was sometimes too tired to eat at night, just fell exhausted onto his cot to sleep only to be awakened at dawn to start the whole routine all over again. He never once mentioned the danger. But Kitty knew that it existed and that every time he went up, he risked injury or death.

Only once had he mentioned something about his life "before" in Virginia. He wrote that one of the fellows had an old gramophone, but only a few records that he played over and over, nearly driving the rest crazy. Kip said he had dreamed about being at a dance during that last Christmas he was home, hearing the music they'd danced to, only to find upon awakening that it was "that blasted, scratchy phonograph." Then he went on to say, "All the fellows complain about it. Sometimes, when it goes on too long, they throw boots, towels, and everything they can find in its direction to stop the music. But short of destroying it, which nobody has the heart to do, we put up with it."

Kitty read the short, scribbled notes again and again, trying to feel close to him. But Kip was living in a world Kitty knew nothing about. The longer he was gone, the more isolated she felt.

That made it equally hard for her to write letters to him. Everything in her daily routine seemed so dull, so tame compared to the life-and-death immediacy of the life Kip was living. America—safe, well-fed, going about its business as usual—was not an appropriate topic for a man living on the edge.

Oh, there was some effort to lend a hand, some activities planned to show interest and compassion for the cause. The church packed boxes of clothing for Belgian orphans and refugees, and the Red Cross held fund drives for medical supplies to be sent overseas. These facts she reported in her letters to Kip, but she kept to herself that life in Virginia went on as though men across the waters were not fighting and dying.

The thought she had had the day that Kip left kept returning to her in increasing intensity. Kitty decided to keep quiet about her plan for a while rather than risk an avalanche of negative arguments to dampen her own enthusiasm for the idea. In the meantime, she wrote to several nurses' training schools for information about qualifications and requirements for entry.

To become a certified nurse, all seemed to demand a commitment of three years of study and a year of actual hospital experience. Kitty realized that being a graduate of one of these schools was probably a requisite for joining the Army Nurse Corps.

A little disheartened, she put the brochures away in her desk drawer to give the idea more thought. She did see, however, that the Mayfield Red Cross Center was giving a six-week course in First Aid and Home Nursing and enrolled in it.

Then something unforeseen happened to replace Kitty's worries about Kip with a more immediate concern.

Late one winter afternoon, when she was trying to compose a letter to him, keeping it optimistic and cheerful, Lynette slipped into her bedroom.

"Kitty—" she began plaintively.

"Yes, honey," Kitty replied automatically, not looking up from her desk.

"Kitty," the little girl said again, coming to stand beside her.

"I'm busy now, darling. Why don't you go play?" Kitty suggested absently.

Lynette placed her small hand on Kitty's arm.

"Don't jiggle me, hon, I'm writing to Kip."

The little girl gave a deep sigh that merged with a racking cough.

"My stars! That sounds awful!" Kitty exclaimed, dropping her pen and turning to look at Lynette.

The child was flushed, her eyes glazed.

Kitty touched Lynette's cheek with the back of her hand. "Why, honey, you're on fire!" she declared. "I think you have a fever."

Lynette nodded solemnly. "I don't feel good."

"I guess not. We better take your temperature and get you into bed." Kitty stood and took Lynette by the hand. "Where did you get such a cough, I wonder?"

Lynette shook her head. "I don't know. I just did."

She settled the child in Cara's twin bed, then went to tell Blythe that she had moved Lynette into her bedroom so she could look after her in case she awoke during the night. Since Kitty had so recently passed her Red Cross home nursing course, she was glad for a chance to use her newly acquired skills.

She expertly applied a hot mustard plaster to ease the congestion in Lynette's chest, then brought her a drink of warm lemon-and-honey to sip.

"You'll be well in a day or two, honey," she assured Lynette as she tucked the bedclothes around her. The child was still shivering, however, and Kitty put a down comforter on top of the blankets.

Lynette stretched out a hot little hand. "Stay with me till I fall asleep, Kitty, please?"

"Of course I will." Kitty drew up a chair beside the bed. "Would you like me to read to you?"

Lynette moved her head slightly in an affirmative nod, and Kitty got out a favorite storybook from her own childhood and began to read: *The Secret Garden*, Chapter One, "When Mary Lennox was sent to Misselthwaite Manor to live with her uncle—"

When she had read five or six pages, Kitty looked over the top of the book and found Lynette's eyes closed. She put a marker in the page and laid the book aside. Leaning over the bed, she frowned. She didn't like the sound of Lynette's hoarse breathing.

During the night Kitty got up several times to hover over the sleeping child, troubled by her labored breathing, the periodic racking cough. Had they caught this cold in time to keep it from developing into bronchitis, or worse?

By morning, however, when the fever had not broken, Kitty suspected that the child was seriously ill. After consulting with Blythe, it was decided that Dr. Rankyn must be called.

"I'll stay with her until he comes. I'll try to get her to drink more liquids," Kitty told her mother and hurried back up the stairs.

Returning to the bedroom, Kitty was alarmed to find that Lynette had awakened but was rambling deliriously. When the doctor arrived and examined her, Kitty's worst fears were realized. Pneumonia!

That day Kitty took her post by Lynette's bedside, a post she barely left for the next two weeks except for brief periods of rest. It was an anxious fortnight for the entire household, particularly because of Lynette's "orphaned" position. With her mother dead, her father thousands of miles away, all the responsibility was upon Blythe, Rod, and Kitty as the child's condition worsened.

Each time the doctor came, he looked grave, making little comment other than "We'll have to wait and see—" Small comfort to the three adults who shared the nightly vigil in the long hours. Not only were they wrenched with anxiety but by the grim prospect of having to bear yet another family tragedy.

Gradually the prayers and skilled care pulled Lynette through. The crisis was reached and safely passed. The family could breathe again as Dr. Rankyn assured them of Lynette's full recovery.

To Kitty's surprise, in front of her parents, Dr. Rankyn praised her excellent sickroom care, then shocked her further by asking abruptly, "Have you ever considered nursing as a profession?"

This confirmation fueled Kitty's desire to pursue nurses' training just as soon as possible. Too much time had already elapsed since Kip left. With no end of the war in sight, no possibility of Kip's coming home anytime soon, if she wanted to see him, she would have to go to him . . .

chapter

8

IT WASN'T LONG after Lynette's recovery was well underway that Kitty learned that Kip had received his commission in the French Flying Corps. And the next communication she received from him was a letter written on the stationery of a Paris hotel.

September 1916

Vaughn and I are here on our first leave as full-fledged officers. His dad's friends are entertaining us royally. Already they've taken us out several times—to cafés, to restaurants for superb meals, to the Opera Comique, and to a play, in French, of all things! But I'm getting better at understanding the spoken language, at least. And there were French people in the company to translate what we didn't get, so it all worked out fine.

We've run into some other aviators in Paris on leave, and when we do, we have a regular gabfest. Some of these men are real "aces" with many downed German planes to their credit. Some of them are very superstitious and each have their eccentricities, mascots, and insignias. All are nonchalant about their exploits. But beyond their careless manner is a courage and gallantry that's rare.

We've learned that there is a code of honor that exists among pilots, Germans as well as French and English. For example, if a plane is shot down over enemy territory, as a courtesy, one of the opposing force's planes flies over the next day and drops a stone on a long, white ribbon with the name of the pilot and the number of his plane. Almost like the knights of old!

There is, of course, a great horror of being captured, as rumor has it that the German prisoner-of-war camps are terrible. Now, don't immediately begin to worry! There is little chance of that in my case. I'm becoming a better pilot all the time, full of confidence in myself and my trusty plane. Yours ever, Kip.

Don't worry! Easy enough for Kip to say, Kitty thought. He had no idea how many sleepless nights she'd spent, her imagination running wild. She was more determined than ever to get her training and go to him.

Then, before Kitty could consult her parents about her plan, a telegram arrived from Jeff Montrose. Her half-brother would be returning with Gareth, now twelve, from New Mexico, where they had been living almost since Faith had died as a result of the sinking of the *Titanic.*

The telegram announcing their imminent arrival sent Blythe into a flurry of activity. Avalon, Jeff's nearby island home, had been closed up for nearly three years and his unexpected announcement had given them little time to get it ready for occupancy again. Naturally, Kitty helped her mother in every way possible. This meant almost daily trips to Arbordale, overseeing the cleaning operations, stocking the kitchen and pantry, and hiring a staff.

After their arrival, Jeff and Gareth stayed at Cameron Hall for a week while Blythe fussed over them, trying to persuade her son to let Gareth live with them, at least during the week. He could attend Brookside Prep and get reacquainted with his little sister, from whom he had been separated since their mother's death.

Brother and sister were overjoyed to be together again. At

last Jeff was persuaded to follow Blythe's suggestion, but not before a compromise was reached. Jeff insisted that both children come to him at Avalon on weekends.

"I've got to get my family, my life together again, Mother," he said to Blythe, passing a hand wearily across his forehead. "Make a home for my children and start painting again."

He didn't mention Bryanne, and Kitty, listening, almost asked about the child. Then she thought better of it. Jeff had enough to deal with at the moment. Besides, since the sinking of the *Lusitania,* it was far too dangerous to think of crossing the Atlantic and bringing his other little daughter to Virginia. Bryanne would have to remain with Aunt Garnet at Birchfields, as safe a place as any in England these fearful days.

Life in Mayfield went on as if there were no war raging in Europe. The fall hunt and the social events surrounding this season were held as usual, with dinner dances on weekends at the country club.

In November, Kitty helped her mother, who was chairwoman of the Ladies Guild, plan the Thanksgiving tea to be given at Cameron Hall. The following Sunday at church came the announcement of a twice-weekly choir practice in preparation for the special Christmas services.

For Kitty, these holiday events to which she used to look forward with anticipation seemed hollow. Without Kip, there was no meaning in much of anything. Mixed with this unseasonal melancholy, Kitty had to admit some resentment. If he had not gone into the Lafayette Escadrille, they would have been married and spending their first Christmas in the cozy little house in the woods.

She had stopped going over there, unlocking the door and walking around inside. It made her too sad, too depressed, and since he had never taken much interest in fixing up the

75

little house, Kip seemed even farther away. So she didn't go any more.

A week before Christmas, Kitty was busy wrapping presents when Blythe stuck her head in the bedroom door. "You have a visitor."

"Who is it?" she asked, but Blythe had disappeared, leaving Kitty mystified.

Puzzled, since she wasn't expecting anyone, Kitty hurried downstairs. To her surprise, she found Thaxton Collingwood in the drawing room.

"Thax!"

"Hello, Kitty. Surprised to see me?"

"Of course, but delighted, too! What are you doing here?"

"I've come to spend the holidays with my cousins, the Langleys." He grinned. "Hope I'll have a chance to see you while I'm here. That is, unless you're all booked up," he said cautiously. "There's a rumor you're engaged."

"Yes, that's right. To Kip Montrose. He's in France. He joined the Lafayette Escadrille, a branch of the French Flying Corps."

Thax looked relieved. "Well, then . . . if you don't think he'd mind, I'd like to take you to some of the parties . . . in particular, the Langleys' Christmas Eve shindig."

"I'd love that, Thax," she replied, genuinely pleased. Kip wouldn't mind. In fact, he'd probably be the first to suggest she keep busy so that she wouldn't miss him so much.

As it turned out, Thax Collingwood became her unexpected escort to all of the various Christmas parties given in Mayfield that season. Kitty appreciated his company, for it helped to keep her mind off how Kip might be spending his holidays.

She went to the parties, the dances held as usual. Those who saw her with Thax seemed puzzled, then a little embarrassed to ask her about Kip. In this part of Virginia, where society was sheltered from news of what was going on in the rest of the world, Kitty supposed they preferred to remain ignorant, feeling ashamed of them, of herself. If they did not have some direct connection, Belgium and France seemed too far away to be of much concern.

She kept up a good front, chatted, smiled, danced. No one would have guessed that beneath the smile, the bright conversation, she was harboring a pervasive feeling of sadness.

The poignant lyrics of a popular song summed up her feelings:

> *Smile awhile, I'll bid you sad adieu.*
> *When the clouds roll by, I'll come to you.*
> *Until then, I'll pray each night for you . . .*
> *Till we meet again.*

Dancing to the music, Kitty kept a smile fastened on her face, but her heart felt as if it were splintering into millions of pieces.

Christmas at Cameron Hall was festive as always. Since Blythe had first come here to live as Rod's wife, she had tried to carry out all the cherished traditions her beloved mother-in-law, Kate Cameron, had observed in her lifetime.

Preparations were started early. Decorations were lavish. Red bayberry candles were set in the sills of all the windows and kept burning throughout the twelve days of the season. Elaborate ribboned wreaths were hung on the double front doors. A blue and white Meissen bowl on the hall table held an arrangement of holly, magnolia leaves, pine cones, and fruit. A six-foot cedar tree filled the house with its spicy scent but was left untrimmed until Christmas Eve.

It helped to have Thax's cheerful presence in on all the family festivities. A few days after Christmas, he volunteered to drive Kitty into Williamsburg, where she had promised to take Lynette and Gareth for a special treat and to spend some of their Christmas gift money.

They took in the annual Christmas puppet show and had lunch at the inn. She was surprised to see that Thax was particularly good with the children. He had a wry sense of humor that kept them laughing uproariously.

On the way back to Mayfield, the children sitting in the back seat grew drowsy. And before they were fifteen minutes out of Williamsburg, Lynette—tired, happy, and with tummy full—was sound asleep.

In the front seat, Thax was talkative, keeping his voice low so as not to disturb her. "I admire Kip for what he's doing. In fact, I've thought of doing something like that myself. But my father's keen on my getting my law degree and coming into practice with him. I hate to let him down, only son and all that." He sighed heavily. "He keeps saying we should stay out of Europe's quarrels, that they'll never be settled anyhow."

When they arrived at Cameron Hall, Lynette had to be carried upstairs to bed.

Blythe insisted Thax stay for supper. "Gareth is staying overnight, and Jeff might join us, too," Blythe added hopefully. She went on to inform the cook of the extra guest for dinner, and Kitty and Thax went into the library, where a fire had just been lit.

Rod, who was sitting in his leather wing chair, stood to greet them, putting down his evening newspaper at their entrance. Inevitably, conversation turned to the recent screaming headlines.

"Those Huns—" He shook his head in disgust. "What they're doing is monstrous."

As horror stories of German atrocities had mounted, Rod's attitude had changed over the last year and a half. His outrage at the inhumanity shown helpless women and children had become a seething anger. He was now impatient that America should go to the aid of the embattled French and English and was now as indignant about President Wilson's policy of non-intervention as he had once been supportive.

"It's a bad situation," Thax agreed. "Do you think we'll get into it, sir?"

"With *our* President?" Rod put the question scornfully.

"But if America *does* come in . . . what then?"

"I think we'd get it over with. The British and French don't seem to know what they're doing."

Just then a boyish voice piped up. "My father says it's a sin to kill."

The adults turned in surprise to see Gareth warming his hands at the fireplace. They had not noticed when the little boy followed them into the library.

"It's the Germans that are doing most of the killing," growled Rod, reddening a little at his grandson's statement. "There's such a thing as defending yourself."

Just then Blythe entered the room and, with a quick sense of the mounting tension, spoke softly to her husband. "Please, darling, no war talk tonight. Shall we go into the dining room now, have supper, and perhaps afterward Kitty will play for us and we'll have some Christmas songs."

Thax left right after New Year's, and Kitty found she missed him. He had filled a void in her life, and now everything seemed bleak and empty again.

Later in the week, she received a much-battered Christmas package from Kip—a lovely silk scarf he had bought for her in Paris and a hand-painted card on which he had scribbled a message. He wrote only that he had a Christmas leave of three days and would be spending it with friends in a village near the airfield. The note was disappointingly brief, and Kip seemed very far away.

Seeing 1917 in had not been like the last New Year's festivities for Kitty. Dread for what the future held now replaced her hope and happiness. Kip's prediction about the war's being over quickly had failed to materialize, as headlines told of German advances, French retreats, British defeats. Now his letters were few and far between, never more than a few lines scribbled in haste.

Kitty decided to wait until things settled down to broach the subject of nurses' training with her parents. But again she was delayed, this time by a telegram from Cara, saying that she was coming for a visit.

chapter
9

ON A GRAY, windswept January afternoon, Kitty drove Kip's runabout to the Mayfield station to pick up her sister. She was eager to see Cara. These days there was never enough time to catch up, and there was so much to share.

Cara stepped off the train, wearing a beige bouclé wool suit, a bright scarf tied in a triangle over her shoulders, a brimmed felt hat cocked at a jaunty angle. She looked smart and elegant, though Kitty recognized the outfit as one she had worn while they were in college. Cara had always had panache, the ability to give anything she wore a flair. By comparison, Kitty, in her casual tweed skirt and sweater, felt almost dowdy. Certainly, her sister looked like anything but a parson's wife!

Rushing to embrace each other, their happy greeting collided with questions, answers.

"I can't believe you're really here!"

"How was Christmas?"

They were interrupted by the redcap bringing Cara's large suitcase and a big canvas bag, filled with gaily wrapped packages. Each grabbed one and, talking a mile a minute, walked down the wooden platform to the space where Kitty had parked the roadster.

Seeing it, Cara raised an eyebrow. "Kip's?"

"Yes, I'm its caretaker until he gets back." Kitty tried to keep her voice light as she lifted the trunk lid to shove Cara's things inside.

"Thought as much. It looks just like something he'd go for—" Cara said with a knowing glance as she got into the passenger seat.

Her sister's tone as much as her remark somehow put Kitty on the defensive. She started to respond to the unspoken criticism in Cara's comment but thought better of it. Anyway, she didn't want to start out her twin's visit with a quarrel, so she decided to ignore it.

Still, Kitty hadn't forgotten that Kip had once been in love with Cara, that since childhood they had been very close. As their old nurse, Lily, used to say, "Them two is lak peas in a pod," or as Jonathan, Kip's father, laughingly tagged them: "Janus—two sides of the same coin." Kitty felt a small stab of jealousy at the memory, but she quickly rebuked it. It was idiotic! What Kip and Cara had felt for each other was over and done with years ago. Cara was married to Owen, and Kip was in love with—

"How *is* Kip, anyhow?" Cara's question interrupted these thoughts as they started down the country road toward Cameron Hall.

"He's completed his fighter training and is flying regular patrols now, from what I can tell," Kitty replied, hoping she sounded cheerful and confident. She had to fight the daily fear of knowing Kip was in all sorts of unimaginable dangers.

"Isn't it just like him to do something as reckless as volunteer to fight in a war that isn't even America's?" demanded Cara. "Of course, I wasn't surprised to hear it. Neither was Owen. He says Kip was born out of his time. He should have been a knight in the Crusades or at King Arthur's Round Table, going out to look for dragons to slay!"

Kitty swallowed over the lump in her throat and changed the subject. "How long can you stay?"

"It depends—" Cara seemed hesitant. They were turning into the driveway of Cameron Hall now and up ahead they could see the house. "I'll tell you all about it later."

The evening was spent with their parents. Cara regaled them with an account of the Christmas program in which she had directed the Sunday school children. Kitty, Blythe, and Rod were all reduced to helpless laughter as Cara recounted some of the hilarious mishaps—the way the beard of one of the three kings, played by a ten-year-old boy, came unglued and hung rakishly by a single strand; how the papier-mâché wings of the angels flapped precariously when they climbed up on high benches to appear over the stable scene; how the shepherds stumbled onstage, tripping over their robes and dropping their staffs with a great clatter while the choir was singing "Silent Night."

"That must have been quite a performance," Rod declared, wiping his eyes when the hilarity had at last subsided.

"It was! In fact, one of the elderly ladies of the congregation came up to me afterward and told me it was the best Christmas pageant they'd ever had—" Cara rolled her eyes heavenward—"which only makes one imagine what the others were like!"

Later, when Kitty had Cara all to herself in the upstairs bedroom they had shared for so many years, she asked, "Are you really happy, Cara? Is being married to Owen what you thought it would be?"

"Oh, yes . . . more . . . better! Owen is so wonderful, Kitty. I can't tell you! He is goodness itself, such spiritual strength, such sweetness of character, such generosity. I don't deserve him, of course. But I've stopped worrying about that. I just thank God for him, and feel so blessed."

"It's just such a different life from the one we all imagined for you."

"I know. But I don't even worry about not living up to what's expected of me anymore. I found something in a marvelous book I've been reading in my morning devotions, and I've been trying to apply it: 'Begin to be now what you will be hereafter.' It's so simple, really. All you can do is try to do your best . . . just for that day."

They got into their kimonos and sat on their twin beds, facing each other.

"I have something to tell you, Kitty. I haven't said anything to Mama or Daddy yet—" Cara began.

Kitty, brushing her hair, halted. "What is it?"

"Owen's submitted his resignation to our church."

"What happened?" Kitty gasped, putting down her hairbrush.

"Nothing. I mean, no problems with the church board or elders or anything like that. It was his own decision—" Cara paused.

Kitty was stunned. "Why?"

"He thinks it's only a matter of time before this country is in the war. He's read about all the atrocities in Belgium and Alsace-Lorraine. He thinks America, as a Christian nation, cannot stand by and continue to be neutral in the face of all that's happening over there. He admires President Wilson but is convinced that honor will compel him to change his mind about our neutrality."

Kitty could only stare at her sister. It was so unlike the Cara of old to be talking so seriously.

"Owen doesn't want to go as a soldier. He's against the killing of course," Cara continued, "but he feels that when we do go in, there will be young men from all over the United States called up ... some of them mere boys from farms, small towns, tiny communities, suddenly thrust into a whole new life. They'll need guidance, someone to offer them some spiritual comfort, strength. So ... he's applied to become an army chaplain."

"When will he go? How soon?"

"He expects to hear very soon ... probably in a matter of weeks."

"Then what will *you* do? Will you come home?"

Cara shook her head. "No, if Owen is sent overseas, I want to go, too. So-o-o—" She paused, her head to one side, weighing the effect of her next words on Kitty—"I've volunteered to go as an ambulance driver for the Red Cross."

This announcement stunned Kitty. What could Cara be thinking?

Then she remembered that just a few years ago, their father had overcome his antipathy to automobiles and bought Scott a small motorcar so he could commute between Mayfield and Charlottesville, where he was a law student at the University. The twins had pestered him to teach them to drive. He was reluctant to do so because the roads around Mayfield were not yet converted to automobiles, and the going was rough over the ruts worn deep by carriage wheels. At last, however, he had given in.

"Don't ride the brake!" and "Engage the clutch *before* you shift gears!" were his commands that they practically heard in their sleep!

Kitty recalled her tendency to dissolve into giggles when this operation wasn't performed smoothly enough and the car leaped forward, bumping and bolting like a rodeo bull while the scraping gears screeched in protest. Cara, intent on proving her brother wrong for once, liked the feeling of power when she took the steering wheel and the sense of being in control when she was in the driver's seat.

Scott was surprised when both of them learned quickly. Finally, through their brother's less-than-patient instruction and her own dogged determination, Cara, especially, had become an excellent driver.

"Is there a good chance of your being sent overseas?" Kitty asked her now.

"A very good chance. In fact, probably *before* Owen goes. Ambulance drivers are in great demand, but they have to be trained in Scotland."

Kitty couldn't hide her conflicting emotions at this news. "Oh, Cara, I don't know what to say!"

"Please don't say *anything* until I have a chance to talk to Mama and Daddy, will you?"

"Of course not."

Cara stifled a yawn, turned back the covers, and slipped into her bed. "I'd better get some sleep. I promised Daddy I'd go riding with him in the morning. So you know how early I'll have to get up!"

Long after Cara's quiet, even breathing told Kitty that her twin was sound asleep, she lay staring into the darkness. The idea of taking nurses' training had never been far from her mind since the day Kip left. She had put it aside until after the holidays. But her experience during Lynette's illness had proved something. Certainly Dr. Rankyn had thought so. Now her resolve to carry through strengthened.

Besides, everyone she knew was now involved in the war in some way. Both Scott and Thax had joined R.O.T.C. and spent one weekend a month in military training at an army camp near the university campus. Kip, of course, was already in the thick of things. And now Owen and Cara. She was determined not to be the last to go.

Part III
Over There

England, 1916

This England ... this fortress built by Nature ...
... this precious stone set in a silver sea....
    —from Shakespeare's Richard II

The Hun is at the Gate! ...
What stands if Freedom fall?"
    —Rudyard Kipling

chapter
10

BECAUSE OF THE uncertainties of maritime travel and the security measures necessary in wartime, arrival and departures of ships were not made public, so no one was there to meet Kitty when her ship docked in Liverpool one typically foggy English morning.

After being checked through the big, drafty terminal, she took a cab to the railroad station to catch the train to London. Her father's sister, Garnet Devlin, had closed her London town house for the "duration" and was living now at her country place, Birchfields, which had been turned into a convalescent home for soldiers. Kitty planned to get in touch with her soon, but first she had to find a place to stay in the city and start the necessary procedures to gain a nursing position.

It was extremely cold in the small compartment. All the things yet to be done began to weigh upon her mind as she hunched her shoulders trying to keep warm. Until now she had been buoyed by the excitement and novelty of her adventure. Suddenly, all Kitty's dauntlessness, so carefully contrived for the benefit of her dubious family and friends, vanished, and in its place were loneliness and apprehension about the future.

It was already dark when the train pulled into London. The huge London station, crowded with uniformed soldiers, was a scene of frenzied activity. Tired and nervous, Kitty pushed through the doors leading out onto the street. After a long wait in the chill dampness, she was able to hail a taxi. Breathless with relief, she gave the driver the first name that came to mind, remembering only that it was a hotel where some of her relatives had stayed while in the city.

In spite of the lateness of the hour, no street lamps were lighted. They crawled in thick traffic through darkened streets.

"It's because of them narsty German Zepplins, miss," said her driver in an almost unintelligible Cockney. "Don't never know when they're comin'."

This information only added to Kitty's overstimulated nervous system, and she sat straight up on the edge of the seat until the cab came to a stop in front of the Savoy Hotel.

In spite of her heightened state, Kitty was physically exhausted from all the hours of travel. She found the soft bed and down quilt in her well-appointed room welcome and soon fell asleep.

The next thing she knew, she was being awakened by the entrance of a chambermaid bringing her tea and the morning paper. With this kind of service, she suspected that this hotel was much too expensive for a prolonged stay. She'd have to look up the small but respectable family-style hotel on Trafalgar Square a fellow passenger on the ship had suggested.

Surely, as soon as she let Volunteer Aides Department—VAD—headquarters know she was here, she'd be assigned to a French hospital. A matter of days perhaps. Or a week at the most. She wouldn't be here very long, but while she was here, she would enjoy her stay.

Looking through the paper, she was pleased and amused to see that Grace Comfort's column, "Inspirational Moments," was in its usual place. She remembered the huge surprise that had become a family secret when it was learned that the *real* Grace Comfort was not the wise old lady who dispensed daily encouragement to thousands of readers but a sophisticated middle-aged *man*, Victor Ridgeway, now married to her cousin, Lenora Bondurant!

Kitty read this day's piece with special interest: "Be strong and of good courage," wrote Victor, quoting the prophet Jeremiah. "I will never leave you nor forsake you." Just what she needed to hear. The word *comfort* meant "to give strength," she knew. Certainly that's what Victor did, day after day, week after week.

She had often heard her mother say that Victor Ridgeway was a very unpretentious person, dismissing his talent as "minor," minimizing the significance or influence of the column. But Lenora often wrote to them, testifying to the hundreds of letters he received from people whose lives he had touched.

As soon as she got dressed, Kitty decided to see London by day. She had not been here since 1914 when she had brought Lynette to visit her Grandmother Devlin and her little sister, Bryanne. But then Garnet had met them and taken them at once to her town house for one night. The next day she had whisked them away to her country estate for the rest of the summer. Since the only other time Kitty had been here was when she and Cara were quite young—the year of Queen Victoria's Jubilee—she remembered very little about the city.

Catching a double-decker bus, Kitty climbed to the top level. From that vantage point, she viewed the London spectacle with mixed emotions. London was colorful and amazing. A panorama of people thronged its streets. All sorts of costumes reflected the variety of life lived in this great city—the stalwart policemen called "bobbies" in blue uniforms and bell-shaped hats with chin straps; boys in their school uniforms, looking as if they might have stepped out of a Dickens novel; smartly dressed businessmen in bowlers, carrying the ubiquitous umbrellas and briefcases. There were dark-bearded men in turbans, probably from some East Indian regiment or another of Britain's far-flung empire, as well as Scots in kilts and puttees.

Yet, London seemed surprisingly peaceful for a country in wartime, Kitty thought. As they passed the park, she saw riders in fashionable habits cantering their horses along the bridle paths as if there were no war at all going on just across the Channel. She remembered reading about the gallant Belgians while she was still in Virginia, and how saddened and horrified she had been at their plight. It had moved her so deeply she had been anxious to come and do her part to help just as Kip was doing his. Here, however, it began to feel like a fantasy.

Later, when she re-entered the hotel lobby, Kitty noted that, at least on the surface, the dignified elegance seemed undisturbed. Uniformed bellmen were going about their duties with quiet efficiency. The luxuriously appointed lobby was filled with well-dressed people, among them a sprinkling of British Army officers in khaki and a few of the more flamboyantly uniformed French or Belgian military. From one of the dining rooms, music was playing, and waiters could be glimpsed carrying trays of delicious food.

Where was all the deprivation, the shortages Kitty had read about? It was as though the war in France was some far-distant episode, unrelated to daily life. It was all very confusing.

Kitty wrote to her Aunt Garnet, telling of her arrival, and

giving her address. She explained that she had registered both with the Red Cross and the English Volunteer Aides Department but had heard nothing from either one and would remain here until she did. She expected to hear any time now, but everything seemed to be taking so much longer than she had thought it would.

Every night before saying her prayers and trying to sleep, Kitty studied her French phrase book religiously. Sooner or later she would need to be fluent in the language. Yet most nights, her mind still churning, sleep evaded her.

Why hadn't she heard from someone at VAD headquarters? Especially when, almost daily, the newspapers reported the critical need for nurses.

Several days passed with still no word. Before she had sailed from America, Kitty had filled out an application, asking for an interview as soon as possible after her arrival. She had enclosed her certificate along with a letter from the Red Cross instructor who had taught the course at the Center in Mayfield, "highly recommending Katherine Maitland Cameron," stating that she had passed "all the required tests, was cooperative and meticulous in carrying out medical orders, was a skilled technician, as well as compassionate and competent."

By now, Kitty's funds were running low, so she decided to make the move to more economical quarters. Once settled in the smaller hotel, she continued her nerve-wracking waiting game.

Finally one day, frustrated with the delay, she acted on a suggestion made by her mother. Before Kitty left home, Blythe had written to Lydia Ainsley in London, telling her about her daughter's plans. She had given Kitty the Ainsleys' town address, extracting Kitty's promise to contact her English friend upon arrival. Suspecting that her mother's motive was to have someone "looking after" her, she had resisted at first, but now Kitty sent a belated note to Belvedere Square.

Almost by return post, Kitty received an invitation to tea.

Lydia welcomed her warmly. "How pretty you are and how grown up! My goodness, the last time I saw you, you were just a little girl!"

The charming woman took her upstairs to her sitting room at once. Seated before a glowing fire, Kitty looked about with pleasure. The room, with its rose-colored watered silk draperies, the elegant French furniture, the exquisite Chinese prints, was as softly feminine as her hostess.

"I had no idea you were already in London, dear. I only got your mother's letter two days ago. Of course, everything is so undependable these days, especially mail from America." Lydia Ainsley poured fragrant scented tea from a graceful silver pot into delicate Sevres cups. "If I had known, we certainly could have arranged to meet your ship."

Kitty took the cup and dainty napkin that Lydia handed her and selected a tiny sandwich from the plate she offered.

"That's very kind of you, Mrs. Ainsley, but we were not allowed to send cablegrams about our arrival. I suppose there are very strict restrictions about telling ship movements, with the submarine threats and all."

Lydia looked distressed. "Yes, everything about this war is so dreadful." Then she composed herself, the fine features resuming their usual serene expression. "How *is* your dear mother? I think of her so often. I still miss her. We were great friends, you know."

Kitty nodded and Lydia went on. "I felt for her so in her awful tragedy. And my darling Jeff. I am his godmother, you know. He was almost like my own son. To lose Faith when they were so happy, so ideally in love. Ah—" Again she struggled for composure. "I shall never forget the lovely luncheon Garnet gave before Faith and Davida left for Southampton to board the *Titanic*—" She sighed deeply. "Who could have known?"

Kitty, not knowing what to say to ease the awkward moment, bent her head over her cup and took a sip of tea.

"It certainly gives us pause to realize how brief our happiness, even our lives, can be. This war, horrible as it is, has made people consider what is really important. The things we used to do seem so inconsequential—driving out, paying calls, shopping— Why do we always have to learn the hard way?" She sighed again, then glancing at Kitty, she said, "Forgive me, dear. I didn't mean to be so gloomy. Tell me about yourself, your plans, and about your sister."

"Cara's in Scotland," Kitty told her. "She's taking a rigorous training course to qualify as an ambulance driver."

Lydia's shock was evident. "You modern young women amaze me! To think of that lovely girl, taking engines apart and changing motorcar tires."

"I'm hoping she'll come back to London before she's sent to France so we can have some time together." Kitty took one more of the delicious little sandwiches Lydia offered her. "Of course, I'm not sure how much longer I'll be here."

"Well, these things take time. Edward says everything is so much more complicated now."

Kitty held out her cup for a refill. "But the need for nurses is so great. At least that's what I thought when I left America. I thought they would be crying for volunteers." She sighed, realizing how weary she was of the waiting.

"Perhaps we could plan a little party. . . . Wouldn't that make a nice little distraction for you?"

"That's very kind of you, Mrs. Ainsley, but I feel sure it

won't be much longer now." Kitty wondered how the woman could possibly think of such things with a war going on!

At last, feeling restless and anxious to check for any messages at the hotel, Kitty dabbed at her mouth with a dainty napkin. "I really must be going. Thank you so much for the lovely tea."

Lydia looked troubled. "Oh, must you go? I hate to think of your being alone in the big city, my dear. We'd love to have you stay with us. We have plenty of room. Wouldn't that be pleasanter than that impersonal hotel?"

"How gracious of you, Mrs. Ainsley. But I'm fine, really, and I honestly expect to hear from the Red Cross or VAD headquarters any day now."

Lydia looked dubious. "Well, do keep in touch, won't you? As I said, these things always take longer than one imagines."

Unfortunately, Mrs. Ainsley's dire prediction proved true. It was another full week before Kitty received her long-awaited summons to an interview.

The starchy "sister," the matron at the headquarters of the Volunteer Aides Department to which she had applied, seemed singularly unimpressed by her favorable recommendations. She questioned Kittly closely, adding a somber note by saying, "Of course, you will have to undergo a period of training with us. Our methods are quite different from—" Here she glanced down at the portfolio of certificates and personal references, running her index finger down along the pages as if to check the name of the hospital nursing school where Kitty had trained—"from that of the States." Even that, Kitty thought, was said with a rather disdainful intonation.

Kitty bit back a retort. She was almost tempted to say something staunchly American but changed her mind. She was too anxious to put her nursing abilities to the supreme test to jeopardize her chances of being accepted. She longed to be where the action was or, to be truthful, where the chance of seeing Kip was more likely. So she kept quiet, not wanting to say or do anything that might negatively influence the matron's approval of her assignment to France.

Still, she waited, wondering if the war would be over before she was ever issued her orders or a sailing date.

Not expecting to be assigned to a hospital in England first, she was at first surprised and dismayed, then resigned when she received a notice to report to St. Albans Hospice.

chapter

11

UPON ARRIVAL at St. Albans, Kitty was given directions to the nurses' hostel across the courtyard from the hospital where she was to share quarters with another VAD. Entering the grimly austere red brick building, she was handed a key and told to go up the stairs to the second floor, Room 8B.

Kitty mounted the uncarpeted stairs, then walked down a long, gray linoleum-covered corridor and tapped once on the door. Since there was no answer, she used her key. The door opened into a narrow room with furnishings as sparse and as spartan as a monk's cell.

One side was already spoken for, as evidenced by a colorful hand-crocheted afghan folded neatly at the bottom of one of the iron cots and some photographs placed on the small chest of drawers. On one side of the closet hung a few garments other than the VAD uniform—a cape, sturdy boots on the floor, some boxes on the shelf above.

Kitty fought a fleeting wave of nostalgia, thinking of her pretty room at Cameron Hall and the luxurious one at the Savoy she had so recently vacated. But quickly she thrust aside such feelings. She was embarking on her great adventure, and this was part of it. With renewed excitement, she began to put her own things away. She was just hanging up her coat when the door burst open and a girl in a VAD uniform entered.

"Hello!" she greeted Kitty cheerfully, displaying deep dimples on either side of a deeply smiling mouth. "You must be my new roomie. I'm Imelda, Imelda Merchant. I'm glad you've come. It's been ever so dreary with no one to chat with since Gladys shipped out."

Almost at once Kitty knew she would like her roommate. Imelda was plump and rosy-cheeked with the kind of openness one could not help warming to, and an irrepressible sense of humor.

"You've met with 'Starchy,' I take it?" Imelda asked, flopping down on the bed opposite Kitty and starting to unlace her high, black shoes. She rolled her bright blue eyes. "She's a ticket, isn't she? Don't let her get you down. She rides all the new ones hard. She has it in for Americans. Thinks you jolly well should come in and help us out of this mess. Gave *me* a hard time, too. Coming from the North like I do, seems I don't have a proper accent, if you can feature that!" Imelda stuck out her feet and wiggled her toes. "Oooh, that feels good! Been on me feet for the last ten hours."

Bursting with questions about VAD life, Kitty asked them and listened to Imelda's frank answers.

"Well, you might as well know at the start that this place is run like a reformatory," Imelda told her with a wry face. "You've heard the expression: 'Cleanliness is next to godliness,' I'm sure, but Starchy truly lives by it. No self-respecting germ would be caught in St. Albans. Floors and walls are scrubbed down twice daily with disinfectant. The air fairly reeks with the stuff. And you can hardly get the smell off your hands, no matter how hard you try!" Imelda wrinkled her nose.

"Besides Matron, you've got to look out for the ward

nurses, called 'sisters,' and don't make the mistake of callin'
them anything else, though I can't say why it's so important.
It's not as though they were Lady Somebody or a duchess or
something! They're tartars and keep you hopping. If you ever
look like you've nothing to do, they'll make good and sure
you do, and that will usually be the dirtiest job of the lot!"

Kitty's expression must have registered some alarm, for
Imelda giggled and quickly reassured her. "Oh, don't worry,
love, you'll do fine, I'm sure. Just keep reminding yourself it's
not the end of the world."

Studying the family photographs Kitty had arranged on her
small bureau, Imelda pointed to one of Blythe. "Is that your
mum?"

"Yes, and that's my brother Scott. And this is my sister."
She held up the snapshot of Cara in her ambulance driver's
uniform.

"Sure, and she's the spittin' image of *you!*"

"We're twins."

"*No!*" Imelda put her hand to her breast in mock surprise,
declaring comically, "I'd never have guessed!" Then she asked,
"So she's over here, too?"

"Yes, in Scotland. She's taking her training there. I'm afraid
she's going to get to France before I do."

"Well, St. Albans is the test," Imelda said, suddenly serious.
"If you pass muster here under Starchy, you'll be in demand
by the army doctors over there. They *know* she'd never send
an unprepared nurse to a French field hospital."

Finally Imelda yawned, pulled the afghan around her
shoulders, and curled up to get "a bit of shut-eye."

The days and weeks that followed proved Kitty's first
impression of Imelda Merchant correct. Besides her obvious
good-natured personality, her roommate also possessed other

invaluable character traits—a generous spirit and an even temper—that made her a genuine friend.

Kitty's duties started the very next morning when she reported to her ward at six o'clock to begin a twelve-hour day.

She soon discovered the routine at St. Albans was more regimented than the Army. Everything was scheduled to the minute—doctors' rounds, bedmaking, patients' baths, meals, rubdowns. All the VADs worked under the eagle-eyed head sisters on each ward. Imelda had not exaggerated. There was never a spare moment in the long, arduous day, and all Kitty's training and skills were put to the test every hour she was on duty.

During the first two weeks, Kitty was so exhausted at the end of her shift that she could barely stumble up the steps to her room to collapse onto her bed. She was even too tired to get up for meals. But Imelda would shake her awake and force her up to walk to the dining hall.

"It's not worth it," Kitty would moan, thinking of the flat, tasteless food served to the staff.

But Imelda was ruthless. "You've got to eat, Kitty. Got to keep up your strength. If your resistance is low, you could get sick. Then you'd *never* get to France!"

This was usually all it took to get Kitty moving again. Then she would force down the unpalatable food, crawl back upstairs to bed again, wake the next morning to another day of relentless work.

Kitty had been at St. Albans for nearly a month when she was sent out for the first time on ambulance duty to the railroad station. Here they parked to wait for the incoming trainloads of wounded men. Nurses boarded first to evaluate the injuries. Most were suffering from shrapnel wounds. Accompanied by the VADs, who carried supplies of cotton, swabs, bandages, disinfectant, and iodine, they did some initial care. But mostly they tagged which men went where.

Those requiring surgery would be sent to the better-equipped hospitals staffed with army doctors and surgeons. Others went to private hospitals, while the less seriously wounded would go to the suburbs, where many of the large residences had been turned into convalescent homes.

It was Kitty's first experience in seeing the actual results of warfare, and she was sickened and shaken. She must have successfully covered her reaction, however, for on their way back to St. Albans at the end of the day, the sister she had assisted said tersely, "Well done, Cameron."

At St. Albans, off-duty hours were equally supervised, allotted, and monitored. No one was allowed to go anywhere or see anyone outside the post without official permission obtained directly from their ward nurse, the matron, or a doctor. VADs were expected to sign in and out, stating their destination and time of check-out and return, and everyone was required to be in by ten at night. Sometimes Kitty and Imelda managed to have the same time off and went to a cinema or to a teashop as a pleasant change from their routine.

One afternoon, after Kitty had been at St. Albans for six weeks, she was summoned by her ward nurse and informed that she had a visitor in the day room and told, "You may take a fifteen-minute break."

"But who—" Kitty started to ask, but Sister Clemmons had already turned away and was busy at her charts.

Who was the mystery caller? she wondered as she hurried out through the ward into the hall. She didn't know anyone in London except Lydia Ainsley. Mrs. Ainsley usually sent a written invitation rather than stopping by the hospital.

As Kitty pushed open the door into the visitors' lounge, she saw a slim woman in a dark blue uniform looking out one of the long windows.

At Kitty's entrance, the young woman whirled around and, seeing her, struck a dramatic pose. "Voilá! Behold, a licensed Red Cross ambulance driver!"

"Cara!" Kitty exclaimed, and the two rushed into each other's arms.

"Oh, Kitty, it's been ages since I saw you last!"

"When did you get here, and how long can you stay?"

"Not long, I'm afraid. I'm leaving day after tomorrow for France."

"*No!*"

"*Yes!* It's official. I have my papers." Cara nodded, holding her twin at arm's length. "But at least we have this evening. I don't have to be back at the hostel until ten. So see if you can get off and we can go out somewhere."

"I'm not sure I can—" Kitty hesitated. "They're awfully strict here."

"But surely *this* is an exception to their rules. Your twin leaving for the war zone? Try, Kitty."

"But you don't know our matron—"

"Oh, do go on. Don't be such a mouse. Every minute counts!"

On her way to the matron's office, Kitty ran into Imelda just getting off her shift. She told her where she was headed and why.

Imelda grabbed her arm. "Come on! I'll go with you to beard the lioness in her den. And don't worry, I'll take the rest of your shift. Now, don't argue," she said, steering her firmly along. "She can't turn you down. After all, it's her patriotic duty, since your sister's on her way to serve the country."

In a matter of minutes, it was settled. Then Kitty took Cara to meet Imelda, and they all went upstairs so Kitty could get her cape and the hat VADs wore outside.

Imelda couldn't get over their striking resemblance. "Did you ever play tricks? Try to fool your boyfriends?"

The twins exchanged a look.

"Not really. But we gave people enough trouble without doing it on purpose."

"Besides, I'm married." Cara held out her left hand to show Imelda her wedding band.

"And he never got the two of you mixed up? Before the wedding, I mean?"

"He's a minister. Has special discernment," replied Cara with pretended sanctimoniousness. Then she laughed gaily, and Imelda joined in a little sheepishly.

"Well, now that I think about it, for all you look so much alike, it's easy enough to tell the two of you apart. Kitty, here, is much—"

"Sweeter, nicer!" Cara filled in for her.

"I wasn't going to say that," protested Imelda. "Just . . . different."

"Cara's a terrible tease, Imelda," Kitty said, smiling affectionately at her sister. "Don't let her get to you."

"Have a good time, you two!" Imelda called after them as the twins linked arms and went out the door.

Soon they were seated in a busy pub near the hospital. Imelda had recommended the place as "quite a respectable spot for ladies dining alone." After ordering meat pies and a pot of tea, the sisters settled down to exchange reports on their new lives.

"Now, tell me all about Scotland and your training," prompted Kitty eagerly.

"Well, I didn't see much of the fabled land of poets and authors. We were billeted at a farm in the Highlands where they've never heard of central heating!" Cara gave a demonstrative shiver. "We were up before dawn, given a breakfast of strong tea and oatmeal porridge—believe me, I felt like Oliver Twist—only I *didn't* ask for 'more'!" She grabbed her spoon and gave a convincing performance of a small boy demanding his dinner.

"Then while it was still dark, we marched out into the cold to work on a bunch of ramshackle Ford trucks. We learned to strip engines, rebuild them, improvise repairs. All of that took days. At night, we had first-aid classes and practiced on each other, splinting broken bones and learning how to use different kinds of bandages. They even had us lifting sacks of potatoes and meal and putting them on stretchers that two women could carry, so that we could get used to lifting heavy bodies." She grimaced and gave another shiver.

"Then on to our French lessons. We studied a kind of phonetic, conversational French that should be enough for us to get by, so we were told—"

Just then the waiter came with their order, and the two turned their attention to the succulent meat pie, a tasty change from hospital fare. As they ate, Kitty gave Cara a sketchy account of her life at St. Albans.

She sighed. "I have no idea when I'll get my orders for France."

"From what I hear, they need all the help they can get over there—doctors, nurses, and drivers." Cara poured more tea, and for a few minutes they sipped it in silence.

"What news do you have from home?" Kitty asked at last. "It seems that mail takes forever to get here."

Cara shrugged. "Only that Scott got his commission as a first lieutenant in the reserves and drills on weekends. He agrees with Owen that it's only a matter of time before America comes in officially. Even Father has taken a different attitude. Oh, yes, and Jeff has finally consented to take a commission to do a poster for the war effort."

At this bit of news, Kitty's brows lifted. Their half-brother's pacifist leanings were well known.

"Oh, not for military recruiting purposes," Cara added quickly, "but a poster supporting War Orphans' Relief."

"And Owen?"

Cara's sparkling brown eyes clouded momentarily. "He's in New Jersey at a training base assigned to a company. We had a weekend together just before I got passage. I've only had one letter from him, but he promised to write every day, so the rest just haven't caught up with me yet. In that one letter, he said his men are the best. He's very dedicated to them and concerned about the bad press America's getting abroad because of President Wilson's stand." Cara shrugged.

The sisters' time together passed all too swiftly and, outside the pub, they hugged each other and said their good-byes.

"Be careful, and don't take any chances or do anything crazy," Kitty whispered over the lump in her throat.

"You, too, Twinny," Cara replied huskily, using the old term of endearment they resented others' using but sometimes used with each other.

"God bless!" they said simultaneously, then laughed a little.

Cara hailed a slow-moving cab back to the hostel from where she would leave with her unit the next morning. Kitty stood at the street corner, watching as it disappeared down the darkened street into the fog. She was overwhelmed with a sensation of abandonment. As had happened many times in their lives, her twin was leading the way into some new adventure while Kitty remained behind.

Walking the short distance back to St. Albans, Kitty wondered when she would see her twin sister again. Quite suddenly Kitty felt desperately homesick—for everyone at home, for the Virginia spring that would soon be blossoming, and for the little house in the woods where she had planned to live with Kip.

Kip. She missed him so much. Where was he tonight? Was he thinking of her, longing to be with her as she was with him? She hoped so, but she couldn't be sure.

chapter
12
Christmas Holiday

Heap on more wood! The wind is chill;
But let it whistle as it will.
We'll keep our Christmas merry still.
Sir Walter Scott
—Sir Walter Scott

WITH THE SEVERE WINTER weather and shortages of fuel and materials for warm clothing, St. Albans was full of patients with respiratory illness. Nurses and VADs were kept quite busy. When one patient was discharged, another quickly replaced him. So when Kitty received a note from Aunt Garnet inviting her to spend the holidays at Birchfields, she did not have much hope of obtaining the time off.

To her surprise, Matron granted her a four-day leave.

"Mrs. Devlin has rendered invaluable support and service to our hospitals and outstanding effort since the war," she explained, "so go, and please give your aunt my regards."

Birchfields, several hours from London by train, had been turned into one of many convalescent homes for British officers, a halfway place where they could recuperate in comfort and seclusion. Most were ambulatory, although not yet well enough to be sent home or return to active duty.

The prospect of a few days away from the hospital sent Kitty's spirits soaring. She had not realized how much stress her daily routine of nursing had placed her under until the thought of being free of it, even for a short time, was exhilarating.

She packed her bag with a sense of anticipation, even putting in an evening dress she'd never had a chance to wear since coming to England, just on the chance there might be an opportunity to wear it.

Kitty was particularly looking forward to seeing Lynette's little sister, her small cousin Bryanne Montrose, who had remained with her grandmother at Birchfields after her mother, Garnet's daughter, Faith, was lost in the sinking of the *Titanic*.

Kitty traveled to the country by train. Upon alighting from her compartment onto the platform, she looked around with interest. The small village showed signs of change brought about by the war. The flowerbeds surrounding the brick station house were neglected. And a lone, elderly man, who under ordinary circumstances would have long been retired, was seeing to tickets as well as luggage. There were no buggies or motorcars waiting for passengers. Noticing that the handful of people who got off when she did were leaving on foot, Kitty set out to walk the mile and a half to the Devlins' manor house.

It was clear and cold, but her VAD cape and brisk pace kept her warm enough. Walking along the winding road brought back memories of the summer she had been here as a child— of going on picnics in a pony cart and of one special day when they'd gone to a village fair, accompanied by Jonathan

110

Montrose and Phoebe, then a governess. Kip hadn't been here that summer. Instead, his mother, Davida, had taken him and his sister, Meredith, to Cape Cod to visit their grandfather. Strange, but Birchfields was the one experience in her entire life that Kip had not shared.

The gates at the end of the drive were open when she arrived at the rambling stone and timbered Tudor mansion. The last time Kitty had been here, it had been summertime. The lawns and meadows had been a velvety green, the old-fashioned formal gardens abloom with primroses and pink and blue hydrangeas. Even now, although the grounds were winter-bare, there was a peaceful serenity here that made the war seem distant and unreal, in drastic contrast to the London she had just left.

There, the winter of 1916 seemed to go on forever. It had become the winter of the world in all its unremitting bleakness. The grim faces of its citizens spoke of the pervasive dread of the nightly threat of German Zeppelins, the wailing of warning signals, the whine of sirens tearing through the darkened streets, and most of all, the long line of ambulances moving toward Charing Cross Station to wait for the incoming trainloads of wounded.

Kitty thrust aside her gloomy thoughts. She had four wonderful free days ahead. It would be foolish to spoil them by dwelling on the harsh realities of her daily life as a nurse. Aunt Garnet had written, "I want this to be a joyous time for you, a few days away from the everyday grind." Kitty was determined that her visit would be just that.

Even so, when she entered the house and saw men on crutches and with canes, or with bandaged eyes, being led about by crisply uniformed nurses, she couldn't help thinking of the cruel irony of it all. That these luxurious surroundings should be ministering to the victims of the unspeakable horrors of war. Within walls where once gala balls and elaborate dinner parties had been given, where even a prince had been entertained, now men with broken bodies and shattered dreams were attempting to put their lives back together.

But maybe, by turning Birchfields into a convalescent home, Aunt Garnet was doing something invaluable for the men sent here to recuperate. By extending to them the gracious hospitality that prevailed here before the war, she was giving them a promise of hope.

While Kitty stood in what was known as the Great Hall, her aunt came rushing to meet her. "Oh, honey, it's so good to see you!"

"You, too, Auntie," Kitty said, thinking Garnet was as handsome and chic as ever, with hardly a wrinkle to show for her years.

"Ever since I heard you were in England, I've been longing to have you down. You're just what's needed around here. What a treat you'll be for these poor souls." She lowered her voice, still soft with a trace of her Virginia accent, as a man in a wheelchair was pushed across the hallway. "But," she went on, regarding Kitty with a frown, "you must get out of that ugly outfit at once!"

Kitty bristled automatically. She was prouder of her VAD uniform than anything she had ever worn in her entire life. But she overlooked her aunt's remark as Garnet rattled on.

"I do hope you've brought something feminine and pretty with you, dear. But, if not, never mind." She patted Kitty's arm. "You may have noticed I've put on a few pounds. It's the wartime diet, you know—too many potatoes! So I have some lovely Paris gowns I can no longer get into. You can take your pick and share some of your beauty with these poor boys who need cheering up." Taking Kitty's arm, she led her toward the stairs. "Come along, I'll show you to your room."

"Wait, Auntie. I'd like to see Bryanne. How is she?"

"Oh, she's fine. I'll take you out to see her in a while. Things have been rearranged, as you'll see. She's staying in the estate manager's house with her governess. Well, actually her nursemaid. There are simply no suitable young women available these days. They're all working for the government in some capacity or as volunteers like you and Cara."

"But why isn't she living here with you, Auntie?" Kitty was confused.

"Well, she is with me, Kitty. Just not in this house. I didn't think it wise for a young child to be subjected to so many distressing sights as she would if she were right here. Naturally, I see her several times a day ... for tea in the afternoon, and, of course, at bedtime."

Kitty's face must have revealed some worry, because Garnet hastened to reassure her. "She's very well taken care of, Kitty. Maureen is a wonderful young woman, devoted to Bryanne. And the child adores her. You'll see for yourself when we go over there. First, let's get you settled."

There was never any use arguing with Aunt Garnet, so she went along submissively and was shown to the room, once Garnet's boudoir, adjoining her bedroom.

"It's tiny, but the bed is comfortable," her aunt told her. "I hope you don't mind."

"If you could see my room at the hospice, Auntie, you wouldn't ask!" Kitty laughed.

"I'll leave you then to unpack. I'll be back in a little while, and we'll go across the lawn and have tea with Bryanne," Garnet said as she left.

Later, when Kitty saw her little cousin, she had to agree she looked healthy, secure, and happy. Her features held the same promise of beauty as her sister Lynette, although their coloring was quite different. Bryanne's hair was a golden maple shade, her eyes a clear lovely blue. She had not seen Kitty since the summer of 1914 and was somewhat shy with her. Two years could seem like an eternity to a child. When Kitty began to tell her about her sister and brother in Virginia, however, the child's curiosity overcame her initial shyness.

"You do remember when I brought Lynette to see you, don't you, Brynnie?" Kitty prompted. "We had such fun together!"

Bryanne nodded solemnly. "She used to send me letters she printed herself and pictures she colored." She squinched up her little face questioningly. "But I haven't got one in a very long time."

"I know. Right now, the mail is very slow coming all the way from America, but I'm sure Lynette keeps writing to you. She would like to see you very much."

Over Bryanne's head, Garnet held up a warning hand and shook her head slightly. Didn't her aunt want her to talk to Bryanne about Lynette and Gareth, or her father? Kitty felt torn. She knew how much *her* mother grieved over her son Jeff's little family, how she regretted their separation. But they were Garnet's grandchildren as well as Blythe's, her beloved daughter Faith's children. Her feelings must be considered, too.

With the war going on, though, nothing could be done about reuniting them, so what was the use of aggravating this controversy between the two grandmothers? Sadly, Kitty did not pursue it further.

chapter
13

By HER SECOND day at Birchfields, Kitty realized how tired she was. Her work schedule at St. Albans had been grueling, not only the physical labor but the added tension to prove herself. One of only a very few Americans on staff, she almost felt that the honor of her country was at stake. There, she had been too busy to think of anything but her duties, and at night, she was too bone-weary to do much but fall into bed.

Now there was time to rest and think. Of course, it was Kip who filled her thoughts. She had not heard from him in weeks and, although he had warned her of this possibility, she worried about him. If he had been injured . . . or worse . . . she would be informed. His family would have received official notification and would have told her.

But deep down, Kitty harbored an apprehension of some unknown danger. Not the recurrent nightmare from which she awoke panting and drenched with cold perspiration, having dreamed that Kip's plane had gone down in a spiraling arrow of flame. No, there was something else, something she could not name.

Before she left London, Kitty had written to him that she was going to spend Christmas with Aunt Garnet. She had even suggested he try to get leave and join them for a family celebration. But by the time she was ready to leave for Birchfields, there had been no letter from him.

Kitty had hoped that perhaps he might write her here. Each morning, she came downstairs in the anticipation that today's mail might bring some word from Kip. She tried to keep busy, volunteering for whatever needed to be done—reading to the men with eye injuries, writing letters home for others. Always a part of her was impatiently counting the minutes until the postman's truck from the village would come puttering up the long drive, and the mail would be sorted and placed on the polished hall table. But there was nothing from Kip.

Knowing that her Aunt Garnet was depending on her to help make Christmas a happy occasion for the men at Birchfields, realizing also that it might be the last some of them would ever have, Kitty tried to bury her own anxiety in activity. She plunged herself into all the holiday preparations, leaving no room for morbid thoughts.

Great armloads of greens from the nearby woods were brought in to be made into garlands to twine through the banisters of the staircase, decorate the fireplace mantels, and drape the balcony overlooking the entrance hall. The doors of the drawing room and music room were opened to form one large space, and a six-foot cedar tree was placed in the center.

A tree-trimming party was planned for Christmas Eve. Early in the evening, Aunt Garnet requested Kitty to play some Christmas carols while the men and staff gathered to participate in decorating the tree. The piano had been moved into an alcove in an adjoining room. While the trimming progressed amid lively chatter and laughter, Kitty seated herself and began to play.

Kitty played dreamily, memories of other Christmases at Cameron Hall filling her with tender nostalgia. In her mind's eye, she could see the snow softly falling on the sweeping lawns of home, frosting the meadows with white, going to church on Christmas morning at the small steepled church in Mayfield. As she played the old familiar carols, she was completely unaware of the lovely glow cast on her hair and face from dozens of candles.

This picture, however, was not lost on the Canadian officer who, drawn by the music, left his card game in an adjoining room and wandered over to listen. He stood in the archway and thought that he had never seen a more enchanting sight. Suddenly for him, Birchfields at Christmas had become a shining, magical place.

Pausing to turn the page of music, Kitty glanced over and saw the tall young man. His left arm was in a sling, and she did not recognize the insignia on his uniform tunic. Their gazes met. He smiled and she returned the smile.

As she went on playing, he walked across the room toward her and leaned into the curve of the piano, still smiling. He nodded and so did she, acknowledging him. His were the kind of good looks sometimes described as Irish—crisp, curling dark hair, high color, and strong, sharply defined features. Later surreptitious glances revealed that he also had the bluest eyes she had ever seen.

When she finished the piece, he leaned forward. "Oh, please don't stop. That is, unless you're tired. I could listen all night. You're quite good, you know."

"Thank you, but I think some people would like to dance. See the group over by the gramophone?"

He turned in the direction of her nod. "Then perhaps you'd do me the honor of dancing with me. I'm Richard Traherne."

"I'm Kitty Cameron. And, yes—" She tipped her head to one side, glancing at his sling quizzically—"if it won't be a problem for you. I take it your injury is not terribly serious."

"Not the kind that merits a medal for bravery." He chuckled. "I hope that doesn't disillusion you in case you thought you might be dancing with a hero." His blue eyes sparkled with good humor. "Actually, it was a motorcycle accident. I'm in Communications and was on my way with a dispatch when my wheel struck a shell hole and I somersaulted over the handle bars, tore some ligaments in my shoulder and leg, broke my wrist . . . . In fact—" He smiled down at her—"as it turns out, I'd say it was a *lucky* break! Otherwise, I'd be spending Christmas in the trenches rather than here at Birchfields!"

He came around to the side of the bench where she was sitting, and bowed slightly. "I hope you don't mind a one-armed partner. The wrist's almost healed. I don't really need the sling any more, but it wins me some sympathy." He laughed and Kitty joined in.

"Then I'd love to dance." She rose from the piano stool. "Shall we go see what records we have? I'm sure Aunt Garnet has brought in a supply of the latest tunes."

"Aunt Garnet?"

"Mrs. Devlin, the lady who owns Birchfields, is my aunt," Kitty explained as they strolled across the room to the record player where a group of soldiers and nurses was already gathered, looking through the stack of phonograph records.

At length a selection was made. The record was placed on the disk, the arm and needle set. Then the handle was cranked, and the music began. It was a piece Kitty remembered from summer dances at Mayfield Hunt Club.

In spite of the sling, Richard was an excellent dancer, leading her smoothly in the latest steps. She followed his strong lead easily, executing an elaborate turn, twirling around and back gracefully.

"I don't think you need any sympathy at all," Kitty teased.

"Vernon Castle better watch out!" She was referring to the male member of the popular ballroom-dancing couple, Vernon and Irene Castle.

They danced four straight dances. When it seemed that those in charge of the phonograph were having some dispute about the next record, Richard suggested they get some punch.

Finding two empty chairs in a corner, they sat down to talk.

"I'm curious," Richard began. "Obviously, you're an American. How do you happen to be here? Or do you make your home with your aunt?"

Kitty shook her head. "I'm a Red Cross nurse's aide with VAD. Right now, I'm attached to St. Albans Hospice in London, hoping to be sent to France eventually."

"I would never have guessed," Richard said quietly, his eyes traveling over her as if finding it hard to believe that this aristocratic-looking young woman, fashionably dressed in a blue velvet dress, with pearls in her ears and around her neck, could possibly be a hard-working hospital nurse.

Kitty blushed a little at the frank admiration in his gaze and quickly changed the subject. "What about you? How did you happen to join the Canadian Army?" By now, she had recognized Richard's distinctive maple-leaf insignia.

"Well, when I was a child, my father was in the diplomatic service and we lived in England for a few years. The summer after I finished college, a friend and I traveled through Europe. After that, I decided to take some courses at Oxford, and I was there when the war broke out. It didn't look as if the United States was coming in, so—" Richard gave a small shrug—"it just seemed the thing to do."

Just like Kip, she thought, then quickly amended the thought. Richard Traherne wasn't in the least like Kip.

"Nobody thought it would last this long," he went on.

"The talk was that the fighting would be over by Christmas, but I guess we didn't give Germany credit for being so tenacious." A grin broke through. "But let's not talk about the war. Not tonight. It's nearly Christmas, and 'tis the season to be jolly,' right?"

Taking her cue from his remark, Kitty groped for some lighter topic. However, it was Richard who turned the conversation by recounting some amusing incidents that took place while he was at Oxford.

"I didn't realize at the time how different our two countries really are until I lived among so many Brits. Wasn't it George Bernard Shaw who said, 'America and England are two countries divided by the same language'? Anyway, I was almost forced to buy a phrase dictionary so I wouldn't miss out on most student discussions!"

He gave a wry grin, Kitty laughed, then told him, "My brother went to Oxford, too."

"Oh? When was that?"

"Years ago. He's much older than my sister and me and our other brother, Scott. It would have been 1895 or '96. As a matter of fact, he didn't graduate. He dropped out to go to France and become an artist . . . much to our parents' dismay, I might add—" She paused. "Of course, now they are more than resigned. In fact, they're extremely proud of him. We all are."

"Why? Is he famous?"

"Well, I guess you could say that. He's won some awards. He's represented by the Waverly Galleries and has exhibited at the Royal Academy."

"I'm impressed. What's his name . . . I mean, besides Cameron, of course."

"Oh, it's not Cameron. He's my mother's son by her first

marriage. Actually, he's my half-brother. His name is Geoffrey Montrose."

Richard put down his punch cup and stared at Kitty. "Geoffrey Montrose is your half-brother?"

Kitty laughed at the look of incredulity on his face. "Yes. Really and truly, he is."

"Well, of *course* I know his work! That is, I've seen reproductions of his paintings in catalogues and art books. When I was at Oxford, I was at least exposed to painting and poetry. The whole place is haunted by poets and artists, you know. I wasn't a very dedicated student, I'm afraid, but I did absorb a great deal of . . . I guess you'd say, 'culture.'"

Just then Kitty caught Aunt Garnet signaling her from the doorway. "I'm sorry, I have to go. My aunt seems to need me."

"My fault for monopolizing you. I assume you're supposed to circulate, spread your grace and beauty among us poor soldier boys—" Then, with a trace of irony in his tone, he added—"who will be returning so soon to the front."

Kitty reacted with spontaneous sympathy. "It must be dreadful for you."

"Sorry. I shouldn't have said that. I didn't mean to spoil one of the loveliest times I've had in months. You'd almost made me forget there *is* a war going on."

Kitty would have liked to say something to take that look out of Richard's eyes. She found him interesting and amusing and very likable, but she caught Aunt Garnet's impatient glance and said apologetically, "I really *must* go."

"Yes, of course. Maybe later? Maybe we could have another dance or two."

"I'd like that, Richard."

With that, Kitty hurried away to join some of the other

young women that Garnet had recruited to be hostesses for the party.

Her aunt had made every effort to make this year's holiday festivities as much as possible like those given in the old days before the war. In the dining room, small tables for six had been decorated with centerpieces of greens, holly, and candles. At each place were poppers, containing paper hats, to be snapped open. The hats would be worn during the evening's festivities. For every man, there was a little gift from the ladies of the local auxiliary.

As a special treat, Garnet had reinstated her own Cameron family tradition of serving "prophecy" cake for this special celebration. This year, so that each group of six would have its own cake, there were individual ones for each table. Inside each cake were baked six tiny symbolic items. A bell meant a wedding soon. A coin promised a financial windfall. There was a horseshoe for good luck, a thimble for a home blessing, and the most coveted of all, a wishbone, granting the finder *any* wish. Great fun ensued as everyone ate his piece of cake and found the symbol foretelling his fortune.

Kitty was busy serving during the meal and, since she was also expected to help clear away afterward, she did not see Richard again until much later in the evening.

He was waiting for her in the hallway by the door when she finally emerged. The party was officially over, the men who had attended in wheelchairs having been rolled back to their rooms and settled for the night. Only a few remained in the lounge and drawing room, chatting in small groups.

"I don't have a curfew," Richard told her. "Ambulatory patients are pretty much on their own. I hope you aren't too tired and we can pick up where we left off."

Nodding in agreement, Kitty led the way to one of the window-seat alcoves in what used to be Uncle Jeremy's study, and sat down. Someone had replenished the wood in the fireplace, and flames rose in brilliant blue peaks in the deep, stone hearth, reflecting on the brass fender guard. For a few moments they were content to bask in the warmth of the fire, relishing the companionable silence.

"I guess I'm being greedy. You're probably exhausted, but I hate to see this evening come to an end," Richard said at last. "It's been so . . . so special." The firelight on his face accentuated its planes, deepening the hollows of his cheeks and making his eyes appear opaque pools of blue. Slowly he turned toward Kitty. "It's helped keep the dark away . . . *dark* being that three days from now when I'll be back in France—"

Unintentionally, Kitty leaned toward him, her expression compassionate.

Richard spoke quietly. "After the hospital, coming here was such an unexpected boon that I'm still making the transition. I'd almost forgotten that there was anything else in the world besides the constant boom of guns, the whine and smash of explosions . . . the mud, the stench, the rats—" He shuddered involuntarily, then looked away from her. "Forgive me, Kitty, I didn't mean to—"

She covered his hand with both of hers. "Don't apologize, Richard. I understand . . . I do know, at least a *little* of what you've been through."

"Of course you do. I forget. It's just hard to imagine you in connection with . . . such dark and terrible things." His eyes took in the lustrous auburn hair swept up from the slender neck, a rhinestone butterfly nestled in its waves, the creamy skin where the folds of her velvet gown outlined the slope of her shoulders.

Her eyes regarded him with sympathetic understanding, and Richard burst out impulsively, "Meeting you tonight seems like such a miracle. But in a way, it makes things worse. I find I'm dreading going back even more now—"

Kitty pressed the hand she was still holding.

Richard shook his head, then with an effort he smiled, and his voice took on an air of forced enthusiasm. "Tell me some more about your family, besides your famous half-brother, that is."

"Well, I've mentioned my brother Scott and a sister, Cara, who is now an ambulance driver in France. Actually, she's my twin."

Richard looked amazed. "*Two* like you? Impossible!"

The sudden solemn gong of the hall clock striking twelve startled them both.

"Midnight!" exclaimed Kitty, jumping to her feet. "It can't be!"

They looked around the room, now nearly empty. Only a few people remained talking and, in one corner, two officers playing chess.

"Have you plans for tomorrow?" Richard asked as he walked with her to the stairway.

"My aunt and I will be going to the village church, but you're welcome to come along, unless you'd prefer to attend the service here. I understand the vicar comes out on Sunday and plans to hold a special Christmas service for the men who can't get out to church."

"Oh, I'd much prefer to worship with you and your aunt, unless I'd be intruding—"

"Not at all," Kitty assured him. She turned to go up the steps. "Well, good night then."

"Wait." He put out his hand to halt her. "Since it's already morning, Merry Christmas, Kitty Cameron."

"Merry Christmas," she replied, looking into the eyes regarding her so steadily.

"Thank you for making this such a special Christmas Eve."

Kitty smiled, then turned and went slowly up the stairs, thinking that it had been a strange, yet a special one for her, too.

chapter
14

THE NEXT MORNING Garnet evidenced only mild surprise when Kitty told her that Richard Traherne would be accompanying them to the Christmas service.

"Oh, yes, that nice Canadian lieutenant."

Kitty excused her aunt's seeming indifference. Holidays must be especially hard for her since the double tragedy of losing both her beloved husband and daughter. Even with her dear little Bryanne's sunny presence to occupy and distract her, there was still a void lurking just beneath the surface.

The interior of the small church was dim and cold. Kitty slipped to her knees in the pew. Her first prayer was for Kip. Where was *he* this Sunday morning? Flying a dawn patrol in the gray skies over hostile territory? *Dear God, keep him safe!* She felt her prayers trite and unspecific and maybe ineffective. Could God really protect Kip from German guns and the skilled enemy pilots with their superior planes and greater experience? *Oh, dear Lord, give me faith to believe you will,* she prayed desperately.

But what about the prayers of German women for their sons and sweethearts? Whose prayers did God hear and answer?

Kitty shivered, and Garnet glanced at her anxiously. Just

127

then there was a stirring and shifting as the congregation stood for the entrance of the vicar, preceded by three small boys in red choir robes carrying lighted candles in tall brass holders.

Kitty tried to concentrate on the service but found that she was more aware of the man beside her. It was astonishing how, in such a short time, she felt she had come to know Richard Traherne. She sensed a quality in him beyond the superficial good looks and manners, the intelligence and charm. Yet even to admit her attraction to him might be dangerous. She was glad when the end of the service also put an end to her troubling thoughts.

That evening Aunt Garnet asked Kitty to entertain for the men once again since many at the Christmas party had requested an encore. This time Kitty selected some of the sheet music on hand.

With the first rippling chords, she began to sing along: "If you were the only girl in the world, and I were the only boy—" She had last sung this song at Montclair on Christmas Day two years ago . . . an age . . . another lifetime ago. She had been singing to Kip, although at the time he'd been too busy talking to Beau Chartyrs to notice. She remembered.

Now as the familiar words flowed, Kitty's eyes drifted toward the door. Richard had just entered and was standing in the shadows, leaning against the wall. The expression on his face was so transparent that she drew in her breath, and her fingers stumbled on the keys, missing a few notes.

She finished the piece, then stood and closed the lid of the piano. Moving to the window, she stared out onto the winter garden, blurred by the gathering darkness.

Soon she heard footsteps behind her, and Richard came up to stand beside her. "Guess what?" he said softly. "My cast comes off tomorrow. What's more, I've got the day off and the loan of a motorcar. Would you come with me to see the countryside?"

Heathercote Inn boasted the English tearoom of the tourist's dreams. While Richard helped her off with her jacket, Kitty looked around. From the small entryway, they stepped down into the main room. Heavy oak beams supported the low ceiling, and rough-textured walls further added a rustic flavor to the room. There were diamond-paned windows, and there was a cozy inglenook fireplace in which a welcoming fire was burning brightly.

As Richard helped her off with her jacket, she unwound her mohair scarf from around her head and neck.

A motherly looking woman with gray hair and rosy cheeks appeared through a door that Kitty presumed was the kitchen, carrying a loaded tray. "I'll be with you in a moment and show you to a table."

"Look, Kitty." Richard took her arm and led her over to a wooden plaque by the entrance. He pointed to the words carved on the surface, then filled in with paint:

TO OUR GUESTS

To all travelers, our door's open wide—
A haven for wanderers, a safe place to hide.
There's always a welcome any day of the year—
This is a haven of love, faith, and cheer.

"How charming," she murmured, looking up at him. Their eyes met and held for a moment, a moment that seemed somehow significant to Kitty but came and went so quickly that its possible meaning was lost.

"I can seat you now." A cheerful voice spoke behind them, and they turned to follow the hostess down two shallow steps and into the main part of the restaurant.

"What would you suggest?" Richard asked her. "You see, we're North Americans—"

At his remark, the woman lifted her eyebrows and beamed knowingly. "I took you to be Yanks." But she was smiling. "Perhaps, then, you might enjoy a typical English tea."

"Kitty?"

"Yes, that would be lovely."

When the woman left to get their tea, Kitty leaned across the table and spoke in a conspiratorial tone. "My Virginia ancestors would turn over in their graves if they'd heard her calling *me* a Yank!"

Richard whispered back, "I wasn't sure how she felt about Canadians, either!"

The ride in the open car had given them both an appetite, so they were ready for their meal when it was served. Kitty exclaimed appreciatively over everything—a squat pink and white teapot, matching cups and saucers, a linen cozy keeping the buttery currant scones warm, soft ginger cookies, and tiny cherry tarts. They devoured every morsel and, even before they had finished, their hostess was back with a fresh pot of tea.

They didn't lack for conversation. Their lively exchange of confidences about their childhood was liberally punctuated with laughter and sprinkled with anecdotes about their lives before the War.

They paused while Kitty poured tea, refilling their cups, and Richard fell silent. His expression was thoughtful, almost pensive.

"Penny for your thoughts," she teased. "Or maybe, since we're in England, I should say, 'sixpence'."

Richard sighed. "I'm afraid I'm going to wake up and find this was all a dream. I wish I could somehow stop the clock, make it all last."

"That's wishful thinking."

He reached into his vest pocket and brought out the small silver wishbone he'd found in his piece of prophecy cake, and dangled it between his thumb and forefinger. "Remember this? I think it means I get any wish I make."

Kitty took a sip of her tea, her eyes smiling at him over the rim of her cup. "Well, anyway, I hope it will be a pleasant memory, a pleasant interlude."

Reaching across the table, he took her hand. "Is that all this has meant to you, Kitty? Just an interlude?"

Kitty felt her face grow warm. But Richard was regarding her with such an imploring gaze that she could not look away.

"Maybe I shouldn't tell you, but I won't regret saying it, because it's true. I've ve fallen in love with you, Kitty—" He paused. "Is there the slightest possibility that you—"

She should have known this was coming . . . a lonely soldier facing who knew what kind of dangers. She should have told him from the first. "Richard—" She took a deep breath. "I'm so sorry . . . I'm engaged—"

He looked surprised, shocked. He picked up her left hand, examined the third finger. "But you're not wearing a ring. I looked right away to be sure. That first night, as a matter of fact, while you were playing the piano—"

Gently Kitty withdrew her hand. "When I knew I was coming to England to be a nurse, my mother suggested I put it in a safe deposit box. I couldn't wear it on duty, and it was too valuable to bring with me. But I *am* engaged, Richard. I should have mentioned it, I suppose. I just didn't think—"

The disappointment on Richard's face was so obvious that Kitty felt obliged to explain. "He's in France, an aviator with the Lafayette Escadrille—"

"And you love him?"

"Yes, of course. We've known each other since we were children."

"I might have known—" Richard's tone was disheartened. "It was foolish to hope. I suppose that's what most of us live on nowadays, though. Hope. The chance to grab a little happiness in all this madness."

He recovered quickly and they talked of other things. Then it was time to go.

Richard was silent as they drove back to Birchfields. Kitty huddled miserably in the passenger seat, feeling the cold wind in her face, and the cold around her heart. She was so sorry she had had to let him down, however gently.

In a way, she wished that Richard hadn't declared himself. Yet knowing that he loved her was strangely comforting. It assuaged some deep hurt in her, wounded by Kip's neglect.

Approaching Birchfields as darkness fell, the estate grounds held a stark kind of beauty. When they swung into the circle of the gravel driveway in front of the house, Richard parked the small car. They sat there, neither of them willing to speak nor move.

Finally, Richard leaned forward and cupped her face in his hands. Then he kissed her. She started to pull away, but the warmth of his lips, the surprising sweetness of his kiss, her unexpected response held her still.

"Kitty, Kitty," she heard him murmur before they went into the house, "why is the timing all wrong for us?"

The next morning, Kitty did not go down to breakfast. Instead, Garnet's maid Myrna brought up a tray with tea and cinnamon toast. Afterward, when Kitty put on her uniform, it felt unusually stiff after the days of soft knits, silk blouses, the satin-lined evening gown borrowed from her aunt.

Aunt Garnet came in to tell her that the chauffeur would

take her to the train station, as there were household supplies for him to pick up in the village.

"I hate to see you go, honey. You've been such a blessing. Your being here helped make the holidays bearable for me. And for others, too—" Garnet gave her a teasing look. "Especially that handsome Canadian officer. I do declare, I believe he's smitten."

"It's been wonderful, Aunt Garnet. Thank you for everything," Kitty said, giving her a hug.

"When this wretched war is over, I'm expecting you . . . and Cara, too . . . for a long stay."

Garnet bustled off with her handful of lists to start another busy day, and Kitty finished packing. Her time at Birchfields was already beginning to feel like a brief, magical respite. Now she had to go back to London, face the reality of her work, begin again the tedious wait for her orders to France.

She wondered where Richard was. Had he gone off somewhere? Last night he had told her he hated good-byes. There was something so hopeless in the way they had parted, a sad ending to their otherwise happy day.

Why did it have to be this way? Only hours before she had met Richard, Kitty had felt so very alone, thousands of miles from anyone she loved. Now, only a stone's throw away, perhaps, was a fine, honorable man who had offered her his whole heart, his love, his life.

She gathered up her cape, folded it over one arm, and picked up her overnight bag and started down the stairway. Halfway down the stairs, she halted. She saw him standing at the hall table, as if looking over the mail. At her footstep, he turned. Kitty knew, in spite of what had been said yesterday, that he was waiting for her.

It was the first time Richard had ever seen Kitty in uniform. The sight of her in her demure gray dress with its starched

133

white collar startled him at first. Then he was aware of his immense longing to take her in his arms, hold her close, to breathe in the sweet fragrance of her hair.

He walked toward her slowly, both hands extended. She set her valise down and held out both her own.

"I don't want you to go," he said.

"I have to."

"But there's so much more I want to say—" he began. "I love you, Kitty. I can't let you go with so much unresolved between us."

"There's no use discussing it, Richard."

"But there may never be another chance," her reminded her gently. "I just want to know . . . *need* to know, Kitty. Before I go . . . do you love me?"

Kitty started to draw away her hands, but he held them tight. "You know I'm promised to someone else, Richard—"

"But . . . if you weren't . . . would you, could you love me?"

"That isn't a possibility, Richard. I never meant to let you think—"

"You didn't, Kitty. All I know is what I feel." He pulled her into his arms so she couldn't turn away. Looking into her eyes, he spoke urgently, "I love you, Kitty; I'd do anything in the world for you. Just give me some hope—"

Kitty closed her eyes to block out the pleading she saw in his, and shook her head. "I–I can't, Richard."

With a sigh, he released her. "Good-bye then, Kitty. Don't forget me, will you?"

"I'll never forget you, Richard—wouldn't want to."

"I don't know why, but I feel somehow, some way—" He paused, then smiled. "That's not fair, is it, Kitty? I do wish you happiness." He hesitated. "Kiss me good-bye?"

"Of course." She lifted her face to his.

His kiss was deeply tender. In it was all the longing of a

passionate heart. Kitty responded to its sweetness, its relin-
quishment.

When it ended, Richard said quietly, "I shall always love
you, Kitty, as long as I live."

Kitty repressed a shudder. His words held such poignant
potential. These days life was so tentative, so precarious. In
another day or two, Richard was going back to France.
Anything could happen.

In the train all the way back to London, Kitty wept softly.
If there were no Kip . . . if there had *never* been Kip . . . she
knew she could love Richard. She *did* love Richard, but she
was not *in love* with him. There was a difference. Richard was
charming, witty, intelligent, considerate—a gentleman in
every sense of the word. Kip was . . . well . . . Kip. He was a
part of her, of all she had ever been. And he would always be a
part of her.

She looked down at her bare third finger on her left hand
and thought of the other things she had left in the bank's safe
deposit box along with the engagement ring—the keys and
deed to Eden Cottage. She felt a chill as though someone had
opened a window and let in a draught of icy air. Would she
ever wear that ring again, or turn the key in the lock of the
little house across the rustic bridge from Montclair?

Kitty had been back in the hospital in London less than a
week when she received a letter marked "Somewhere in
France." She scanned the unfamiliar handwriting and guessed
before opening it that it was from Richard.

Inside, he had written:

> I told you that at Oxford I dabbled in painting and poetry, but
> I'll never be able to capture in words what last week meant to me,
> only to say it was like a dream, with timelessness and joy I've

135

never experienced before. Maybe it was a romantic illusion of what I imagine life could be with someone you love.

I enclose something I found recently and want to share with you, written by a Winifred Mary Letts:

> I saw the spires of Oxford
> As I was passing by;
> The grey spires of Oxford
> Against a pearl-grey sky.
> My heart was with the Oxford men
> Who went abroad to die.

I love you, Kitty Cameron.

Always, Richard Traherne

Kitty folded the letter and replaced it in its envelope. She hated the depression she sensed in Richard's words. She knew the awful waste of the young men whom the poet had written about. Didn't she see them every day? Some scarcely out of high school, others fresh from college campuses. But there was something else that disturbed her deeply, a kind of fatalism. Did Richard expect to die?

Suddenly Kitty was reminded of something that old Lily used to say when she'd received bad news, "Somthin' jest walked ober mah grave."

Kitty forced back the superstitious thought. She was being foolishly morbid. What did the Bible say about fear? She couldn't manage chapter and verse, but she knew there were many admonitions to trust God and not be afraid. Quickly she whispered a prayer of protection for Richard, for Kip and Scott and all the unnamed, unknown soldiers facing death. Then she went on duty with determined cheerfulness.

Only a few weeks later, Kitty received her orders to go to France.

Part IV
No Coward Soul

Somewhere in France

No coward soul is mine,
No trembler in the world's storm-troubled sphere:
I see Heaven's glories shine,
And faith shines equal, arming me from fear—
—Emily Bronte

chapter
15

PALE WISPS of fog swirled about like shreds of gray cotton wool in the cold dark pre-dawn. Kitty shivered even under her nurse's cape, its warmth useless against the deep shudders she was powerless to control. She found herself praying, *Please, Lord, don't let anything happen to prevent my going to France!* No incidental error on her papers, no question about her eligibility, no last-minute hitch.

Her initial excitement at receiving her orders had been lost in the frenetic rush to complete all the necessary papers, send word of her transfer home, get her duty release from "Starchy," and pack. Now all that was left, after a hurried trip by train to this seaport town of embarkation, was a bad case of nerves.

At the train station her Red Cross certification and signed release from St. Albans had not been sufficient identification to offset a thorough search. She had been requested, though politely, to take off her shoes and empty her purse while another matron ran expert hands along the lining of her cape.

It was already past midnight. Heart in her throat, Kitty followed the straggling crowd of passengers and joined the line forming on the jetty under the shed.

"Ladies and gentlemen, please have your passports ready,"

instructed someone in a precise British voice. With a shaky hand, Kitty drew hers out of her handbag. An irrelevant fear gripped her that here, at this last minute, she might be turned back. Ridiculous, she told herself, glancing about at the others standing with her. Their faces looked ghostly in the yellow light, mirroring her own anxiety.

The line moved forward silently and slowly. Credentials were presented to the officer standing at the gangplank. Kitty tried to think of other, more pleasant thoughts. Then at last it was her turn. Her passport was studied for what seemed an inordinate amount of time, then the officer gave her a brisk nod and handed it back to her.

"All right, Miss," he said. "Next, please."

She moved quickly past him, up the gangplank. Then she was on deck. She moved over to the railing, leaned against it. Only then did Kitty realize that she had been holding her breath.

The wind off the Channel, moist with sea spray, was freezing. Gradually she felt the vibration of the engine starting up, the slow, rocking movement of the boat beneath her, sliding out from the dock, edging its way out from the harbor. As she gripped the rail, the boat plowed through the dark, dangerous waters of the Channel. She was on her way to France at last!

The wind grew bitingly cold, and Kitty left the deck, seeking the warmth of the lounge below. It was furnished only with plain wooden benches. Many of the other passengers had already taken refuge here.

Her fellow travelers were a mixed lot. About ten VADs from other training centers were also on their way to field hospitals. Kitty did not know any of the young women, merely recognized them from their uniforms identical to her own—the red-lined capes, the short-brimmed blue hats, the Red Cross insignia on the armband.

There were soldiers, too, some who looked heartbreakingly young, obviously on their first tour of duty. These men, laughing and joking among themselves, offered a sharp contrast to others with glazed eyes and hunched shoulders, perhaps returning to battle after leave.

It was a strange night, one that Kitty would always remember. Though some slept, her mind was roiled with many thoughts, interspersed with prayer. For some reason, a poem by Emily Bronte that she had learned in college came to her:

> *No coward soul is mine,*
> *No trembler in the world's storm-troubled sphere:*
> *I see heaven's glories shine,*
> *And faith shines equal, arming me from fear—*

Kitty hoped that she would be brave, hoped that she would not be found to have a "coward's soul" when she was faced with whatever lay ahead.

A gray dawn was breaking over a pewter sea when the boat nosed into the landing dock. Groggy and feeling rather queasy from hunger, Kitty followed the line of passengers trailing off the boat onto the dock.

After landing, the VADs were instructed to line up to have their papers checked by the French port authorities and once more by an officer from the medical corps. When their identities were established, verified by double-checking against a long list, they were given the name of the post to which they would be assigned. Kitty and four other young women were directed to a bus, which they boarded silently.

They acknowledged each other with stiff little nods and

nervous smiles, but no one spoke. Soon a sergeant swung on to the bus and got behind the wheel, announcing cheerfully, "Right-o, ladies, off we go," and with a great grinding of gears and the noisy scratchy sound of a rusty ignition, they started off.

It was getting lighter now. Kitty looked out the smeared window of the bus and saw the bleak, unfamiliar landscape.

From Dunkirk to the front, the road was lightly guarded. They passed village after village that appeared to be deserted. Beyond lay fields flanked by groves of poplar trees, and beside them a muddy canal slithered through the scene like a venomous serpent.

Even above the rattle of the vehicle, Kitty was aware of the distant sound of booming artillery. This was really it. She was in France. Not far away was the war zone. Her heart hammered in her throat, her palms under the woolen gloves grew clammy.

They must have driven for two hours. Kitty lost all track of time. Her head ached dully from lack of food, and every nerve in her body tingled with tension.

"Well, ladies," boomed the driver, "we're almost to our destination—formerly the Chateau Rougeret, now officially an evacuation 'ospital. This buildin' was once the home of the Rougeret family, who are, I'm told, quite the hoi-poloi, leastways until most of 'em lost their bloomin' 'eads in the Revolooshun!" He laughed heartily at his own joke.

Amused, Kitty could not help wondering if the sergeant had been a music-hall comedian before the war.

"Madame Rougeret still lives in part of the chateau," he went on, "although I don't know anyone who's actually seen her ladyship!" Once again, he stopped to enjoy his humor. "Maybe she's a 'eadless ghost! Who knows? Maybe the 'ouse is 'aunted!"

One of the other VADs sitting across the aisle from Kitty leaned toward her, winked, and asked in a stage whisper, "Do you suppose he's trying to cheer us up?"

Kitty shrugged and returned her mischievous smile.

The young woman thrust out a mittened hand. "I'm Dora Bradon."

"Kitty Cameron." She started to ask where she'd trained, but just then there was another announcement from their driver.

"For your information, ladies, the chateau is situated only ten miles behind the Allied lines, so don't worry, you'll have plenty of business, as they say."

At that moment the bus lurched, and everyone had to grab the back of the seat ahead to keep from sliding into the aisle and onto the floor.

As their vehicle chugged into a village which, from the look of it, had been the target of heavy bombardment, their driver began weaving crazily to avoid the deep shell holes blasted out of the street. In the field to one side, Kitty saw many little crosses, and the sight chilled her heart.

A little farther along, a platoon of men came marching alongside, their eyes fixed, faces grave and determined. A wagon loaded with artillery rumbled past them down the rutted road.

Protesting in backfires, the bus began a long uphill climb. Flanking them were dense woods. At the top, a turreted stone building was silhouetted against the overcast morning sky.

The bus braked at last to a groaning stop.

"Here we are, ladies—Chateau Rougeret!"

Stiff and shaky, Kitty emerged from the bus. She took a few steps and glanced around. On what must have once been terraced lawns and formal gardens stood several wooden buildings, looking as though they had been hastily erected.

143

"This way, ladies." The sergeant motioned them forward, and the little group followed him up some shallow stone steps and into a gloomy entrance hall.

Kitty's first impression was of impregnable cold. The great hall had the feeling of a fortress, untouched by sunlight for centuries.

"Wait here. I'll go fetch Matron." The sergeant left them and disappeared down a narrow vaulted hallway.

"Suppose that's the way to the dungeon?" quipped Dora Bradon, the young woman who had introduced herself to Kitty.

Unexpectedly, Kitty burst out laughing. Soon all four VADs had joined in, welcoming the input of some humor into this alien situation. With the laughter came a release of tension, followed by a round of introductions.

They had just completed this exchange when a tall, handsome woman in a nursing sister's uniform walked briskly toward them.

"Good morning, ladies. I'm Matron Elizabeth Harrison. What you've undertaken is far from easy, but I believe you are all well qualified to take on this challenge or you would not have been sent here by your supervisors. We run a tight ship here, but we're supportive of each other and work as a team. We expect discipline, strict adherence to duty, and unquestioned obedience to orders. I commend you for your patriotism."

Her bright eyes traveled over the group, and she gave a little nod. "You will be assigned two to a room, so choose your roommates, and settle in. Shift assignments will be posted as soon as you report to your ward nurse. Thank you, ladies." With that, she turned and walked back down the hall.

There was a moment of silence when they looked at each

other before Dora arranged the painting. "Let's go find our room, Kitty."

The Chateau Rougeret, once the palatial home of a noble family, had been transformed into a model British field hospital. On their way through the great halls, where patients lay on cots lining the walls, Kitty could see that most of the rooms had been converted into spaces accommodating four patients each. The staff, the VADs, and ambulance drivers were billeted to the top floor, which had once been the Rougeret servants' quarters.

At the top of what felt like thousands of stone steps up a twisting stairway, Kitty and Dora found the room they were to share. It was hardly more than a closet. As they unpacked, they bumped into each other repeatedly, at length bursting into helpless laughter.

"I don't mind telling you," Dora admitted, "I'm scared stiff! I've never tended war injuries before."

It was a relief to Kitty to put into words what they both were feeling.

After a cold supper taken in the staff dining room where they were barely acknowledged by weary nurses just coming off duty, they returned to their room. They got ready for bed quietly. Soon both were in their narrow cots, too absorbed in their own thoughts for further conversation.

Awakening well before 4:00 A.M., the hour she was to report for duty, Kitty left her cot and began to dress. She had not slept well. She had been too cold, for one thing, and too apprehensive, for another. Her fingers were numb as she buttoned on her coverall apron, laced up her shoes, adjusted her cap with its crisp veil, and pinned it in place.

As she dressed, all her self-doubts rose to taunt her, the questions pouncing upon her from the deep well of her own insecurities. Would she measure up to the Matron's expectations? Had her training at a civilian hospital equipped her to handle the kinds of wounds and injuries she would soon be seeing?

Dora was sleepy but cheerful when she finally joined Kitty in the dining room for a breakfast of coffee and chunks of toasted French bread. Except for a few sips of the scalding brew, however, Kitty could not swallow a thing.

When Dora left to receive her assignment in another ward, Kitty met the kind-eyed woman who would be her immediate supervisor. "Welcome, Nurse Cameron. I'm Sister Ferris."

She began by reviewing the duties Kitty would be expected to perform, showing her where supplies were kept and apprising her of daily routines and schedules. In response, Kitty warmed to her gentle instruction, feeling a returning of self-confidence.

Kitty soon learned that everyone admired Sister Ferris. She issued orders in a soft but authoritative voice and knew how to correct in a quiet manner, suggesting alternative tasks. Consequently, Sister Ferris was a favorite, adored and respected by doctors, nurses, and orderlies alike.

At the end of the day, Kitty found that Dora had not been so lucky. Her roommate had drawn a real tyrant for a ward nurse and soon came in at night, smarting from sharp reprimands, or reporting some hilarious encounter.

There was little time for the new group of VADs to become acclimated, for the first week, a big drive at the front brought a convoy of ambulances pouring into the courtyard. They came at night, the only time vehicles could safely transport the wounded without being the sure targets of enemy fire.

Nothing Kitty had yet experienced had prepared her for this carnage. As ambulance after ambulance deposited its victims, a barrage of moans and sharp outcries assaulted her ears. The sight of so much human suffering was permanently imprinted on her brain—the pain-contorted faces, the cries of agony, the panicked pleas for help.

Kitty and the other nurses did their best to handle the wounded as gently as possible, cutting off mud- and blood-soaked uniforms and making the men comfortable until a doctor could make a diagnosis and determine the treatment needed.

Up and down the crowded aisles they raced—from the hissing sterilizer to the bandage store to the sinks for antiseptic soap. From the operating room annex next to the ward, the odor of disinfectant and ether drifted in, making Kitty's nostrils prickle and making her stomach lurch uneasily.

Still, despite the grim realities she was facing, she was determined to remain calm, not become maudlin or ineffective. More than anything now, she wanted to become a highly skilled professional without losing her compassion.

For all her own discomfort, Kitty knew the suffering of these men was far more intense. Many of them had lain out in the cold and rain for hours, waiting to be picked up and driven to the hospital under the cover of darkness. So besides shrapnel wounds, the nurses soon began to see gangrene of the extremities, the result of standing knee-deep in muddy trenches, and dozens of cases of pneumonia and bronchitis from the abominable winter weather.

The painkillers and narcotics, kept under lock and key in the pharmacy, were reserved for the post-operative and amputation patients, so there was little to do for the others except rely on the remedies Kitty had learned in her Red Cross First Aid training—rub the feet and legs with oil, wrap them in soft cotton wool, and apply linseed poultices to the chest cases.

Kitty prayed as she worked, grateful for the skills she had

been taught that could alleviate even in small ways the agony of these men. The fact that they were all so grateful, often even apologetic for the trouble they were causing, humbled her, knowing how much more they had given.

The bone-chilling cold Kitty had noticed the first day never abated. At one time or another, almost all the staff succumbed to coughs or colds. But as long as the nurses could stay on their feet, there was no thought of taking a well-earned day off.

To make matters even worse, the weather turned really miserable—the coldest winter in fifty years—so said the French orderlies and ambulance drivers. Dora wrote her mother to send woolen long-johns, and a package from Blythe, containing beautifully knit sweaters, finally reached Kitty.

The added layers helped a little, but crawling out from the blankets on chill mornings became harder and harder. They dressed quickly, shivering convulsively, their breath frosty plumes in the frigid air.

After being on duty for twenty hours at a time, the long climb up the steep stone steps seemed an impossible challenge. Only the prospect of a few hours of dead sleep enabled Kitty to put one foot in front of the other.

In her room at the end of a day on the wards, Kitty was usually too physically drained to think about Kip. Not until she was finally in bed at night or had awakened in the eerie light of dawn, did her thoughts center on him. She had hoped to hear from him after she sent her letter telling him that she was now stationed in France. She hoped that he would find a way to come see her. Of course, she didn't know exactly where he was, or whether her letter had reached him. He might have been transferred to another airfield, or . . . and a deep shudder would tremble through her body. Surely if anything had happened to him, she would *know!*

Often Kitty had to fight the waves of homesickness that sometimes unexpectedly engulfed her. It was a kind of agonized aching for all the faraway beauty of Virginia, especially the blossoming woods between her home and Montclair where their little honeymoon house, Eden Cottage, awaited their return. The pink impatiens she had planted all along the flagstone path to the blue-painted door, seemed an almost comical reminder of a virtue she herself must cultivate.

Remembering it all, Kitty would close her eyes, feeling the awful urge to cry—for all the lost days, the lost happiness, the lost innocence before she had known about war and blood and the terrible dailiness of death.

chapter
16

In February came the news that after the sinking of an American freighter, the *Housatonic,* by a German submarine, President Wilson had broken off diplomatic relations with Germany. "Surely now the Americans will come in" was the opinion voiced most often by members of the medical staff at the chateau. But when weeks went by with no further word that the United States would join the Allies, Kitty and some of the other Americans attached to the British Red Cross unit felt an undercurrent of hostility beginning to surface.

Later in the month, a brutal German attack on Verdun sent the number of casualties soaring into the hundreds of thousands on both sides, and the staff was taxed to the utmost. News of the fierce battle brought an urgent demand for more ambulances to bring the wounded to the hospital. French as well as British units were alerted for service.

Soon a steady stream of ambulances was arriving at the chateau. To Kitty's mingled delight and dismay, knowing the risks of such duty, Cara was one of the drivers. The twins had a brief ecstatic reunion before the orders for dispatch were announced.

Since a VAD would be assigned to each ambulance, Kitty kept track of the posted assignments. When she saw that another VAD had been given the number of Cara's vehicle, Kitty quickly traded with her.

As they hurried out into the darkness and scrambled into the high cab of the ambulance, Cara spoke for the first time. "Thank God, there's no moon." She did not need to explain. Kitty understood her sister's remark. It was more than a statement. It was a heartfelt prayer of gratitude. Both knew that the Red Cross symbol painted on the top was not always the international protection it was designed to be, but at least the moonless night would give them a chance to move undetected past enemy fire.

If either twin had been struck by the incongruity of their presence here in France, neither said so. Only a year ago, that they should be setting out on such a mission would have seemed incredible.

Cara turned the vehicle expertly out into the line of ambulances. Kitty, sitting silent beside her, was gripped with anxiety. Was she up to what would be demanded of her before this night was over? She glanced over at her twin hunched over the wheel, saw her profile under the beaked cap—the small chin thrust out, her lips tightly compressed.

They drove through the night, in convoy, following the other three ambulances in front of theirs. Kitty felt her palms grow sweaty inside the woolen gloves. She squinted through the grimy windshield at the narrow winding road ahead.

When the signal came to stop, Cara slid into low gear and braked. The dull thud of bombs could be heard constantly in the distance now. Then came the whine followed by an explosion, and the sky lighted up for a split-second.

Kitty's stomach cramped, her heart banging against her ribs. *I'll never get used to it*, she thought, wondering how many men had been hit by that last shell.

They remained parked, waiting for another signal to move

forward. Sitting in tense silence, they heard the dull shuffling sound of marching boots.

As the men in the trenches were relieved, columns of weary soldiers trudged by on either side of the road. They moved like sleepwalkers, shoulders bent beneath heavy packs and guns, not talking, not looking to right or left. Their faces—haggard and gray, eyes glazed—mirrored the horror and hopelessness of all they had endured.

Kitty had never felt so frightened, so filled with defeat. Were the Allies losing the war?

Hearing a rustling noise, she turned to see several of the men leaving the ranks and falling wearily to the ground. Where were their officers? Was the whole army in retreat?

Just then Kitty heard Cara mumble something under her breath. She could not make out the words but knew that her sister was echoing her own reaction. What was it all for? She reached over and pressed Cara's hand. There was no need for words.

They waited tensely. There was a stirring of activity, felt rather than observed. A soldier moved alongside the line of ambulances, motioning them forward. Kitty felt her stomach muscles contract as Cara moved her foot alternately from accelerator to brake, struggling to steer the vehicle straight ahead, fearful that one of the men, blinded by exhaustion, might stumble under the wheels.

At a short blast from a whistle, Cara jammed on the brakes and the ambulance came to an abrupt stop. There was movement, low voices. Through the murky darkness, they could see figures emerging from the woods—medical corpsmen bringing out stretchers bearing wounded men.

Kitty jumped out, aware that Cara's orders were to remain at the wheel, ready to get going at a moment's notice if the bombardment started again.

153

Amid the cries of the injured, Kitty helped the stretcher-bearers load the ambulance. Quickly, and as gently as possible, they laid the men on the double layer of benches inside. Kitty spoke soothingly, assuring those who were conscious enough to understand, that they were on their way to help.

The ride back to the chateau was a nightmare. Every rut and bump and shell hole in the road brought fresh cries from the wounded men. Kitty bit her lip, holding onto the railing of the back door as the vehicle rocked back and forth.

When the torturous ride ended at the chateau, the waiting staff helped unload the men and made quick judgments as to which wards they should go for treatment. Kitty had no time to speak again to Cara but went directly on duty, helping with those assigned to her ward.

The activity was frantic. Uniforms had to be removed or cut away, the wounds washed and loosely bandaged, at least until the doctors could make their own examinations.

It was early morning before Kitty was relieved. Numb with fatigue, she staggered dizzily into the staff dining room to gulp down some strong, sweet tea.

When she asked about the ambulance drivers, she was told they had gone back for another run. But she knew the chateau had reached its capacity, and that the next load would be taken to another field hospital. Kitty felt a wave of sadness. She had not even had a chance to tell Cara good-bye. Nor did she know when . . . or if . . . they would see each other again.

chapter

17

WITH THE ADVENT of spring, the German flyers became more daring. Even in daytime, they flew so low over the chateau that the black cross on each wing was clearly visible. But it was at night when the moon was cruelly bright that they returned to dispatch their deadly bombs. Able to find their targets in its cold light, the pilots flew low. First, there would be a roar of engines, then a whistling whine, followed by a deafening explosion.

On such nights Kitty wondered why she had ever loved the moonlight, thought it romantic! For at last she was beginning to understand war, the wanton waste of it—the dead or damaged, the destruction of homes and land, the women and children deprived of husbands and fathers. When would it all end?

One afternoon while she was out for a rare breath of fresh air, Kitty saw a German plane meet its fate. It must have been returning after dropping its load of bombs, she decided, since the sound of its engine was different from those on the way to a bombing raid.

On the edge of the woods, she stopped to listen, looked up at the sky, and saw the plane with its recognizable insignia come into sight. Then she heard the rackety sound of anti-aircraft artillery. A minute later a red flame cut through the clouds almost directly above. The plane spiraled down in a spinning rocket of fire and disappeared. She held her breath, waiting for the muffled explosion.

Rooted to the ground, Kitty began to shake. She could picture the young man pinned in the horrible inferno of the crash. What if that had been Kip instead of the German pilot?

In the next few weeks, a shocking rumor began to circulate that the Germans were using poison gas. At first, no one believed it. Then the rumor was verified. Against all international law, the Germans had sent clouds of poison against the Allied troops with no other purpose than to inflict cruel suffering and death. Kitty was stunned.

At first, the only protection against the noxious fumes was primitive—squares of folded gauze, soaked in some sort of solution and tied with tapes around mouth and nose. Since these had to be kept moist to fit, the soldiers were forced to use polluted water from the trenches. Even then, the gas could seep in around the contrived masks. It was the ultimate in the war's degradation.

When the first victims came pouring into the hospital, writhing in pain, their lungs seared from the exploding fumes they had inhaled, Kitty's rage knew no bounds. When she was assigned to the German prisoner ward, going on duty became a daily test of will.

Kitty fought her anger for a government that would conceive and implement such a demonic weapon. As a nurse, however, her compassion extended to any soldier whose wounds she dressed. It was difficult to know when one emotion left off and another took its place. They were, after all, the enemy. Men who if, given the chance, were pledged to kill those she loved—Kip and all the others.

Not only that, but Kitty could see the ongoing questions in the eyes of her fellow nurses. Why didn't America—rich, powerful, strong—come in and help before it was too late?

She buried her own wondering. As a Christian, she must not hate. She must somehow forgive her own country for their failures, and she must learn to love her enemies, "do good" to those who persecuted her. So she surrendered to backbreaking work, stumbling exhaustion, and sleepless nights until she was too numb to feel.

In April America declared war on Germany. Shortly after that Kitty learned that Scott was in England, had seen Aunt Garnet and would soon be in France. Daily she expected some words from him.

One afternoon, just as she was finishing her shift, the matron sent for her. "You have a visitor, Cameron."

"It must be my brother!" Kitty exclaimed.

"Oh?" Matron lifted a skeptical eyebrow. "Most say they're *cousins*."

Kitty tried not to laugh, wondering how many times her supervisor had heard that likely story.

"Well, take the rest of the afternoon off, Cameron," she was told and rushed off before Matron could change her mind.

At the main entrance she saw Scott, looking fit and trim in a natty United States Army officer's uniform.

"Scott!" she cried and was caught up in a bear hug. "How marvelous to see you!"

"You, too, little sister!" He held her at arm's length. "Just look at you! How professional you look, but much too thin and pale. I'm going to kidnap you and make sure you have a square meal. Can you get some time off?"

"Only a few hours—"

"Try for longer. I've requisitioned a vehicle. We can drive

up to Paris. I'd planned to take you to one of the finest restaurants, force some of those delectable French pastries on you. Surely your commanding officer would allow you to spend some time with a long-lost brother!"

Kitty was dubious. "I'll see, but you don't know Matron—"

"Shall I pull rank?" Scott struck a Napoleonic stance.

She grinned in spite of her fatigue. All at once, she felt younger, freer than she had in ages. It *would* be good to get away, catch up on old times. "I'll ask. All she can do is say no, right?"

When Kitty returned to her ward, Matron looked up from a batch of reports on her office desk and gave Kitty a long thoughtful look. "I realize this is a special occasion, Cameron, but I can only grant you a short leave. You know the situation here." She made a notation on a chart, then said brusquely, "Twenty-four hours—no more."

Paris, even in wartime, still held its legendary magic. Driving up the tree-lined boulevard into the center of the city, Kitty's spirits lifted. Although damp and cold at this time of year, the city was all she had imagined it would be—the Champs Elysees, the Eiffel Tower soaring against the gray sky, the Arc de Triomphe, reminding her of a victorious ending of another war.

They left the requisitioned vehicle at army headquarters, once a luxury hotel, and started off on foot. There was so much to see. The sidewalks were filled with people strolling, most of them in uniform. Many were Americans, looking healthy and vigorous in comparison to some of the British and French officers. After all, she realized with a pang of guilt, the Americans had not been fighting a seemingly invincible enemy for four long years.

To Kitty's amazement, the shop windows were filled with all sorts of items. There seemed no shortages or lack of any kind. Upon closer inspection, however, she could see that the displays consisted mostly of luxuries—"haute couture" fashions, beaded purses, feathered hats, jewelry, leather goods.

Still, it was fun to see all the lovely things. Kitty could almost forget why she and Scott were in this city, so far from home.

"Tired?" he asked when they had spent an hour sight-seeing and window shopping.

"Not really!"

"I'm sure you've worked up an appetite by now. You're way too thin, you know, Kit," he commented in a concerned, big-brotherly tone. "Shall we find that restaurant now?"

"I'm not about to turn you down. Not after my steady diet of hospital food." She took Scott's arm. "Ready any time you are."

"One of the attachés in our unit gave me the name of a place he says offers the epitome in French cuisine. So I think we should head in that direction." Scott paused to study a street sign. "It's quite near here, I think."

"Fine. We can do some more touristing after we eat."

They had just crossed the street and were walking down the sidewalk when Kitty stopped abruptly. Her hand tightened on Scott's arm. Puzzled, he halted, glancing at his sister, who had turned suddenly pale. Then he looked in the direction she was staring.

Kip Montrose! Scott almost called his name until he saw that Kip was not alone. He was coming out of a hotel, arm in arm with a young woman wearing the gray-blue uniform of a French ambulance driver. They were laughing, her face turned up toward his. Scott turned to look at Kitty and saw his sister's stricken expression.

Kitty stood motionless, unable to believe her eyes. At a glance, she took in the woman's dark sparkling eyes, the rosy-red mouth, the dark hair cut in a straight bang across her forehead. But it was the radiant look on her face rather than her beauty that struck Kitty. She recognized that look. It was the look of a woman in love.

For a minute Kitty couldn't breathe. Her fingers dug into Scott's arm. Instinctively, she stepped back so that her brother's body shielded her from view in case Kip should turn and see them.

But Kip was much too involved in his conversation with the girl on his arm to be aware that anyone else existed. Still laughing, he hailed a taxi and, when it drew up at the curb, he handed his companion inside and hopped in after her. Then the cab pulled away and rolled down the street.

Kitty remained transfixed, her face chalk-white, her eyes reflecting her bewilderment and hurt.

"I'm sorry, Kitty—" Scott began.

"Don't," she ordered from between clenched teeth. "Don't. Please just don't say anything."

Slowly they resumed walking down the street and into the first café.

The Café D'Auberge was bustling with activity. Nurses were identifiable by their white veils, the red cross emblazoned on the headband. They sat at tables across from aviators in leather jackets. Mixed with the sound of voices and laughter was their determined air of seizing this moment.

Other couples in various types of uniforms were enjoying a brief respite from wartime danger and anxiety. Scott found a table for two in the corner.

Kitty stared fixedly into space. Scott's attempts at conversation failed miserably, and they sat in numbed silence until a mustachioed waiter came to take their order.

"Two brandies."

When Kitty protested, Scott said firmly, "For medicinal purposes. You're in shock." He put his hand over her small one. "Kitty, it's wartime. A man like Kip—"

She stopped him with an upraised hand. "Don't make excuses for him, Scott. I don't need that. I just need some time to absorb what's happened—"

Kitty *was* in shock. But the brandy did not help. Nor did the genuine sympathy in Scott's eyes or his insistence that she eat every bite of the succulent *coque au vin* the waiter set before her.

Afterward they drove from Paris back through the dark countryside. Sitting beside her brother, still unable to speak, Kitty looked up at the stars and at the tall trees that lined the road like sentinels. She wondered if, when the numbness wore off, would she feel unbearable pain? How long would it take her to get over Kip?

When they reached the chateau, Scott got out of the car, came around and helped Kitty out. Then he put his arms around her, cradling her head against his shoulder. "I'm so sorry, little sister."

Kitty shook her head. "No, Scott. I knew . . . I *felt* something was wrong. I have for weeks. I just wouldn't admit it to myself. It's been ages since I heard from Kip even though he knew I was here. If he could get leave to go to Paris . . . he could have come here, if he'd wanted to. No, I've just been denying it."

Scott tried again. "Maybe there's some explanation—"

A rush of emotion threatened to overwhelm Kitty, but she managed to say, "I'm only sorry it spoiled our day together."

"It didn't, not really. It was wonderful to be with you, Kitty." Scott's voice was husky. "I'll try to get another leave. I'm not sure where the colonel will be sent, but of course, I'll have to go with him. So good-bye for now. And . . . take care."

He hugged Kitty hard, wishing with all his heart he could have spared her today's heartbreak, wishing also that he could keep her safe from the horrors to which she was returning.

The letter that Kitty had anticipated but dreaded came a few weeks later. She recognized Kip's familiar scrawl immediately but sat holding the envelope, postponing the inevitable. Even so, it was a shock to see the truth in writing.

"I would give anything not to have to write this, Kitty," Kip began.

> I know this is going to hurt. . . . But I've fallen in love with a wonderful French girl. Her name is Etienette Boulanger. She's an ambulance driver and, strangely enough, thinks she has met Cara. Small world, eh?
>
> If circumstances were different, I know you'd like her. She's everything we've always admired—courageous, fun-loving, good. We've know each other only a short time, but we're very sure it's right. We're going to be married in her village church. She's at home now telling her family, and I'll follow in a few days as soon as my leave is approved.

For a long, desolate time, Kitty sat immobilized. Then the letter dropped from her fingers, and she buried her face in her hands.

She was still sitting on the edge of her bed when Dora came into the room from her shift. "You're due on the ward, Kitty. Better hurry. Matron's in a foul mood." She hardly glanced in Kitty's direction, but flopped wearily onto her cot, dragged up her blanket, and closed her eyes.

With effort, Kitty got to her feet. She reached for her apron, buttoned it, put on her headband and veil and left the room. She moved along the corridor and down the steps like an automaton. Signing in on the duty chart, she made her rounds, attending to her patients, all the time trying to make some sense of what had happened.

It all seemed so pointless now. Despite her growing nursing skill, Kip was the reason she had come here in the first place. He was the reason for everything, the driving force that made it possible to put up with all this hellish life—the blood, the mud, the never-ending cold, the boom of guns. If it were not for her love for Kip, she would be safely home in Virginia right now—

Now everything had come crashing in around her. After everything she had hoped and dreamed all these years, Kip loved someone else, someone he had just met, a *stranger*. And he was going to marry her—

But in her heart Kitty knew that there were other reasons she had come to this place. There must be! She was becoming a better nurse. She was doing some good, wasn't she? In spite of what had happened, in spite of Kip, she had to believe that.

Work was Kitty's anesthetic. Still, she dreaded the moment it would wear off, no longer able to kill the pain. In her nursing duties with the amputees, she had heard the doctors talk about "phantom pain," the kind suffered after amputation. Even when a damaged limb was removed, patients complained of feeling pain in it and begged for something to stop it. But there was no one, nothing to stop the pain for Kitty.

After that day in Paris, after Kip's letter, Kitty moved through her days relying on her training, her instincts to do her job. But a part of her mind was always preoccupied with what had happened to her dreams. Ever since Kip had left to join the French Flying Corps, Kitty's thoughts were *after the war, when Kip and I* will do this or that. Now there was only the "I." She had no idea what she would do with the rest of her life.

Coming off her shift one afternoon, Kitty went to her room for a much-needed nap. As she started to remove her headband, it caught on a hairpin and held fast. She tugged at it irritably but, as she did, pulled out more hairpins, and her hair tumbled down onto her shoulders.

Impulsively she reached into her apron pocket for her surgical scissors, grabbed a handful of hair, and whacked it off. It hung there in a jagged clump.

Suddenly the realization of what she had done struck Kitty. She stared into the small wavy mirror above the bureau. One side of her hair was cut off below her ear, the rest fell nearly to her waist. What should she do now?

Just then Dora came in off duty, saw her, and gasped. "Good grief, Kitty! Are you out of your mind?"

"No, I had an uncontrollable urge, that's all." Kitty turned around to face her roommate, then put on a pitiable face. "Help!"

"Oh, Kitty!" Dora moaned. "Your beautiful hair!"

"Cut the rest of it off for me, will you, please?"

"Oh, no, Kitty! Don't ask me to do that!"

"You'll have to. I can't leave it like this." Kitty held out the scissors.

Reluctantly Dora took them and began to cut.

"Shorter," Kitty ordered.

"Shorter?"

"Yes." Kitty's voice was firm.

"Well, you've got naturally curly hair at least, and it's such a lovely color. Besides," Dora continued philosophically, "your cap and veil will cover most of it."

But Kitty eyed her newly cropped head sadly. It was a far

cry from the sleek, dark "bobbed" cap of hair she had seen on Etienette Boulanger.

Still, her rash decision had achieved something else. Something important. She wasn't quite sure why, but she felt as different as she looked. It was as if cutting off her hair had freed her in some strange way.

Part V

Keep the home fires burning,
Though the hearts are yearning,
Turn those dark clouds inside out
Till the boys come home.
—a popular song of 1917

chapter

18

Mayfield, Virginia

Late Summer 1917 at Cameron Hall

"WHEN WILL THE war be over, Gran?" Lynette asked Blythe.

"I wish I knew, darling." Blythe glanced up from the letter she was reading and looked fondly at her little granddaughter and beyond to the lovely sweep of lawn. The hydrangeas were in full bloom and a soft breeze gently stirred the leaves of the trees that shaded the veranda where they were sitting. On this mid-summer afternoon, here in the peaceful Virginia countryside, it was hard to imagine a war raging on the other side of the world. "We must just keep praying it will end soon."

The little girl nodded earnestly. "I do. Every night."

Blythe sighed. All three of her Cameron children were in the thick of it—Scott, stationed in Paris, which was constantly threatened by German invasion; Cara and Kitty, near the front lines.

As if reading her grandmother's thoughts, Lynette said plaintively, "I miss Kitty very much. She doesn't even know I've learned to jump and am riding a horse instead of a pony now."

"Why don't you write her a letter and tell her so? Better still, why don't you draw her a picture of yourself on Princess, going over the stone wall at the end of the driveway? I know she'd love that."

"What a good idea, Gran. I'll go get my crayons."

Blythe smiled as the child scrambled up and ran into the house. Her granddaughter was really quite talented artistically. She wished that Jeff noticed her more, encouraged her. Even after six years, he was not yet over Faith's tragic death. Sadly, he seemed to have lost interest in everything—his children, his art, even life itself.

Blythe sighed again, this time a sigh so deep it was almost painful. All she had ever wanted for her children was happiness, but now all of their lives had been touched by some deep tragedy—Jeff's wife's death, Kitty's broken engagement, and now Cara.

She dreaded writing Scott the latest news that Cara's husband, Owen Brandt, had been killed in action. He had died while bringing a wounded soldier to safety from the battlefield. Of course, the fact that he had died a hero wouldn't ease the young widow's sorrow or make his death any easier to bear.

Between the lines of Scott's letter, Blythe sensed *his* heart's loneliness, for Scott had not yet found a love of his own. She read the poignant last paragraph of her son's letter:

To keep myself sane, I try to remember what it was like as short a time ago as summer before last. In my mind, I see the smooth, green lawn where we used to play croquet, the men in their blue blazers and white flannels, the girls in fluffy white dresses . . . flowers everywhere . . . eating strawberries and drinking iced lemonade by the gallon . . . I'm thirsty for it all!

And I think about the twins a great deal. How alike they were and yet how different . . . their glossy curls bobbing, the sound of their giggles. And somewhere there is music . . . there always seems to be music in my dreams . . . and Kitty's sweet face, her eyes—and Cara dancing . . .

Well, Cara isn't dancing now. Would she ever want to dance again? Blythe remembered her own young widowhood and prayed Cara would not grieve too long or too irreconcilably. She was still young enough to find another love, begin a new life. And Kitty, what about dear Kitty?

*   *   *

Somewhere in France

Chateau Rougeret Hosptial
December 1917

The strains of "Minuit Chritiens" echoed from the small chapel where midnight services were being held for the Catholic members of the hospital staff. Listening to the clear voices ringing out onto the crisp night air, Kitty hummed along with the melody, mentally substituting for the French words the familiar English ones: "O holy night, the stars are brightly shining./It is the night of the dear Savior's birth—"

Earlier she had left the scene of New Year's Eve merrymaking in the staff room. It had seemed so artificial, so forced that, overcome with emotion, she had felt the need to escape. Throwing her cape around her shoulders, Kitty went out into the starry night to walk along the stone terrace of the chateau.

Out here it was as still as it might have been that long-ago night in Bethlehem. For once the guns were silent. It seemed so peaceful that one could almost forget—but that was an illusion. There was no peace, although it was rumored that the Germans were as desperate for it as the Allies. There was even a report that on Christmas Eve, both the German and French soldiers had joined in singing "Silent Night" in their own language from their trenches.

How much longer could this dreadful war go on?

Kitty thought of the poem Richard Traherne had enclosed in a recent letter:

> *The snow is falling softly on the earth,*
> *Grown hushed beneath its covering of white;*
> *O Father, let another peace descend*
> *On all of troubled hearts this winter night.*
>
> *Look down upon them in their anxious dark,*
> *On those who sleep not for their fear and care,*
> *On those with tremulous prayers on their lips,*
> *The prayers that stand between them and despair.*
>
> *Let fall Thy comfort as this soundless snow:*
> *Make troubled hearts aware in Thine own way*
> *Of love beside them in this quiet hour,*
> *Of strength with which to meet the coming day.*

The enclosure had seemed so timely. Just that morning she had been reading in her small devotional book, trying to snatch a scrap of serenity before going on duty. The Scripture for meditation had been John 14:27: "Let not your heart be troubled, neither let it be afraid."

What a coincidence! Kitty thought when she received Richard's letter with the poem that same afternoon. It was almost as if he had sensed her discouragement and fear.

But then Richard was very perceptive. Ever since Birchfields last year, he had written to her occasionally, friendly letters, often enclosing poetry or some quotation from a newspaper or magazine. Then a few weeks ago, she had a letter from him saying he had met Scott in Paris and had been so pleased to hear news of her. Kitty could not help wondering if her brother had told him about her broken engagement.

She checked her watch. It was nearly midnight. Maybe she should go back inside and try to blend in with the others, find a little joy in whatever time was left.

The party was still going strong when Kitty entered the staff room. Twisted lengths of faded red and green crepe paper festooned the walls where a big sign had been hung proclaiming in tarnished gilt letters: "HAPPY NEW YEAR! WELCOME 1918!"

The small group remaining had formed a circle, and someone was trying to find the right pitch for "Auld Lang Syne." Seeing Kitty, a VAD broke the circle and made room for her. She moved forward, clasping her hand on one side, the hand of an orderly on the other.

"Should auld acquaintance be forgot and never brought to mind—" sang a mixed chorus of voices. Kitty found it difficult to sing with the hard lump in her throat. Memories of other New Year's Eves back home at Cameron Hall flooded her mind. She had welcomed most of them with Kip. How many New Year's Eves would she have to greet without him?

The song ended with a round of cheers and applause. Then with an exchange of greetings, hugs, and kisses, some departed to go back on duty. In a few minutes another group just finishing their shift, straggled into the staff room. This bunch did not linger, their slumped shoulders and heavy-lidded eyes proclaiming their need for sleep more than holiday cheer. One by one, they left. Everyone, that is, except Dora, who insisted on helping with the cleanup.

The two began gathering up tattered streamers and

discarded poppers, then collected glasses and cups, carrying them out to the adjoining kitchen.

"Dora, I can manage here. You go on up to bed," Kitty suggested. "You've already worked a full shift and must be tired. I don't go on until seven A.M."

"I *am* beat," admitted Dora, stifling a yawn. "Are you sure you don't mind?"

"Positive. I'm not sleepy at all. And this won't take long."

"Well, if you're sure—" She eyed the clutter, the dirty dishes still to be washed.

"Dora!" Kitty shooed her off. "Do go on."

When her roommate left, Kitty stacked the dishes and cups, waiting while the water heated. She was pouring liquid soap into the sink, stirring it with her hands into sud when she heard a movement behind her. Thinking that Dora had returned, feeling guilty for leaving her with the work.

Without looking, Kitty called over her shoulder. "Dora, I meant it! Go along to bed! What's it going to take to convince you I can handle—"

She half-turned her head to confront her. But instead of Dora, there was Richard Traherne standing in the doorway.

She whirled around. "*Richard!* What in the world are you doing here?"

"Is that any way to greet a fellow who's driven three hours straight across the worst roads imaginable to wish you a Happy New Year?" he demanded, smiling.

"But—but—" she stammered. "Of course, it's wonderful to see you, but how did you manage it?"

"The colonel decided to see the new year in with some friends in the country not far from here, so I drove him over." He grinned. "Then he gave me leave to spend the rest of the holiday as I like." He came toward her, holding out both hands.

174

"Oh, I'm all soapy," she apologized, starting to wipe her hands on her skirt.

"Never mind. I won't shake hands. I'll just kiss you instead. Happy New Year, Kitty." His lips brushed hers lightly, then he looked down at her, regarding her. "It's so *good* to see you again."

"And you, Richard," Kitty murmured, knowing it was true. "I've appreciated your letters so much. Especially the poetry." She looked into his eyes and felt a kind of joy welling up inside.

His eyes moved over her as if taking inventory. "You've cut your hair . . . your beautiful hair! But I think I like it. It suits you."

She ran her hand through the crop of curls. "It's ever so comfortable and convenient." Feeling a little self-conscious under his admiring gaze, she asked rather breathlessly, "Are you starved? We've been having a party and there's plenty of cake left . . . and I can make some cocoa—"

"Sounds just right, Kitty. Reminds me of the homey feeling of coming into a warm kitchen and sitting down at the kitchen table after a day of ice-skating or sledding."

She laughed gaily. "It will only take a minute!"

Richard watched her reflectively. Although she was thinner than he remembered, there was a new sort of grace about her as she moved about, pouring milk into a saucepan, spooning in the powdered chocolate. As she turned to look at him, he was struck by the fact that in spite of what she must have endured, Kitty had a kind of innocence, a purity that remained untouched. A hope he had tried to banish came alive in him again. After all, her brother *had* told him she was no longer engaged to the childhood sweetheart back home. Dare he risk another rejection?

Kitty arranged a tray with two mugs, a beverage server, a

plate with slices of the dark, rich fruitcake that Dora's mother had sent them. "Come along, we'll go into the staff room. We even have a little decorated tree in there, and we might as well enjoy it."

"Let me carry that." Richard took the tray from her, then followed as she led the way, setting it down on one of the tables.

Kitty proceeded to pour the cocoa. "Here you are." She placed the mug before him, its chocolaty steam rising tantalizingly, then poured herself a mug and sat down opposite him.

Richard felt his heart lift recklessly. How lovely she was— the warm brown eyes with their direct gaze, the curve of her cheek, the compassionate mouth. Even in the ugly gunmetal-gray uniform, she had astonishing beauty.

They talked easily, like old friends unexpectedly reunited. She asked how he and Scott had met and learned that they had been stationed in the same Paris hotel, now the headquarters of the joint Allied communications team. After a few questions, Kitty was brought up to date on her brother, and they moved to other topics. Mostly they spoke of the past, of their lives before they had met at Birchfields.

Surprisingly, they found much more in common. Richard knew Cape Cod well, had summered at Martha's Vineyard with his grandparents as a little boy. He told her of losing his mother when he was ten, of boarding school, of school holidays. His grandfather had been a history professor at a small New England college, and Richard had been at the university when his father remarried. Although he was fond of his stepmother, the family was not close.

"I'm a little envious . . . your having such an extended family, I mean," Richard said. "My brother Brad is a lieutenant in the U. S. navy now. But I haven't seen him since I enlisted in the Canadian army."

Kitty touched the double bars on his uniform jacket. "I see that you made captain."

"Yes . . . well, I wish the whole awful thing were over."

They were quiet for a minute, then Kitty held up her empty cup. "More?"

"No, thanks. But I see a gramophone over there. Would we disturb anyone if we played it?"

"Not at all. The wards are quite a distance from here, and the walls of the chateau are thick."

Richard got up and went over to look through the meager stack of records.

"They're all pretty scratchy, I'm afraid," Kitty told him. "They've been played so much."

He studied the labels, then cranked the handle and carefully put a record on the turntable. Then he was holding out his arms to her, and Kitty moved into them as the record began, spinning out the strains of "If you were the only girl in the world—"

Suddenly it was last Christmas at Birchfields, the scent of cedar, the soft glow of candles—

Richard's arm was around her waist, her hand in his. They moved as one, around and around, the music flowing over and through them in harmony.

Kitty felt Richard's lips on her hair, felt his fingers tighten on her hand, felt his arm drawing her closer. "Kitty, Kitty, if you only knew how often I've dreamed of this," he murmured.

The music stopped, but they went on dancing. Richard led her back to the gramophone and flipped the record to the other side. "I'm always chasing rainbows," the vocalist crooned.

"Is that what I'm doing, Kitty? Chasing rainbows?" Richard asked.

She looked up at him, not knowing quite what to say.

"Scott told me you're no longer engaged."

Kitty felt her face flame with remembered humiliation.

"Don't blame Scott for betraying a confidence. I asked him point-blank—" He paused. "Ever since Birchfields . . . well, I've never been able to get you out of my mind, Kitty. Is it too soon? Should I have kept quiet?"

"No, Richard, it's all right. Really. Of course, it hurt at the time . . . even now, when I know it's over, that he loves someone else. I guess I haven't dealt with the reality yet—" She shook her head. "I just go on from day to day, doing my work. . . . It's just that Kip was so much a part of my life . . . at least my life back home—"

She hesitated. "I've thought a lot about it and now realize it might have happened anyway after the war, when we were back in Virginia. We may have both changed, and it wouldn't be right for either of us anymore. It's better that it happened now before . . . well, before we made a worse mistake—"

"Come, let's sit down," Richard suggested. "There's much to talk about."

They found much to say to each other as the hours slipped by. Time passed, and still there was more. They never even noticed when the eerie gray of winter dawn crept through the narrow windows. It wasn't until a nurse came in for coffee before going on duty and snapped off the light switch, that they realized they had talked through the night.

Richard was all concern. "You'll be dead on your feet."

Kitty dismissed that and asked, "How much leave do you have?"

"I have to pick the colonel up tomorrow morning."

Kitty hesitated only briefly before suggesting, "What if I

ask Matron for the day off? I can take someone else's shift another day."

"Would you do that, Kitty? It would mean the world to me if we could spend the next twenty-four hours together."

"I think . . . I'm sure I can arrange it. Look, we'll both get a few hours' rest, then you come back for me at . . . three o'clock?"

At Kitty's request, there was a glimmer of amusement and understanding in Matron's eyes. She pursed her lips as if considering. "I wouldn't want you to make a habit of this, Cameron. But you *are* one of my best VADs, and you haven't had a day off in a long time. So, permission granted."

Richard was back promptly at three. He had rented a room at the village inn, and told Kitty that the innkeeper's wife had suggested he bring his "amie" back for dinner. "The villagers think you American and British nurses are *magnifique*. I told her I heartily agree, especially where *one* of them is concerned." He grinned. "But then I'm prejudiced."

Kitty had the grace to blush a little. "Let's walk, Richard. I hardly ever get a chance to be out in the fresh air." She fastened on her cape.

They started down the road from the chateau, stepping carefully over the frozen ruts, patches of snow still clinging to the hard brown winter ground. But the sky was a washed blue and the air was cold and sharp.

Kitty felt lightheaded and strangely invigorated. *Sleep deprivation,* she told herself with clinical objectivity. But when Richard took her hand and drew it through his arm, she felt a pleasant tingling sensation. They walked on, saying little, finding conversation unnecessary.

When they reached the village inn, Madame Julienne welcomed them. She beamed at Richard and fluttered over Kitty as she led them through the main restaurant to a

179

secluded alcove. There a single table had been set at a window in a pool of winter sunshine.

After serving them a superb omelet and croissants still warm from the oven, Madame wished them "Bon appetit!" and left.

Kitty had not realized that she was so hungry and relished the delicious food, then pushed back her plate with a sigh. "That was the best meal I've had since . . . since I don't know when."

Richard poured her a cup of coffee from the white porcelain coffeepot. He added cream to his and stirred it slowly, gathering his thoughts, pacing his words. "You know I love you, Kitty. I've never stopped. Even when I thought there was no chance, I couldn't help myself."

He reached for her hand, brought it up to his lips, kissed her fingertips. "Maybe it's too soon, but time is so precious now. I have to know. Is there a chance? Could you give me some hope?"

Kitty returned his searching gaze. "I don't know, Richard. I honestly don't know. I wouldn't want to say yes and give you second-best, a rebound love."

Richard smiled. "I'll take whatever I can get, Kitty."

"But you're too good for that. Love should be so much more."

"That's what I'm trying to tell you. We don't have time for dwelling in the past, trying to make sense out of what happens. You and I . . . all of us in our generation . . . are caught up in this tangled web of history. We may not have a future. The world may blow itself up any day. Can't you see?" His grip tightened on her hand. "You do care for me, don't you, Kitty? At Birchfields you said you did. I don't think that's changed."

"I do *care* for you, Richard—" She paused. "It just seems to have happened so fast . . . I'm not sure—"

"Kitty, nothing in life is guaranteed. The only thing I'm sure of is that I love you. Let's be happy together for whatever time we have. Please say yes."

Richard's eyes were so full of tenderness that Kitty felt a stirring within her. She so wanted to return the devotion she saw there. But was that enough? Was it the kind of love he deserved? Or was it only gratitude for filling the aching void she had felt in the aftermath of heartbreak?

What Richard wanted was an enduring commitment. Marriage. Such a major decision in life had its consequences, Kitty knew, making a wartime wedding even more hazardous. She had to be honest with him and with herself. To tell Richard she loved him meant that she must pull away from the hold of the past . . . let Kip go.

She thought of the years stretching back to Virginia, to those she had dreamed of sharing with Kip at Eden Cottage. Then she thought of the years ahead, reaching into an unknown future . . . with Richard?

Looking again into his eyes, Kitty felt a warmth, a tenderness beginning to build within her. Why not accept this fine, honorable man's love, his desire to cherish and protect her? Suddenly it seemed so right. She smiled, and watched the anxiety in his eyes give way to hope.

"Kitty?"

"Yes, Richard, yes, if you're willing to take a chance—"

As soon as the words were out of her mouth, Kitty felt her heart leap. Maybe this marriage *was* a risk, particularly now in the middle of a war, but this kind of happiness was worth it. Hadn't someone said that love demands all, that one must not count the cost?

When they left the restaurant, they walked slowly past the

village and up the hill toward the hospital—still talking, saying all the things that people newly aware of each other say.

In sight of the chateau, Richard stopped and pointed to the arched cloister leading to the small Gothic building beside it. "What is that?"

"That's the chapel."

He regarded Kitty for a moment, his eyes thoughtful. "Let's see if it's open."

Surprised, Kitty hesitated. "Oh, I don't know if we should. I believe it's Madame Rougeret's private family chapel."

"It's God's house, isn't it?" Richard countered.

"Yes, I suppose—"

"Come on then." He took her hand.

The heavy, carved door squeaked as they pushed it open. Stepping inside, they blinked as their eyes became accustomed to the dim interior. There were no pews here, only chairs with racks on the back for prayerbooks. The room smelled of beeswax candles, of ancient stones and incense. Slowly, still holding hands, they moved quietly forward.

At the curved steps leading up to the altar there were a few wooden kneelers. Over the altar, a large brass crucifix gleamed in the shafts of light filtering down through the arched windows.

"Kitty, let's ask a blessing on our love, that it becomes what Scripture tells us it should be . . . whatever the future holds for us. I believe we've been given a special gift, and I just want to give thanks."

Richard was so serious, so sincere, that Kitty felt humbled, touched. Wordlessly she nodded, and they knelt down on the stone steps together and bowed their heads, praying silently.

At first Kitty's mind was a blank. Lately her prayers had been inarticulate cries for help—help for getting over Kip, for the men whose shattered bodies she was responsible for nursing back to health.

As she knelt beside Richard, her heart began to swell with gratitude. Richard had said they had been given a gift. Love was *always* a gift. And what does one do when one receives a gift? One says "Thank you." Kitty smiled at the simplicity of the revelation. Almost at once, words of thanksgiving rushed into her mind. They seemed childish, yet somehow she believed that God understood and was pleased. With one last plea for Richard's protection as he returned to the front, she got to her feet.

Hand in hand, they walked out of the chapel and back into the sunlight.

"Oh, Kitty, don't you think it's significant we started out this new year together?" Richard asked, taking her into his arms when it was time for him to leave. "Starting a brand-new life together, remembering all the rest of our lives that it began on New Year's Day 1918?"

Not until after Richard in a haze of happiness had given her one last lingering kiss and climbed back into the colonel's car, did Kitty have second thoughts. Not until much later did she wonder if her decision had been made in a moment of reckless euphoria.

No, wartime had nothing to do with it, Kitty argued with herself. She loved Richard and he loved her, deeply. If she had met him another time, another place, she would still have been attracted to him. Even last Christmas, with Kip still in the picture, she had found Richard charming, everything she admired in a man. After the war, they would have a wonderful, fulfilling life together—

Dora was enthusiastically happy for her when Kitty shared

the news. "What a looker your fellow is! You're a lucky girl, I'd say, Kitty."

That's what Kitty kept telling herself, too, when letters from Richard began to come regularly. Letters filled with loving concern, plans for their future, declarations of the joy her promise had given him. One day a small package arrived, containing an initialed gold signet ring Kitty had noticed on his little finger.

With it was a note:

Darling Kitty, This ring was my mother's. I want to set my seal on you so that none of those dashing doctors or patients who think you're the reincarnation of Florence Nightingale get any ideas! Wear it until the time we can pick out a proper engagement ring together at Tiffany's in New York or maybe in Paris, if you'll agree to marry me on my next leave!

Kitty could not wear the ring on her finger because her hands were too often in disinfectant or rubber gloves. Instead, she put it on a chain that she wore around her neck under her uniform, beside the little cross that Blythe had given her before she'd gone overseas. Feeling it there made her feel loved, cherished, protected, and helped banish any lingering doubts that she and Richard may have acted too hastily. Remembering their time in the chapel together comforted her. Surely the Lord had brought him into her life, hadn't He?

chapter

19

IN MAY, the Allies—France, Britain, and now the United States—were united under one joint commander, the French General Foch, and there was growing optimism that the entrance of the American forces would turn the tide of the war.

There seemed no weakening of resolve within the German army, however, and hoping to crush the Allies before the full benefit of the American alliance could be felt, they mounted a huge campaign. By the end of the month they had reached the banks of the Marne River. Here they met resistance in the form of a brigade of American marines at Belleau Woods on the road to Paris.

Discussions of the war in the staff room were electrified. For Kitty it was a time of pride in her countrymen and dismay in the growing number of casualties. Now many Americans were among the wounded brought in by ambulance. It saddened her to see how young they were. Only a few short months ago they had been playing football on the high school team, going to proms, having sodas at the local drugstore with their sweethearts. Now they were dying.

A second fierce battle between the Americans and Germans took place at Chateau Thierry and there, by enormous effort,

American troops prevented the enemy from sweeping across the Marne into Paris. At this point, even Dr. Marchand, one of the French surgeons reputed to be an anti-American, favored Kitty with his version of a smile.

During July, five battles raged simultaneously, with news bulletins reporting the progress of the Allies posted each day in the staff room. Then in August, the fighting intensified.

One hot day, coming off duty, Kitty learned of an offensive led by Canadian and Australian troops deep into the enemy stronghold at Amiens. She felt her blood run cold. Was Richard involved? As an aide to the colonel in Communications, he might well be. *Oh, dear God, keep him safe!* she prayed, terrified.

A few days later she received several letters at once from him. But they were undated, hastily written, and gave her no comfort. She could do nothing but follow Paul's exhortation to "pray without ceasing" as she went about her duties.

The days dragged on. Early in September, Kitty was assigned to the ward for the hopelessly wounded. The French called it *Salle de Mort,* the "room of death." Patients remained here only a few days before being replaced by other terminal cases. There was little the nursing staff could do for them except keep them as comfortable as possible.

One of Kitty's most painful duties was to write letters home for some of these soldiers, often dictated in their dying breath. Of if there was no time, Kitty herself, hoping to spare some wife or mother the pain of an official notice, wrote to tell how nobly her loved one had fought and died for his country.

But more and more Kitty became sickened, her illusions shattered. War was not ennobling or glorious. It was horrible, useless!

The day she learned of Thax Collinwood's death, Kitty had just pulled the sheet over the face of a boy barely eighteen and had signaled the orderly to carry him out of the ward. Taking a brief break, she had checked her mail and found a letter from her mother.

"Thax and his commanding officer were standing at the top of their trench, getting a breath of air, when a shell landed nearby," Blythe wrote. "They were both killed instantly in the explosion."

Thax—always fun-loving, gracious, a considerate friend. He had enjoyed everything about life—theater, picnics, sailing . . . That his bright presence was gone, that she would never see his smile or listen to his latest funny story seemed impossible. Thax was part of her youth, of some of the happiest times of her life. How could he be gone?

Head down, choking back tears, she walked aimlessly, and found herself on the other side of the chapel in the garden that must have once been the showplace of the estate. Although now overgrown and neglected, its ornate Italian statuary chipped and broken where shells had fallen, the garden still had a certain forlorn beauty.

The day was unusually quiet, with a stillness that was in odd contrast to the turmoil within Kitty. She felt a hundred years old. What peace was possible in this war-torn world? Hot tears started, rolling helplessly down her cheeks.

Then from behind her a voice spoke. *"Tu est triste, mademoiselle?"*

Startled, Kitty wiped her eyes and turned around. Standing behind her in the shadows of the cloistered passageway was an elderly lady in black. Instinctively, she knew it must be Madame Rougeret.

Wondering if this part of the grounds was off-limits to hospital personnel and fearing that she might be trespassing, Kitty stood guiltily. *"Excusez-moi, Madame."*

"Non, mademoiselle, il n'y pas quoi." The woman shook her

head and made a ges ~ e of dismissal with one graceful hand. Then in accented bu rfect English, she continued, "Do not apologize for tears. i icy are God's gift to ease the pain of heartbreak. If you did not sometimes weep . . . with what you see every day . . . surely it would be more than one could bear."

Madame Rougeret took a few steps toward Kitty, studying her closely. "I believe I have seen you before, have I not? Were you not in the chapel one day some time ago with a Canadian officer?"

Surprised, Kitty nodded, recalling the day that she and Richard had gone there to pray.

"I thought so." Madame Rougeret smiled faintly. "I was in the back of the church that day and saw you come in. I prayed for you both."

"That was very kind of you, Madame."

"Well, what else can an old woman do in these terrible times? What can any of us do, really, but pray?" She sighed. "And your young man, he is all right?"

"Yes, thank God . . . so far."

"*Oui, très bien.*" Madame turned to go, then paused and gave Kitty a look of infinite pity. "*Pauvre petite.*" She shook her head sadly and walked slowly away.

chapter
20

"KITTY, WAKE UP!" Dora's urgent voice penetrated Kitty's drugged-like slumber.

Having fallen into bed after fifteen straight hours on duty, she resisted being awakened like this, but Dora's fingers dug into her shoulders, shaking her insistently. "Come on, old girl. This is an emergency!"

Kitty dragged herself to a sitting position. "What is it, Dora? Why are you waking me? I just got to bed—"

Dora sat down on the edge of the cot and caught Kitty just as she was about to drop back onto the pillows. "It's Richard! I'm sorry to have to break the news this way. But he's been badly wounded. I knew you'd want to know, be with him—"

Instantly Kitty was awake. "How bad is he?"

"Pretty bad. They're evaluating him now."

Dazed, Kitty stumbled out of bed and stood swaying with fatigue.

Dora steadied her, then handed her her dress and apron. "Here, I'll help you." Then, kneeling down in front of her as Kitty tugged on her stockings, Dora shoved each foot into the high-top black shoes, and began to lace and tie them.

When Kitty was on her feet, Dora studied her face. "You all right?"

"I think so—" Richard was here, wounded. She must get to him.

"I'm right behind you, Kitty. Let's go." Dora helped her out to the corridor, down the two flights of stairs, and into the pre-op ward.

Kitty had expected to see Dr. Marchand, but it was one of the British doctors, Captain Hayford, bending over the stretcher where Richard lay, making a preliminary examination. Bracing herself for the worst, Kitty clenched her hands and took her place beside the assisting nurse. This was the crucial point for any wounded man. Here the doctor made the decision to operate or . . . if it was hopeless . . . to allow the man to die in as much comfort as possible.

A nurse with a clipboard stood by, ready to jot down his orders.

When Kitty stepped up, the doctor gave her a quick glance before he dictated his diagnosis. "Hit in the lower lumbar section. Hard to say how many vertebrae may be involved . . . no movement . . . no feeling in lower extremities. Probable paralysis." He straightened and looked Kitty in the eye. "He needs surgery, but it's too delicate a procedure to do here. If he lives through the night, we'll tag him for evacuation. Dr. Manston in London is the only one I know who can tackle this kind of operation."

Kitty looked at Richard's expressionless face, drained of color, his handsome features pinched. She tried to see the man lying on the stretcher as she would have viewed any other wounded soldier. But it was *Richard!*

"We've shot him full of morphine." The doctor turned his attention to the recording nurse. "Keep him immobilized in splints and heavily sedated. That's all we can do for now."

Kitty cleared her throat as the doctor turned away to move

on to the next man. "Permission requested to remain on special duty with Captain Traherne, sir."

"Captain Traherne?"

"The wounded man, sir."

The doctor frowned. "You know him?"

Kitty swallowed. "He's my . . . we're engaged, sir."

The doctor's face remained impassive, but there was a flicker in the steely gray eyes. "What you're asking is highly unusual, Nurse. Not recommended at all!" he snapped but hesitated. "But it will have to be Matron's decision." With that, he moved on.

Kitty's request was quickly granted by the matron with the promise of authorization papers allowing her to accompany Richard to England, and she remained at his bedside most of the night.

It had been established that Richard had sustained trauma to his central nervous system, so he was heavily sedated to prevent further injury to his spine. Kitty learned that his legs were paralyzed, at least temporarily. The success of an operation to restore their use was an unknown at this time.

Reading his chart, Kitty knew his condition was poor, his prognosis negative. There was barely a chance that Richard would live at all, much less survive the trip to England.

By morning, when Richard's condition was unchanged and it was decided to chance the evacuation, Kitty left him long enough to pack a few things and change into her traveling uniform for the trip to Calais. From there they would board a steamer for England.

When she returned to the main floor, Dr. Hayford beckoned her into his office directly off the ward and handed her a small leather carrying case. Its lid was open to display several small vials of clear liquid, a syringe, and some hypodermic needles.

"Use these at your discretion, Nurse. I cannot overemphasize the necessity of keeping the patient as immobile as possible. Any movement might bring on a seizure or muscle spasm that could injure him fatally." The doctor speared her with his eyes. "The object is to keep him still, not to keep him entirely free from pain. He is anesthetized as much as is safe. When he wakes, he may beg for relief. I do not need to tell you that morphine is a very potent drug—" He halted abruptly, breaking off his thought. He closed the case and handed it to Kitty. "Administering this drug in proper amounts is critical, Nurse Cameron. I hope you're up to it."

His warning was clear. It would be imperative that she maintain professional distance and not give way to natural sympathy. She returned his steady gaze without wavering. "Yes, Doctor."

When Kitty entered Richard's ward to supervise his move to the ambulance, he was wrapped in bandages like an Egyptian mummy. His head was held rigid by splints on either side, his body tucked tightly into blankets, then buckled by canvas belts to restrict his movements.

Dora helped them out to the waiting ambulance. Once Richard was on board, she gave Kitty a fierce hug. "We'll all be praying. I know everything will be all right."

The ambulance jolted its way down the hill, Kitty wincing with each bump. Glancing at Richard, she was relieved to see that he was still too deeply sedated to feel anything.

Out the back window of the vehicle, Kitty glimpsed the charming little restaurant where Richard had told her he loved her and asked her to marry him. It was hard to believe that was only a few short months ago.

Huddled beside Richard's stretcher as the ambulance made

its way over the shell-pocked road, Kitty prayed desperately. "Please, God, please," she begged from between tightly clenched lips. She had been taught that it was wrong to bargain with God, but she couldn't help it.

The hours passed in a haze of unreality. From time to time, Richard moaned. His eyelids fluttered, but still he did not awaken. Fearfully Kitty took his pulse, counted his respiration. How much morphine had they given him? It was such a dangerous drug, often lethal—a blessing to those in agony, but also a curse, for it could be addictive.

It was dark when they reached the dock where Richard was to be carried aboard the ship to begin the treacherous Channel crossing.

Muscles aching, weary from the constant strain of watching over him so intently, Kitty got stiffly out of the ambulance to supervise Richard's unloading. "Careful now, please!" she cautioned the two orderlies who grabbed the handles of the stretcher and lifted it clear, then shifted to begin their awkward progress up the gangplank.

The sudden movement brought Richard to consciousness. When he cried out, Kitty leaned over him. "I'm here, Richard, dear. We're on our way to England. It will be just a little longer, then they'll take good care of you, make you well. Just hold on, dear."

They maneuvered up the narrow gangplank and onto the deck, Kitty walking beside him. On board, while there was a discussion of the cabin they would occupy during the voyage, Richard began to moan. His eyes, though glazed, roamed wildly. His face was contorted with pain. His breath came in short gasps.

Kitty got out the small leather case containing the vials of morphine. Her fingers fumbled with the buckles. By the time she got out the hypodermic needle, her hands were steady.

Just as she was about to draw sterilized water into the syringe, a voice spoke beside her.

"Why don't you do the poor bloke a favor and put 'im out of 'is misery?"

Kitty jerked about to see a British infantryman with a corporal's chevron on his uniform sleeve. A second look revealed that he was on crutches, one trouser leg pinned up. An amputee. Having assisted in many such operations, Kitty recognized the sarcasm, understood the bitterness.

"But he's going to have an operation," she replied quietly. "He's got a good chance of recovery if he can make it to England."

"Ha!" grunted the man. "Then wot kinda life 'as 'e got, I arsk ya? Look at me, will ya? I drove a lorry in civilian life and after I got in the Army. Then, one day we wuz drivin' down a road and . . . Pow! . . . it's Good-night, Irene, for me! Wot kinda job is there for a one-legged man? Not drivin' no vehicle! I might as well 'ave been blown up in me lorry," he said acidly, stumping off across the deck.

Richard moaned again, louder. Kitty turned to him, reminding herself of Dr. Hayford's warning. Biting her lip nervously, she dropped the correct number of tablets into the syringe. She rolled up his sleeve, swabbed his arm with alcohol, positioned the needle, and pushed down the plunger. Gradually his moans lessened as the drug brought merciful oblivion.

When the problem with the cabin was settled, two corpsmen came to move Richard, stowing him as gently as possible in the lower bunk. Kitty pulled a blanket and pillow from the top bunk and settled herself on the floor beside him to take up her vigil.

Looking at Richard's face, the lines of pain erased by the drug, Kitty was filled with compassion. This was the man she had promised to marry, the man who had promised to love and care for her for the rest of their lives. If he lived, it was far more likely that it would be she who would be doing the caretaking.

But there was no resentment in that thought, nor any self-pity. During that long night a strange and beautiful thing happened as she kept watch by Richard's side. The love she had not been sure of, the commitment she had not quite been ready to make, became a reality. This was the love freely given, the love that would endure "for better or worse, in sickness or in health."

"Oh, Richard, my darling," she murmured, resting her head on the wooden slat of the bunk, "I do take you now until death do us part."

They docked in the fog-shrouded early morning and were taken by ambulance to the train station where they boarded the train for London. There, at the private hospital of the recommended surgeon, Richard was to be examined. Then it would be decided whether he could undergo the operation that might enable him to walk again.

The London streets seemed very different this time. No flag-waving, cheering crowds lined the sidewalks. None of the glitter or glory. Four years of war had drained the country of the optimism she had observed in the people then as they embarked on what was to be a short war, "over by Christmas."

Richard's eyelids stirred, slowly opened. He moistened his parched lips with his tongue. Gradually his dulled eyes focused on her, then a glimmer of recognition came into them. "Kitty, love," he rasped.

A sharp, wild hope sped through Kitty. He knew her! He was going to be all right! He would get well! *Thank God! Oh, thank You, God!*

chapter
21

There's a long, long trail awinding unto the land
of my dreams,
Where the nightingale is singing, and the white moon beams.
There's a long, long time of waiting until my dreams
all come true,
Till the day when I'll be going down that long, long trail
with you.

THE SONG THAT had been so popular early in the war played
over and over in Kitty's mind as she left Richard at the
London hospital to return to France. He was in good hands.
Although the operation had been a surgical success, it was
uncertain whether or not he would ever regain the use of his
legs. Only time would tell.

Please, God, please was the only prayer Kitty could manage.
Everything felt unreal to her as she retraced the route she had
taken nearly two years ago. The Channel crossing, the jolting
bus ride back to Chateau Rougeret hospital were endured in a
kind of trance-like state.

She had asked for and received an extended leave to see
Richard through the surgery and the critical post-operative
days. She had even briefly considered resigning so that she
could stay with Richard and nurse him herself. But in the end,

197

her sense of duty, knowing the acute need for nurses at the chateau hospital, would not allow her to do so.

All the way on the train from London, Kitty thought back over their last conversation before she left. She had gone into Richard's hospital room to say good-bye, and he'd taken her hand:

"Kitty, I want you to know I don't hold you to any promise you made . . . before this happened. You aren't under any obligation to me."

"Hush, Richard, don't say things like that. Don't even think them," Kitty had admonished, placing her fingertips on his mouth.

"Kitty, I mean it. There's no way of knowing how I'm going to come out of this. And I don't want you . . . wouldn't want anyone . . . tied to a man . . . who's no longer a real man."

"Richard, you're the man I love, the most real man I know, the bravest, the most—"

"Kitty, promise me . . . when the doctors give me the final outcome on all this . . . if it's negative—" He had halted. "You know I may never walk again—"

Glimpsing her reflection in the train window, Kitty hoped with all her heart that her expression had not betrayed her like this at Richard's bedside. As a nurse she had seen enough, learned enough in her experience to know that Richard's prognosis was not optimistic.

But it didn't matter. It wouldn't change her love, her loyalty to him. She thought of the day they had slipped into the little chateau chapel. In retrospect, their prayer, their pledge seemed as meaningful, as binding as the betrothal ceremonies of olden times. Whatever happened, she would never desert Richard, never renege on the promise she had freely given him.

* * *

November 1918

Kitty was in the small annex off her ward, writing one of the letters that had become her bittersweet duty in her assignment on the Salle de Mort, when news came of the armistice.

"Cameron, it's over! The war's over!" announced one of the VADs over the wild clanging of the chapel bell. "The Germans have surrendered. Come on out to the staff room and celebrate with us! Hurry up!"

Kitty let her go. As if from a long distance, she heard the sound of excited voices, the shouts, the rush of running feet along the stone corridors. Oddly, she felt nothing.

Of course, she was glad it was over—relieved that there would be no more killing, no mutilated bodies, no crippling wounds. But it would never be over for some. Not for Mrs. Benson to whom Kitty was finishing a letter about her son Bill. Kitty blinked back tears.

And it wasn't over for Richard. Or for her. They still had a long way to go. "There's a long, long trail awinding—" The refrain spun into her mind once more. Kitty straightened her shoulders and, with a sigh, continued writing.

After that, things happened quickly. By the end of the week all the VADs had been dismissed, for the hospital would soon be evacuated and closed. French nurses would take over the patient care, and all others would be sent home, to England and America.

The last day, Dora and Kitty packed up their belongings in the crowded little room they had shared for almost two years. Together, they went down the winding stone steps and gathered with the other members of the staff. The head French doctor and Matron each said a few words, commend-

199

ing the VADs for their excellent work. There was much shaking of hands, kissing, and hugging before the English VADs, Kitty with them, boarded the bus and departed for the two-hour trip to Calais for the Channel crossing.

Dora's family was waiting on the dock to greet her, and Kitty was introduced all around. She and Dora exchanged addresses, said a tearful good-bye, and Dora went off with her proud Mum and Dad. Kitty took the train up to London . . . and Richard.

chapter

22

Mayfield, Virginia
Fall 1919

> _There's a silver lining,_
> _Through the dark clouds shining . . ._
> _When our boys come home._
> _—a popular song of World War I_

CARA CAMERON BRANDT stood on the terrace of Cameron Hall and breathed deeply of the crisp autumn air. Lines of a poem she had memorized as a child came to mind, something about purple gentians, sunshine, and "October's bright blue weather." She was suddenly happy in a way that she had not been happy in a long time.

Once in a sermon Owen had tried to explain the difference between joy and contentment. Then she had not really understood. She did know, however, that what she was feeling now was pure, lighthearted joy. It had nothing to do with loving Owen or their life together that was so earnest and so worthwhile and, yes, sanctifying.

She walked down to the stables and greeted the groom who had brought out her horse, Valor. Cara mounted, and the old spark of excitement stirred. It had been ages since she had been off for an afternoon's canter on a fine horse.

The air was sharp with the tang of autumn. The horse's ear twitched and he tugged at the reins, eager to take the stone fence at the end of the meadow.

A rush of remembrance coursed through Cara. She threw back her head and laughed, letting the reins slide forward in her hands, giving the horse his head.

She had not gone far along the bridle path when she heard the sound of hoofbeats. She reined sharply, listening, then turned in her saddle to see a man on horseback.

Kip! Kip Montrose. She had not seen him in five years.

As he came in sight of her, he drew up short, sending his horse rearing and tossing his mane. He circled, then leaning forward to calm his mount, Kip looked at her. An expression of disbelief crossed his face.

"Cara! Is it really you? I thought I was having some sort of delusion."

She laughed. "No, Kip, it's me."

He walked his horse nearer so they were side by side.

"How are you, Kip?" Cara asked, thinking he looked older, his eyes haunted. "I didn't know you were back."

"I didn't let anyone know I was coming."

"Didn't want a hero's welcome, eh?"

"Are there any heroes?"

She thought of Owen, who had given his life for someone he didn't even know. "A few."

Kip looked stricken. "I'm sorry, Cara. I didn't mean . . . He was a fine, fine man." He halted, frowning. "You're looking well, Cara. Are you here to stay?"

"No, just to see my parents. Actually, I'm going back to

France. I have a job in an orphanage there." She sighed. "There are so many orphans—" Her voice trailed away as she leaned down and patted her horse's bronze mane. "Somehow, I thought that going back, doing something to help might make it all seem worthwhile, after all."

Kip did not say anything. What was there to say?

"The truth is, Kip, this isn't home anymore. I've changed. I don't seem to belong here."

"I know what you mean. I'm not sure I do, either."

Cara smiled ruefully. "Perhaps *we* are casualties of the war, as well."

Kip looked straight ahead for a moment then turned and looked at Cara. "Everyone blames everything on the war—with justification in many cases. It *did* change things, changed the way people look at life. And it changed people. I suppose none of us will ever be the same."

Cara was surprised. This didn't sound like the old Kip. That Kip had rarely had such introspection. But then, he was right. The war had changed everyone.

"Well, I must go now. Mama will be wondering where I've been so long. I'm leaving in the morning. First, to Washington, D.C., to get all my papers in order, then to New York. I sail on the eighteenth of this month." She untied the horse's reins and hesitated, not knowing quite what to say. "I'm sorry about Etienette, Kip—"

There was nothing else to say. No word of sympathy or comfort would help, she knew too well. For both of them, there was a grave "somewhere in France" where all their young hopes and passions were buried.

Kip watched Cara go as horse and rider disappeared through the thick autumn woods. He had meant to ask her when Kitty was coming home, but being with the new Cara, the woman she had become, had distracted him. The girl he had once thought he loved had vanished, and it had shaken him.

His world, the one he'd missed and longed for, hoped to bring Etienette back to, was gone. He was left adrift. Maybe when Kitty came, he could get his bearings again—

chapter

23

Washington, D.C.

October 1919

THE MORNING she was to leave for Virginia, Kitty went out to see Richard at the hospital. Although the visit on the whole was cheerful, when it came time for her to leave she was aware of his mounting anxiety.

Checking her watch, she finally had to say, "I'll have to be going, Richard. Scott is treating me to lunch at some fancy Washington restaurant before taking me to the train." She got to her feet, leaned down to kiss him good-bye.

He looked up at her with those truth-seeking eyes. "Are you sure, Kitty?"

"Of course, I'm sure. I can't wait for you to see Mayfield, to meet my parents. And to show you our little house. It will be all snug and cozy, ready and waiting for you when they release you."

She kissed him then, and he drew her face down to his once more. "I love you."

"And I love you—" She smiled at him—"very much."

Scott met her at the entrance of the smart Georgetown

restaurant where he had made reservations for them. It was unadvertised but well-known and patronized by an elite clientele. A dignified headwaiter showed them to a table for two in the corner.

Everything was muted—the soft colors, the carpeted floor, the pearl-gray walls, even the lowered voices of the other luncheon guests. Kitty felt almost as if she should whisper.

"How was Richard?" Scott asked after he had ordered for them and handed back the oversized menus to their waiter.

"Better, I think. His spirits are good." Kitty tried to sound optimistic.

Scott leaned forward, looking at his sister earnestly. "This marriage is ill-advised, Kitty. You'll be marrying an invalid, you know, a desperately sick man who will never be able to give you what you've always wanted—a home, real love, children—"

"Scott, please. My mind is made up. It's what I want to do. I love Richard and he loves me . . . he *needs* me—"

"That's just it. Isn't it his condition that is motivating you to sacrifice yourself? Don't let sympathy or pity drive you to do something you may both regret."

"I'm not sacrificing myself. It's not as though either of us is being *forced* to do anything. We knew each other, fell in love *before* Richard was wounded, remember? That hasn't changed."

"But so much *has* changed. If you can't see that, you're being deliberately blind."

"You're wrong, Scott. Richard and I have so much in common. We understand each other."

Scott was silent for a minute as if considering something he wanted to say. "Kitty, let's be honest. You fell in love with Richard . . . or *thought* you did . . . *after* Kip—" Scott hesitated. "You know Kip is free again, don't you? That has to make a difference. Don't let some mistaken sense of honor or loyalty bind you to Richard now. Surely he, as *any* man in his situation would understand, would want you to—"

Kitty's heart wrenched at her brother's words. Just then the waiter came with their soup, and neither of them spoke while it was placed before them.

When the waiter left, Kitty leaned forward, speaking in a low voice. "It doesn't matter, Scott. I'm going to marry Richard. Please let's not discuss it any more." She picked up her spoon. "Umm, this smells delicious."

But Scott made one more try. "What about Cara? What does she think of this?"

"Cara understands." Kitty smiled, thinking her twin was the only one who did. "Now are we finished talking about this?"

"I tried to talk *her* out of going overseas again." Scott shook his head, lifted an eyebrow. "But she didn't listen to me any more than you have."

"Dear Scott. You mean well, and we *do* appreciate all your brotherly concern for us, but we're grown women now, you know. You have to let us go, make our own mistakes if that's what we're doing. I really and truly believe that both of us have made the right choices."

"I hope so," Scott said doubtfully, unwilling to concede that his little sisters were adults now.

At the train station he thrust a box of chocolate-covered mints and a newspaper at her before seeing her to her seat.

"You will be at the wedding, won't you?" Kitty asked as Scott kissed her cheek.

He gave her a long look. "Of course. It wouldn't be official if I weren't."

Settled in her compartment as the train slid smoothly along the tracks from the station, out past the city toward Virginia,

Kitty recalled their conversation at lunch. She knew her brother's love and concern for her had prompted his words, wise and logical as they were. And he was partly right. Whenever she had dreamed of marriage, she had always thought of passionate love—what she had once felt for Kip Montrose. To be honest, she had never imagined caring for a disabled husband, one permanently crippled and confined to a wheelchair.

Yet Kitty knew she did love Richard. Maybe not the head-over-heels passion of her youth but with a deep caring and commitment. After all, she and Richard had been through a war together, had been tempered by loss, strengthened by surviving the unbearable. Their bond was deeper than perhaps anyone else could understand.

In that dark time after Kip's letter telling her he was going to marry Etienette, Richard had given her back a part of herself she thought was lost. When she had needed someone badly, he had been there. By loving her, he had restored her shattered confidence, given her something to live for. Scott simply did not know how much she owed Richard. But Kitty knew, and she was willing to pay that debt, if it took the rest of her life.

She stared out the train window. The landscape was growing more familiar as the miles rolled by. Richard loved her, needed her, and they were going to start a new life together, supporting each other, strengthening each other, giving to each other.

No doubt some lingering hurt might haunt her when she returned to Eden Cottage, but she was determined not to let memories of what might have been with Kip spoil the life she would share with Richard. It was going to be a good life, a good marriage.

After her broken engagement, Kitty had thought of Eden Cottage as described in a line from a poem by Tennyson:

Make me a cottage in the vale,
Where I may mourn and pray.

That quotation no longer applied. *It will not be a place of mourning,* she resolved to herself. *We'll be happy there. We will!*

Several days after her arrival at Cameron Hall, Kitty packed up the boxes of household goods and other belongings she was taking over to Eden Cottage. As she came downstairs from the bedroom she had shared with Cara, carrying a large cardboard carton, her mother was standing in the lower hall.

"Is that the last?" Blythe asked.

"Except for a few odds and ends of mine," Kitty replied, setting the box down beside several others near the front door.

"You've been working awfully hard, darling. Is it almost finished?"

"Oh, there are a few last-minute touches, of course. For one thing, I want to fill the house with flowers before Richard arrives. But I'll do that tomorrow."

Blythe gave her daughter a long, thoughtful look. "I hope you're doing the right thing, dear."

"Now, Mama, don't *you* start in on me." Kitty came over and put her arms around her mother. "Believe me, this is the right thing. You'll see."

"All I want is your happiness."

"I know, Mama, I love Richard, and we're going to be *very* happy," she assured her mother, and gave her another hug. "Now, I've got to go. I have lots to do. I'll just carry these out to the car and be on my way."

Upon her return to Virginia, Kitty had acquired a small station wagon. The dealer had made necessary adjustments to accommodate a wheelchair in the back. Now she filled the empty space with her boxes, got into the driver's seat, and drove down the curving drive to the gates.

After Kip and Kitty's engagement, when Eden Cottage was being renovated for their occupancy, their fathers had commissioned the construction of a road beginning where the Montrose and Cameron property lines converged. This had made the little house accessible from the county road.

As Kitty made the turn into the narrow lane leading to Eden Cottage, she caught sight of Montclair, viewing it through the foliage now tinged with the first colors of autumn. The Montrose home, like Cameron Hall, had been built in the early eighteenth century but retained an imperishable beauty. These two were among the few houses in the area still occupied by the same family who had built them, in spite of so many changes in the world.

Kitty slowed the car to gaze at it, thinking how many memories both great houses must hold—all the arrivals and farewells, the births and deaths, the christenings and funerals, the trials and triumphs of each generation. Yet both remained as a symbol of the strength of family love and loyalty and endurance.

It was thrilling to be a part of it. Kitty couldn't wait to introduce Richard to all that was hers, the heritage she might have failed to appreciate fully before the war.

She parked the station wagon at the side of the house where the sloping ramp had recently been built to accommodate Richard's wheelchair. She got out and stood for a moment, breathing in the familiar, indescribable smells of the woodland—the tree bark, pine needles, the spicy scent of marigolds and shaggy chrysanthemums along the low stone wall.

It was a glorious day. A golden haze gilded the maple leaves and fired the dogwoods with touches of scarlet. The grapevines on the arbor were glistening clusters of ripe color—gold, purple, emerald.

Stepping up on the porch, Kitty took out her key, inserted it into the brass latch, and opened the door. It squeaked a little, and Kitty smiled. She had meant to bring some oil to ease the ancient hinges, but it had slipped her mind. Oh, well, next time. She was about to enter the house when someone called her name.

"Kitty?"

For a moment, she could not move. She knew that voice, and her heart began to hammer wildly. Very slowly she turned around.

Standing only a few yards away was Kip. He was in his riding clothes—worn tweed jacket, beige jodphurs, leather boots. The sun slanted through the trees and enveloped his tall figure in an aura of unreality.

Kitty put one hand on the door frame to steady herself, for she was trembling. "Hello, Kip."

He came forward, stood at the foot of the porch steps. "Kitty! It's really you! I wasn't sure. I saw Cara near here the other day, and I thought at first it might be—"

"No, she's gone."

"When did you come?"

"Last week." Kitty was surprised that her voice sounded so normal.

"What are you doing here?"

"Didn't you know? I'm going to live here. That is, Richard and I are." She paused, seeing his brows furrow in a puzzled frown. "You *did* know I was being married . . . to Richard Traherne, didn't you?"

He shook his head. "No, I mean, yes. I didn't realize—" He halted. "Father and Fiona are away, in Bermuda. I just got home myself. I haven't actually seen anyone, talked to anyone—" He paused again. "When is the wedding?"

"Saturday."

"That soon?"

She nodded.

"And you're going to live *here*? At Eden Cottage?"

There was so much emotion in his voice that Kitty's hand gripped the porch railing tightly. What did she hear in it? Shock? Disbelief? Regret?

"You *do* remember deeding the house to me, don't you, Kip?" she reminded him gently.

He shook his head as if to clear it. "That was before the war . . . so much has happened—" His voice broke. He bent his head, drew a circle with the toe of one boot in the gravel path.

Kitty knew he was remembering more than that.

A silence fell. It was suddenly so quiet that the buzzing of bees among the flowers along the side of the porch droned loudly. Kitty stiffened.

Finally Kip raised his head and looked at her. "Let's take a walk. I think we should talk."

Kitty hesitated. Was it wise? What would they talk about— the past, old times, what might have been? Recalling them could only bring back the bittersweet memories, the anguish of their break-up, but would not change anything. She remained where she was until Kip held out a hand to her.

"Please, Kitty?"

She had never been able to refuse Kip anything. The pleading in his eyes drew her now, against her better judgment.

She ignored his hand, thrust both hers into the pockets of her sweater, and stepped down from the porch. They started down the walk along the pine-needled path leading down to the brook that eventually ran to the river.

"You know Etienette is dead." Kip spoke quietly, matter-of-factly.

"Yes. I'm sorry."

"I have a son. Her parents are keeping him until he's old enough for me to bring him home to Virginia. His name is Lucien."

Kitty said nothing. What was there to say in the face of the tragedy Kip had suffered?

"A lot of people died . . . young people, like Etienette . . . most of my friends in the Escadrille. I never told you, but the average life of a flyer was three weeks." When Kip spoke again, his tone was charged with irony. "We were lucky, Kitty, you and I. At least, I guess we were."

They walked on a little farther.

"When Etienette died, I didn't want to go on living. Then an old priest, the parish priest in the little village where she lived, the same one who married us, actually, said something I've tried to hold onto. He said that the Lord had left me here for some purpose. Most people never know why they're in this world. But he told me that since I have a son, maybe my purpose is to teach him that war is madness, that I should bring him up to be the kind of man who'll help the world learn that lesson."

Kip stopped abruptly and turned to face Kitty. "I could see what he meant. That's what I plan to do. Why I wanted to come back here, to Virginia, to Montclair, to my roots. I mean to bring Luc up with the values and traditions our families have held onto all these years." He paused, studying

213

her face intently. "I'd hoped to have some help doing that, Kitty."

He let the words hang between them, but their meaning was unmistakable. And when she looked into his eyes, she saw in them what she had always longed to see there—love, longing, need. Suddenly Kitty was aware of the danger they were in, and she was frightened.

What did she really want from Kip? Did she want him to say he was sorry, that marrying Etienette had been a mistake, that he wanted to pick up with Kitty where they had left off, just as if nothing had happened in all the years in between?

It was tempting to read into all of this what she might have wanted months ago. But if she allowed Kip to say what she sensed he was on the brink of saying and she listened— She halted suddenly, saying, "We'd better turn back."

"Wait, Kitty." Kip caught her arm, "There's something I have to say."

"Maybe it would be better not to say it, Kip."

"But I should have said it before," Kip insisted. "I wasn't too sensitive, was I? I've always been impulsive, thoughtless—I didn't realize at the time—how much—"

"It's all right, Kip. I suppose we've both learned a lot, to appreciate happiness now more than we did before the war."

"That's not all I wanted to say, Kitty—"

Kitty knew that they were on dangerous ground and she interrupted him.

"It was a long time ago, Kip, no need to—"

"I *am* sorry, Kitty. Truly sorry."

Did Kip just mean sorry that he had hurt her or did he mean more than that? If she looked into Kip's eyes, what would she really see? Simply loss and loneliness or really love? Kitty dared not look. Instead she turned away, saying softly, "I must go, it's late, Kip."

"You mean that it's too late, don't you, Kitty?" she heard him say as she started down the path leading back to Eden Cottage.

He fell in step with her, and they walked the rest of the way in silence.

At the small herb garden, a miniature of the one at Montclair planted by the first Montrose bride, Noramary, Kitty bent and plucked a sprig of rosemary, held it for a moment, then handed it to Kip. "Rosemary for remembrance. Let's just remember the happy times."

They were standing close together, and he put his hand on her shoulder, letting it rest there for a moment, then leaned down and kissed her tenderly.

"I hope you'll be happy, Kitty. You deserve it."

Watching him walk slowly away, Kitty knew in her heart that she needed only to call his name to recapture her once-cherished dream. Then she glanced at the little house. It had a waiting look.

With an awful certainty Kitty realized that a step in either direction would change her life irrevocably. Was there a choice? Had life really handed her a second chance? The longing of the moment seemed irresistible. Or would there be an eternity of regret? The wind rustled the boughs in the tall pines overhead, making a sighing sound. Kitty shivered slightly, then she stepped out of the shadows and into the sunshine.

Cast of Characters for *Hero's Bride*

Mayfield, Virginia

Kip Montrose
Kitty Cameron
Cara (Kitty's twin)
Blythe and Rod Cameron (the twins' parents)
Lynette Montrose (the twins' grandparents)

In England

Lydia Ainsley (an old family friend)
Garnet Cameron Devlin (Kitty's aunt)
Bryanne Montrose (Garnet's granddaughter,
    Kitty's cousin)
Richard Trahern (a Canadian officer)
Scott Cameron (Kitty's brother)

People Making A Difference

Family Bookshelf offers the finest in good wholesome Christian literature, written by best-selling authors. All books are recommended by an Advisory Board of distinguished writers and editors.

We are also a vital part of a compassionate outreach called **Bowery Mission Ministries**. Our evangelical mission is devoted to helping the destitute of the inner city.

Our ministries date back more than a century and began by aiding homeless men lost in alcoholism. Now we also offer hope and Gospel strength to homeless, inner-city women and children. Our goal, in fact, is to end homelessness by teaching these deprived people how to be independent with the Lord by their side.

Downtrodden, homeless men are fed and clothed and may enter a discipleship program of one-on-one professional counseling, nutrition therapy and Bible study. This same Christian care is provided at our women and children's shelter.

We also welcome nearly 1,000 underprivileged children each summer at our Mont Lawn Camp located in Pennsylvania's beautiful Poconos. Here, impoverished youngsters enjoy the serenity of nature and an opportunity to receive the teachings of Jesus Christ. We also provide year-round assistance through teen activities, tutoring in reading and writing, Bible study, family counseling, college scholarships and vocational training.

During the spring, fall and winter months, our children's camp becomes a lovely retreat for religious gatherings of up to 200. Excellent accommodations include heated cabins, chapel, country-style meals and recreational facilities. Write to Paradise Lake Retreat Center, Box 252, Bushkill, PA 18324 or call: (717) 588-6067.

Bowery Mission Ministries are supported by voluntary contributions of individuals and bequests. Contributions are tax deductible. Checks should be made payable to Bowery Mission.

 **Fully accredited Member
of the Evangelical Council
for Financial Accountability**

Every Monday morning, our ministries staff joins together in prayer. If you have a prayer request for yourself or a loved one, simply write to us.

 **Administrative Office:
40 Overlook Drive, Chappaqua,
New York 10514 Telephone: (914) 769-9000**